A
TAINTED
MIND

TAMSEN SCHULTZ

*everafter*ROMANCE

EverAfter Romance
A Division of Diversion Publishing Corp.
443 Park Avenue South, Suite 1008
New York, New York 10016
www.EverAfterRomance.com

Cover Design by Sian Foulkes
Edited by Julie Molinari

This is a work of fiction. Names, characters, places and incidents either are the
product of the author's imagination or are used fictitiously. Any resemblance to
actual persons, living or dead, events or locales is entirely coincidental.

For more information, email info@everafterromance.com

First EverAfter Romance edition March 2017.
Print ISBN: 978-1-63576-035-4

To Nav, even though you don't share my love
of white wine and country music

and

To the boys, because you inspire such a range of
emotions and give me lots to work with

CHAPTER 1

VIVIENNE DEMARCO GUIDED HER CAR onto the shoulder of the country road and peered out through the windshield into the black night. Her eyes skirted to the side windows as she tried to see something, anything. When that failed, she turned her gaze to the rearview mirror then let out a long, slow breath. There was nothing. Nothing but the darkness and the deafening sound of rain hammering her car.

It was a dark and stormy night, she thought to herself with a rueful sort of inevitability as she loosened her grip on the steering wheel. Here she was alone, in the dark, on a deserted road, and in the middle of a torrential spring downpour. Her life had become a series of clichés lately and tonight was no different. As if in a bad movie, she'd been felled by a simple flat tire.

She craned her head forward and looked up through the windshield again, debating whether or not to risk the pelting rain. She knew storms like this moved on as fast as they came in. And so, after listening to rain drops the size of New Hampshire lash at her car, Vivi put her faith in experience and opted to wait.

Still, as she sat listening to the metallic sound of her roof taking a beating, the cliché-ness of the situation—of the past year—did not escape her. She was just a woman who'd thrown herself into her job after a searing loss—a job that had propelled her to the brink and finally catalyzed a meltdown of epic proportions. A meltdown that drove her away from everything she knew in an effort to find herself again. Honestly, all Vivi needed now was the urban legend hitchhiker scratching his hook along her window. But at least the hitchhiker would make a good story. As it was, her life story was all so prosaic that, if it were a book, it would never make it past an agent's slush pile.

With a sigh, she pulled her mind from her uninspiring existence and glanced at her GPS. Judging by the tiny map, she wasn't all that far from her destination, a place her aunt had been telling her about for years. Windsor, New York, was a small town in the Hudson Valley and, having been in her fair share of small towns, Vivi figured that if she saw anyone on this night, he or she was more likely to stop and help than to stop and slit her throat. But either way, the storm was letting up and she wasn't going to sit around and wait for help, or anything else, that may or may not come. She knew how to change her own tire.

However in the dark and wet, what should have taken her no more than twenty minutes took forty and, after tightening the last bolt, she needed to stand and stretch out the kinks in her back and shoulders. The now gentle rainfall had soaked her clothes, and water was running under her jacket's hood, down her neck, and onto her back. At least the job was done.

With the smell of wet earth hanging in the humidity, Vivi paused. Taking a deep breath of the heavy air, she inhaled the cleanness of it, the purity of the scent. No pollution, no smells of the dead and decomposing. And knowing Windsor would have somewhere she could stay for the night, Vivi ignored how uncomfortable she was for a moment and savored the peace as a sense of calm settled over her.

But as if to object to her enjoying such a small luxury, an owl screeched in the night, jarring Vivi back to the here and now. Gathering her flashlight and tools, she tossed the jack into the car, wiped the grease from her hands with a wet rag, and shut the trunk. She turned toward the driver's door as a sound behind her, muffled by the dense air, caught her attention. Vivi stilled and cocked her head. It wasn't a car and it hadn't sounded like footsteps either.

There, she heard it again. Vivi frowned. Judging by the gentle thuds and cracks, it was nothing but a few rocks tumbling down the shoulder behind her. But there wasn't much wind to speak of now that the storm had reduced to a drizzle, nothing strong enough to move rocks around. Shining her flashlight onto the water-soaked road, she realized that it was possible the runoff from the storm was stronger than she thought and that the rain had dumped enough water to loosen the soil under the asphalt. Or maybe there was something else causing the disruption.

This thought came out of nowhere and disturbed her more than the sound itself. Despite her experiences, despite her job, she was *not* one of those people who saw danger or evil everywhere she looked. And, more to the point, she didn't ever *want* to be one of them. So, forcing herself to come up with some alternate logic for her errant thought, she remembered her aunt telling her that bears were endemic to the area. Maybe one had come out for the night, dislodging the earth as it made its way into the field across the road?

Yes, a bear—or maybe even a deer or a fox. That made more sense than anything else out here on this quiet road. This option gave her a small sense of relief until she realized that, while she might know how to change a tire, she knew nothing about bears. What did someone do when encountering a bear? Run? Stay still? Vivi's mind had just started spinning when she brought it to a purposeful halt. She was getting ahead of herself. She had no idea what, if anything, was out there. And so, with some trepidation, she made a half turn and swept her flashlight across the road. Nothing.

She glanced to her left. A forest of elm and birch trees lined the road. Even if she shined her flashlight in that direction, which she did, she couldn't see more than a few feet into the dense woods. To her right, and steeper than she had originally thought, the side of the road dropped down about ten feet before leveling out onto a cornfield filled with stalks about a foot high. Curiosity got the better of her, and she moved a step away from her car. She'd seen lots of deer in her time, but she had never seen a bear, or even a fox, in the wild. As long as she knew an animal wasn't right next to her, she wouldn't mind catching a glimpse of one moving about in nature.

She pointed her light along the line of corn at the edge of the field, looking for some sign an animal had disturbed the crops. After two passes, the only thing she saw were neat rows of baby stalks, their tops and leaves battered by the heavy rain. Vivi should have felt comforted by the lack of wildlife, but she didn't.

As she took another step away from her car, the night encompassed her. Steamy fog was rising from the road, casting eerie shadows that drifted in the weighty air and made the hairs on her neck stand up. She thought about getting in her car and driving away; she hadn't gathered up the courage a few weeks ago to take a much-needed leave of absence from all the violence of her work only to step right back into the thing she was trying to get away from.

But it wasn't in her makeup to let fear guide her response, so Vivi took a deep breath, moved away from her car toward where she thought the sound had originated, and stopped. Standing silent and still, she let the night become familiar. After a few moments of hearing nothing but cicadas and frogs, Vivi directed her beam down the edge of the road as far as the light would go. But the fog and shadows blended with the black of the night and the darkened roadway, so it was hard to see much of anything.

Rather than move farther along the road, she redirected the light down the side of the slope to the field's edge, the contrast of the lighter dirt making it easier, just a bit, to see any anomalies. Starting below where she stood, she swept an area in a straight line away from her as far as the beam would go. Then, shifting it up a foot or two, she brought it back toward her, searching the area in a grid-like way, looking for what might have made the noise.

Standing on the side of the road, wet and exposed, combing the area for something unknown, Vivi couldn't ignore the reality that, to her dismay, she *had* become one of those people—one of those people she never wanted to be. She no more expected to find a simple little rock slide than she expected to see Santa Claus. The pain and death and evil she worked with every day had filtered into her life and colored her experiences.

The irony of her situation did not escape her. Whatever was compelling her to stay and find answers on the side of this country road was the same thing that had gotten her here in the first place. She didn't like to let things go, and because she couldn't let things go, she had almost destroyed herself with her last case. She'd taken to the road to escape, maybe to find some balance. If she were to hazard a guess, though, she'd say that whatever balance she'd found in the past few weeks was about to be tipped.

And, as if to give weight to the direction of her thoughts, about fifteen feet away from her position and about halfway down the embankment, her light landed on a small collection of rocks. No, not rocks, pieces of road that had broken away from the win-ter-weakened, rain-pummeled lane and tumbled down to rest a few feet away.

Vivi kept her beam trained on the pile as she walked closer. Tracing a line up the embankment, she could see an approximately two-foot by one-foot section of the road cracked and starting to cave in, the edge beginning to break away.

As she contemplated the small sinkhole illuminated by her flashlight, a gust of wind picked up. Her wet jeans pressed against her legs, her ponytail lifted, and her skin broke out in bumps from the sudden chill. Another piece of the road cracked and tumbled down the slope.

And there, at that crumbling edge, barely visible in the dark and shadows, was the unmistakable form of a human hand.

CHAPTER 2

VIVI MADE A GENTLE LEFT turn onto Windsor's quiet Main Street where, according to her GPS, she would find the police station. She had thought about calling in what she'd found; thought about staying on the side of the road and dialing 911. But even if she'd had cell service—which she hadn't—she knew from experience how short staffed local law enforcement probably was in this small town, especially after a hard rain had slicked up roads and downed power lines. And besides, as glib as it sounded, what she had found was no emergency. A tragedy? Yes. An emergency? No.

From where she sat at the south end of town, Main Street looked so short it was hard to tell if she would find her destination in one block or three. Easing her foot off the accelerator, she slowed to a crawl. As she passed through town, Vivi took in the solid-looking brick, stone, and mortar buildings that lined the streets—buildings built long before the whimsies of the Victorian era by men and women who seemed to have had every intention of staying. She was used to seeing the old clapboard towns that littered New England, but this was different. The sturdiness of the place, the permanence, shouldn't have come as a surprise, but for some reason, it did.

And the fact that the shops she drove by looked well maintained led her to believe that, while this might be a small town, it wasn't as desperate a place as some other small towns. She passed a restaurant called Frank's Fed-Up-And-Fulfilled Café on the left, followed by a bakery and a used bookstore. After passing several more darkened shops, she saw the only two lively-looking places—a movie theater and an ice cream shop. Judging by the times on the marquee, the movie was in progress. Vivi suspected the streets would fill with people in an hour or so when the movie let out, but as it was, the old-fashioned sign, which Vivi noted carried the name of a recent movie, and the lights from the ice cream shop were the only signs of life she could see this time of night.

One more block down, she pulled through a wayward roundabout and up to the front of the police station. There was no question in her mind that she needed to stop and report what she had seen, but she wasn't looking forward to having the conversation. Mostly because she didn't have any answers. It was always harder when she didn't have answers.

Anchoring the north end of Main Street, the aging brick police station had white trim and was built in much the same style as the rest of the buildings she'd passed, functional and solid, if somewhat sagging around the edges.

She spared a thought for the charm of the village but didn't stop walking until she was at the entrance. Wanting to get the meeting over, she pushed the door only to have it refuse. She paused, thinking that couldn't be, and then tried again with the same result. The police station was closed.

Stepping back from her determination to unburden herself, Vivi took a closer look at her surroundings. Except for maybe one or two lights that looked more like safety lighting than anything else, the building looked quiet. The street was also empty of any police or sheriff cars. In fact, the street was empty of all cars except the few parked in front of the theater.

For a moment, she imagined calling 911 and hearing it ring inside the station, unanswered. But her snarky thought was mostly due to the fact that she was tired, cold, and wet. The reality was most small towns consolidated their switchboards after hours; if she called, she knew someone would answer.

Looking at her cell, she noted that she had service. But after a quick internal debate, she opted to try one more discreet way of locating the local police before dialing 911. If the police were out on calls that affected the safety of living people, she didn't want to take them away from that. And though she knew that any more road that caved in or fell away, or any car that drove over the sinkhole could compromise the remains, she held little hope that the local law enforcement, or even a more sophisticated team, would find much after such a long a time—and it had been a long time. And so, she made her decision.

She'd passed a place called The Tavern before hitting Main Street; it wasn't hopping, but she remembered a few cars and trucks in the parking lot and light filtering out through the windows. Climbing into her car, she headed back south down Main Street. After pulling in next to a mud-splattered Jeep, Vivi gave a thought to her hair and wet clothes before giving up; there wasn't much she could do about them anyway.

As she entered, the handful of patrons turned to see who'd come in. They took in her clothes, took in the fact she wasn't local, and turned away. Only the bartender kept an eye on her. She acknowledged his watchful interest with a small nod then gestured toward the opposite end of the room.

"Can I help you?" the man asked, meeting her at the end of the bar furthest away from the other customers.

"I'm looking for the local police. I was just down at the police station and they appear to be closed." She couldn't help the bit of wry cynicism that crept into her voice.

"Everything all right?" he asked, drying a glass.

"I would just like to the talk to the local law enforcement."

He set the dry glass on the rack and studied her for a long moment, but she wasn't about to say more. "You can call 911," he offered, picking up another glass and indicating the pay phone against the wall with a jerk of his head.

"I could but would rather not. It's urgent but not an emergency." She didn't have to, but she pulled out two IDs and slid them across the bar. He glanced down at the items before tipping his head in acknowledgement.

"I'll call Ian for you," he said, moving away and pulling out

his cell. Two minutes later he came back. "He'll be here in fifteen minutes. In the meantime, you can hang your coat up there," he pointed to an empty coat rack. "And can I get you something to drink? Coffee? A beer?"

"Thanks," she responded, removing her damp coat. She had noticed the sign for The Tavern *and* Inn when she'd entered and hoped that it wasn't just an antique advertisement. "I'll take coffee for now and a room, if you have one? And a glass of whiskey would be nice once I've talked to...?"

"Ian MacAllister, Deputy Police Chief," he supplied. "I'll bring you some coffee and make sure we have a room ready." He was already moving away before he'd even finished the sentence.

Vivi waited at the end of the bar, watching the people around her, sipping the strong coffee the bartender, who'd introduced himself as Rob, had brought. A few folks gave her a look or two, but most seemed more interested in their drinks or their friends than her. After a short wait, Rob stopped back by with some paperwork and handed her a room key. Once she'd spoken with Deputy Police Chief MacAllister, Vivi planned to down the shot of whiskey to warm her bones, pop into a hot shower, and slide into some dry sheets.

She was fantasizing about dry sheets when the door opened, followed by a gust of wind. Rather than looking toward the entrance, Vivi watched Rob, the bartender. When she saw him jerk his head in her direction, she turned in her seat.

Striding toward her with water dripping from his long coat, Ian MacAllister looked like a small-town cop who'd already had a long night. He wasn't particularly tall, somewhere just shy of six feet, but was built fit and solid. His hair was cut short and, even though it looked brown, Vivi could see streaks of a reddish gold in it. His jaw and general facial features were strong, both in structure and in bearing, and he was younger than she had expected, probably just a few years older than her own thirty-three. His heritage, at some point in time, was likely Scottish. Or, more precisely, she amended to herself as he stopped before her, Celtic.

"Ma'am?" he said, holding out his hand. "Ian MacAllister, Deputy Chief of Police."

"Vivienne DeMarco," she responded, standing up to shake his hand. Vivi motioned him toward an empty table in the back. When they reached it, he waited for her to sit then joined her as she pulled out a piece of paper and handed it to him.

"GPS coordinates," he said, frowning at the numbers.

"I had a flat tire outside of town a bit ago. After I changed it, I heard something—thought it might be a bear, so I took a look around. There is no easy way to say this, but you have a body, or at least part of one, buried under the road at these coordinates."

Ian MacAllister stared at her for a good long while. His eyes were green, an arresting and unusual shade—almost pastel. And though the color was soft and muted, his expression was not. Vivi had been around long enough to know he was taking stock. Finally, he spoke.

"You seem awfully calm to have just discovered a dead body, Ms. DeMarco."

Reaching into her bag she pulled out her IDs again. He glanced at the card on top, the one identifying her as member of the Boston Police Department and Medical Examiner for the county. He pushed it aside and took a closer look at the second ID, the one granted to her as a permanent consultant with the FBI.

"So you see a lot of dead bodies, don't you, Dr. DeMarco?" He pushed the IDs back across the table.

"My fair share, yes."

"I assume, since you didn't call 911, this isn't an emergency?"

She shook her head and told him everything she knew. He listened to the sparse information, taking notes and asking questions. There wasn't much she had to offer, so the interview lasted less than ten minutes.

"Thank you for your assistance," he said, rising from his seat. "If I need to speak with you again, how can I reach you?"

"My number is on the paper with the coordinates," she said, following his lead and standing. "I'll be staying here tonight, but

I'm on vacation and don't plan to stay in this area for more than a night. If you need to talk to me in person, try to reach me in the morning."

"Please do us both a favor and stick around until I give you the official okay to leave." It wasn't a request.

Vivi stared at the Deputy Chief of Police for a long moment. His intensity, his commanding confidence, and, not to mention, the fact that he didn't seem all that upset about the thought of a dead body made her think he had seen his fair share too. Her eyes swept him in a study. Military of some sort, she would guess. But whatever his background, there was no doubt in her mind he was more than a small-town cop.

"I'll stick around tomorrow, but if I don't hear from you either way, I'll be out of here the day after," she conceded.

They both knew she wasn't a suspect and he was getting more than what she was obligated to give, so he gave her a curt nod then turned to leave. She watched the door close behind him then signaled Rob for that whiskey.

After she'd downed the shot, Vivi relaxed for a moment as the warmth traveled through her body. *Nice*, she thought with no small dose of sarcasm. Everyone was always telling her to take a vacation, take a break, take some time to herself. Go figure that when she'd finally gotten in a car and just started driving—with no plan other than *not to work*—she'd landed right back in the thick of it.

***

Nice, just what I need, he thought to himself. Ian fingered the piece of paper in his jacket pocket as he made his way to the station. A dead body buried under one of his roads. No doubt Vic Ballard, the Chief of Police, would find some way to blame him for it. Not for the actual murder, but for letting it happen in the first place. For some reason Ian had yet to grasp, the older man was convinced that Ian was out to take his job. Nothing could be further from the truth. Hell, Ian hardly wanted the job he had. But it was a job—something the therapist at Walter Reed recommended.

Of course, from what it sounded like from Vivienne DeMarco, the body had been there a good long while. He had only been back stateside for a year, and only back in town for six months. But even that wouldn't stop Vic from trying to blame him for something. At least the chief was away on vacation, Ian could be thankful for that. Maybe, he thought as he pulled up to the station, he could get everything wrapped up by the time Vic came back.

He slid the key into the station door and entered the main room. Hanging his jacket up on the rack to dry, he moved toward his desk and the map of the county that lay spread across it. Based on the map and the GPS coordinates, he corroborated what she'd told him about the location. Not that he doubted Vivienne DeMarco. No, she looked like a woman who knew a thing or two about this sort of thing.

Since she hadn't seen a full skeleton and he wasn't sure what to expect when he got out there, Ian began to gather a variety of supplies. As he went through the motions, on impulse he pulled out his cell and dialed a familiar number.

"Ten o'clock on a Saturday night. What makes you think I'm not out doing something—or someone—fun?" came the voice at the other end of the line.

"Because our idea of fun is completely fucked. So, for the safety of our good citizens, we're better off working late," Ian replied with a smile.

"I'd say you have no idea, but that would be a lie," Special Agent Damian Rodriguez, and Ian's former brother-in-arms, answered. "What can your friendly FBI help you with this evening, Deputy Chief MacAllister?"

"One of yours rode into town tonight," Ian answered. "Found a body, reported it to me. Seems a bit too coincidental so I thought I might check her out." He gave Damian her name and waited, packing more supplies, while listening to computer keys click away.

"Huh, that's interesting," Damian said.

Ian paused. "That's interesting, as in, I've been snowed? Or that's interesting in a good way?"

Damian took a moment to respond. "Definitely in a good way if you can get her to help you. She's done a lot of work for my assistant director." Damian paused again then let out a low whistle and continued. "She's a medical examiner who somehow also holds the rank of detective with Boston PD. How that works, I'm not sure, since one is a county position and the other with the city. But in addition to her MD, she has a PhD in forensic psychology, and she also volunteers a lot outside the US with the Red Cross and Mercy Corps. Her domestic specialty seems to be violent crimes, which is what it looks like she does a lot of for us. Internationally, I'm not sure, but based on her background and the organizations she works with, I'd guess body identification, disaster response, and search and rescue stuff."

"A regular saint."

"She's good looking, too. Kind of has a young Sophia Loren thing going on. Great eyes. Nice hair. Oh, and she's an artist. She also does facial reconstructions."

"I thought reconstructions were done with computers?" Ian asked, not all that interested in the answer for now but knowing it might be useful later.

"Some of the places she's been have probably never even heard of a computer before."

"So you're saying this really is a coincidence?" Ian shoved the last of his gear into the supply bag and zipped it up.

"I'm about as much a fan of coincidences as you are, but we've seen stranger things."

Ian couldn't argue with that.

"Maybe she'll help. Can't imagine you guys get too many dead bodies up there," Damian suggested.

"I'm sure she could. Whether she wants to or not is another issue. She's on vacation, doesn't seem to want to get involved."

"A woman like her? She probably works harder than we ever have. From her file it looks like she is on her first leave of absence since she started consulting with us eight years ago. In her spare time she travels to natural disasters. Can't say whether she's a saint or not, but she definitely has some demons riding her. I'm betting you can use that to your advantage. If you want to, that is," Damian added.

"Guilt her into helping." Hearing the contemplation in his own voice made Ian cringe.

"I like to think of it as encouragement."

Ian cringed again when it hit him—just how fucked up he'd become over the past decade-plus. The idea of using guilt on a stand-up fellow law-enforcement officer who was trying to take what seemed like a much-needed vacation had actually held some appeal, if only for a moment.

Nice. If he ever had any doubt about what a dick he could be, he didn't now.

"Thanks, Damian. I appreciate the intel."

"No problem. Let me know how it goes." They disconnected and Ian gathered the last of his supplies. He placed a few calls to the off-duty deputies to request assistance and headed out into the night.

CHAPTER 3

Ian walked into The Tavern and approached the bar.

"You look like you need a drink, Ian," Rob commented more than offered.

"Thanks, Rob. Wish I could, but the day's not done yet." He'd confirmed Dr. DeMarco's find, but there hadn't been much they could do in the middle of the night. As a result, he and a couple of cops from the state police had been up at first light and had spent much of the morning and afternoon removing the road piece by piece to see what they had. And what they had was indeed a complete skeleton.

"I'm looking for Vivienne DeMarco. I know she's staying here. I tried her cell, but she isn't answering."

"Most likely can't," Rob answered, handing Ian a cup of coffee in a to-go cup even though he hadn't asked for it. "She came in this morning asking about hiking trails. I pointed her to the Taconic Trail. If she's up there, she won't have cell coverage."

"Thanks, Rob," Ian answered, taking a sip of the hot coffee. It wasn't cold out, not like the winter, and the rain had stopped, but it was still cool for early May. "Did you point her to a specific access point?" Rob nodded and mentioned the entry point off the Taconic Parkway about twelve miles south of town.

Twenty minutes later, Ian drove to the end of a short dirt road, pulled into a secluded parking lot that sat halfway up a hill, and considered what he was doing. According to Rob, she'd left five hours ago. If she was still hiking, she could be gone for hours. He hadn't thought much about it; he figured he would just wait for her. But when he'd pulled into the lot and seen her car, he realized his approach was a throwback to his old life, when he'd had one mission and stuck to it—even if he'd had to wait hours, or days, or weeks. He got out of his Jeep and leaned against the hood, wondering if there was something else he should be doing—some coordination, some oversight, something that, as the Deputy Chief of Police, he should be thinking about.

And not for the first time, he questioned his position on the force. From his vantage point, he stared out over the rural Hudson Valley and contemplated his situation. While the skills he'd developed over the past several years were valued by various law enforcement agencies, the truth was it wasn't an easy transition from soldier to police. As a soldier, he and his team spent a lot of time planning and executing missions. As a police officer, he came in to clean things up—which required an entirely different set of skills. And at times like this, times when he wasn't sure if he was doing what he should be doing, he was very aware of how different the two roles were. In fact, he sometimes thought the only things they had in common were guns and testosterone.

Ian was pondering how long he should wait when a figure emerged at the top of the hill. Dr. DeMarco moved with the ease and familiarity of an expert hiker as she made her way down toward the parking lot. She spotted him, paused, looked behind her, then continued down. Seeing her in her jeans, hiking boots, and a long-sleeved shirt with a backpack slung over her shoulder, Damian's comment about her floated into Ian's mind. She was an attractive woman. Athletic and strong looking with long brown hair pulled back into a ponytail, olive skin, and brown eyes that confirmed the Italian heritage her last name hinted at. She didn't look like she wore makeup or needed to. But then again, he was a guy—what did he know about makeup? To him, whatever she did or didn't do was irrelevant; she looked good.

"Dr. DeMarco," he said, straightening off his Jeep.

She walked toward him, taking a sip from a metal water bottle. "Deputy Chief MacAllister," she acknowledged as she stopped in front of him. He studied her for a moment, not thinking anything in particular, but taking her measure nonetheless.

"So, did you find her?" she asked, turning away from him and opening the trunk of her car.

"How do you know it's a her?"

"I don't." She dumped her backpack into the trunk, unzipped the main pocket, and pulled out a lightweight pullover. "But given the size of the wrist bones I saw and what looked like a thin, gold bracelet, I'm presuming. Of course it could be a young person or a cross dresser or the bracelet could have been placed there. It could be anything. Was it a whole body?"

Ian nodded, watching her pull on the sweater.

"Sorry about that," she said as her head emerged. "My guess is that you don't see a lot of murder up here. Sorry you have to see it now."

"I could use your help."

She froze for a moment, a split second, then shook her head. "I'm sorry, I really am, but I'm on vacation. The New York lab is excellent—the doctor who runs it is a good friend of mine. They'll be able to help you."

"But I hear you're one of the best."

Crossing her arms over her chest and leaning against her car, Dr. DeMarco eyed him. He could see the honest debate in her eyes. He could try the guilt card and, at this point, he was pretty certain it would work. But he caught a glimpse of the dark circles under her eyes and something stopped him. Not from asking, but from trying to manipulate her.

"Look, the truth is my boss is on vacation now—something we should both be glad about," he added as an aside. "He thinks I'm out for his job—"

"Are you?"

Ian shook his head. "Half the time I'm not even sure I want *my* job. But he thinks I'm after his anyway. He's a real prick about it. If he comes back and this isn't resolved, or heading in that direction, he'll derail it. I'm not going to disguise the fact that asking you to get involved is as much for the victim as it is for me."

"I get the sense, Deputy Chief MacAllister, that whether I help or not, you're going to do a thorough job. My guess is that doing it any other way isn't even an option for you." A ghost of a smile touched her lips. The first he'd seen from her.

"Believe me, I will do everything in my power to find out who this person is, what happened to him or her, and who did it. But, given that I think Vic will do more harm than good, both to me and the case, you can't blame me for wanting to stack the cards in my favor by using you and your skills." Ian watched her ponder him and his request. It still left him feeling a little slimy—she looked like she deserved her vacation, not a murder investigation. But at least it felt better being honest with her about his situation than trying to manipulate her. His therapist would be so proud.

After a long moment when the sounds of nearby birds and the distant cars on the Taconic Parkway seemed impossibly loud, she conceded. "I'll take a look. I'm not promising anything and I'm not going to process any evidence for you because I'm not authorized to. But I'll take a look and tell you what I can."

"Thank you," he nodded, more grateful than he expected. He didn't know Vivienne DeMarco from Adam, but still, he felt he now had an ally. "We're still working to clear the debris away, but they should be close to done."

"I want to shower and change. We have plenty of light, so give me forty-five minutes and meet me at The Tavern. I'll be ready then." Again, Ian nodded then watched as she climbed into her car and drove away. She wasn't warm to the idea, but she was going to do it. He couldn't ask for much more.

A little over an hour later, Ian and Dr. DeMarco pulled up to the spot on County Route 8. He glanced at his passenger who was checking out the scene. The car ride had been silent, but not uncomfortable.

"Must look a bit different than last night," he broke in. She inclined her head.

"It was dark and pouring rain most of the time—it was hard to see much of anything that wasn't ten feet in front of me. In the daylight, if you ignore the crime scene tape and the knowledge that someone was buried here, it's pretty." She sounded surprised.

"You've never been to this area before?"

She shook her head. "I know, crazy, right? I grew up in Boston and I know it's only a few hours away, but well, when I get home, I like to stay there. I travel a lot."

"What made you come here now?"

She was quiet for a moment and he couldn't tell whether she was debating how much to tell him about herself or if she just didn't know the answer. Then she shrugged. "I have a close family friend, kind of like an aunt. She and her husband come here all the time. She's always talking about it. When I was passing through New York City, I saw the sign for the Taconic State Parkway and on a whim I decided to take it."

"You regret that decision?"

"I'm here," she shrugged again and reached for the door handle. "Doesn't matter whether I regret it or not."

They exited the car and headed toward the primary scene. Ducking under the crime scene tape, Ian caught a few speculative glances cast at Dr. DeMarco. Heading it off at the pass, he announced, "Everyone, this is Dr. DeMarco, FBI consultant. She's not here officially but happens to be traveling through the area and has been nice enough to stop and give us her opinion." He didn't mention she was the one who found the body. He didn't feel like having to explain it to everyone else, so he took the path of least resistance.

He watched her scope out the area as they made their way to the grave. When they arrived at the side of the hole dug by the crew, she went down on her haunches. She studied the skeleton for a long time. He didn't know what she was looking at or for, but her obvious competence reassured him. And so he studied her.

She had changed into another pair of jeans and a different pair of boots—the kind of boots that were made for a woman, with heels and all. She had on a light green sweater and her hair was pulled back again and still damp. Her curves were hard to miss, as was her confidence. The combination of the two made it hard for him to ignore the fact that Dr. Vivienne DeMarco was most definitely a woman.

Not taking her eyes from the body, she held her hand up and asked for a flashlight. The daylight was still good, but he didn't question her as he handed one over. He watched as she swept the beam over the body. Finally, she spoke.

"It's a female. Between the ages of twenty-five and thirty-five. I can't tell for certain from this angle, but there does not appear to be any severe trauma to the bones. I also can't see it from here, but when you get her out, I'd take a close look at the hyoid bone."

"Strangulation?" Ian asked.

"Possibly, but she could have been starved to death, or suffocated, in which case the hyoid will likely be intact. But in cases like this, with no obvious trauma, it's the first place I look.

"She's Caucasian," she continued. "And has had at least one child," she added, shining the light on the pelvis area.

"Then there is probably family looking for her? Husband, boyfriend? Maybe even the kid?" interjected Wyatt Granger, one of Ian's officers. Dr. DeMarco looked up at the young man as if just now realizing other people were around.

"Not if the husband or boyfriend did it, or there is even a husband or boyfriend at all," Ian stated. Wyatt's questions were nice but naïve. "And the kid, if it's still alive, might not even know who his or her mother is. For all we know, she might have been a migrant prostitute with no family to speak of."

Ian felt, more than saw, Vivienne's gaze bounce to him. He didn't need to look at her to feel her censure. Without a word, she swung her light back to the body.

"She was restrained," she stated. *That* got his attention. He came down onto his haunches beside her. "You can see where there is some damage to the bones." She shined the light on each wrist and each ankle in turn. He examined the illuminated bones and, sure enough, he could see a couple of small, straight lines, each about a half an inch long.

His stomach went flat. "She fought the restraints."

"Yes, she did," came the quiet confirmation.

"Can you tell what it was? Rope?"

She shook her head. "With a mark like that, it's more likely to be something like a metal shackle."

"A shackle?"

"Hhmm, and," she paused again, leaning forward, "it looks like she was restrained lying down with her arms up over her head."

"As opposed to sitting or standing?"

"I wouldn't rule anything out, but based on the location of the damage, I'd look at a restraint system that tied her down from below."

"So she might have been tortured?" he asked. At this, her eyes swung to his and he realized he'd just given her more information about himself, about his life, than he'd intended. Torture probably wasn't the first thing your average small-town cop would've come up with.

"And possibly sexually assaulted," she agreed, returning her gaze to the body.

"Any indication of that?"

She shook her head. "Not from what I can see, but given her age and the evidence of restraints, I would say it's a possibility. When was the last time this road was repaved?" she asked, shining the flashlight onto the layers of blacktop Ian's crew had sliced through to reach the body.

"Three years ago, after a big storm. Is that the time of death?"

Dr. DeMarco shook her head. "You'll have to run more tests to know the time of death, but at least you know the dump date."

"Can you do a reconstruction?"

Her eyes shot to his again, and a look of annoyance crossed her features. He was pushing and he knew it. Asking her in front of everyone else, making it harder to say no, was a strategic move. And, judging by her expression, a bad strategic move at that.

"I think I'm done here," she said, turning away from him in more ways than one. After one last look at the body, she stood, handed Ian the flashlight, then moved to read Wyatt's badge.

"Officer Granger," she said. "You should know I've been doing this kind of work for a while now, and it can get to you." Wyatt's eyes darted to Ian's, but the young man was listening to Dr. DeMarco. "All the successful agents I know," she continued, "all the best detectives and everyone else who works these kinds of cases—every single one of them—they all have the same thing in common."

"What's that, ma'am?" he asked, as if asking for her permission to ask the question.

"They have all somehow learned how to preserve their humanity—to keep themselves from assuming the worst in every person or every situation, to maintain their belief that there are good people in the world. It's a unique ability in this field and sometimes the only thing that keeps us sane. Keep it, Officer Granger, it will serve you well, I promise." Her words were spoken to Wyatt, but Ian knew they were meant as much, if not more, for him.

"Thank you, ma'am," the young officer smiled. Ian was certain Wyatt fell a little bit in love with Vivienne DeMarco in that moment.

"You're welcome. And don't let anyone else tell you otherwise," she added as she turned toward the Jeep. "I'm ready to go, Deputy Chief MacAllister."

"I need another few minutes. Go ahead and wait in the car." It was childish, he knew. He didn't need another few minutes, but he also didn't like being reprimanded, veiled or not, in front of his reports. Especially when she was right. Without a word, she ducked under the tape and headed back toward his Jeep.

Forty-five minutes later, he made his way toward his car. His empty car. He ran a hand over his face and cursed himself. And then he laughed—for the first time in a long time. He had to admit, she had style. She didn't like the way he'd handled her, so rather than sulk, she'd taken matters into her own hands.

He found her walking alongside the road about a half mile from town. He slowed his Jeep and rolled down the window.

"Want a lift?"

"No thanks, I'm almost there." She didn't bother to look at him.

"Sorry I put you on the spot."

"Call me crazy, MacAllister, but I don't like being manipulated or lied to." Her pace didn't slow.

"I didn't lie to you."

"Yes, you did. You're not sorry you put me on the spot asking for the reconstruction. You may be disappointed that I didn't cave, but you're not sorry you tried."

He let out a huff of air. Dr. DeMarco was right. But it was easy for her to say no. She didn't have an unidentified body to deal with. And he told her so. For some reason that stopped her cold.

"You think this is *easy* for me?"

Ian put his car in park and hit the emergency blinkers as she crossed the road and halted at his window. "How many murders has this area seen in the last ten years?" she asked.

He had looked into it as soon as they'd found the body so he didn't have to think about his answer. "Two."

"Let me guess, bar brawls or domestic violence?"

Wherever this was going, it wasn't good. "One of each," he answered.

"Now I'm not saying you haven't seen your fair share of death, MacAllister. I'll bet you have. Special Forces of some sort?"

"Rangers," he answered with a frown. "How did you know?"

"Because you seem the sort." She waved a dismissive hand at him that he liked even less than the comment, but before he could respond, she continued. "I've been working cases like this for over eight years. More if you count my work while I was still in residency. Do you know how many bodies I worked on last year?" It was a rhetorical question. "Over 300," she supplied. "Think about that, MacAllister. Think about how many bodies I have worked with over the years. How many murders—how many children, parents, wives, and husbands that is. How much anger, pain, anguish, and guilt I've seen.

"I literally can't remember the last time I had more than a day off because there is always, *always* someone new that can use my help. Some husband who needs closure for the murder of his wife. Parents who are desperate to find their child, even if they know that child is dead. How do you say no to that? How can *anyone* possibly say no to that? So no, this isn't easy for me. It's not easy stepping away and taking the break everyone says I so desperately need. It's not easy knowing that I could be somewhere helping someone bring closure or justice to a senseless death. But I have finally found the courage to take that time for myself before I'm useless to everyone. Before I'm useless to myself."

She was breathing hard and he could see her pulse beating a rapid rhythm in the hollow of her throat. And, though she probably wouldn't admit it, she was blinking back tears.

"Believe me, MacAllister," her voice quieted. "Nothing about this is easy."

It wasn't often that Ian was speechless, but she had rendered him that. Taking advantage of it, she turned and walked away. He let her go, watching her figure disappear down the road, and sat thinking about her words.

When he walked into The Tavern, his eyes found the doctor's before the door closed behind him. She was nursing a beer at the bar, staring into the empty space between her and the bottles stacked neatly behind the counter across from her. She looked up when he approached her, a look of disinterested curiosity on her face.

"I'm sorry," he said.

Her expressionless eyes gazed back at him. Then she shrugged it off.

"Have you ordered dinner?" he asked.

She arched an eyebrow at his gall, and he almost smiled.

"I need to eat. I thought maybe we could eat together. I promise not to talk about the case."

She gave him a look, as if wondering what they might talk about if not the case, but then accepted with a nod of her head. After telling him she'd already ordered, she motioned toward a table in the back. He placed his dinner order with Rob, grabbed a beer, and joined her.

"So, how was your hike this morning?"

She looked surprised by the question but rolled with it. "It was good. It's beautiful around here. I can see why my aunt loves it. Very bucolic, reminds me of England."

"Did you meet Angus?"

"Angus?"

"Old guy, looks a little crazy, but—"

"Mostly harmless?" She finished his sentence and he nodded. "Yes, I did. How did you know?"

"You paused on your way back down to the lot and looked up the hill, like you were looking for someone."

"Ah," she said with a small smile. "He seemed an interesting character. Offered me a dram of whiskey from his flask. Said I looked like I needed it." She paused. "I'm pretty sure that was an insult, but it was hard to tell with him."

Ian smiled. "If he offered you a drink, it wasn't an insult. So, tell me how you ended up here in Windsor?"

"Like I said, I'm on a leave of absence. I was just driving through."

"On your way where?" He was trying to be chatty, but his skills were rusty and he knew his questions came out sounding more like an interrogation.

"To wherever I decide to go next."

He smiled again. "Not much of a conversationalist, are you?"

She let out a small laugh at that. "Now, are you the kettle or the pot?"

"I'm trying," he pointed out. She gave him a look. "I've just never met anyone like you before," he offered. One of her eyebrows shot up. "And I don't mean that as a pickup line. I mean I've never met a forensic psychologist before. I've never met anyone who has managed to work for both federal and state law enforcement."

"I'm good at what I do."

"I'm sure you are, and you don't need to get defensive with me."

"That remains to be seen."

She had a point, given what he'd done to her earlier in the day. But still, he was a fixer, so he asked. "Is it just with me or are you always on the defensive?"

She let out a long-suffering breath. "Do you know what percentage of women work in the Boston PD?"

Ian shook his head.

"A small fraction of a minority percent," she answered. "I'd finished my medical residency, my PhD, and the police academy when I joined up at the age of twenty-eight. I'm pretty good at not letting things get to me, but sometimes they do."

He sat back and took a sip of his beer. It couldn't have been easy joining such a predominantly male organization with her credentials and at her age. Come to think of it, it probably wouldn't have been easy to join any professional organization with her credentials at her age. Doing the math, he realized she must have started college early and finished fast. A regular child prodigy. It gave a little insight into Dr. DeMarco's character and he could deal with that.

"Like I said, you don't have to be defensive around me." He had no problems accepting highly capable women in law enforcement or anywhere else. Good was good, regardless of gender.

"Well, as I said, that remains to be seen. How did you find out about me?"

"I have a buddy with the FBI."

"Which team?"

"His Assistant Director is a woman by the name of Sharon Titus."

"He must be good, Sharon only works with the best."

"He said the same thing about you."

"And what about you? How did you end up here?"

Which reminded him. "What did you mean that I 'seem the type' to have been special forces?"

Rob chose that moment to bring their dinners. She took a sip of beer while the food was laid out. He'd ordered a big shepherd's pie. She'd ordered the ploughman's meal of local cheeses, homemade Irish bread, and a salad. No frills and entirely serviceable—some protein, carbs, and greens, nothing more or less. It told him something about the woman across the table and while it hadn't been a line when he'd told her he'd never met anyone like her, the more these little details interested him, the more it was beginning to feel like one.

"Your intensity and confidence that borders on arrogance," she said, answering his earlier question.

"What?" he asked, coming back to the conversation.

"It's what gave you away as special forces of some type."

"Arrogance?"

"It's not a bad thing. Given what you guys do, a little arrogance can go a long way to saving your ass, or someone else's," she added. "You were injured." It wasn't a question.

"IED."

"In the left leg?"

He nodded.

"You have a slight limp—nothing too noticeable to someone not in my line of business. So, how did you end up here, in Windsor?" she parroted his question.

"After my stint recovering in Walter Reed, I needed a place to recover." Both mentally and physically was unspoken, but judging by the look on her face, understood. "I grew up here. My parents have a farm, a couple of hundred acres out off of County Route 9. It's quiet."

"You live with them?"

He had to smile at the surprise in her voice. "No. My sister and her husband, when they first got married twenty years ago, built a small place on the north forty, so to speak. They moved out about seven years ago and I live there now."

"And the job?"

He shrugged, a little uncomfortable. "I needed something to do."

"But you don't like it all that much?" He was of a mind to tell her tit for tat; if he talked about himself, it was only fair that she do the same. But something held him back and he answered.

"It's not always an easy transition from being a soldier to being the police. People think it's a no-brainer, but the skills are different. It's not that I don't like it, per se, but breaking up bar fights and stopping underage drinking is a far cry from what I was doing."

"Then why do you do it?"

That was the million-dollar question. "Right now, I do it because they need someone to do it. Will I do it forever? I don't know. Maybe it will be different when I settle in more."

"When your boss decides to back off and leave you alone. *If* your boss ever decides to back off and leave you alone." He was surprised she'd remembered that, and there was some truth to what she was saying. He liked the other officers he worked with. And he liked feeling like part of a bigger community. But Vic made things, well, difficult.

"There is that."

They had both finished their meals and drinks. She didn't strike him as a dessert person and so they had reached that awkward moment of goodbye. Not friends, not colleagues either, Ian didn't quite know what to do.

"Thank you," he said. "For today and no, I don't mean that facetiously. We have more now than we did before, so I wanted to say thank you."

She regarded him in silence and he wished like hell he knew how to read her, but she was a tough person to read.

"Where did you take her?" she asked.

"The Community Hospital at Riverside. It's the next town over. Not a much bigger town, but it has the hospital and morgue."

"I'll take a look tomorrow if you want me to. I'll do my best with a reconstruction, but I'm not authorized to work with you, so I'll be limited in what I can do since I won't be able to touch her."

Ian wasn't sure he'd heard right—it took a few seconds to sink in before he nodded in acknowledgement of Dr. DeMarco's offer. "I can pick you up at ten," he proposed.

"Why don't you give me directions and I'll meet you there at two? I spoke to my aunt this morning—the family friend I mentioned that loves this area," she reminded him. "Anyway, she insisted I visit a few places she loves while I'm out here. The Martin Van Buren house, some Shaker village north of here, and some lunch place in West Stockbridge that's run by a family friend. I know, it seems petty compared to what you're dealing with—"

"I'll take any help I can get. She's not scheduled to be transported to the state lab for two days, so a few hours here or there isn't going to make a difference."

And, with this new development, saying goodbye was a little easier. He had a plan, and he liked plans. He gave her directions to the hospital as well as his contact information. And when he walked out of The Tavern, he was feeling better than he had any right to.

CHAPTER 4

"DEPUTY CHIEF MACALLISTER, SORRY I'M late," Vivi said as she walked into the hospital morgue the next day, fifteen minutes late. "I got stuck behind a tractor trailer somewhere between West Stockbridge and here."

"Call me Ian, and it's not a problem." His clipped tone told her otherwise. She cast a glance at him as she scanned the room. No, it looked like it was a big problem. But, even with his tense jaw and tight fists, standing there in his uniform, he was a striking figure.

"Need a hand with anything?" he asked as she set her workbag down on a table.

She shook her head. "Is that her?" Vivi motioned toward a shroud-covered table and Ian nodded. The room was standard-issue hospital morgue, complete with linoleum tile floors, body storage for six, and that unique scent of industrial cleaner and human waste. In addition to the table that now held her things and the gurney holding the skeleton, the only other pieces of furniture were an outdated chunky wood desk and a red padded chair on wheels.

"Did you think I wasn't going to come?" she asked as she began removing her equipment. She wouldn't have access to entire bag of tricks, but she did have an excellent camera, her computer, and a sketchpad. She would rely more on the camera and computer, but she liked having the option of the sketchpad.

"No, you said you were coming."

"Then why the look when I walked in the room?" Vivi should have dropped it, but something nagged her not to. And she hoped that if she was casual about the question, he would feel casual about answering. Psychology 101. But when Ian didn't answer for a long moment, she looked up from her computer and focused on the man.

He lifted a shoulder and turned his back to her on the pretense of picking up some papers from the desk. "Most folks around here are familiar with the roads, sometimes too familiar, and sometimes they aren't used to seeing other people on them. They drive crazier than I would like."

He'd been worried about her—about her safety. Not whether she would bail on him. The realization brought her up short, though she didn't show it. Vivi didn't often work with people who cared about her outside of what she could bring to a case. It was new and kind of sweet, but judging by his posture, something told her he wouldn't appreciate the sentiment if she said so.

"I'm sorry you have to stay," she commented instead, dropping it. She wasn't officially part of the investigation so couldn't be left alone with the evidence. "I'll try to work quickly but it could take a few hours."

"Not a problem. Mind if I watch?"

She shook her head and Ian approached her side. "I'll take a detailed set of pictures first," she started explaining. "Normally I like to handle the skull itself, but since that isn't possible right now, this should be pretty good. Once I have a complete set of pictures, I'll upload them to my computer and then start running the reconstruction software. It's a little bit art and a little bit science, so it can take some time, depending on how things go."

"Fair enough," he said, stepping aside as she began to take pictures. She chatted with him as she snapped away, telling him about her day and other inconsequential things.

Forty-five minutes later, Vivi popped the camera's memory card into her computer, created a file, and dumped all the pictures into it. One by one, she pulled out images that gave her detail or insight she needed. There had been a few long strands of brown hair still attached to the scalp so she was using that information, along with basic statistics, to justify making the eyes brown and the skin not exactly dark, but not fair either.

"This is the part that might take a while and I'll be a lot less chatty now," she preemptively warned Ian. This part of what she did would take much more concentration than the photos had. When he didn't respond, Vivi glanced up at him. He was leaning against a wall, ankles and arms crossed, looking for all the world like he could stay there for another twelve hours without so much as blinking. He raised an eyebrow at her.

"Sorry, that was unnecessary," she added with a rueful shake of her head. There was no way Ian MacAllister was going to start complaining. This was a cakewalk compared to some of the things he had probably been through.

She worked on her computer for three hours before she was satisfied with her product. It might not be an exact image, but she hoped it was close enough to get some hits off the missing persons database, provided someone had reported her missing. Vivi sat back and stretched her arms over her head, working out the kinks in her neck and back.

"Done?" Ian asked from behind her. She jumped at the sound of his voice. He'd been so quiet the entire time she'd been working, she had all but forgotten he was even in the room.

"Yes," she said, getting her bearings again. "Come have a look," she added, sliding her chair to the side. She looked at the picture, then up at the man standing at her shoulder. His arms were crossed over his chest and he was frowning.

"She looks like you," he commented. She laughed.

"A large portion of the population has brown hair and brown eyes and, I'll grant you, we both have those." But beyond that, Vivi couldn't see much of a likeness.

"You made her on the younger end of your age range."

Vivi tilted her head and examined the picture again. "I did. I'm not sure why. Without examining the bones, her age can't be precisely determined."

"Is that the 'art' part of the process?"

"I suppose so. Again, I have to tell you, this may not be accurate."

"But it might be accurate enough to get some hits," he finished her sentence. "And then we'll have to do some testing to be sure." She nodded at his assessment.

"Do you still have the bracelet she wore?" she asked.

"Yes, there is a storage locker here where we put the little evidence, other than the remains, that we have. Do you want to see it?" When she nodded, Ian turned and walked toward the back of the room without a word. He returned to her side a few minutes later with a box from the locker. After signing the sheet, he cut the tape and pulled out a small plastic bag, which he held up for her to see.

Inside it was a plain, gold chain bracelet, nothing distinctive about it. "Is there a tag on the clasp?" she asked.

He fingered the evidence through the plastic until the clasp came into view. "Nothing."

"Too bad. My cousins and I all had bracelets like that. Our moms gave them to us for confirmation. But ours all had small tags with the name of the jeweler and the date of the confirmation. Guess you aren't that lucky."

"Guess not," he agreed, placing the bag back in the box and taping everything back together. When he moved to return the box to the locker, she turned her gaze back to the body. It was such a loss. It always was. Yes, it was possible that the woman these bones had been was a terrible person, but chances were she wasn't. Chances were she'd had people in her life who'd loved her—and at least one person in her life who'd hated her.

"You're thinking about asking to be officially put on this case, aren't you?" Lost in her thoughts about the Jane Doe on the table, Vivi hadn't noticed that Ian had come back to stand beside her. They both stared at the remains of the young woman.

"I could," she said, testing it more with herself than with him. "It's not like I have somewhere I need to be."

"It's also not like you've had a vacation in years," Ian pointed out, much to her surprise.

"It's an old crime, there might not be much to go on. You might wrap it up quickly if there aren't any leads," she countered.

"If there aren't any leads, then it won't matter if you're here or in Tahiti."

Vivi smiled. "Now, if I were in Tahiti, that would be another issue, but since I'm not, and I'm here, I can stay if you want."

She felt Ian studying her, no doubt weighing whether to look a gift horse in the mouth or not. She knew where he would come out.

"I can't authorize you to come on board."

"Vic?"

He nodded. "I'm in charge, but because I'm so new, my authority only goes so far, unless he is incapacitated rather than just difficult to reach."

"Who else can authorize me?"

"I suppose Vic's boss, but she'll want to know why I don't have Vic's approval."

"The governor can authorize me."

"I'm sure she could," he laughed. Then he caught her meaning. "Shit, you know the governor, don't you?" he said, running a hand through his hair.

Vivi smiled again, pulled her cell from her purse, and dialed. Ian crossed his arms and leaned his hip against the table as Vivi put the phone on speaker.

"Vivi!" came the governor's voice without preamble.

"Hi, Kathryn. How are you?" Vivi always loved talking to Kathryn. The woman was more astute than anyone had a right to be, but what Vivi admired most was her compassion.

"I'm fine," she answered. "And how is my prodigal son, Daniel? He hasn't blown up anything in your lab again has he?"

"Daniel is doing great. And he only blew up that one experiment that one time." Vivi laughed, remembering the look on her student's face when his experiment hadn't gone quite right.

"You wouldn't tell me if he weren't doing well anyway, would you, Professor?"

Vivi laughed. "No, I would not. I leave it to your son to tell you what he wants you to know."

"You're far too ethical for my liking, Dr. DeMarco," the governor rejoined in mock censure.

"And Henry?" Vivi asked. "How is your handsome husband?"

"My handsome husband has been talked into being interim dean of the engineering college and is regretting every moment of it. He can't wait to find a new permanent dean and get back into the classroom."

"He is a great professor. I'm sure the students will be glad to have him back."

"They will—but enough about us, what are you up to, my dear?"

"Well, I'm in your neck of the woods." Even without seeing Kathryn's face, she could feel the string of questions forming in the woman's head. They'd known each other long enough for Kathryn to know that Vivi wouldn't just find herself in the Hudson Valley. "Given everything that has happened in the past year, I thought I might take some time to wander around and lose myself a little bit."

Across the line, they heard Kathryn sigh and Vivi felt Ian's eyes on her, no doubt wondering what she meant about the last year. "No less than you deserve, my dear. But you do know what they say about losing oneself. You might not like what you find."

"Well, in this case it happens to be true. I found a dead body outside of Windsor."

Vivi glanced at Ian in the silence that followed. They could hear the governor clicking away on her keyboard.

"Hhmm, so that was you?"

"Did you pull up the report?" Vivi asked.

"Yes, of course. Doesn't look like you have much to go on."

"We don't, but I just finished the reconstruction and I'd like to be authorized to work on the case."

"I can't imagine you need my approval for an authorization?"

"The current chief of police is out of town and the acting chief is new and doesn't have the authority. We could have gone one step higher, but I figured this was faster and easier."

"Hhmm, well, Vic Ballard *is* a piece of work. I assume," she paused, presumably scrolling through her files, "I assume Deputy Chief MacAllister is in charge?"

"Yes, Ma'am," he answered.

"And you've convinced Vivi to look into the case for you?"

"Dr. DeMarco offered to look into the case with me," he clarified.

"Well, if you've got her, hold onto her in every sense of the word, MacAllister. She's one in a million." Vivi cut a glance to Ian, whose lips quirked into a grin. No chance he'd missed the governor's not-so-subtle attempt at matchmaking.

"Totally inappropriate, Kathryn," Vivi interjected.

"Nonsense, dear. Someone has to look out for your love life since you don't."

"Really, Kathryn?" Vivi retorted with affectionate resignation. "He could be sixty and ugly."

"He's not. I have his file in front of me. Deputy Chief MacAllister?"

"Yes, Ma'am?"

"Please don't take this the wrong way, but you are a very good looking young man."

"I'm not sure there is a wrong way to take that, but thank you."

"You're welcome. Now, it's actually a jurisdictional pain in the ass to authorize you, Vivi, so I'll do it under one condition."

Vivi groaned, knowing the condition wasn't going to have anything to do with the case. "Of course, name it."

"You have to come to dinner while you're in the area."

That wasn't so bad.

"And bring MacAllister with you."

"He's very busy, Kathryn."

"Fine, I'll have Henry invite that nice new assistant dean from the school."

Vivi cast him a questioning glance. She didn't know Ian MacAllister well, but she was sure he would be a better dinner companion than one of Henry's colleagues. Still, it was his call if he wanted to pay the price for getting her on the case.

"I'd be happy to join you," Ian said.

"Excellent," Kathryn commented, sounding way too pleased with herself. "MacAllister, email me the resource request and I'll have it back to you by the morning. Vivi, call Henry and set up a dinner."

They both agreed and when Vivi hung up she cast a wary look at Ian. "Sorry?" she offered.

"That was not at all like I thought it would be," he answered. "And I didn't know you were a professor, too?"

"Adjunct," she qualified. "I only take a couple of doctoral students at any given time. Kathryn's son, Daniel, is one of them. We've known each other for a while."

"I can tell. How did you meet?" he asked as she moved to gather her things.

"Sad story, really. Daniel is a grad student of mine now. But back when he was sixteen, before his mother was even in politics, he contacted me to help with a cold case. When he was six, his twin sister was kidnapped from their home."

"I think I remember my parents saying something about that when she was running for election."

"Yes, the kidnapping came up a lot during her campaign, as I'm sure you can imagine. But you were probably out of the country at the time." Knowing he wouldn't confirm or deny, she continued. "Anyway, Daniel read some article about me and some case I'd worked on. He contacted me to ask for help, and how could I say no to a sixteen-year-old who only wanted to find his sister? So I took the case."

She paused while Ian slid the table that held their Jane Doe into one of the wall crypts and checked the locks on everything.

"Did you find her?" he asked.

"We did." They resumed the conversation as they headed out

of the hospital. "It wasn't a happy ending. Kristen had been killed within hours of when she was taken. But we did find her body and we did find at least one of the people involved."

"At least one?"

"If you ask me, there were at least two, maybe three people involved. But the only one we caught was a former student of Henry's. Turns out she was obsessed with him and thought that if she took his daughter they could run off and have a family together. When Kristen fought, the woman struck her. The blow knocked Kristen down and she hit her head on a rock, killing her instantly."

"That's shitty."

"Yeah, understatement. But Kathryn and I have been friends ever since. Despite the fact that she keeps trying to marry me off."

They reached their cars and stopped. "Is that such a bad thing?" Ian asked.

"Not really, but except for Henry, she doesn't have very good taste. Don't get me wrong, the men she tries to set me up with are all great. Nice guys, accomplished and all that. But they are like younger versions of Henry."

"Which worked for her."

"But isn't my type," Vivi ended the sentence then realized where the conversation had gone. "I should go."

"Do you want to grab some dinner first? It's close to seven."

She shook her head. "I need to get back and make some calls—let my family know where I am, that sort of thing. I have some errands to run in the morning, but I'll come back down to the hospital after lunch and begin my investigation."

"Sounds good," Ian said, opening her door for her.

"I'll call you in the morning to make sure I'm cleared first," she added.

He nodded. "You know where to find me."

***

Ian watched Vivienne drive away before getting into his own car.

He was attracted to her, no way around it. And on more than a physical level. She was a woman of contradictions. To call her intriguing was too cliché, but there was no other way he could describe her. She was friends with the governor, an international traveler, an FBI consultant, a professor, and a medical examiner. But when she relaxed, she was quick with a smile, more empathetic than was probably healthy, and felt too obligated to the dead and to the living they left behind—not that he had any right to fault her for that since he was benefiting from it at the moment. Ian couldn't help but identify with her; he knew a thing or two about feeling obligated and what it could do to a person. He reached down and rubbed his thigh and, even through his pants, he could feel the raised scars along his leg. Letting out a breath, he brought his hand up to turn the key in the ignition and started for home.

Obligation wasn't always a bad thing. For him, and he suspected for Vivienne too, obligation wasn't wrapped in martyrdom, but rather in guilt mixed with a genuine belief in the good he was doing. He'd bet she was driven to do what she did because she could, and her moral code wouldn't let her do otherwise. At least, if she was anything like him.

Passing the mini–Statue of Liberty that marked the edge of Riverside, Ian headed north toward Windsor and wondered about Vivienne's conversation with the governor and what might have happened to her in the past year. Maybe it had something to do with one too many bodies, he thought, remembering what she'd said yesterday. Her practical nature and obvious work ethic made him think she wasn't a woman who'd make the decision to walk away easily. So, whatever it was, it must have been big. It had taken an IED to make him to walk away.

Whatever brought her here, he wasn't going to speculate or look a gift horse in the mouth. But maybe he could hedge his bets and at least try to make it easier for her. He couldn't change the facts of the case, but there were other things he could do for Vivienne.

CHAPTER 5

VIVI WALKED INTO THE TAVERN and caught Rob's eye. They'd talked enough over the past few days that she could call him an acquaintance, if not a friend-in-the-making.

"Hey, Rob. I have some things to take care of, but I was wondering if I could get a ploughman's plate and salad in my room?"

"Already there," he answered, drying a glass and stacking it back in a perfect line.

"Ah, okay. Thanks?"

Rob smiled. "Ian called. Said you were on your way back and hadn't eaten dinner. He asked me to get a plate ready for you."

Vivi gave this bit of information some thought. It made her feel a little strange because he didn't need to take care of her, or even look out for her. But he had and hadn't made big deal out of it. A small luxury she didn't often experience.

"So, you're going to help him with that murder case?" Rob's voice interrupted her thoughts.

"As much as I can," she answered. "He's a good cop, isn't he?"

Rob nodded. "How long will you stick around?"

"We'll have to see how things go. It's too early yet to have any ideas about where the evidence will take us."

"But there is evidence?"

"There's always evidence," she answered without answering.

"Fair enough," he said, sliding a pint in front of her. "And when you're done, are you going to head home?" She shrugged in response, not having given it much thought.

"Boston's not far," he continued. "Just a couple of hours away."

She nodded at his obvious statement. "Go ahead and take that upstairs," Rob added with a nod to the glass in her hand. "I'll collect it with the rest of dishes when you're done. Just give me a call."

She thanked him and turned toward the stairs. She was halfway up when she realized something. Coming back down, she stopped at the end of the bar. Rob looked up, drying yet another glass. The man was always on the move.

"Are you trying to play matchmaker for Ian and me?" She should have let it go, but on the heels of her conversation with Kathryn, she couldn't do that.

"Men don't play matchmaker, Dr. DeMarco."

"Call me Vivienne or Vivi. Then were you doing whatever it is men do to try to get their friends, uh," she paused, not quite sure of the word she wanted to use.

"Laid?" he offered, his lips tilting into a smile, teasing her.

"Maybe not quite the word I was looking for, but something like that," she conceded. She didn't think Rob was out to help his friend along on that front—she was pretty sure Ian didn't need any help *on that front*—but something between a one-night stand and marriage was more likely.

"Maybe."

She thought about asking him why her, or why not someone else, but she wasn't sure she wanted to know the answer.

"Okay, just, uh, checking," she said instead and made a beeline for the stairs. She hadn't missed how attractive Ian was. And she'd sensed his awareness of her, in a subtle, tentative sort of way, like he was testing out whether the interest was mutual. But she hadn't let her mind go any further than an almost clinical analysis of the situation—interest noted, felt, and filed away. It was different now though, with Kathryn's conversation still hovering in her mind, followed by Rob's very male inquiry, and she knew it would be harder to ignore the whole thing. The next time she saw Ian, it—whatever *it* was—would be lingering there on the fringes of her mind like a pesky bug, flittering in and out of her line of sight at random moments.

She pushed the door to her room open a little harder than necessary then grabbed it to keep it from hitting the opposite wall. Setting all her stuff down, Vivi stripped off her clothes and jumped into the shower. When she no longer smelled like a morgue, she dried off, slipped into a nightshirt, and propped her dinner tray on the bed. It was early, but she didn't feel like getting dressed in something else only to get undressed again in a few hours.

Picking up her cell, Vivi dialed her Aunt Mary, who would, no doubt, want a minute-by-minute account of her morning excursion. And an hour later, she hung up with Mary and dialed her Uncle Michael.

"Darling girl, is that you?"

"You know it's me, Uncle Michael, you have caller ID," she answered with a laugh. Uncle Mike, was one of her father's three brothers, all of whom had become cops. He'd married an Irish girl, back in the day, and so, while Vivi's dad was firmly rooted in the Italian community in Boston, Uncle Mike and his wife Nancy straddled the Irish-Italian divide.

"What's doing, young lady? Are we going to see your gorgeous face here any time soon?"

In response, Vivi gave him a brief overview of her situation. Not surprisingly, he was upset that she had landed herself in yet another murder investigation. But she could also tell he was pleased that she was no longer driving around the country alone with no rhyme or reason—that kind of spontaneity worried him. And, since it hadn't been in her character either until a month ago, she was pretty sure he might have given himself an ulcer over her little road trip.

She gave him the rundown on the players, the victim, and the evidence. He mulled it over with her for a bit, tossing ideas back and forth, but since there was so little to go on at this point, the conversation was fairly short.

"Well, if anyone can help bring that girl some peace, you can," he offered in blind support of Vivi. "Your Aunt Nancy is grabbing the phone from me, now. I'll talk to you soon, Vivi. You keep in touch," he added. There was a shuffle of the phone being handed around, then Nancy DeMarco's voice came on the line.

"Luv, it is you!" her Aunt Nancy started. "I'm so glad you called. I just walked in the door, I was out shopping for Kiera's baby shower. It's a few days away and I'm leaving for Los Angeles tomorrow— any chance you will change your mind and come with me?" Kiera was Nancy and Mike's eldest daughter and only a year older than Vivi. Because they were the closest cousins in age, they'd been like sisters as long as Vivi could remember. But even so, Vivi couldn't bring herself to make the trip. Not now.

"I'm in the middle of a case, Aunt Nancy. But even if I weren't, well…" her voice trailed off.

Nancy sighed in understanding. "I know, dear. We all know." She absolved Vivi with those few words. "We're all glad you're finally taking some time to yourself. Even though it sounds like maybe you aren't, right now." Vivi opened her mouth to make excuses, but her aunt kept talking. "Vivi, dear, you do what you need to do. If it's work, work. If it's driving all over the world, then go ahead and do that, even if it gives your uncle an ulcer. The shower is a shower. Kiera knows you're thinking of her. Of course, if you don't come for the christening, that might be a bit of an issue, since you're the godmother."

"I'll be there," Vivi promised. And she would. There was no way she was going to miss her goddaughter's christening.

"I know you will." The certainty in her aunt's voice was comforting. Vivi may be on a different path right now, but her family still considered her family—still *expected* her to be family, as well.

"Well, I'll be letting you go. But you be careful. I ran into Mary today and, though she swears that Windsor is the most beautiful, peaceful place, obviously it isn't, since they've had a murder."

Vivi promised to be careful and to stay in touch, then hung up. She made a few more calls, and by the time she finished the last, it was late and she was tired. She called Rob, and he sent someone to pick up the dishes. Once that was out of the way, she brushed her teeth and climbed into bed, wondering just what she was getting herself into.

***

Vivi, feeling agitated by either her fitful night of sleep or, more likely, a guilty conscience about not going to Kiera's shower, decided to spend the next morning doing something "normal"—shopping for her cousin's baby. She had already sent a gift, but still, she wanted to do more. And after perusing the stores on Main Street, she hit the quilt shop, searching for something unique to send and hoping that Kiera wouldn't see it for what it was, a guilt offering.

"Ah, Rebecca," a woman called as she opened the door. "I was wondering when you might come in for your fabric. Oh wait, I beg your pardon." The woman stopped short a few feet away from Vivi. "I took you for one of my regulars. I apologize."

Vivi smiled at the stylishly-dressed woman in her sixties. "No problem. They say everyone has their doppelgänger somewhere in the world."

"That they do. I'm Julie, the owner. Can I help you with something?" She stepped forward and they shook hands.

"Hi Julie, I'm Vivienne. Do you have baby quilts?" Vivi looked around and didn't know where to let her eyes land. The shop was filled with fabric and rows and rows of shelves with everything from needles to books to thread. Even the walls were covered to the ceiling with folded, hanging quilts.

"To make or to buy?"

"Definitely buy." Vivi turned back to Julie.

The woman smiled at Vivi's self-deprecating comment. "On this wall here," she said, pointing to a line of quilts hanging along the back wall. "Most are locally made. But we do carry a few from Amish friends I have. Do you know if it's a boy or a girl?"

Vivi answered that it was a girl and Julie spent the next several minutes walking her through some of the quilts that might fit what she was looking for. Finally she settled on a soft-colored quilt of green and lavender.

"I assume you want this wrapped?" Julie asked as they headed for the counter.

"Please," Vivi answered, looking around the store. "Have you been here long?" she asked, making conversation as Julie went about taking care of her purchase.

"Yes, nearly forty years."

"Wow. And have you always had this shop?"

"More or less. I opened it about thirty-six years ago."

"That's impressive—to keep a small business going so long. Is it hard in a town of this size?"

"It has its ups and downs to be sure. The fall is always a big season for us. We get a little bump at Christmas and on the week-ends when all the folks come up to their weekend homes. Though I have a string of regulars that kind of smooth things out for me. Not every business is so lucky."

"Like Rebecca?" Vivi commented, her eyes still surveying the larger quilts hanging on the wall behind the counter.

"She's sort of a regular. Lives up here in the wintertime. She's a costume designer in New York City and spends her winters up here doing her own projects."

"Sounds nice."

"It is if you don't mind the cold and snow."

"It must be hard for the other businesses that might depend more on the tourists? Is there a lot of turnover?"

"About as much as you would expect," Julie replied, turning back to the counter and placing the beautifully-wrapped quilt on the counter. "The jewelry store does reasonably well, the bakery does good business. The Tavern has been doing well for several years. But we used to have a chocolate shop, a few more cafes, and a local grocery store down here. Anything that is too overpriced for the locals doesn't last long. The weekenders' money is good, but not usually good enough to sustain a business on its own."

"The bane of small-town economics, I suppose," Vivi responded as she signed her credit card receipt.

"You're not from around here?" It wasn't a real question but Vivi answered anyway.

"No, Boston. But I travel a lot and spend a lot of time in small towns all over the country. I like them. I think it's kind of nice to know most of your neighbors."

"Whether you want to or not," Julie added with a smile.

"There is that," Vivi conceded. "Now, if I want to mail this somewhere, I know I saw a post office."

"Go to the end of the street, turn left, and it will be on your right. I don't have a large selection of cards, but if you want a great baby shower card, Madelyn across the street has some fun ones."

Vivi thanked the woman and, taking her advice, jogged across the street and bought a card to send with the quilt. Once that errand was complete, she headed to the post office and sent off the entire package. Realizing how close she was to the police station, she opted to stop by rather than call Ian to check on her clearance.

"Officer Granger," she said, walking into the main office.

"Dr. DeMarco," he answered, standing as she walked toward him. He was young, probably not even twenty-five, and his tall, gangly body hadn't come anywhere close to filling out yet. Still, his soft brown eyes were kind and inquisitive, and his eager but sweet demeanor made him easy to like on sight.

"How are you today?" he asked.

"Well, thank you. Is Deputy Chief MacAllister in?" she asked, reverting to his title in his workplace.

"I'm in here, and call me Ian, everyone does," came a voice to her right. Officer Granger made a motion to a door that was open a crack. She walked over and peered in.

"Is this a good time?" she asked. He looked up from his paperwork and she was caught again by the color of his eyes.

"You're our Hail Mary on this murder, any time is a good time for you," he answered.

"I was out running some errands," she said, stepping into

the room and closing the door behind her. "Met two very helpful shopkeepers, by the way," she said as an aside. "And I was walking through town so figured I would stop by and check to make sure you have what you need from Kathryn before I head down to Riverside?"

"I do, thanks for checking. You're good to go. What errands did you run?" he asked, closing a case file on his desk.

She must have given him a funny look because, really, it was an odd question.

"There's not a lot of shopping to do in town. Call me curious," he shrugged. She took a few more steps into the room and stopped next to the chair in front of his desk.

"Or call you an investigator," she suggested with a lopsided smile. "One of my cousins is having a baby, and the shower is next weekend. I'm going to be the godmother but can't make the shower, so I popped into Julie's quilt shop and picked something up to send," she explained.

"Glad you found something and sorry you can't make the shower. It's not this case is it?" Ian sounded concerned and, again, she was struck by how novel it was to work with someone who seemed to care about her, not just her skills.

She shook her head and took a seat. "No, it's a long story I don't want to get into, but I wasn't going to attend anyway. The only thing this case is taking me from is a random journey through the Finger Lakes."

"Well, glad to hear it. Are you headed down to Riverside now?"

She nodded. "Any hits from the missing persons database?"

He shook his head. "I'm not sure they're running the picture you came up with yesterday through everything they could be running it through. Backlogs, all the time. Anyway, I have a couple of things I need to do this afternoon, and then I'll meet you down at the hospital. Once you're done, there's a good Mexican restaurant in town. We can pop over there and you can fill me in."

Vivi frowned. He wasn't exactly asking her on a date. In fact he wasn't asking her anything. For a moment, she thought to protest but then realized how petty that would be. She did need to eat.

"Fine, sounds good. Although I may be a while. Why don't you come around six-ish?" she suggested, rising from the chair.

He nodded and stood, following her lead. "Be careful," he said as she headed toward the door.

His concern reminded her. "Thanks for calling Rob last night," she said, turning back. "It was nice to have dinner waiting." Ian shrugged in response but said nothing. She studied him for a moment, acknowledging to herself that the man before her was probably more complex than the average male. And she found that interesting. More interesting than a professional colleague should.

"I'll see you at six," she reaffirmed before turning and walking away.

***

Ian paused at the door to the morgue and watched Vivienne through the small window. She sat, very still, on a stool beside the table that held the bones of their Jane Doe. Vivienne's hands were folded in her lap and she looked to be lost in thought as she gazed at the skeleton. Something about her stillness bothered Ian. He didn't believe in ghosts, but watching Vivienne, it was almost as if she was in deep conversation with someone, if only herself.

He gave the door a soft knock to let her know he was there, then stepped inside. Vivienne's head swung up on his entry, but other than that, nothing about her moved. He paused several feet away from her and tried to read her expression.

"I'm not going to like what you've found today, am I?"

She pursed her lips. "I don't know that I've actually *found* anything."

He glanced at a box that looked to be filled with evidence bags, slides, and other objects. "Um, it looks like you found a lot," he countered.

"I collected a lot of things, but I don't have the equipment here to know if what I collected will tell us anything or is meaningful in any way," she clarified.

Ian's eyes lingered for a moment on the box before he turned them back to Vivienne and spoke again. "Granger will be by later tonight to pick up the samples and drive them to the lab in Albany." Ian watched as she nodded. Her own gaze turned to the box and then back to the bones. "But that's not what's bothering you, is it?" he asked.

She shook her head. "It's too early to be bothered by much of anything other than the fact this woman was murdered."

"Vivienne," he said, trying out her first name. "Something's on your mind. I can see it in your expression, in your body language. And it has nothing to do with the evidence that may or may not be in that box."

She gave him a ghost of a smile. "I think you're a better cop than you think you are."

"I think, after all the time I spent doing the things I did, I got pretty good at reading people," he responded, careful not to show how close to the target she'd come in her assessment of him and his own self-doubt.

"Fair enough," she conceded. Again, her gaze swung back to the bones.

"Vivienne."

She sighed. "You're not going to like it and it's all speculation anyway."

He stepped forward, saying nothing, but coming close enough to examine the body himself.

"You see these marks here and here," she said, pointing to the marks she'd noticed the first time she had viewed the body. There were two on each wrist, two on one ankle, and three on the other.

"Shackles, you said."

She nodded. "But these kinds of shackles aren't something you would use for an impulse kill."

"So the perpetrator planned the attack."

"In all likelihood, yes."

"But that's not what's bothering you."

She shook her head. "He—and while it could be a she, it's more likely to be he so I'm going to use that pronoun—he not only planned the attack but prepared for it. It's pretty safe to say this young woman wasn't local, so he probably either lured her here or brought her here himself."

Ian was following her so far. "Which means he might be local."

"Maybe, but he could be a weekender. He could also be someone who has access to facilities up here. But he is someone who is, at the very least, familiar with the area."

"And that's what bothers you?"

Vivienne frowned and shook her head again. "No, what bothers me is that I don't think this was his first kill."

CHAPTER 6

IAN BLINKED AND TRIED TO take in what he was hearing. "You think we might have a serial killer? Here? In Windsor?"

"That's not what I said," Vivienne jumped in.

His mind was racing and he couldn't get past his first reaction: *impossible.* But still, he forced himself to stop the objections. Studying the woman in front of him, he took a deep breath.

"Okay, tell me what you think and why," he said. While he may know his town, he had no problem acknowledging that she knew a hell of a lot more about this sort of thing than he did.

She eyed him for a long moment before deciding to speak. "In my opinion, this kill wasn't personal, not in the sense he was going after this specific woman. He was definitely going after someone, but I doubt it was her."

"Meaning?"

"We've already established that this kill wasn't an impulse kill. It was planned. Which means it was either personal to the victim—something he planned for her—or it was the kill itself that was personal, personal to him."

"And?"

Vivienne glanced down at the body and he saw the sadness in her eyes, grief for their unknown victim. She sighed. "When a kill is personal to the victim, the whole process is personal. He would have planned everything out, from his initial contact to the way she was killed to the disposal of her body."

Ian shifted, moved a little closer and examined the body again. "But the disposal couldn't have been planned. Or at least not for long. No one could have known that the storm that washed away that part of the road was going to be as strong as it was or that that specific section would wash away when it did," he said.

"How long did it take to fix?"

"I looked into that this morning. Because it was such a big washout, the crews went to work the next day. It took a few more days to clean up and get everything back in order, but the time between when it washed away and when the road was repaved was only six days. Could that have been enough time to plan and execute the killing *and* dispose of the body?"

Shaking her head, she spoke. "Unlikely. With the setup he probably had—finding a location and setting it up with the shackles and whatever else he might have had, not to mention finding the victim and taking her—it would likely take more than six days."

"So then he just took advantage of a situation to dispose of her and that means the kill wasn't about her at all but was just a kill for the sake of killing?"

"A kill for his own personal gratification," Vivienne clarified. He could see the subtle difference she was pointing out, but killing for gratification was so far outside of his reality, he had a hard time accepting that difference.

"And because the kill provides him some personal gratification," Ian all but choked on the word, "and it isn't specific to this victim…" His voice trailed off, unwilling to finish what he was saying.

"And because his method is so advanced," she added.

"You think he's done this before, to other women."

She gave a grim nod. Her reasoning made sense, but he still wasn't ready to admit to the possibility of a serial killer in Windsor. "Isn't there some component of sex in most serial kills?" he asked, remembering her comment about a potential sexual assault.

"Not always, but it is common. And sexual gratification can be a big part of a kill. Not sex in the way we normally think of sex, but gratification can come in many ways, whether an actual rape or ejaculation occurs or not."

"There is nothing normal about sexual gratification and killing," he commented.

"On that we agree, but we're not serial killers, are we? So my initial comments still stand. I do think she was sexually assaulted. Based on my findings today, I believe the actual cause of death is strangulation. But given the fact she was chained down, I do think there was a sexual component that manifested itself physically with the victim."

That he could understand. It wasn't too far-fetched to imagine that a young, beautiful woman chained down was also sexually assaulted. In fact he would have found it hard to believe otherwise. But that was still a far cry from having a serial killer on the loose.

"I get that. But what makes you think this isn't his first kill? You said his method was advanced, but what does that mean?"

"Think about the psychology of it. Or," Vivienne paused, tilting her head in thought. "Do you hunt?"

He nodded.

"It's a horrible analogy, I know. But hunting people isn't unlike hunting animals. How clean was your first kill?" Ian was thankful she didn't seem to want to wait for his answer. "I bet it wasn't as efficient as it was after five hunting seasons. With each hunt, you gain insight into what works and what doesn't. If you're organized, and I'd bet my life we're dealing with an organized killer here, rather than a disorganized one, you'll become more methodical over time. The kill is still the kill, but part of the rush comes in how expertly you execute the plan."

Everything in him rejected what she was saying. But in rapid fire, Ian's mind flashed through his first few hunting seasons, then sped forward to his first few missions as a Ranger. During his early years, the rush came in just being successful—being able to check the box and get out alive. But by the time he left, he rarely deemed a mission a success unless everything about it went according to plan. Getting the target wasn't enough.

"It's a kill that took time and planning. It's not personal to *this* victim. And the execution and dump itself was very successful. What does that tell you?" she challenged him.

Ian wanted to argue. He wanted to point out that maybe it was a fluke. But he couldn't. He wanted to point out that they didn't have any more bodies, but that would be too much like tempting the fates. He wanted to argue that she must have missed something. But everything she'd said pointed to one thing. A killer that not only knew what to do and how to do it, but one that had experienced it, probably multiple times.

"Fuck," he said, running a hand through his hair.

"I could be all wrong, you know," Vivienne offered.

"But you don't think you are?"

She shook her head.

"So, what now?" he asked.

"Now we run the pertinent points through the similar crimes database and see if anything pops," she answered.

"If it's someone local doing this, don't you think we would have had a least one missing person from this area? Because we haven't had any missing persons reported in the county that fit her profile."

"First off, it could be anyone. Just because he happened to dump a body here once does not mean he lives here or is even from here. Maybe he rented a house here one season? Maybe he's a truck driver and comes through the area a lot, has friends here. All we know right now is that we have one body. And, as for the profile of the victim, we'll run that through the database too. We only have one body, so we can't really come up with a victim profile. Serial killers usually have at least one victim that is different from the rest. I don't think that's the case now, but if she *was* his, we may find it harder to connect her with other similar crimes."

"Right, isn't that what they call the stresser? The person who triggers the killing?"

"A stresser can be any number of things. It can be a person, but it can also be an event. If it's an event, usually the first kill will be a reaction to that event."

"But if it's a person?"

"Then the one different victim may come at any time during their career. But like I said, I don't think she is the first, nor do I think she is the trigger. This murder was too well planned to be a first, and the disposal of the body was too unceremonious for it to be symbolic to the killer. And if she was the trigger, it would be symbolic."

"So, the bad news is he's probably killed people before her, but the good news is she may be similar enough to the other victims that we might be able to come up with some hits in the database."

"We can hope."

"Shit."

"Yeah. My thoughts exactly."

CHAPTER 7

VIVI AWOKE THE NEXT MORNING, groggy and hungry. Neither she nor Ian had had much of an appetite after their conversation in the morgue, so they'd come back to The Tavern, had a drink, talked a little about next steps, and then she'd gone to bed. Only to be haunted by images and dreams that kept her up most of the night.

Shaking the remaining darkness from her mind, Vivi crawled out of bed. Within a few minutes she found herself standing in the lobby of The Tavern in her running clothes wondering which way to go. When she wasn't working, she preferred to eat before a run, but given everything that was going on and how new this situation was to Ian and his whole department, she knew that if she took the time to eat first, something would come up with the case and she would never make it out for a run. And at this point, she needed to burn off some anxiety with exercise more than she needed to linger over breakfast.

"Going for a run?" Rob asked, emerging from the back office, rifling through a stack of mail.

Vivi gave a nod. "I was also thinking about stopping at Frank's Café on my way back for breakfast. Thoughts?"

He glanced up, a half smile playing on his lips. "You're thinking of going to Frank's?"

"Uh, yeah, is there a problem?"

A beat passed before he answered. "No, no problem. Just don't bring your cell in and you'll be fine."

She gave him a questioning look, but he waved her off. She didn't carry her cell when she ran anyway, so she let it go. Starting out through town, she ran past Frank's Café and the bakery. A few folks were out and about and those that were seemed to be headed into the café. Comforted by that, figuring it couldn't be all *that* bad if people were going there, Vivi turned her attention back to the rest of Main Street.

Passing by the quilt shop, something nagged at her. She didn't stop but let her mind wander, hoping she might pick up the thread. Another fifteen minutes into the run, it came to her. It was such a crazy idea that she was tempted to reject it outright. But even though she wanted to, she knew she wouldn't.

The quilt shop wasn't open yet and wouldn't be until ten, so Vivi continued her run, heading through the north part of town. She waved at Officer Granger as she passed the police station and headed onto a narrow road that took her west of town. Twenty minutes down the picturesque lane, dotted with farmhouses and fields, she turned back. Slowing to a walk as she hit the roundabout by the police station, she caught her breath and walked the last few blocks to Frank's Café.

By the time she reached the café, her breathing was more or less back to normal. As she took her time finishing her cooldown out front, she watched a number of people walk through Frank's doors. All of them carried disposable coffee cups as they left. And judging by the numbers, Vivi guessed Frank must have good coffee—the thought almost made her head spin.

Following a group of three older men, Vivi entered the café and stood in line. She eyed the case of gelato to her right as she listened to what people before her ordered. And, while the food orders were varied, she noted that everyone ordered a mocha.

Taking her cue, she did the same when her turn came.

"Anything else?" the man behind the counter asked. She didn't know if he was Frank, but she guessed he probably was—no one would hire such a gruff man as a hospitality employee.

"Uh, an egg and bagel sandwich, please?"

"What kind of bagel?"

"What kind do you have?"

He sighed, looked at her without raising his head, and pointed to the sign behind him.

"Plain, please?"

"Anything else?"

"No?" Everything she said came out sounding like a question. *Nice.* Frank—assuming it was Frank—reduced her to a self-conscious teenager. In an effort to take back some pride as he rang up her order, she asked, in a very assertive voice, if his gelato was good.

His finger froze over the keys of his cash register and he looked at her, raising his head this time. His eyes narrowed. "Did you just ask me if my gelato was good?"

She wished she hadn't but couldn't stop herself from nodding. He planted his hands on his hips and drew himself up.

"That's about the dumbest thing anyone has ever asked me. What do you think I'm going to say?"

Vivi blinked in surprise. She was pretty sure no one had ever said anything like that to her before. But on reflection, she had to admit he was right.

"How much?" she asked, with a nod to the register. He looked at her for a moment longer before giving an audible sniff and turning back to his machine. Two minutes later she was standing off to the side waiting for her order.

"Don't take it personally, dear," the woman beside her offered. "Frank takes a little getting used to." Vivi thought he might take a lot of getting used to, but she smiled at the woman.

"You!" Frank's voice bellowed. Vivi jumped, feeling inexplicably guilty.

"You know you're not allowed back in here!" he continued, pointing an accusatory finger at an older woman standing halfway in the door. Without a word, the woman dropped her gaze and left.

When the door closed, Vivi turned to the woman beside her again, hoping for some sort of explanation.

"She was in here a week ago and suggested that Frank had used day-old bread for her sandwich. She's not allowed back for another week. I'd feel bad for her, but honestly, you'd think she would know better. Her husband was banned last year for answering his cell in the middle of his order. He hasn't been back since," she added.

"Does Frank have *any* redeeming qualities?" Vivi asked, wondering why people would take such abuse.

"Oh, he's not that bad. Once you know his rules. And the food, well, you'll see." Vivi opted to withhold judgment. It would have to be one hell of an egg and bagel sandwich to bring her back here.

And, unfortunately, it was. As she sat out on the patio at The Tavern, she decided that whatever Frank did with his eggs and bagels must be magic. Even living in Boston, with the enormous Jewish population, she had never in her life tasted such a good bagel. Or egg. There was something in it, or on it, that made it taste, well, heavenly.

Vivi sighed in resignation. She'd have to figure out what the rest of his rules were. She had a feeling she'd be going back a time or two in the days to come.

A couple of hours later she was showered and heading back into town, to the quilt shop. Officer Granger was running the evidence she'd collected the night before to the state lab in Albany where they would run the tests. In return, a van was being sent down from Albany to collect the skeleton from the hospital in the early afternoon. The head of the lab was a former student of hers so she knew her evidence would be made a priority, but still, she wanted to give him and his team at least a day to process things without her starting to look over his shoulder. Which left her with a day to do nothing. Except maybe, just maybe, track down a lead.

"Oh, hello again. Vivienne, right?" Julie at the quilt shop greeted her when she walked in the door. "I hope nothing was wrong with your purchase?" A look of concern crossed her face.

Vivi smiled. "Call me Vivi, please. And no, the quilt was beautiful. So beautiful, in fact, that I was thinking of buying one for myself."

"Oh," Julie beamed. "Then by all means, come in."

Vivi spent the next thirty minutes talking quilts and, every now and then, interjecting questions about fabrics and fabric choices. So, by the time she got around to asking what she'd originally come in for, the question seemed to flow.

"You mentioned a woman yesterday, said she looked like me?" Vivi started, remembering full well her name was Rebecca.

"Yes, Rebecca Cole. Now she is a woman who knows her fabric. Has an incredible eye."

"That must be fun for you, to work with someone so talented?"

"Oh, it's great. She'll come in here and we'll talk for hours. She always has new ideas for how to display things. And the things she orders are, well, let's just say I think I get as much pleasure out of handling them as she does."

"So, you must enjoy having a little bit of extra time with the pieces she hasn't picked up yet?"

Julie's smile turned to a frown. "I have to admit I'm getting a little worried. Rebecca is a good customer and has always picked up her orders or called me if she was going to be delayed."

Just the opening Vivi was looking for. "Worried?"

"Yes, she's never left an order with me for so long. I've called her, but she hasn't called me back."

"Maybe she's changed her mind and is embarrassed? Or doesn't want to pay for it?"

Julie shook her head. "Even if she did change her mind, she's such a great customer, I would only ask that she cover my costs for returning it. But in this case, it wouldn't be anything. I can sell the fabric myself online and make more than what she owes me."

"Hmm, that is odd. Do you know where she lives? Can you stop by and see if she's okay?"

It was apparent the woman had already contemplated this. "I know she lives on Old Bailey Road. Or at least when she is in town. But I don't know the house and I don't know where she lives in the city. We've always used the phone or email."

Vivi had the information she needed, but she chatted about inconsequential things for a few more minutes anyway. And by the time she walked out she also had something she didn't need but had fallen in love with, a king-size quilt all her own.

Dropping the quilt off in her room, she thought about stopping at Frank's Café for lunch, but she hadn't eaten her breakfast all that long ago and she wanted to speak with Ian. So, going with plan B, she walked back through town, plopped herself into a seat at one of the few shops she hadn't yet been in, and pulled out her cell.

"Yeah," Ian answered gruffly.

"You need to work on your phone manners, MacAllister."

"Good afternoon, Dr. DeMarco. What can you do for me today?" he complied, tongue in cheek.

"Nice. You can meet me at What's the Scoop."

"When?"

She liked that he didn't ask why. "As soon as you can," she answered. "I ordered some ice cream after opting out of gelato at Frank's Café."

"You went to Frank's?"

She could hear the smile in his voice. "Yes, and while he didn't yell at me, I did get to see him kick someone out."

"Must have been Mary Smythe."

"Small woman. Round face, short curly hair, and glasses."

Ian laughed in assent. "Order me something, I'll be over in five minutes."

And he was. Sliding into the seat across from her, he eyed her ice cream.

"Don't even think about it, MacAllister," she held her spoon over her bowl protectively. They were the only two people in the shop—other than the woman working there, who arrived at that moment to save the day, or at least Vivi's ice cream.

"Saved by the bell," Ian smiled, switching his hungry gaze from her ice cream to the banana split being placed in front of him.

"Thank you, Meghan," he said, looking up. "Did you decide I should have this?"

The petite young woman shook her head and nodded toward Vivi. "She must know you well."

He glanced at Vivi and she wondered what he was thinking about her choice. It had been a guess, and a good one, judging by the look on his face. But he said nothing.

"How is Davey?" he asked Meghan.

"He's doing great, thanks." Meghan's face lit up when she answered, and if Vivi had to guess, she'd bet Davey was the shop owner's son.

"And your mom?"

Her smile faltered a little bit and she tucked a lock of her short blonde hair behind her ear. "She's hanging in there. Good days and bad days. You know how it goes. Your mom dropped off some food today. I'll be sure to give a call and thank her."

"She'd be happy to hear from you, and probably even happier to take Davey for a few hours, if you need it."

"Thanks, Mr. MacAllister. I'll keep that in mind." Meghan moved away, saying she would be in the back making more ice cream, but to call if they needed anything.

"She's had a rough go of it," Ian said when he and Vivi were alone. "Good kid. Bad parents. Her dad ran off, her mother was a smoker and drinker all her life. Has lung cancer now. Meghan went a little wild a few years ago. Has a kid who is cute as a button but without a father—she's never said who he is. Now she takes care of her son and her mom, runs this shop—started it herself—and is trying to take some college classes online when she can."

"Tough kid," Vivi commented. Ian nodded in agreement.

"So, I assume you have something you want to tell me?" he said, taking a big bite of his sundae.

Vivi fingered the piece of paper she held, before sliding it across the table.

"What's this?" he asked.

"It's probably nothing."

"But?"

"But I got to thinking about what we talked about last night and then, when I was out for a run this morning, I remembered something Julie said when I was in the quilt shop yesterday. So I popped in and, very discreetly, asked about a woman she'd mentioned to me. A regular that hasn't been in for a while."

Ian's spoon hung from his fingers as he stared at her. "Once again, I'm probably not going to like what I'm about to hear, am I?"

She dropped her eyes to her ice cream. It was much nicer to make him smile than to deliver bad news all the time. But that was the job. She looked up.

"Since you pointed out that our Jane Doe looks like me, and Julie said her absent regular looks like me, I thought it might be worth looking into."

Ian glanced at the name on the sheet. "I don't recognize the name."

"That's why it could be nothing. Apparently, she stays at a friend's house up here in the winter. So she's a regular during that time, but she's not from here. She's from the city."

"So, she could just be home? Wouldn't her friend report her missing?"

"She could be home, but Julie ordered this fabric especially for her and she hasn't been in to pick it up yet, despite it having been four weeks since it arrived. And as for her friend, again according to Julie, the friend spends his winters in Argentina and only comes up here in the summer, which is why the house is empty. But you're right, it could be nothing and she could be back at home, safe and sound, in the city."

"Or she could be another missing person."

"Or she could be another missing person," Vivi echoed.

"Any idea where this friend's house is?"

"Julie didn't know which one it was, but she said it was up on Old Bailey Road. I have no idea where that is, but I assume you do?"

"I do, and I probably know the house. There aren't a lot of them up there and I'm pretty sure most are owned by locals." He paused and stared at the piece of paper. "I suppose we should take a drive?"

"It can't hurt."

"We can't do much without a warrant and we can't get that without more cause. I'll call Granger though and have him call this in, see if any missing persons reports have been placed on her."

"I hope she's safe in the city and I hope this is a fool's errand, but thank you for considering it."

"I hope you're right, but you're welcome. Let's go. I'll drive."

Twenty minutes later they pulled Ian's Jeep up to a large farmhouse. The house, like most in the area, was originally built sometime in the late 1700s. But the clean siding, perfect shutters, and geometric gardens all pointed to a recent remodel—to the nines.

"Nice place," Vivi commented, her eyes fixed on the window and the land unfolding before them.

"Yeah, it is. Used to be the old Calloway farm, but a few decades ago the three kids all up and moved out of the area. They kept the house for a while. But it was too big for their mother, who was a widow by then. When she got too old to be here by herself, they moved her to an assisted living place over in Stockbridge and sold the house to a builder. He did the remodel about ten years ago." Ian put his car in park and killed the engine.

"And sold it to a weekender?" She studied the house, as if it might tell her something.

"At the time, they were the only ones who could afford to buy something like this. Not many people who live around here full time can afford a two-million-dollar house."

"Not many people living anywhere can afford a two-million-dollar house," she pointed out.

"True enough," he conceded, opening his door. "You ready?"

"A bit of a loaded question, MacAllister, but yes, I'm ready."

They approached the door and Ian knocked. No one answered. They waited a minute before trying again. Still nothing.

"Want to look around the outside?" Vivi suggested.

In response, Ian stepped off the porch and headed toward the side of the house. Looking in a window, he spoke. "There's a blue, late-model Subaru in the garage, but I can't see the plates." They tried looking in another window and though they could see into the house, they saw very little to help them. No obvious signs of a struggle. With the exception of the car and a single glass in the kitchen sink visible through a window, there were no signs of anyone even living there. They walked the perimeter, and when they'd completed the circuit, they stopped in front of his Jeep.

"Not much to go on until we hear if she's officially missing or not," Ian said.

Vivi crossed her arms and leaned against the grill. Gazing up behind the house, her eyes swept over a large, sloped hill that ended about a third of a mile away in a thick copse of trees.

"Is that land part of this property?" she asked.

Ian shook his head. "The pasture is, but the woods belong to the Mayfields."

"Any chance we can go up there?"

"You think we might find something in the woods?"

"In a perfect world where killers are stupid, it would be a good place to hide a body. Provided the woods aren't used on a regular basis. At the very least, we might get a different view of the house, especially if you have binoculars." Silence met her suggestion. She turned to give Ian a questioning look and found him staring at her.

"What?" she said, feeling self-conscious.

"Just that the same thought crossed my mind. Higher ground is usually better ground. I'm just surprised, though I probably shouldn't be, that you thought of it too."

"You weren't going to say anything?"

"I didn't want to seem like a perv, peeking in second-floor bedroom windows through binoculars. I figured I'd come back out when I was alone."

She stared at him for a beat before responding. "I think we should go up there."

"Good thinking, but you aren't dressed for it," he pointed out.

Vivi had on jeans, a pair of sandals, and a white tank top. The hill was a long slope but nothing she couldn't handle.

"I'll live. As long as you don't mind slowing down a bit to account for my shoes."

"It might rain."

"I won't melt, MacAllister. I'll be fine."

He shrugged in acceptance and went to get a pair of binoculars from his car as she headed up the hill.

"Do we need to get permission from the Mayfields?" she asked when he caught up with her.

"On it," he answered, pulling his cell off his belt. His voice mumbled behind her as they made their way toward the tree line. By the time they were halfway there, Vivi was wishing she had her hiking boots. The walk wasn't all that difficult, but every time she stepped down, something—a branch, a twig, or some other sharp, spiky thing—wormed its way into one or the other of her sandals. Still, she'd been adamant about being fine, so she kept her complaints to herself as they continued up.

When they reached the top of the hill, Ian came to stand beside her and they turned to look at the house from the back. He pulled out the binoculars and began scanning the windows. There wasn't much Vivi could see from her vantage point so she let her eyes skim the horizon. And her heart sank.

"It's going to rain, isn't it?"

"Yep," he said, not taking the binoculars from his eyes. She could see a line of black clouds making its way toward them from the south. It was a quintessential northeast storm; it would move in quick, rain hard, and then move on. Just like it had the night she'd discovered the Jane Doe. The good news was it wouldn't last. The bad news, judging by the increasing darkness, was that they were going to get soaked.

"Shit," she huffed. Ian chuckled. And the first drops hit.

"You were trying to tell me about this, weren't you? When you were hinting that I wasn't prepared to come up here."

He pulled the glasses away from his eyes and gave her a half smile in response.

She sighed. "Nice. For future reference, when you know something I don't, or think I'm being dumb, I would appreciate it if you just told me."

"Yes, ma'am," he replied.

A few minutes passed and it was raining in a steady flow—at this point, even with the binoculars, they couldn't see into the house. She stared down at the Jeep thinking about how dry and warm it would be inside. It wasn't the worst storm, but wet jeans sucked.

She was still fixating on her jeans when a loud crack erupted across the valley. She jumped and suddenly found herself pinned between Ian and a large tree. Stunned, it took her a moment to sort out what had just happened. Thunder. She looked up at Ian and saw in a split second everything that haunted him—all the fear, all the memories. He must have sorted out what was going on at the same time; his expression shuttered, then turned grim.

Vivi wanted to make it all go away for him—the pain and confusion of everything that had happened to him, everything he'd done as a Ranger, everything he'd experienced just doing his job. But even if he wanted her to, it wasn't something she, or anyone other than Ian, had the power to do. So she did the best she could.

"It's nice to know you'd put your body between mine and a bullet if it ever came to it. Although, if it did come to it, I would rather you didn't. I'm Catholic; I don't think I could live with the guilt." Her tone was intentional and light.

His eyes searched hers and he looked like he was trying to sort out how to take her words. She didn't know what he'd concluded, but he stepped away, keeping a hand on her shoulder. "It's the training. What can I say?" He lifted a shoulder with deliberate carelessness.

She thought it was a bit more than his training that was bothering him—like the fact that it was kicking in when he was no longer in the line of fire.

71

"Are we safe from the storm here in the woods?" Changing the subject, she turned to look down over the valley.

"Safer than out there." Ian gestured toward the open field.

As if to make his point, Mother Nature chose that moment to send a bolt of lightning no more than a half mile away.

"Fair enough," Vivi conceded. Looking around, she found a low stone wall and perched on it to wait out the storm. Ian came and sat beside her. "Is this an old fence?" she asked to pass the time.

He looked around the area before answering. "Probably not. It looks more like the foundation of an old house."

That surprised Vivi, who turned her head to see what Ian saw. Sure enough, she could make out a few other rows of stones that would have formed the outline of a building. "It's amazing how something can be here and then be gone, with no one knowing much about it," she commented, wondering who might have lived in the house and what had happened to them.

"Happens more than we'd like to think."

Something in Ian's tone drew her eyes back to him. He continued looking forward and she studied his profile. He looked watchful, silent, and still, but she knew his mind was working fast, assessing the situation.

"I suppose it does," she said, turning away. She tried to hitch her knees up but her wet jeans made it impossible. Sighing, she propped her elbows on her thighs instead and watched the storm unfold.

"You're going to freeze," he said.

"It's seventy degrees. Between the wind and the rain, I'll get chilled, but it's better than being a human divining rod," she added with a nod toward the empty field.

"Still," he said, unbuttoning his uniform shirt and handing it to her. She didn't think she needed it, much less deserved it. After all, she was the one traipsing through the woods with only a tank top.

"Your gun will get wet."

"My gun will be fine," he responded, untucking his white cotton undershirt and pulling it over his belt.

She held the shirt for a moment longer before sliding it on. The poly-cotton fabric was damp, but the lingering heat from Ian warmed her. And it smelled of him. In a good way. "You like to take care of people, don't you?"

Ian inclined his head, whether in agreement or not, she didn't know. "Everyone needs to be taken care of at some point or another."

Another glimpse into the man who was Ian MacAllister.

Vivi jumped when his cell buzzed between them. He cast her a glance, as if to make sure she was okay, then pulled it from his belt and answered.

"MacAllister. Yes? Shit. Okay, go ahead and start filling out the warrant papers based on what we know from Julie Fitzpatrick and the report." He paused and listened. She didn't need him to tell her what the conversation was about. She knew and her heart sank. "No," he continued. "Don't talk to Mrs. Fitzpatrick. Just use the information we already have. Do what you can and leave it on my desk. I'll take care of it when I come back tonight. And Granger, I know I don't need to say this, but not a word to anyone. You got that?"

He hung up then waited a heartbeat. "Fuck."

"Rebecca Cole is missing."

"Yep. Her boss reported it a few weeks back. A couple of friends have called to check in with the police in the city over the last few days."

"I'm sorry."

"Why is it we can know so quickly with Rebecca but still be waiting on the Jane Doe?"

"Different databases. With Rebecca we have a name and know where she lives. It's a lot easier. Facial recognition matches take more time, especially when we have no other information to narrow down the search."

They sat in silence for a long time. The rain turned to a drizzle, then after another few minutes, stopped altogether.

"How do you do this?" he asked. She didn't need him to clarify what *this* was. *This* was the business of death, often violent and senseless death. He had probably seen a lot in his previous career, but war was war—it was different, psychologically, when it was at home. It was harder to separate yourself from the victims and sometimes even the killers. And she had a whole repertoire of bullshit she often fed herself to make it easier, or at least manageable. But Ian didn't need her patronization.

"Because someone has to do it and I happen to be good at it," she said instead as she shifted her weight.

"I'll grant you that, but it doesn't mean it's easy. What do you tell yourself to make this better?"

"A whole host of things," Vivi muttered, mostly to herself.

"What?"

"Nothing."

"Tell me, Vivienne," he said in earnest. "I've been to war, I've seen some of the worst of the worst. But, somehow, this is different."

She shrugged, not entirely comfortable sharing this part of herself with him. Still, she knew she would. Ian needed to have this conversation, and she doubted there was anyone else who would understand. Or who would be honest with him, given everything else he'd already gone through.

"These ones are easier," she started. "Or so I tell myself. Rebecca Cole went missing long before I came onto the scene. Long before you came onto the scene. She was missing before we even knew there was one murder, let alone suspected there might be two. There was nothing I could have done to stop what happened to her. So I tell myself," she added as she stood and moved away, needing some space.

"But the others," she continued quietly. "The ones where we know, we just *know* someone is going to die and we can't do a thing to stop it. Those are worse. Those are the ones that I try not to think about too much."

"The ones that haunt you."

"They all haunt me, Ian. Everyone last one of them."

They lingered there in a macabre kind of silence. He stayed still on the old foundation and she stared at the middle space between her and an old decaying log. One last distant rumble of thunder brought her reverie, their moment of quiet, to an end. She shook her head. There was work to do.

"Ian," she said, turning toward him. He looked up at her voice and she watched as his expression changed to surprise then fear. Then she heard the crack and hit the ground.

CHAPTER 8

VIVI LAY ON THE GROUND trying to catch her breath. For a space of several seconds her mind was a complete blank. And then her breath came back and an awareness that, while she was in pain, there wasn't anything wrong with her that might spell the end of her days.

She turned her head against the dirt to see Ian. Having hit the ground at the same time she did, he lay a few feet away. He looked up from his position on his belly. His gaze swept over her, taking everything in. Including the fact that they weren't under fire.

"Fuck," he said, rolling over onto his back and wiping a hand across his face.

"Don't knock yourself out for doing what years of training taught you to do," she retorted, still on her back. Something had collapsed under her foot and it *had* sounded like a gunshot. She didn't know what'd actually happened, but she wasn't about to let him feel like a fool for reacting the way he had. He glanced over at her and then seemed to pull himself together.

"Are you okay?" he asked, coming to her side.

Vivi's head hurt from hitting the ground, her right ankle was twisted, and her left leg—from her knee down—was stuck in some kind of hole.

"I'll be fine. Especially if you help me get my foot out of the hole it's in. Lord knows how deep or dark it is in there."

"Good news is we don't have a lot of poisonous snakes around here," Ian offered. That didn't make her feel any better.

When she sat up she could feel something dripping down

her buried leg—something she was pretty sure wasn't water. She wanted to yank it free, but Ian kept a hand on her knee until he'd cleared around the hole and made it large enough to pull her foot out without scraping it up any more. When it was loose, she lay back again, catching her breath.

"You okay?" he asked again. Concern laced his voice, even as he peered over her and into the hole.

"A little more banged up than I thought."

He looked up, and again his eyes swept over her. "Your leg is a mess. We need to get it cleaned and put some antiseptic on it. You may even want to get some antibiotics. What else hurts?"

"My head and my other ankle."

He scooted to her other foot. As gentle as he was, she couldn't stop the hiss that escaped when he tested it with his fingers.

"Sprain?"

She shook her head. "I'm pretty sure it's just a twist. A little ice and some ibuprofen and I should be good to go. Can you help me up?" she asked, already struggling.

He stood, then took her hand in his and leaned down to wrap an arm around her torso, pulling her up with him. "I should carry you."

"I have no doubt you could, but please don't," she answered. Now standing, Vivi balanced on her scraped-up leg and put her arm over Ian's shoulders. Her leg hurt like hell, but she knew it would bear her weight better than her foot with the twisted ankle.

Ian looped an arm around her waist and they began to inch their way down the hill and back to the car—a distance that seemed at least twice as far as it had on their way up.

"What was that anyway? Do I want to know?" She didn't care at this point, but anything to take her mind off their slow progress would work for her.

"Probably the old well to the house. At least that's what it looked like from what I saw." They hobbled their way closer to the Jeep. "Really, I can carry you," Ian offered again.

"I'm sure you can, but I already messed up once today," she

said with a motion toward her soaking wet clothes and now man-
gled sandals. "Please let me keep at least a shred of dignity."

Vivi thought he might be contemplating swinging her up into
his arms. If he did, there wouldn't be a whole lot she could do
about it. But he surprised her.

"Okay." He didn't seem put out or bothered at all about
humoring her. She was beginning to realize that while some things
bothered Ian MacAllister, they were only the things that should
bother him. Not petty things like having to take an extra ten minutes to descend a hill so she could maintain some dignity.

"You're very accommodating." Vivi meant it as a compliment,
but he let out a bark of laugher.

"I wish some of my Army buddies could hear you say that."

"Well, you are," she defended him as they reached the car.

"For the record, you're easy to accommodate since you don't
ask for much. Especially considering what you're giving me in
return." Ian opened the door and helped her hop in. As soon as she
was seated, he got a good look at her leg and did not look happy.
His jaw ticked as he held her ankle, turning her leg back and forth,
investigating the damage the best he could without wrestling with
her wet jeans too much. He looked like he was contemplating
pushing them up to see better, but something stopped him. He let
out a huff, jammed a fist on his hip, and continued to contemplate
her bloodied calf.

"What am I giving you in return?" she asked, perched on
the side of the seat, her other foot dangling. She didn't like the
expression coming over his face. He was worrying; she wanted him
to stop.

"Huh?" he looked up, as if remembering her leg was attached
to the rest of her. "Oh, your time, expertise, skills. Your vacation,"
he elaborated with a wave of his hand. His eyes went back to
her calf.

Vivi looked down at the blood dripping from her leg down
her sandal and over his hand. "Seems like the only thing I've been
giving you is bad news and grief."

"You're just the messenger. Somebody at some point would have found that body and the same thing with Rebecca Cole. It just happened to be you." His eyes never left her leg.

"You're a very focused man," she commented, more to herself than to him.

Ian looked up with a frown, "I beg your pardon?"

"In the space of a few days we've found a body, suspect we might find another with our missing person, think a serial killer is at work, and gimped down a hill trailing blood. Do you ever get flustered?" Everything that had happened was all a little out of left field for him, if not for her. And people asked her the same thing all the time. For the first time, Vivi saw in Ian what others must see in her. She was the queen of cool when she was in the field, her focus absolute. But when she was alone it was a different story. She wondered if it was the same with him. His military training and experience would require control in situations of stress—situations like this. And she knew what that kind of control cost—how she withdrew from everyone, even herself. Was Ian the same? Did he ever fall apart? Did he ever let himself go?

His eyes watched her for a time.

"Yes." His single syllable answer to her question was laced with so much more. She opened her mouth to ask when, but he cut her off. "In you go," he motioned toward her legs. "Unless you want me to get the first aid kit out right here?"

She shook her head, letting him change the subject. "My jeans are too wet to hike up and, while it's superficial, these are my favorite pair so I don't want to cut them off. If you get me back to my room, I can change and clean up there."

"Fair enough," he motioned again toward her legs, urging her to swing them into the Jeep.

"There's blood all over my foot. Do you have a rag or something to put under it?"

"It's fine."

"Ian."

He sighed. "Here," he said, reaching behind her seat to grab a copy of the local newspaper. Setting it down on the floor, he stepped back.

"Happy?" he asked, resting his hands on his hips.

"Yes, thank you." Vivi pulled her bloody leg in, placing it on the paper, then brought her other foot into place and braced herself as it made contact with the floor. Ian shut the door, rounded the car, and slid into the driver's seat.

"My place is five minutes away and a lot easier to navigate than the stairs at The Tavern. We'll go there. You can shower, warm up, and clean up. My sister has a dresser full of clothes. You can borrow something while I put your clothes through a rinse and dry cycle. I'll check in with my office and the warrant, we can eat, then I'll drop you off at The Tavern on my way in to finalize the paperwork."

They were bumping down the dirt road, and for a moment, Vivi looked at him. When she didn't say anything, he glanced her way.

"What? I plan. I make plans. It's what I do."

"I guessed," she responded, trying to hide a grin at his defensiveness.

"You have a problem with the plan?"

She could have. She could have insisted on going back to The Tavern. But for a whole host of reasons, including the fact that her own first aid kit probably wasn't as extensive as his and was sitting in the trunk of her car, she didn't. She also knew what his plan really was. It was his way of dealing with—of controlling—the stress of the situation. It was useful, to be sure. She'd get clean faster, warm faster, dry faster. But more importantly, if she went along with it, he'd feel like he was doing something to fix the problem.

"No." She shook her head and turned her eyes back toward the road.

"Good." They drove in silence for the short time it took to get to his house, a cute bungalow with a sweeping view of the valley from the screened-in front porch. He pulled around back, and while there was a front door from the front porch, it was obvious from the shoes lining the slate patio that the back door was used more often. He helped Vivi out of the Jeep, through the back door, and into a bathroom. It had tile floors and would be easy to clean so she didn't feel too bad setting her bloody foot down.

"Holler when you're in the shower. I'll come grab your clothes and leave some of my sister's."

She glanced at the opaque shower curtain before nodding. He handed her a black beach towel and left, closing the door behind him. She sat on the lid of the toilet seat and managed to pull off her jeans without causing too much pain or making too much of a mess. Then, after piling her clothes on the floor by the door, she flipped on the shower and stepped into its warmth. She heard Ian come in to gather her things and gave a fleeting thought to how familiar their actions felt. Not that she was reading anything into it, but the way they were handling this situation seemed pretty in sync for two people who had just met a few days ago. But then again, once Ian had gotten past his suspicions of her and his moment of manipulation, he'd been nothing but straightforward, practical, and for lack of a better word, strong. There wasn't any doubt in her mind, even after such a short time, that Ian was a man who could be counted on. Which was kind of nice.

***

Ian flipped the lid on the washer, set it to rinse, and hit the switch. He acknowledged that in a perfect world, or even a nice one, he might spend some time thinking about the attractive woman in his guest shower. But the reality was, while he wouldn't be able to shut down that awareness altogether, now was not the time or the place. Back in his room, he stripped out of his own clothes and jumped into the shower. Five minutes later, he emerged, pulled on some jeans and a t-shirt, and made some calls. He had just hung up from his last conversation when he heard Vivienne calling. He left his bedroom, headed down the hall, and stopped outside the bathroom.

"Everything okay?" he called through the door.

"Sort of. I'm fine, but I'm going to bleed all over everything so it might be better if you brought me the first aid kit and I took care of it in here."

Ian remembered the splintered wood and dirt around her leg and didn't think it was a good idea for her to do her own patching up. "Are you decent?"

"I'm wrapped in a towel the size of a bedsheet."

"Good enough," he said, entering the room. Vivienne's head whipped around in surprise. She sat perched on the edge of the tub with her back to him and her legs still inside. He walked over and peered in. Her right ankle was swollen and her left leg looked good and chewed up.

"Here," he said, grabbing a hand towel. "Wrap this around your leg." She frowned but did as she was told. Without asking, he reached down and scooped her up into his arms. Her cry was more of surprise than protest, though he didn't miss the unhappy grumble that followed as he carried her down the hall.

"I thought women liked to be swept off their feet," he teased as he placed her on the guest bed.

"We like to be carried off to bed for all the good reasons, not because we're invalids. We're not all that different than men when it comes to bruised egos."

"Bruised ego?" His lips lifted into a smile even as he plucked her left leg up to examine it more closely.

"Oh, right. You would probably have to be missing two legs *and* an arm before you let one of your colleagues carry you anywhere," she said with a roll of her brown eyes.

Ian smiled but couldn't argue her point so he said nothing, taking a moment to step away and grab the first aid kit.

"What are you doing?" Vivienne asked when he returned to the bed.

"I'm going to clean you up. There are splinters and dirt in some of the scratches." Ian slid onto the edge of the bed and lifted her left ankle. Resting her calf and foot across his lap, it didn't escape his notice that he was almost literally between her thighs. God would surely reward him for his restraint, he thought as he broke an instant ice pack and placed it on her swollen ankle. After handing her a bottle of water and some ibuprofen, he turned his attention to her other leg.

"When was your last tetanus?"

"About a year and a half ago."

"Good," he said, starting to clean the wounded area. Vivienne let out a surprising litany of curses when he sprayed some disinfectant on it, making him laugh.

"I'm glad you find this amusing." Her remark could have been bitchy but wasn't—for which he was glad.

"I'll do the best I can and we'll put some antibiotic ointment on it, but you might want to get some oral antibiotics just in case." She mumbled something in assent and he kept picking and pulling and cleaning. It wasn't a horrible set of scratches, but a lot of dirt and splinters had been embedded in her skin. He could feel Vivienne's tension under his hands so he tried to distract her by filling her in on his phone conversations.

"I made a couple of calls while you were in the shower. Wyatt got the warrant paperwork filled out. Depending on when he can track Judge Edgars down, we should have a decision by tomorrow morning, at the latest. This is probably the most exciting thing Edgars will do in his career."

"Such as it is," Vivienne commented on the car-crash appeal this case would have to many folks who would work on it in the days to come.

"I called the NYPD precinct that took the missing persons report and filled them in. They aren't all that concerned and just want to be kept in the loop. They're emailing me the original report so we can take a look at what her friends said."

Ian paused and, for a moment, stared at his large hand lying across her leg. "What do you think the chances are that Rebecca's disappearance has nothing to do with the body you found?" He knew the answer. He knew it in his gut. But he needed to hear her opinion. Her opinion that held so much more experience than his in this type of death.

He glanced up when she sighed. "I've seen stranger things happen. TV shows are always making comments about coincidences not being coincidences, but weird things do happen. It's possible the two things are completely unrelated."

He searched Vivienne's eyes, forcing her to say what she wasn't saying. She bit her lower lip and turned to look out the window. "I can't give you any stats, but I would be surprised if they weren't related. Two women who look alike, both with ties to this area, one recently missing and one long dead. It doesn't look good."

"We don't know that the Jane Doe has ties to this area."

"No, we don't, but it's not really about her having ties in the traditional sense to Windsor, it's about the killer having ties here and extending those, even in death, to the victims."

Ian went back to her wounds for several minutes. When the last splinter he could see was out, he wiped her leg clean with an antiseptic cloth and bandaged the whole area. He mulled the case over in his own mind—who, what, why—and as the questions faded and he acknowledged he had no answers, Ian realized he'd been lost in thought.

Looking down, he found his left hand resting on Vivienne's bare inner thigh. He hadn't even noticed that his other hand had been rubbing her calf. And she hadn't moved or said a word. He turned to meet her gaze.

Her dark brown eyes, open and frank, met his. The end of her damp ponytail fell over her bare shoulder. He felt her watching him as his eyes traveled, unbidden, from her face to her shoulders, down over the beach towel, under which he knew she was naked, then back up again—pausing for a moment on the little knot holding the towel together above her breasts. It would be so easy to get lost, to make it all go away, if only for an hour or two. And she looked like she knew it, too.

"Dinner," Ian said, clearing his throat and forcing himself to extricate his body from hers. "Why don't you get dressed," he said, gesturing to the clothes he'd grabbed from his sister's dresser, "and come into the kitchen. I'll throw some steaks on the grill."

Vivienne nodded and he left, fighting the urge to go back to her every step of the way.

***

Vivi entered the kitchen wearing a pair of sweatpants and an NYU sweatshirt. Although she wasn't all that hungry—she always seemed to lose her appetite when working a case—she felt she needed to make the effort. If she declined, she was pretty sure he would think she was making too much out of that moment in the bedroom.

Ian was talking on the phone when she caught his eye. She motioned an offer of help. He shook his head and gestured toward a bar stool as he continued listening to the call while pulling potatoes out of the microwave.

She laid her cell down on the counter and watched him move around the kitchen then step outside. When he returned, he had a plate with a steak on it and his cell was off. He set everything down on the counter in front of them and spoke only when he was seated on a stool himself.

"We got a hit on the facial recognition database for our Jane Doe."

That brought her up short. "And?" she prompted, fork halfway to her mouth.

"Her name is Jessica Akers. She's been missing three years. A nurse from New York City. Her parents filed the report, but they live in DC."

Vivi frowned. "That name sounds familiar. Prominent family?"

He shrugged. "I'm not sure, but the department down there is sending us what they have. They also have the unenviable job of going to talk to the family."

"We're ordering a DNA comparison, right?"

He nodded as her cell rang. She glanced at the number then frowned, hitting the ignore button. One of Ian's eyebrows went up in question. She ignored him too and turned back to her steak. Until her phone rang again. She cursed on an exhale.

She told Ian to listen in, then hit the speakerphone button. "Yes."

"Hello, Luv."

"Hello, Nick. What do you want? I'm in the middle of dinner."

"I'm on speakerphone, where are you?"

"Nowhere public, now talk." Vivi was keenly aware of Ian watching her, though she kept her own eyes focused on the phone.

"Imagine my surprise when your name turned up on one of the cases I've been keeping an eye on." It was hard to believe that she'd once found Nick's British accent, and the way he used it, charming.

"My name is probably on a lot of cases you keep your eye on, Nick."

"Jessica Akers," Nick responded.

She glanced up at Ian. She was as confused as he was. "What about her?"

"You found her?" Nick asked.

"Yes."

"And did the preliminary, including the reconstruction," he added.

She didn't like where this was heading. "She army?" Vivi asked, trying to suss out why Nick, an Army CID agent, would be involved in a missing persons case and how much she should tell him.

"No, but her family is," he answered. "Now, why don't you tell me what you know?"

"Or," she paused for effect, "you can tell me what you know, and then I'll decide if I want to share."

"Ah, Luv. You're breaking my heart."

"Were that the case, Nick," Vivi said under her breath. Across from her, Ian set his knife and fork down.

"Ah, that must be the enigmatic Deputy Chief MacAllister I hear scraping around in the background," Nick said.

"Tell me what you know," Vivi said before Ian could answer.

"And then you'll tell me what you know?"

"No, then I'll verify what you know with my reliable sources and then *maybe* I'll share with you what I know," she corrected.

"You were never this territorial, Viv. It doesn't become you."

"I never had to watch my back with a colleague before, now did I, Nick?"

His sigh came over the line, and when he spoke again, he still spoke with his native accent, but the cajoling jocularity was gone. In its place was the seasoned agent she knew him to be. "Jessica Akers is the daughter of Hammond Akers. *General* Hammond Akers. He has a proclivity for young girls that, embarrassingly enough, escaped without notice until someone provided evidence against him. He's in Leavenworth now, having very quietly and discreetly been court marshaled a year and half ago."

"And Jessica provided the evidence?" Vivi asked.

"Yes, three weeks before she disappeared."

Vivi glanced at Ian. "I'll see what information I can get you," she said.

"Ah, Viv, you're really going to make me wait?"

"Goodbye, Nick. I know where to find you." She hung up.

"Will he call back?" Ian asked, curiosity written in his expression.

"No, he knows better now," she said, shaking her head.

"*Now*?" Ian asked. "As in, there was a point in time when he *didn't* know better?"

"It's a long story. We were involved at one point. Together, not on a case," Vivi clarified. "We used to talk shop. A few years ago he was working a complicated, awful case. He bounced ideas off me, and when I gave him my feedback, he laughed. Well, not literally. But he didn't take me seriously. Didn't want to believe that psychology could explain anything. It caused a—well, to call it a rift is a bit of an understatement. He was ridiculing half my life's work. He had full confidence in all the science, but not in anything else.

"The long and short of it is the case got worse, and I was called in, by his superiors mind you, to consult. I walked into the briefing room to hear him espousing my theories and taking the credit for them." Vivi paused, taking a bite of her dinner. That moment, when she'd walked into the briefing room had felt so profound all those years ago. Now, here in this homey kitchen, it felt like nothing but a mild, unpleasant memory.

"To be honest," she continued. "I don't care who gets credit and who doesn't but—"

"But when he used you after being so condescending, it was kind of hard to let that part go," Ian finished.

She nodded. "Nick is very good at what he does. But the case was more my specialty than his. The fact that he was so disrespectful to me personally and professionally ended our relationship, which has, for obvious reasons, made our subsequent dealings a bit tense. Even though he is one of the best agents I know."

"I can understand that. But, all that aside, do you think he's onto something? With Jessica Akers's death being linked to her father's crimes?"

"Before we jump the gun on that, I want to confirm his story." Vivi picked up her cell, scrolled through the phonebook, hit a number, then put it on speaker.

"Danielson," came the voice picking up the line.

"Karen, it's Vivi."

"Vivi," Karen's voice warmed. "Good to hear from you. What did Nick do now?"

"I'm sitting here with the Deputy Chief of Police of Windsor, New York, and we have a case Nick is interested in. I wanted to verify his story." Vivi gave her friend the rundown of what Nick had told her. When she was done, Karen spoke.

"It's the truth. But not all of it. Jessica Akers has been his white whale for the past three years. Nick was the one who interviewed her. He wanted to put her in protective custody, given the information she'd brought us. She declined and then she disappeared. It wasn't our case, NYPD was handling it, and we were moving ahead on the case against her father. Our focus was elsewhere."

"But he's never been able to forgive himself, has he," Vivi commented.

"You know Nick," Karen commented.

And despite everything, she did. "Thanks, Karen."

"Are you going to work with him?"

"Work with him? No," Vivi answered. "But we will keep him updated. We all know what it's like to be haunted. Despite what a cad he can be, no one deserves that."

They hung up and Ian sat back. "Who was that?" he asked.

Vivi smiled. "Nick's partner. She likes me."

He laughed for a moment then sobered. "So, do you think her father had anything to do with it now?"

"It's always possible," she answered. The ibuprofen and ice had kicked in so Vivi was a bit more comfortable putting weight on her ankle. She gathered up their dinner plates and took them to the sink. Glancing around, Vivi noticed that Ian didn't have a dishwasher, so she stacked the dishes and began running the hot water.

"But?" he said, coming up beside her with their glasses.

"I have no problem seeing a man cornered the way her father probably was, or feeling cornered the way he was, lashing out and killing. But I don't see him killing her in the way I think she was killed." She washed and rinsed a plate, then handed it to Ian.

"Meaning?" Ian pressed, taking the wet plate from her and wiping it dry with a white dish towel.

"He's a pedophile. Of course that doesn't mean he can't or won't commit other crimes, but being a pedophile isn't the same thing as chaining up an adult woman and killing her. Two very different psychologies at work."

"But not always mutually exclusive?" he commented, drying dishes and putting them away as they came to him.

"I haven't seen it, but that's not to say it couldn't, or doesn't, exist. But like I said, a pedophile is more likely to kill an adult out of rage or impulse or fear. Jessica's death involved thought, planning, and execution."

"What if he wanted to torture her for turning him in?"

"Possible, but unlikely. Torture probably isn't something that interests him," she said washing the last of the dishes.

"Sex with young girls isn't torture?"

"It's torture for them, I'm sure. But not in his mind." She handed him the last plate, then turned to find a towel to dry her hands.

"You said you thought there was a sexual component to Jessica's murder. Would that fit with her father? What if he was abusing her?" Ian asked, gesturing with his head to another dish towel hanging on the oven door.

"He probably did, when she was younger. But that's the thing. If there was a sexual component to Jessica's murder, and we don't have any physical evidence of that, then it's even more unlikely that her father would be involved. His sexual satisfaction comes from young girls. Once they reach a certain age, they aren't interesting to him in that way. He might not even be able to perform well, if at all, with an adult woman." Vivi folded and rehung the dish towel, then leaned against the kitchen counter, as Ian put the last of the dishes away.

"But what if it's about the power, and it's the power that, well, for lack of a better word, does it for him?" Ian crossed his arms over his chest as he rested against the counter opposite her.

"It's always about power. But it's hard for me to see a pedophile being interested in holding the kind of power that whoever killed Jessica held over her. Again, I'm not saying it's *not* possible…" Her voice trailed off.

"But you think it isn't likely," Ian finished.

"Keep an open mind, but I would be surprised," she said.

"Shit," Ian said, running a hand through his hair.

Vivi concurred.

"So, in all likelihood, we're back to the serial killer theory?" he asked.

"I am," she said reaching for her cell. "But you should be more thorough. Come to think of it, Nick might handle that part of the investigation for us if you want him to."

"What part?" Ian asked.

Vivi walked toward the back door but paused in front of Ian to answer. "He'll want to prove her father was involved once I tell him what we know. We can let him follow that trail while we continue looking at the connections between Jessica and Rebecca."

"You think you're sending him off on a wild goose chase, don't you?" Ian asked as one side of his mouth tilted up into a half grin.

"I like to think of it more along the lines of giving him an excuse to exorcise a demon."

"And we'll stick together?"

She nodded.

Ian grinned fully. "Then it sounds like a plan."

CHAPTER 9

AT NINE O'CLOCK THE NEXT morning, Ian, Vivi, and Wyatt stood at the front door of the house where Rebecca Cole stayed while in Windsor. Ian had sent two other officers—Carly Drummond, a tall, fit woman with blonde curly hair and vivid hazel eyes, and Marcus Brown, an even taller man with broad shoulders and light brown eyes that contrasted with his military-short dark hair —to stand perimeter. No one expected anyone to go jumping out windows or bolting out the back door, but as protocol and caution dictated, they weren't going to take any chances.

No one answered when Ian knocked and announced their presence. Wyatt debated with Marcus, who was visible from where they stood, about breaking down the locked door, but Vivi lifted a flowerpot and found a key. Holding it up, she handed it to Ian.

"The first lesson of the day: never make things more complicated than they already are," Vivi chided. It was, in fact, a lesson, and she knew it would be the first of many that day. While she had little doubt that the three younger deputies were good cops, all of them were new to this. From what she could tell, they were more interested in learning and doing the right thing than in trying to prove themselves in an area where they were so obviously out of their depth, and for that she was grateful. So, they took her announcement with good humor while Ian unlocked the front door.

Vivi, Ian, and Wyatt stood to the side, lingering on the threshold for a moment as the door swung open revealing a center hall staircase to the left and a hall to the right. When no one came barreling out and no weapons were discharged, Ian, who held his service weapon, and Vivi, who'd brought hers along too, entered the house in the choreographed movement of a team who had cleared a building or two in their time. Leaving Wyatt to stand guard at the door and the stairs, they systematically went through the rooms before meeting up again in the center hall. Certain the house was clear, Ian called in the other officers, and when they were all assembled, Vivi proposed her plan.

"Why don't Carly, Wyatt, and I take the upstairs, and you and Marcus can take the downstairs? We'll photograph everything first and then start documenting and collecting?" she suggested. Ian was new to this, too—evidence collection. But she trusted his cautious nature and skills of observation to lead him. He nodded and she handed out the equipment—gloves and booties for everyone. In addition to her own evidence collection kit, she carried a camera. Ian held both the department's kit and camera. All three of the other officers were several years younger than Vivi—she would peg Marcus as the oldest of the three and Wyatt as the youngest—but they looked intelligent and alert and, more importantly, clearly and comfortably under Ian's command.

"Ready, folks?" Vivi asked with a nod to Carly and Wyatt, who both nodded back. "Good, follow me, stay to the outside, and keep your eyes open as we photograph. It's unlikely we're going to find a smoking gun here, but we may find something useful, so look for anything that might look out of place. Don't touch smooth surfaces until we know there aren't prints on them, and if you see something, don't waste any time wondering if it *is* something. Once we start collecting evidence, just document it, collect it, bag it, and tag it." Everyone nodded again and they all went to work.

Four hours later, they had several boxes full of evidence and, at least for Vivi, not a lot of hope that they were going to find anything useful. While the deputies seemed excited about random hairs and fingerprints, she had enough experience to know that if the person responsible for Rebecca's disappearance ever set foot in the house he would have been too smart to leave any evidence of it. No, to her the most exciting thing was not the hair, but a small spot of oil in the garage. It looked like there had been a second car in the garage, at some point. Judging from the spatter, it was something taller than Rebecca's own Subaru. But then again, even that oil spot could be nothing. It was possible that the owner had a truck he drove up on occasion. But to be on the safe side, they had photographed, documented, and collected a sample. It sat in box number two, waiting to be dropped at the lab in Albany.

Vivi watched as Carly and Marcus drove away, headed back to the police station. Wyatt had the afternoon off, so he departed for home.

"Want to come to Albany with me?" Ian asked from behind her. She turned and considered, then shook her head.

"Yes, but I won't. Sam needs some time alone with the evidence. He knows his team and his equipment. I'll let him do his job without me standing over his shoulder like I did when he was my student."

"He may want your help."

"And he'll get it tomorrow, if he wants it."

Ian studied her face for a moment then gave a short nod. "I'll take you back to The Tavern then, before I head up to the lab to drop everything off."

They climbed into the Jeep and headed back into town. "So, what will you do this afternoon?" he asked.

"I have some research I want to do on the case and some people to call."

"Anything I should know about?"

"I'm going to log in to the similar crimes database and also the VICAP, the FBI violent crimes database, and the missing persons database, to see if anything comes up. I'm also going to call Nick."

"You didn't call him last night?"

Vivi shook her head. "No, call me petty but I wanted to make him sweat a little, and then we were a bit busy this morning. I'll fill him in now though."

They pulled up to The Tavern and Ian put the Jeep in park. "Is there anything more we should be doing? It feels like we should be doing something."

Vivi turned and held his gaze. His face was expressionless, but she could hear the frustration in his voice. "Unfortunately, all is not like what we see on television. In real life things move slower, especially on cases like this where so much time has passed."

"It's only been a few weeks since Rebecca Cole disappeared," he pointed out.

"And without a body, she's still just another missing adult who could have run off to the Bahamas with the love of her life," she countered. "Unless we find something in the evidence we collected today, we don't have much to go on."

"Or until we have a body, Rebecca's or someone else's."

"Hopefully, Rebecca's alive," Vivi commented, not wanting to think about yet another woman being involved. Even though she suspected that between now and when they caught the killer, *if* they caught the killer, there would be more than a few more bodies. "Dogs," she said, a thought suddenly occurring to her.

"Pardon me?" he asked, turning in his seat to look at her.

"Dogs. If you want to do something, and you have access to search and rescue dogs, or cadaver dogs, maybe you could get them out to the house."

Ian considered the suggestion then frowned. "Won't it be too late? We know it's been a few weeks since she was in the house. Wouldn't any trail left outside be gone by now?"

Vivi lifted her shoulders. "No, you don't want sniffing dogs. Those trails do go cold after several days, but dogs trained to air scent can come in sometimes weeks later. And the scents associated with decomposition can be identified by cadaver dogs for years. But what will have an impact is getting the dogs in the right area to catch any scent. We don't know where she went missing from, but if you start with either air scent search and rescue dogs or cadaver dogs, we might get an idea of whether or not she was in the house or died there. It's not common to find dogs who do both, but since we don't know if she's alive or dead at this point, if you had access to one who can sniff out both, it might be worth a try."

"And it might give us something. I'll make a few calls while I drive to Albany and see what I can pull together. Dinner?"

"Sounds good. Meet back here at seven?" she answered, before thinking or even considering how easy her response came.

"Seven it is. Call me if you find anything."

"You too." She gave Ian one last look and had the sudden urge to lean over and give him a kiss goodbye. Startled by her instinct, Vivi opened her door, climbed out of the car, and quickly shut the door behind her. After a sharp wave goodbye, she turned and went inside.

Rob was at the bar when she entered. He held up a glass, asking her if she wanted a drink before heading up. Vivi shook her head but approached the bar and ordered a salad instead.

When it was ready, she headed upstairs to her room, and after plopping herself, her computer, and her lunch on the bed, she propped her ankle up and called Nick.

"You can be vindictive, can't you?" he answered.

"Yes, but that's not why it's taken me eighteen hours to call you back. We had to collect some evidence this morning. I was busy."

"Evidence relating to Jessica Akers?"

"No. We have another missing woman." Vivi went on to tell him about Rebecca Cole.

"Could be she's just missing," Nick pointed out.

"Could be."

"But you think it's related to Jessica?"

"Yes, I do."

"If they are related, then Jessica's father isn't involved, since he's been in Leavenworth and will stay there."

"I could be wrong," Vivi offered.

"As much as it pains me to admit it, you're rarely wrong, Viv."

"True, at least when it comes to murder." She didn't doubt he'd pick up on her subtle jibe that she'd been wrong in her judgment of him.

"You know I regret that, don't you?" Nick said.

She sighed. She hadn't called him to rehash things and wished that she hadn't let the insinuation slide from her mouth. It just wasn't relevant anymore.

"Water under the bridge, Nick."

"Then why don't I come up there and help you?"

"Because we don't need your help. And it's not your jurisdiction. She's not army, it's probably not related to her father, there's no reason for you to come up here."

"Unless you're wrong."

"If I'm wrong, I'll call."

He let out a frustrated breath. "You won't call."

"Nick, I may have been furious with you, but I know what she meant to you. I know you wanted her in protective custody and I know she declined. I also know that you probably blame yourself."

"It wasn't my bloody fault she ran off," he responded.

"Of course it wasn't, but that doesn't mean we don't blame ourselves for other people's mistakes. Come on, Nick. Think of who you're talking to here. We do it all the time. The one that got away, the one we couldn't catch in time. I know what that feels like, Nick. And despite the fact that you used me, I wouldn't wish that feeling on anyone. Not even you. If I think this case is related, I'll call."

Nick was silent and, after a long moment, Vivi began to think he might have actually hung up on her. But then he spoke.

"I would appreciate that," he said, very formally, making her nervous.

"Nick," she warned.

"It's too late for us, isn't it, Viv?"

"A long time ago, Nick."

"I should have tried harder."

"There's a lesson for next time then."

He paused again. "Call me."

"If it looks related, I will," she gave one last promise before hanging up. She stared at the phone in her hand for a moment and was almost certain that wasn't the last she would hear from Nick.

Shaking her head, shaking off the conversation, she booted up her computer and began picking at her lunch. Combing through databases wasn't as simple as it sounded on television. There were so many variables that brought up different results that Vivi often felt it was a bit like playing the slots. Only there wasn't one big payout, but lots of little ones, and even those needed to be sorted through to find the real gems.

Several hours later, she stretched and took a break consisting of taking her plate back down to Rob then coming back up to jump in the shower. Within thirty minutes she was back on her computer, weeding through more missing persons reports than she cared to acknowledge.

Lost in thought, she jumped when she heard a knock on her door. She glanced at the clock and shot up. It was ten after seven.

"Sorry about that," she said, opening the door. Ian stepped through and glanced around.

"Everything okay?"

"Everything is fine, I just got hung up on the research. Give me five minutes and I'll be ready."

***

Ian nodded in agreement and watched Vivienne disappear into the bathroom. She'd showered and changed and her hair was still damp. And for the first time since he'd met her, it wasn't pulled back but rather fell, in long locks, down her back. It was the kind of hair a man could get tangled in. For a moment he considered suggesting they skip dinner. But as appealing as that sounded, it was a bit presumptuous, even for his arrogant Ranger-self. He was pretty sure the attraction was mutual, but he couldn't get a read on how far Vivienne was interested in taking it, if anywhere at all.

He glanced down at the table in the room, littered with files and printouts. They were case related, judging by the few sheets he saw, so he picked one up. It was a report of a woman missing from DC. Same basic stats as both Jessica and Rebecca and the picture accompanying the report looked similar enough to Jessica that, if the killer did prefer a certain look, she would definitely fall into that category. He frowned and picked up a second sheet of paper.

This one was different. This one was a printout of a report regarding the murder of yet another woman. There was no photo, but the report included height, approximate weight, hair and eye color, and means of death. Again, the stats fit Jessica, but more alarming, so did the method of death. Manual strangulation, signs of a shackle or manacle-like restraint, and likely sexual assault.

"How did you find these?" he asked, spinning around when the bathroom door opened.

"FBI databases. I know you put in the request a few days ago to run them, but I have direct access, and since I'm now officially on the case, I figured I would handle the database information."

"It looks like you might have found more than you bargained for," he said, motioning to the pages scattered across the desk. There had to be a hundred of them. The thought made him sick.

She came to his side, took the two pages he held, and placed them back with the others. "Not all of these will be related to our case. In fact most of them won't be related. But the thing is, I've been doing this long enough that I like to keep the parameters open and explore probably more than I need to. I figure I would rather put in the extra time and cast a wider net in the hopes I don't miss something than stick to the bare facts."

"And you do this yourself?" Ian was both stunned and humbled by the thought. When Vivienne DeMarco stepped into a case, she stepped in 110 percent.

"Like I said, I like to cast a wide net. The people who run the database queries are good, but they don't always have the time to explore the unexpected, or even if they do, they generally don't have the inside information I have. Don't get me wrong, they do a good job of maintaining the databases, an excellent job. But the databases—and the information we get out of them—are only as good as what is put in, and sometimes people don't put everything in. I've been around long enough to know when it's worth looking at a case that might, at first glance, not look like a good fit."

"So what now?"

"I'll go down and eat dinner with you, tell you what I've found so far. Which isn't much," she warned. "You'll tell me about anything that might have come up with you this afternoon. Then when you leave, I'll come back up here and start combing through these reports," she said with a gesture to the table and its contents. "By morning, hopefully, I'll have a short list of cases we should take a closer look at."

"Hopefully, a very short list," he muttered.

She gave a last look at the scattered reports. "Amen to that."

***

When Vivi's cell rang at seven in the morning, she ignored it and burrowed deeper into the blankets. She knew the dogs were on their way later that day, the evidence was at the lab, and the results of her own digging were scattered around the room. She'd spent hours after dinner going through the various reports and had narrowed the list down to twelve women—three bodies and nine missing persons—she wanted to look into further. And she was exhausted. But the ringing wouldn't stop. So, with a groan, she slapped her hand over the device and answered.

"Yes?" she sounded grumpy, but four hours of sleep did that to her.

"We have a body."

Nothing quite woke her up like that phrase. She bolted upright and looked at the clock. "The dogs aren't supposed to be there until this afternoon."

"Didn't need them," came Ian's reply. "I called Owen Mayfield yesterday to tell him about the well you stepped into. Offered to pay for a new cover. He took a hike up there this morning."

"And found her inside," Vivi finished his sentence, her stomach turning. They were so close and hadn't sensed a thing.

"Any plans for the day?"

"Oh, you know, wash my hair, do my laundry," she replied. "Actually, I do need to do laundry, but that can wait until tonight. I'll be out in twenty minutes."

"Dump your stuff in my washer. My house is on the way, it won't add five minutes to your trip. We're waiting for the assistance team from the firehouse, so we're not doing anything yet anyway."

Vivi considered the offer for all of two seconds before agreeing. Assuming they got the body out this morning, she could swing back by Ian's afterward, dump the clothes into the dryer, then head up to the lab to do the autopsy and talk with Sam about the evidence collected yesterday. Within five minutes she was out the door and headed downstairs. Rob stopped her on the way with a cup of coffee and a bag of goodies ready to go. She smiled her thanks, knowing Ian had probably called him to ask the favor.

When she pulled up to the house Rebecca had stayed in, Vivi was better equipped for the walk up the hill than she'd been the first time, and despite the ache in her ankle, she made decent time. The scene was quiet when she arrived, even though close to ten people were present. Ian made his way toward her.

"Doing okay?" he asked with a nod to her ankle.

"I'll be fine," she answered. She liked that he'd asked but hadn't made a big deal out of it. "Tell me what's going on."

"Carly and Marcus are here. This is Carly's first murder but she's doing well. Marcus was an MP in the Army so he's seen a bit more, but this is different. Still, they are both doing great. Over there," he motioned with his head, "is the fire assist team. I called them in because I think we're going to need help getting her out, and they have more equipment than we do."

"And him?" Vivi asked with a nod toward a man standing with Wyatt.

"Owen Mayfield. He found the body."

She studied him for a moment. He was an older gentleman,

wearing a red flannel jacket, jeans, and workman's boots. But he stood straight and appeared calm as he talked to Wyatt. "He seems to be holding up fine," Vivi commented.

"He's been better, but like me and a lot of guys around here, he did a stint in the military, so this isn't his first dead body."

"But the first on his property, I'd imagine." Ian inclined his head in assent. She studied the surroundings again for a moment, then in silent agreement, they made their way to the side of the well. Ian handed her a powerful flashlight; even in the daylight hours the area was darkened by the shadows of the surrounding trees. Ian stood beside her as she sank to her haunches; everyone else stayed a respectful distance away.

Over the years, the well had filled in, leaving it only about twenty feet deep. At the bottom lay the body of what Vivi presumed was Rebecca Cole. There wasn't enough flesh left to make a visual ID, and DNA would come later, but for all intents and purposes, Vivi was certain it was their missing woman. The body was in an upright fetal position with one leg splayed to the side, the other tucked up against her chest. Her arms lay at her sides and the back of her head rested against the wall of the well. She looked as if she'd simply been tossed down, like trash.

"Has anyone been down there?" she asked. Ian shook his head and Vivi shined her light on Rebecca's wrists and then ankles.

"It's hard to tell from here what kind of damage she sustained and what might have occurred before her death versus after or when she was dumped. I'm stating the obvious, but we need to get her out."

"Yeah, we're on it." In his usual way, Ian already had a plan. After sliding the body onto a makeshift platform, they were going to pull a large plastic cover over it for protection. The fire assist team had a lift, and once everything was positioned, they would pull the platform up. Because of the size of the well, Vivi knew it would have to be her or Carly who went down to prepare everything. And she wasn't surprised at all when Carly volunteered. The woman was quiet, but from what Vivi could tell, she was capable and conscientious.

Using a rope, Carly was lowered into the well where she managed to get the platform under the body and the protective cover in place. After a few fits and starts, Ian and Marcus carefully guided the body over the lip of the well and onto the ground.

"She make it?" Carly called from her position in the well. Marcus gave her the thumbs up. "If you hand down some collection bags and a good light, I'll see what I can find down here," she offered.

"Good thinking, Carly," Ian said, directing Wyatt to assist her.

"If we have a ladder that will fit down there, we may want to use it now, so Carly can examine the walls of the well on her way up," Vivi suggested. There was no way they could have fit one in the well with the victim and Carly, but now that the body was gone, they were able to slide a long, metal ladder down.

Joining Ian and Marcus, Vivi slid on a pair of booties and gloves. After asking for a pair of scissors, she gently cut the protective plastic away, revealing the mostly decomposed body of the woman they were assuming was Rebecca Cole. Vivi did an initial examination of her in the fetal position, and then, with Ian's assistance, they straightened her out.

"There's not a lot left," Marcus commented, keeping an appropriate distance.

"Have you had a wet spring?" Vivi asked. Ian and Marcus both responded in the positive. "The decomp is affected by the moisture that likely built up in the well. Have Carly collect some soil samples, and we'll see if anything got washed off while she was down there. You can see here and here," she said, pointing to the wrists and ankles, "are marks similar to those we found on Jessica Akers."

"So she was restrained too," Ian commented.

"And here," Vivi continued, leaning way over to take a closer look at the neck area. "It's hard to see much right now, but there are signs of strangulation too." She sat back and regarded the body again before standing and giving Ian an apologetic look.

"I'm sorry this is happening here," she said.

He held her gaze for a moment and then glanced back at the body. "I'm sorry it's happening at all."

Vivi concurred with that. After taking one last look, she began directing Ian and Marcus on how best to preserve the evidence for transport. By eleven thirty, Carly was done with her collection, and both the body and the evidence were on their way to the lab.

"Carly, Wyatt, you two are on today. Marcus, take the afternoon off. We need to rest while we can. Vivienne and I will drive up to the lab in Albany to oversee that part of the investigation. We'll keep you updated," Ian directed his team. They took his word without complaint and headed in their respective directions. Then Ian turned to her.

"Lunch at my place, you can switch your laundry, then we'll head up to the lab together?"

"That your plan?" she responded, her lips lifting into a small smile.

"Come on," he lifted his eyes at her teasing. "Let's get cleaned up and fed."

When they entered the house he offered to switch her laundry for her, claiming a finicky dryer. But modesty got the best of her and she didn't want him handling her lingerie any more than he already had the other day, so she declined. It wasn't that what she was washing was embarrassing—it wasn't too sexy or too plain—it was just a little more personal than she was willing to get at the moment. Ian gave her a look that suggested he knew what she was doing and thought her ridiculous, but he didn't say anything.

He popped back into the laundry room a few minutes later, as she shut the door to the dryer. Startled by his sudden appearance, she spun around. Three bras were hanging from her first two fingers and several panties dangled from the rest. She froze in that tableau for a moment. His eyes went to her undergarments and fixed there for long enough to let his, and her, imaginations go to work, then they traveled back to her face. He hitched his hip against the dryer, crossed his arms over his chest, and looked every bit the male he was.

"You can hang those to dry," he said with a nod to the rod and hangers behind her. But it wasn't a suggestion, it was almost a dare.

She narrowed her eyes on him. "You just want to see my underwear."

He tilted his head. "I'd rather see them on, but I do have a good imagination."

It wasn't often that she was speechless, but she was now. Flirting had never been her strong point; having started college at sixteen and never having gone through that stage of discovery with boys her own age, she'd never had any practice, never really had the chance to develop the skill. And because of that, she intentionally tried to keep games, and flirting, out of all her relationships.

She cleared her throat. "I'll take these outside to dry. You can start the machine."

CHAPTER 10

VIVI TOOK LONGER THAN NECESSARY to lay her clothes out in the trunk of her car. It wasn't ideal, but it was the best place to dry her things out of the view of someone who was supposed to be a professional colleague. Although, even before his explicit comment, she suspected they were headed in the more-than-colleagues direction.

Ian came out the back door as she was headed toward it. He had two paper bags with him, one of which he handed to her.

"Turkey sandwich with Swiss cheese, mayo, and mustard, an apple, and a bottle of water," he said, heading toward his Jeep without breaking stride. "I figure we can eat in the car, if you don't mind?" He seemed to be asking more because manners dictated it than because he thought she might object. Which she didn't.

They headed out, turning toward the Taconic Parkway, which would take them to Interstate 90 and into Albany. Once they were on the parkway, Ian reached for his lunch bag. Rather than watch him juggle the driving and the unpacking of his lunch, Vivi grabbed it from him, pulled everything out, including the paper towel he'd packed—which made her smile—and set it all up within his reach. Once his was ready, she did the same with hers; she hadn't realized how hungry she was until she took her first bite of the sandwich.

"Thanks for the lunch. And the use of your washer and dryer," she added.

"Thanks for helping me solve a crime spree," he countered.

They ate in silence for several miles, and then she asked the question that had been on her mind since they'd gotten back in the Jeep. "Why did you say that?"

Ian cast her a glance before returning his eyes to the road. "Say what?" He wasn't playing dumb; he wanted to hear her say it.

"That thing about wanting to see me in my underwear," Vivi said.

"Because it's true." His answer was annoyingly simple.

"I don't mean why did you say it, I meant *why* did you *say* it?"

He slid her another look, this one a bit longer. "Is this one of those woman things where if you say something twice, it has a completely different meaning than if you say it only once?"

Vivi was pretty sure her expression was about as blank as her mind.

"You know," Ian motioned with his hand. "I don't *like* him like him, but I like him? Or, did you kiss him or *kiss him* kiss him?"

Vivi's lips twitched. "Hang out with girls much when you were a kid?"

"Evelyn Greene was my sister's best friend. Four years older than me and the undisputed hottest girl in town. I used to eavesdrop a lot."

Vivi laughed softly, picturing it, which wasn't hard to do. "I don't mean why did you think it, I meant why did you put your thoughts into words," she clarified, going back to the original question.

He changed lanes as they merged onto I-90 and shrugged. "Because I thought you should know. I thought I should put it out there."

Vivi's eyebrow shot up. "Why would you think I should know that you want to see me all but naked. Because really, thanks, now I'm going be self-conscious about my butt every time I walk in front of you," she grumbled.

"Believe me, you have nothing to be self-conscious about."

"Was that supposed to make it better?"

She saw his lips fighting a grin before he spoke.

"Look, I don't think I'm too crazy to think that there's an attraction between the two of us. I put it out there in case you were thinking of ever doing anything about it. This way, if you do decide you want to do something about it, you won't have to spend any time wondering how I'll react. You'll know."

"So you did it for me?"

Ian half shrugged. "You could say that. But it's not entirely selfless either. Obviously."

"And if I don't want to do anything about it?"

"Your call."

"Why can't it be yours? Why can't you make the first move?"

"Seems to me I did."

Vivi regarded him before commenting with complete honesty. "You have way more guts than I do, MacAllister."

"Optimism is probably a better word." They drove for a few more miles as she considered the situation. He must have been doing the same because he asked, "You okay with this?"

Normally, she wouldn't be okay. Not at all. She wasn't very good at dealing with feelings, at least not her own, anyway. They made her uncomfortable because she didn't always understand them—or couldn't always rationally explain them—and so she did her best to minimize their intrusion on her life. But Ian had gone and laid it all out there—an attraction, a curiosity about each other that was more than professional. It was different, that's for sure. And she wasn't quite sure what to do with it.

But she hadn't been lying when she'd said that what he'd done had taken guts. She had a certain amount of respect for his approach. And that's what she sensed it was—an approach to dealing with something he wasn't quite sure about either.

"Yeah, I'm okay," Vivi responded.

Ian turned his head and gave her a quick glance. "That's it? You're okay?" The incredulity in his voice made her laugh.

"Yes, I promise, I'm okay. Everything is fine."

She felt him study her out of the corner of his eye, even as he kept his eyes on the highway. And then his lips curled up into a very male smile. "Good then. We're okay."

***

Ian kept a wary eye, and ear, on Vivienne for the rest of the drive. His gamble in the laundry room had been just that, a gamble. He hadn't been sure how she would take it. She could have laughed, or she could have outright told him he was out of line, and she wouldn't have been wrong.

But he hadn't been attracted to a woman in a long time. Not in the way he was attracted to her. He wasn't a monk and had had his fair share of girlfriends and female companions. But there had been no one since he'd been hit by the IED. A year ago.

By the time he made it back to the states, he was pretty fucked up, both mentally and physically. And he hadn't allowed himself to consider any kind of relationship with any woman. Until Vivienne. He still wasn't sure if it would go anywhere, but he recognized a kindred spirit of sorts in her and so had to try.

He turned his head for another quick look. She was gazing out the window, lost in her own thoughts. She may not see herself as a warrior, but she was. In every sense of the word. And maybe that was what he was responding to. Maybe it was because he sensed she would understand. She'd been in the trenches. She would know.

He exited I-90 and made his way to the lab. After showing their IDs at the security gate, they parked and walked into the lobby.

"Have you been here before?" he asked Vivienne as he produced his ID again for the receptionist.

"Not to this lab, no." She handed her ID over as well.

"And you're here to see?" the receptionist asked.

Ian looked to Vivienne to answer. He'd worked with the lab techs the day before but hadn't met her friend.

"Dr. Buckley," she answered then turned to Ian. "He was one of my first students. It will be good to see him again."

"Small world. Does that mean we'll get special treatment?"

"Yes, it does," a voice behind them answered. Ian turned around to see a man entering the room. He was tall and looked to be part Southeast Asian, part something else. His facial features looked Indian, but his coloring was fair and his eyes were a lighter brown than the dark, almost black, of most Indian people.

"Sam." Vivienne smiled and stepped forward. The two hugged and Ian caught a glimpse of the student in Dr. Buckley's eyes, still looking at Vivienne for approval, praise.

"Ian, this is Dr. Sameer Buckley. Sam, this is Deputy Chief Ian MacAllister."

Ian held his hand out, and the good doctor had a straightforward, solid handshake with an expression to match it on his face.

"Have you signed in?" Dr. Buckley asked.

They hadn't, so Ian moved to do that. When he was done, he handed Vivienne the pen to do the same. "What's the date?" she asked.

"The seventeenth," he answered. He expected a casual "thanks," and when she said nothing, he turned. Vivi stood at the counter, pen in hand, with her back to him. An unusual stillness had come over her. "Vivienne, are you okay?"

She gave a little start, then finished signing in. "Yes, I'm fine. Everything is fine."

Her tone was flat, as was her expression when she turned. She looked at Ian, then her eyes darted away. He frowned.

"Ready?" she asked, facing Sam. He nodded and led them through a door and into the main part of the lab. Ian followed behind Vivienne, only half listening to what the younger doctor was saying. Something had happened when she'd signed in, and whatever it was, it wasn't good.

He'd pulled her into this investigation; was she doing something she wasn't ready to do? The more he knew her, the more he realized how hard it must have been for her to step away, even for a month or two. But something had happened that had taken her to that point.

Ian tried to think of her in a detached way but couldn't. She was healthy—he knew she ran, knew she was eating. But that was all taking care of her body. What about her mind?

"Ian?"

He came up short when Sam and Vivienne stopped. She was looking at him, a question in her eyes. He'd missed something.

"Sorry, woolgathering," he said.

She tilted her head and studied him for a moment before speaking. "Not a problem. Sam and I are going to do the autopsy. Once we're done, we thought it might be a good time to go over all the evidence together."

Ian gave a curt nod. "Sounds like a plan."

A ghost of a smile touched her lips. "Do you want to watch?"

He thought about it for a split second. "Not if there is something more useful I could be doing."

Vivienne glanced at Sam, who nodded. "We'll set you up with a computer that has access to all the databases I have access to," she said. "I think it would be a good idea if you culled through some of the databases, like I did last night, to see what you can come up with."

That sounded reasonable. "Do you want me to use the same parameters you used?" he asked.

She shook her head. "No, I want you to use what seems logical to you. Then I think we should compare what I came up with and what you came up with and see if we have any overlaps."

Ian nodded in agreement and, fifteen minutes later, found himself sitting in front of a computer looking at empty query fields. He took a second to watch Vivienne walk away and thought that maybe the best thing he could do for her was solve this case. So, after giving himself an overview of the extensive databases open to him, he devised a plan to go to each and try as systematically as he could to find something—anything—that might help them.

**

Vivi stood at the door for a moment and watched Ian work. His eyes were fixed on the computer screen; he had one hand on the mouse and the other holding up a sheet of paper. She glanced at the clock. Four hours had passed and he didn't look any worse for wear.

"Ian?"

His head came around.

"We're done," she said.

"Is it Rebecca?" he asked, still seated.

She nodded. "We were able to get a partial fingerprint. We matched it to a print she had on file for some work she did with a children's theater in New York."

She watched a myriad of emotions flicker across Ian's face before he gathered all the printouts, slid them into a folder, and rose. She gestured with her head and he followed her out. They entered another room where Sam had taken over a table and spread out a number of the reports on the evidence collected from both victims. It wasn't the worst case Vivi had seen, but that wasn't saying much.

Ian held out his file to her. She shook her head. "I'll look at it later. I want to go over what physical evidence we have first. We can look at that information tonight."

"So we do have evidence?"

She frowned at the reports, wishing they held more than they did. "Not much, but yes, we do have some."

Ian put his folder down when she handed him a set of papers. "That's the report of trace evidence found in the injuries caused by the binding. It's a lot of scientific stuff, but basically, they're iron. New or very well preserved. There were no rust particles."

"Found on both women?" Ian looked up and Vivi nodded.

"These," she said, handing him two small vials, "are slivers we found on each victim. Jessica's were found in what was left of her hair, and Rebecca's were found in some flesh behind her elbow joint."

"Like where she might rub her arm if she was struggling against being chained down. And they're the same wood, aren't they?" Ian asked, holding the vials up to the light for a better look.

Again, Vivi nodded.

"Okay. Can we tell if they came from the same piece of wood or table?" Ian asked. "And what was Rebecca's cause of death?" He handed the small containers back to her and she passed them back to Sam, who rechecked the evidence seals and placed them on the table.

"No, the wood is standard issue plywood." Vivi answered. "No way to tell for certain if they came from the same board unless we had that board and could match the pieces. As to Rebecca, her COD was strangulation."

"And any sexual assault?" Ian raised the question while skimming one of the reports lying open on the table.

Vivi nodded. "Yes. Again, it is hard to tell to what extent, but there was evidence of aggressive sexual behavior."

"It must have been extremely aggressive if there was still evidence of it after the decomp," Ian pointed out, a hard look crossing his features.

Neither she nor Sam answered.

"So, what else?" Ian prompted.

Sam answered this time, picking up another folder and handing it to Ian. "No donor fluids, so the obvious DNA is out. Although Rebecca had some scrapings under her nails that are being tested now. I didn't see any evidence of skin cells, but I didn't look at every scraping. We'll let the computer do that."

Ian flipped through the DNA report Sam had handed him, then closed it, and placed it with the others. Sam then handed Ian another set of papers.

"What's this?" Ian asked, scanning the documents.

"It's the initial analysis on the trace soil found on both victims," Sam answered.

"What will it give us, given that both women were found lying on dirt? I mean, how will you be able to know if the dirt you find is relevant or not?"

"We have soil samples from both dump sites. We'll run those against what we found on Rebecca and Jessica. If we only find soil from the dump sites on them, we may have nothing," Vivi answered.

"But if you find something that isn't a match, we might have something? Something that can give us an idea of where they might have been held?" Ian asked, working it out in his mind.

Vivi didn't want to get his hopes up too high. "If we find soil that is foreign to the dump sites, it will tell us something, but what that is depends on what we find. In other words, if what we find is common soil, we'll be able to eliminate places like industrial areas that would have a different makeup. But the possibilities would still be wide open."

"But if it's something more unique, we might be able to narrow it down more?" Ian pressed.

She nodded then looked down at the table. Unlike on TV, a body didn't always tell them enough to solve a crime. Sometimes evidence wasn't enough. Or they didn't have enough of it to make a difference.

"And what if you find the same soil on both women?" Ian asked.

"If we find the same soil on both women and that soil is foreign to both dump sites, we might be able to postulate that they were held in the same place," Sam responded.

"But we can't confirm, can we, unless the soil is so unique as to point to only one location." The defeat in Ian's voice echoed Vivi's feelings. Physical evidence was vital, but they needed more.

"Then I guess we'll need to keep looking at these." Ian said, putting down the soil report and picking up the folder he'd created of similar crimes. "We'll take what we can get as far as the physical evidence goes, but it doesn't look like it's going to give us a smoking gun, so we'll keep working this from all angles. Dr. Buckley, I assume you'll continue to drive things here?"

Sam nodded.

"Then we can focus on finding similar victims," Ian said, holding up his folder. "We'll see what we can dig up. I can put Carly and Marcus on tracing the last movements of both of the victims we have, looking for any intersections between them. And Wyatt can work with the sheriff's office to look into possible locations where someone might have been held. We probably won't find a torture shack, but we can also probably eliminate a lot of land around the county."

Ian held up a hand to stop Vivi from speaking. "And yes, before you point it out, that is my plan."

She managed to smile.

"Then I think we're good. Or as good as we're going to get right now," Ian said.

Vivi had to give him credit; he was becoming more and more of an investigator every day. Not that it surprised her, but she wondered if he even noticed. Knowing him, she doubted it.

"You'll keep us posted?" she asked, turning to her former student.

"Of course." Sam wagged his head in a distinctly Indian way, something he'd no doubt picked up from his mother.

His *mother*.

Vivi looked down at her shoes and blinked back the moisture gathering in her eyes.

"Vivienne?" Ian was at her shoulder, one of his hands gentle but solid on her waist.

"I'm fine. I, uh. Let's leave Sam. I need to get back to my room." She could feel Ian looking at her, but she couldn't bring herself to look back because he would see too much. So she stepped away, gave Sam a hug goodbye, thanked him for his help, and headed for the door. Behind her, she heard the men exchange their own goodbyes as she kept on walking.

***

The tension in Ian's body ratcheted up with every mile they drove on the way home. Vivienne said no more than two words, and for the life of him, he couldn't figure out what was wrong. If she didn't tell him, how could he fix it?

He put the Jeep in park in his driveway and climbed out. His clothes felt raw against his skin as he slammed the driver's side door and walked toward his house. He flinched when Vivienne's door echoed his. He hated this.

Ian thought about pressing her, about cornering her and making her tell him what was going on. He thought about taking her to bed, about working everything out physically. And while that thought held great appeal, one look at Vivienne stopped him cold.

She avoided him as she gathered up her clothes from his dryer, not once raising her eyes to his. She looked alone, isolated, even though he was standing not five feet away. He was feeling a growing sense of helplessness that did not sit well on his shoulders.

"Vivienne," he said, taking a step forward and reaching for her.

She ducked away, still not meeting his eyes, and tucked the last of her laundry into her laundry bag.

"Thanks for the use of your machines. I have some things to do this afternoon. I'll—" she paused and, for the first time since they left the lab, looked at him. He saw her throat working and she swallowed before speaking. "I'll call you tomorrow."

And she was gone.

Ian cursed to himself as he watched her car fly down his driveway. He'd followed her outside and now stood in his yard, frozen in indecision. Go after her or leave her be? He'd seen pain in her eyes and wanted to make it go away. But he knew himself well enough to know that if he went to her now he'd demand answers—because he needed them, because he needed to feel better about whatever was going on—and that wouldn't be a good thing for either of them.

Feeling the need to steady his nerves before making any decisions, he changed into his workout clothes and went for a long run. It wasn't quite the same as working out his frustrations in bed with Vivienne, but it was probably healthier for the both of them. Or so he told himself.

When he came back from his run, Ian stripped on his back patio and stepped into his outdoor shower—one of the perks of living in the country with no neighbors. He was standing with his face in the streaming water, still trying to clear his mind, when he heard a car pull up his driveway. Frowning at the interruption, he shut off the water, wrapped a towel around his waist, and stepped out of the shower.

Ian took a few steps to the edge of his back lawn and watched Vivienne's car reappear. Pulling alongside his house, she jerked the car to a stop twenty feet away. He crossed his arms over his bare chest and waited.

Not moving a muscle, he watched as she unfolded herself from the driver's seat. Closing the door behind her, she turned and looked straight at him.

She'd changed from her jeans into a dress—and it wasn't a cute summertime dress. Vivienne's long legs were showcased by the short skirt and high platform sandals. Her hair was pulled back and the eyes that met his were not those of the woman who had left his house just over an hour ago. No, this woman was on a mission. And every fiber in his being knew what that mission was.

She stalked toward him, never taking her eyes from his. With every step, his body reacted in a primal way. Just the way she wanted him to, judging by the way she took him in. By the time she stopped, six inches away from him, he was ready—in every sense of the word—to give her whatever she wanted. And to take what he needed.

Vivienne laid a hand on his chest and his skin jumped. His pulse was beating a rapid rhythm that kicked up when her finger circled his nipple. Then she slid her hand up and curled it behind his neck. Her eyes met his and he knew she didn't want to talk. She didn't want to discuss a thing. She wanted oblivion. And she wanted it from him.

Before Ian had a chance to respond, she closed the distance between them and pulled his mouth down to hers. And everything exploded from there.

He wrapped one hand around her waist and pulled her body flush against him. His other hand tangled in her hair, drawing her closer as their mouths opened to deepen the kiss. Vivienne's fingers dug into his shoulders as his hand fisted in the back of her dress. They battled each other for control over something that was so far out of control that neither was going to win. Or lose.

He turned and forced her backward until she was up against his house. No longer needing his hands to keep her close as he pressed against her, he reached down, slid a hand up her thigh, and pulled her dress up along with it. His stomach contracted when he felt her knuckles graze his abdomen and her fingers slip under his towel, yanking it loose. The towel fell to the ground in a heap.

Naked and needing to feel her, more of her, he reached around and tugged her leg up, wrapping it around his waist. Feeling skin against skin, she ran her hands down his back and pulled him to her, pressing him against her heat. She let out a little moan and his hand tightened on her waist.

"Ian," she whispered, taking his earlobe between her teeth. Need surged through him, and grabbing two handfuls of her dress, he pulled back just enough to tug it over her head. His breath coming in fast, he drew back and looked at her.

His imagination hadn't done her justice.

Standing there, trapped between him and the wall with her leg wrapped around his waist, Vivienne looked up. At that moment, Ian was pretty sure he'd never been so happy to be a man in his life. He could see everything through her sheer bra and panties. And when he looked down, he could now see, and feel against his skin, where he wanted more than anything to be.

She had caught her dress in one hand and pulled out a strip of condoms from some hidden pocket. He almost lost it right there, thinking of what it was going to feel like to slide into her. Without a word, she unhooked her bra with one hand, slid it off, and dropped it. Then she tore open one of the condoms, dropped her leg back down, and pushed him back a step.

She took him in her hand and stroked him once, then again.

"Vivienne," he said, taking her mouth again. Unable to keep his hands to himself, he reached between her thighs. Not bothering to remove her panties, he pushed them to the side and pressed a finger into her eager body.

"Oh god," she breathed, leaning her forehead against his shoulder. She rested her hands on his waist as he stroked her. Her legs started to tremble and her head fell back as she let out a quiet plea.

"Now, Vivienne," he ordered.

He would have put the condom on himself, but he didn't want to take his hands off of her. After a few tries, she managed to roll it on him. And he couldn't wait any longer.

Dipping his knees, Ian positioned himself. With the hand not inside her, he pulled her thigh up again and then, in a single, swift motion, he replaced his finger with what they both wanted and lifted her whole body up against the wall, burying himself inside her.

Her head fell onto his shoulder as she wrapped herself around him. His head came forward to rest on the wall behind her. They stayed there for a heartbeat and he absorbed the feel of her around him. Vivienne was hot and wet and tight, and he thought for a moment that he could stay there forever. Then her muscles twitched around him, her ankles tightened, and she whispered a little "please."

And there was no way he could stay still. Bracing his hands on her hips, Ian slid out and pushed back in again. And again. And again.

Her ankles locked over his lower back, making it harder for him to stroke in and out, making every stroke that much more gratifying. He ignored the feel of her nails biting into his skin while her hands gripped his shoulders. Her thighs fell open, her head lolled back, and he felt the telltale quiver begin, jacking him up even more. Primal instinct took over and Ian was moving in and out of her fast—faster than he probably should, sooner than he probably should—but when he felt her insides start to grab him, he no longer cared. As Vivienne curled up to meet him and her body locked onto his, she cried out and he slammed into her one more time, releasing everything he'd been holding back as she squeezed him dry.

They were both breathing hard when their world settled again. When Ian had the strength to open his eyes, he pulled back and looked at Vivienne. Her eyes were still closed. Loose tendrils of hair were pressed against the damp skin of her face and neck. She had a red mark on her shoulder from a particularly aggressive kiss and she looked stunning.

Everything inside him shuddered and tightened. She might not have come to him out of love, but she had needed him. And though he was more than happy to have given her what she'd needed, what they'd both wanted, he wasn't going to let it end there on his back patio.

Gathering her up in his arms, Ian took a tentative step back, testing his ability to walk after such a rush. Her eyes opened, but she didn't let go. She didn't make a move to get away. More sure of his ability now, he carried her into his room. And after following Vivienne down onto the bed, stripping her of whatever she had left on, Ian started all over again.

CHAPTER 11

Vivi rolled to the side of the bed and sat up. Looking over her shoulder through the window, she realized she had no idea how much time had passed. It had been dusk when she'd arrived and it was dark now, with a full moon casting shadows in Ian's room.

She scanned the floor, looking for her clothes before remembering that the only pieces she'd find in the bedroom were her underwear and shoes. Everything else was outside.

She was rising from the bed when Ian's hand shot out from under the sheet and caught her arm. She turned to find him watching her.

"Leaving?" he asked.

"Do you want me to stay?" She wanted to, but didn't want to push him. When he didn't answer, she pushed aside the disappointment and made another attempt to rise.

"Wait, Vivienne," he said, holding onto her arm as he sat up.

"It's okay, Ian. There are a lot of reasons for me not to stay. It's fine."

"No, it's not that." His grip on her arm tightened for a split second and she sensed he had more to say. Something he needed to say, even if he didn't want to. She sat back down, pulled a blanket that had been cast aside around her, and waited.

The sheet fell to his waist as he sat all the way up, revealing his bare chest. Vivi would have taken a moment to admire it if the look of dismay on Ian's face hadn't grabbed her attention. He ran a hand through his mussed hair, sighed, then propped his knees up and rested his arms across them.

"I want you to stay, Vivienne. But I—" he stopped and turned away. Then with a rueful shake of his head, he continued. "I have nightmares sometimes. They're not, well, they aren't pretty. And I haven't slept next to anyone since I started having them. I haven't slept with anyone period since I got back." A self-deprecating smile touched his lips as he turned to face her.

His admissions, both of them, surprised her. But one was far more important than the other.

"PTSD?" It wasn't much of a guess considering how he had reacted that day up in the woods. But still, he nodded and ran a hand over his face again.

"And you're afraid you might hurt me," she said.

He nodded again and she saw the pain and shame in his eyes.

"You won't," she said with certainty.

"I don't know that, Vivienne." Ian's voice was soft in the dark night hour.

"No, but I do."

His eyes searched hers and she held his gaze, sure of her convictions. She had no idea what his nightmares were like or what they might do to him, but she knew he would never hurt her.

"Then stay." She knew it cost him to make the offer. Not because he didn't want her there, but because she might see a part of him that wasn't strong, a part of him he saw as a failure. She didn't see PTSD that way at all, but she knew any words to that effect, any words to assure him his experiences, his nightmares, weren't his fault or a weakness of his character, would fall on deaf ears. Her trust in him, her belief in him as a man, was something that, at this point, she could only show him. And so, when he held his hand out to her, she came back down onto the bed and tucked herself in next to him.

She let him settle into his decision as she traced designs on his chest with her fingertip. When she felt his heart rate return to normal, she propped her chin on his chest.

"There is one problem though, if I stay," Vivi sighed. Ian

looked down at her and arched a brow in question. "I'm starving and you'll have to feed me."

His chuckle rumbled under her and warmed through her.

"I think I might be able to handle that."

Vivi grinned. "I thought you might. I should probably pick up my clothes while we're up, too."

"Now I wouldn't waste my time on something like that." Ian's hand slid down and patted her bare behind. "Here," he said, jack-knifing off the bed and displacing her. He tossed her one of his t-shirts. "You can wear this."

There was something appealing about sliding into one of his shirts. The large size made her feel small and feminine. And the masculine scent reminded her of whom she was with. She rose from the bed and the shirt fell to mid-thigh, it was a bit cool and breezy, but she liked it.

Glancing up, she saw Ian watching her. He'd pulled on a pair of boxers and was leaning against the doorframe regarding her.

"It looks good on you."

A sudden wave of shyness crept over her. She looked away as she felt herself blushing in the moonlight.

"Vivienne?"

She met his gaze again.

"I'd like for you to tell me what happened today. I'm glad you're here, and to say I'm glad you came to me would be an understatement, but something was bothering you today. Something drove you here. I'd like to know what that was."

Vivi froze. But Ian didn't push any further. He walked toward her, gave her a soft kiss, then left. She was still standing in the middle of his bedroom when she heard him pop the microwave open in the kitchen. She could hear him pulling out dishes then opening a bottle of wine. He was giving her space. He was giving her time. And she knew, without a doubt, he would give her all the time she needed. But standing there, in his room, in his shirt, she realized she didn't need the time. He deserved to know, and whether she told him now, or weeks from now, wouldn't make it any easier. Taking a deep breath, she moved to join him in the kitchen.

Vivi walked in as Ian was setting plates of lasagna and glasses of red wine on the table. She sat down, took a healthy sip of wine, and watched him as he sat down across from her. Her dress was folded and sitting at the other end of the table.

"I don't have any greens, sorry."

"It's ten o'clock, and given what we've been doing, I think I'm good with the carbs."

His lips twitched and they dug in. She was glad for the casual chitchat as they ate, but when they'd finished and pushed the plates away, she knew it was time. Reaching for her wineglass, Vivi started to talk.

"This year has been, well, to put it mildly, it's been rough. Remember when I told you how many cases I'd worked in the past twelve months?"

She looked up from her wine to find Ian sitting forward, elbows propped up on the table, fingering his glass. "Over 300," he recalled. "That's a lot."

"It is, and I probably underestimated. But it wasn't the cases that were the problem. Not at the beginning, anyway." She took another sip of wine and, for the first time, recognized the sound of rain on the roof. She glanced out the French doors that were open onto Ian's screened-in front porch and wondered when the clouds had moved in. Light flashed in the distance, bringing her back to the here and now.

"A year ago today, I lost my family." Vivi's chest tightened, and for a moment she struggled to breathe. Picking up her glass, she noted with detachment that her hands were shaking.

"Vivienne?"

She brought the glass to her lips and managed to choke down another sip. "I had a brother. Special Forces. Not unlike you, I imagine. Sometimes we knew where he was, most of the time we didn't. Because of the work I do, I know a lot of people in the military. Jeff and I had an agreement that if anything were to happen to him, I would be notified as his next of kin and it would be my job to tell our parents."

If she stopped talking, she might not start again, but she couldn't just sit there, so she stood and walked to the French doors. The cool, night air washed over her and the smell of the rain brought a measure of familiar comfort.

"I got a call from his base commander, a friend of mine. He'd gone around protocol so he could tell me that Jeff had been shot by insurgents that morning. They were still trying to figure out what had happened, but he wanted me to know about Jeff right away."

She stared out into the night and watched lightning off in the distant sky. "That call was the worst call I have ever received." Vivi still remembered the gut-wrenching pain that ripped through her body and soul when she'd heard that her brother was dead. She rubbed her chest now, still feeling it.

"But I knew what I had to do. I had a friend come pick me up and drive me over to my parents' house. I knew they were on their way back to Boston after being down at the Cape for a few days, enjoying the quiet before the summer season. Something they did every year."

Vivi remembered sitting with her friend on her parents' sofa waiting for them to come home. The familiar smells of their house, the comfort of being home. And they waited. And waited. Just sitting there.

"They didn't come," she whispered.

"Vivienne." Ian was behind her, his hands on her shoulders, easing her against him.

"We waited and waited and when we finally heard someone at the door, it was the state police. My parents had been hit by a drunk driver on their way home."

She closed her eyes to the memories. Ian's arms came around her, but she was so lost in time, reliving that day a year ago, that she couldn't respond.

"One day. In one day I lost my entire family." Her voice broke and tears cascaded down her cheeks. "I tell myself that at least it was a blessing my parents never knew about Jeff. At least they died believing both their children were safe."

The rain continued as they stood where they were. Exhausted, Vivi leaned against Ian and watched the storm move across the valley. Lightning flashed in the sky, thunder shook the house, wind whipped the branches of trees. And they stayed.

When the violence of Mother Nature quieted down, Vivi finished her story. "I didn't know what to do with myself so I threw myself into work. I was on a plane every time they called. I went to Haiti, Bangladesh, Guatemala, Los Angeles, anywhere and everywhere they needed me. Anything to not be at home.

"I don't know if it was good or bad, but it gave me a reason to get up every morning." She paused. "And then I went to Seattle."

The rain had changed to a slow drizzle, but the runoff dripped steadily down the gutters.

"What happened in Seattle, Vivienne?"

"A family was murdered. At first it looked like the father did it—like he'd shot his daughter, his wife, and then himself. They'd all been killed by single gunshot wounds to the head."

"Why were you called in if it was straightforward?"

"Because the father was a scientist I'd worked with in the past. His sister didn't think he could have done it, so she begged to have me come in. It was such a horrific crime in an area that doesn't experience a lot of that kind of violence. The Seattle police, some of whom I'd worked with in the past, let me in to make her happy."

"And what did you find?"

"What I wanted to find was that she was right." God, how she'd wanted that. "I didn't want to believe that a man could wipe out his whole family. That someone would *choose* to rid the planet of his child and life partner. After having lost my family, I would have given anything to have them back. And it seemed incomprehensible to me that anyone could feel differently."

"And?"

"I bird-dogged that case like you wouldn't believe. I'm surprised my friends at the SPD are still talking to me. But in the end, the sister was wrong. My friend, Dr. Howard, held a pillow over his sleeping twelve-year-old daughter's face and shot her. He then proceeded to shoot his wife as she slept in their bedroom, before lying down beside her and shooting himself.

"It was—" Vivi paused and took a deep breath of the rain-cleaned air. "It was too much for me and I walked away. I flew down to LA to see my cousin Kiera, then rented a car, and just started driving. I drove from California through Arizona, Texas, Georgia—all through the South as I made my way east. I was thinking of heading into Canada when I passed through New York City and saw the sign for the Taconic Parkway," she added.

"And then you ended up here." Ian's cheek came to rest against her head.

"And, for a little while, I was able to forget. Not my parents or my brother, but the pain, the emptiness of it all."

"And when it all came back this afternoon, not only did it all come back, but the guilt came too, didn't it?" Ian asked. "The guilt for having allowed yourself to forget for even a second."

Tears filled her eyes and poured down her face as she nodded. When a choked sob escaped her, he turned her around and held her close. Vivi clung to him, buried her face against his chest, and cried. For the first time in a long time, she just cried. For her parents, for her brother, for herself. And for everything good the world lost the day they died.

CHAPTER 12

IT WAS STILL DARK WHEN a ringing phone roused Vivi. Half awake and half asleep, she struggled to a sitting position and thought for a moment that it couldn't possibly be her cell. Her eyes were gritty from crying earlier, and next to her, Ian looked as confused as she felt. Then the phone rang again, and she remembered that Ian had brought her purse in from her car when they'd come back to bed. They'd lain together for a long time until she'd needed him to remind her of some of the good things in life. After that, they'd fallen asleep.

Slapping her hand on the bedside table, she located the nuisance and answered without looking at the number.

"It's three in the morning, Viv, luv. And you're not in bed. Not your bed anyway."

"Nick."

Beside her, Ian sat up and switched on a lamp. They both blinked in the sudden flood of light.

"I decided you could use my help," Nick said.

"You decided not to trust me." Vivi ran her fingers through her hair and rubbed her aching eyes. Nick was the last thing she needed right now.

"I always trusted you, Viv. I just didn't always believe in you. But I learn from my mistakes."

"What do you want, Nick?"

"Right now? A place to crash. Tomorrow, maybe we can talk."

"Fine, help yourself to my room. But if you call me before I call you tomorrow, you'll be dead in the water."

She ended the call and slid back into bed. Ian looked down at her. She closed her eyes, then cracked one open when he didn't move in to lie next to her. "He's fine, Ian. Nick's not going to do anything too dumb."

"How is he going to get into your room and how does he even know where you're staying?"

"Nick knows all sorts of things, and believe me, we don't have to worry about how he'll get into my room."

Ian frowned. "Okay. Do I need to worry about him? About the investigation?"

She opened both eyes and looked at Ian. Really looked at him. He *was* worried. "In what way?" She propped herself up on her elbows.

"Is he going to try to run roughshod over me? Believe me, I have no problem putting and keeping a man in his place, but this, well, it's all the legal stuff…" His voice trailed off.

Vivi lifted a hand and touched his cheek. "It does take some time to figure out how to use the system and, you're right, the legal ins and outs. But between your common sense and my experience, I don't think Nick will be able to get away with anything."

"But he'll try?"

She gave him a rueful smile. "Nick will always try. But once he has the measure of the man, so to speak, he'll back off and play nice."

Ian lifted a hand and traced a finger down the tip of her nose to her lips, then brushed it across them, soft and slow. Leaning down, he replaced it with his lips. "Promise?" he asked against her mouth.

She slipped a hand behind his neck and pulled him in for a proper kiss, then let him pull back as she spoke. "I'm not going to promise something I'm not certain I can deliver, but I can promise that you can count on me to see this thing through the best way we decide how."

He studied her eyes. His chest brushed against her with his every breath. Then he reached behind him and turned the lamp back off, casting them into darkness. She felt his lips brush her neck. She threaded her fingers into his hair and pulled him down to her.

"Sound like a plan, MacAllister?"

She felt his smile against her lips. "Sounds like a plan, DeMarco."

***

Even from twenty feet away, Ian sensed Vivienne's discomfort. Lingering in the hallway, he watched her reach for her dress, still on the kitchen table, and pull it over her head. Her shoulders were set and she hadn't looked at him for more than a fleeting second all morning. He had an idea of what was going on. A strong independent woman like Vivienne would feel awkward, if not embarrassed, by her breakdown the night before. It was ridiculous, but she didn't know that. Or didn't trust that he wouldn't make her feel bad about it, or use it against her.

"Will you make some coffee?" he asked from his position. She spun, startled to see him there, and after staring for a moment, gave a reluctant nod. He'd bet she was planning on leaving at the first chance. Now he'd made her stay. As he climbed into the shower, he devised a plan to make her okay with everything that had happened, everything that had been said the night before.

Dressed in his uniform, he entered the kitchen. Vivienne was standing with her back to him, cup in hand, looking out onto the backyard. She was back in the clothes she'd come in last night, shoes and all, and her hair was loose, falling well below her shoulders. His eyes skimmed her from behind.

"I was a little preoccupied last night, but how is your ankle? And the cuts?"

She looked over her shoulder, but didn't turn to face him. "The ankle is fine. It was fine after a few hours. The cuts are ugly, but don't hurt at all. Thanks for asking."

Her tone wasn't cold but didn't hold anything personal either.

"Thanks for staying," Ian said, approaching her. Stopping about a foot away, he saw her body tense. "I don't know if you noticed, but I didn't have any nightmares. Thanks for that."

"Except for having a hysterical woman clinging to you."

He had hoped to remind her that she wasn't the only one who had shared vulnerabilities last night. That she wasn't alone. But, judging by her grumbled answer, he hadn't. Truth be told, he wasn't very comfortable with his diagnosis of PTSD and was even less comfortable with the fact that he was still experiencing episodes. But if he could use it to make her feel better, he would. Too bad it hadn't worked.

He put his hands on her shoulders and forced her to turn around. When she was facing him, he slid his hands up to frame her face.

"Look at me, Vivienne," he ordered. Her eyes went left, then right. When it became clear he wasn't going to let it go, she let out a deep sigh and met his gaze.

"You fell apart last night. You broke down, you lost it, you sobbed, and you clung to me." He could feel her jaw clenching under his palms, but he continued, knowing she needed to hear what he had to say to her. Knowing he needed her to know how he felt. "You lost your family, Vivienne. Your family." His voice was quiet.

She didn't relax under his hands, but there was a shadow of curiosity creeping into her eyes and so he went on. "Everything you're feeling—every ounce of anger, of sadness, of emptiness, of guilt—you're entitled to feel, Vivienne."

Her eyes were watching his intently now. "There is nothing to be ashamed of, nothing to be embarrassed about. I'm not going to tell the world about what happened. And you should know that when I look at you now, after last night, I still see an amazing woman. You're a professor, a cop, an ME, an FBI consultant, a psychologist. You're not weak, Vivienne, you're human."

A single tear trickled out of her eye, slid down her cheek, and landed on his thumb. He brushed it away.

"You came from your family. They are a part of you. And knowing what I know of you, they must have been good people. People you have every right to mourn in whatever way you need to."

Vivienne's dark eyes stared back at him. And after several heartbeats, when he was sure she believed him, he leaned in and gave her a light kiss.

"Now that that is out of way, shall we get back to work?" Ian coupled his comment with an easy smile. It did the job and she gave him a tentative one in response. He moved to pour himself a cup of coffee to go, but she grabbed the front of his shirt and pulled him back.

"Thank you, Ian." Her voice was soft, but strong. "Not just for doing what you just did, but for being there for me last night, for listening to me, for holding me. And, most of all, for letting me be all those things I am. For making it okay to be all those things."

Something shifted in the range of his chest as he looked down at her. He dipped his head and gave her another kiss. And then another. And then her hands came around his neck and he let her pull him into a kiss that was anything but soft and sweet.

"God, when you kiss me like that I want to crawl inside you," she said when they pulled apart. Everything, except one strategic part of him, went still. She must have noticed.

"Uh, was that kind of creepy?" She looked cute when she was embarrassed.

"No," he responded, wrapping his arms around her. "But you can't say something like that and then not expect me to react." And react he did. Not happy with sitting her on the kitchen table, he stripped her down, again, and took her back to bed, again, so he could feel every inch of her against and around him, again.

***

Having left Ian to talk to Rob about something or another, Vivi walked up the steps of The Tavern to her room. She slid the key in the lock and the door swung open, revealing Nick. Lost in thought about the night before, she'd almost forgotten about him. Wearing jeans and a white t-shirt, he lounged in one of the chairs. His dark hair was damp and his cowboy boot–clad feet were propped up on the desk.

"Hello, luv." The smile he gave her was more knowing than friendly.

"Nick."

They eyed each other for a long moment—Vivi feeling like she wasn't quite sure what to do with him, and Nick not bothering to hide the fact that he was taking her in. High heels, short dress, messy hair, and, she was pretty sure, a mark or two on her neck.

"Well, darling, you look well and truly—"

"Finish that sentence and you *will* regret it." Ian said, stepping up behind her. Vivi said nothing, watching as Nick's eyes went from her to Ian and lingered there for a while.

Then Nick gave a small nod. "I was going to say 'rested,' darling. You look well and truly rested."

Vivi rolled her eyes but stepped into the room. "Nick, Deputy Chief Ian MacAllister. Ian, Agent Nick Larrimore, Army Investigation Division." Ian closed the door behind them; neither man bothered to shake hands.

"Rob doesn't have any more rooms," Ian commented.

"I can always stay with you, luv," Nick interjected.

"Shut up, Nick. You don't have any jurisdiction here so remember where your bread is buttered." She didn't bother looking at him as she said this—he'd spoken only to get a rise out of Ian. Instead, she moved toward her luggage and started gathering her clothes.

"So, it looks like you're certain Jessica Akers was a victim of a serial killer," Nick said from behind her. She assumed he was referring to the files she'd left lying on her desk. He probably knew them better than she did at this point.

"We have another body. Vivienne did the autopsy yesterday," Ian answered as she dug through her bag looking for a clean pair of socks.

"Same method of death?" Nick asked.

"Down to the type of shackles," Ian answered.

"Sorry about that," Nick commiserated with Ian. "Are you going to call in the FBI?"

Vivi turned around at that and almost bumped into Ian who was standing right behind her. Startled at his closeness, she looked at him, then at Nick, who gave her a crooked grin, then back at Ian, who shrugged.

"I was admiring your backside, luv. Deputy Chief MacAllister thought maybe I shouldn't."

Vivi's eyes went back to Ian, who looked a little embarrassed, then back again to Nick, who was grinning openly now. She sighed.

"Be nice. I'm going to take a shower and then we can head to the station to start the geographic analysis." She gave each man a pointed look before disappearing into the bathroom. She wasn't sure about the wisdom of leaving both men in the same room unattended, but what could she do? Ian might not like Nick ogling her, but Nick was only doing it to egg him on. And, once he got over his juvenile need to needle Ian, it might be okay to have Nick on their side. He was good. Really good. And maybe removing herself from the room—removing the pawn, so to speak—would actually be a good thing. She hoped.

When Vivi re-entered the room in jeans and a lightweight sweater with her hair pulled back into a ponytail, both men were almost where she'd left them. Ian stood, leaning against the wall beside her luggage, arms and ankles crossed. Nick was in the same chair, a file open on his lap.

"Ready?" she asked, pulling on her boots. Ian shoved away from the wall, Nick swung his feet down and unfolded his lean six-foot-two frame from the chair. "Can you gather those up?" she added to Nick, with a nod to the files. "You have yours in the car, right?" she said to Ian. He nodded.

"I haven't eaten, Viv darling. The man who runs this place gets up at some god-awful hour and I didn't have a chance to sneak out before then," Nick complained.

Vivi looked at Ian in silent question. He smiled and nodded.

"Come on," she said, ushering everyone out of her room. "I know just the place. I'll even let you order."

***

"I hate that man. Hasn't he ever heard of a sense of humor?" Nick demanded as they exited Frank's Café.

"Oh, I don't know," Vivi grinned at Ian. "He has his own charm."

"Of a snake, darling. Although, I will grant he makes good coffee," Nick added, taking a sip.

Vivi glanced at the two men walking with her as they crossed the street. They were so different in almost every way, from looks to approach, that the case was bound to stay interesting. She was pondering how Carly, Marcus, and Wyatt would take to Nick, and he to them, when she heard a familiar voice.

"Dr. DeMarco!"

Vivi stopped so fast that Nick, still grumbling about Frank's treatment of him, bumped into her shoulder.

"Daniel?" A sinking sensation hit her stomach as she looked at the young man in front of her. And it was heightened by Ian's muttered curse behind her. It didn't take a genius to know why Kathryn's son was standing before them.

"Hi?" Daniel said. Vivi had known him for so long that, especially when he looked at her the way he was looking at her now, chagrined but hopeful, she sometimes forgot he wasn't a boy anymore.

"Vivienne," Ian warned, as if he could change what was coming.

"What are you doing here?" she asked the young man.

"Well, I," Daniel shuffled his feet a little bit, and in the sunlight, Vivi noticed that he had golden streaks in his blond hair, just like his mother. "I have a break in my studies and my mom mentioned you were up here working on a case. I thought maybe I could, you know, help out."

Vivi arched a brow.

"I mean, you know, if you need it or anything."

She sighed and looked at Ian. After a moment, he threw up his hands. "Sure, why not." His tone was not exactly pleased, but turning down the governor's son would not be a good political move.

"Daniel Westerbrook, Deputy Chief MacAllister and Agent Nick Larrimore. Nick, Ian, this is Daniel, one of my students." She didn't point out his parentage; Daniel wasn't the kind of kid to ride his mother's coattails and his mother wasn't the kind of woman who let him. But, on that point, Vivi thought, the less said the better.

"Come on," she said as she began walking again. "We're headed to the police station to meet with the other officers and review some files. I'll go over the physical evidence with you this afternoon and maybe we can go back to the lab and I can introduce you to Dr. Sameer Buckley, one of my former students, as well."

A few minutes later they all stepped into the police station. Carly and Marcus were on their feet before the door closed behind them, eager to get going on the case.

"Wyatt?" Vivi asked.

"On patrol with one of our part-time officers," Ian answered.

"How many do you have?" Daniel ventured.

"Five full-time officers and four part-timers," Ian answered. "Though Vic Ballard, our Chief, is out of town for a couple of weeks," he added.

Vivi let Ian make the introductions. Then he directed Carly and Marcus to clear out one of the upstairs rooms to work in. He introduced Vivi, Nick, and Daniel to Sharon, the police receptionist and dispatcher, before heading out to his Jeep to grab his files. When he returned, he handed the files to Sharon, asking her to make copies for everyone.

They left her to make the copies and trucked upstairs. Vivi figured Ian's decision to move them off the main floor was a strategic one. There was space on the first floor, but what was there was easily accessible to anyone who might wander in off the streets.

Before she entered the room upstairs, Ian held her back. They were alone in the hallway and she saw the doubt in his eyes.

"Any words of advice?" he asked.

She wanted to touch him, to reassure him and tell him he'd be fine. But the situation wasn't conducive to that. There was a room full of people waiting for him to tell them what to do. And at least one of them was waiting for him to mess up.

But despite not being able to reassure him the way she'd like to, Vivi knew he'd be okay. Ian would be good at this, of that she was certain.

"It's like planning a mission, Ian. That's all there is to it." Not that she'd planned any military missions herself, but using common sense, she'd wager that they had a lot in common with murder investigations. Both required a thorough examination of the facts and the people involved; both required a plan to get from point A (where they were) to point B (finding and catching the killer), and both required a plan B and probably a plan C.

He seemed to think about what she said as if he'd never thought of it that way before, then gave a bob of his head and turned to enter the room.

"Carly, thanks for picking up the map," he started, with a nod to the large map of the United States that now hung on a board at the front of the room. Sharon walked in at that moment and handed him the stacks of collated pages.

"Perfect timing, Sharon. Thanks." She nodded and left room to return to her post. Handing each person a complete set, Ian moved back to the front of the room.

"We all know the basics," he said, taking two small red pins and pushing them into the area representing Windsor. "We have two bodies here that appear to be victims of the same killer." He paused to look at the board, then turned back to the room.

"In the first stack of files are the nine women that Vivienne identified as being similar to our victims. Three are confirmed dead and six are missing. In the second stack," Ian said, holding his up, "are the women I found. I'm not as experienced as Vivienne in this, so my parameters were probably wider than hers. I found four confirmed dead and eleven missing.

"Now, what I would like to do is figure out how many, if any, Vivienne and I found in common. Then we'll get all those women up on the map. We need to mark where they went missing from and, if there was a body, the dump site of that body. Once we have them all up on the board, we'll split up and take a look at what we have from a geographic perspective and then dig deeper into the cases themselves."

Ian looked around the room and everyone nodded. His eyes landed on Vivi's, and she allowed herself a small smile for him.

"Once we have more information on the individual cases, we'll reconvene and talk about each—see if there are any we all agree can be weeded out. When we have a final list, we can begin contacting divisions responsible and see if we can get some more extensive case files."

"And what about the FBI? Aren't they usually called in on serial cases?" Marcus asked with a glance at Vivi. Ian also looked to her. This wasn't his strength; he had no experience in this area and wasn't hesitant to ask her to step in. She turned to Ian's colleagues.

"Yes, the FBI can handle serial killer cases and generally does if the killer has crossed state lines. If the killer is local, they will usually wait to be invited in. But we aren't there yet. We may get there, maybe even by the end of the day. But right now, we have two bodies and what we *think* might be a multiple killer, but we don't know and we don't have any more evidence to point toward it. That's what we need to do today. We need to look through these files and see if we're going in the right direction or if maybe this whole idea is way off base."

"You don't think it is," Carly pointed out.

"I don't," Vivi conceded. "But I've been wrong before. Quite recently, actually. And while I don't discount intuition, I don't want to base an investigation on it." She glanced at Ian, who was watching her, then gestured for him to take over again.

"Okay folks, let's get to work," Ian directed.

Twenty minutes later, they had eighteen pins in place—the two women found in Windsor, plus sixteen more. Out of the sixteen, eight were women Ian and Vivi had both identified as potential victims—three were confirmed dead and five were missing. The remaining eight were ones that either Vivi or Ian identified, but not both.

Everyone sat back and studied the map. The pins were spread across the US. Two in Windsor, two each in Seattle, Chicago, New York, and Savannah, one each in Miami and LA, and three each in New Orleans and Boston.

"Well, they're all urban vacation spots," Marcus offered.

"Except Windsor," Carly pointed out.

"You're kind of a vacation spot but not urban, and it's a good point, Carly, that Windsor is definitely the odd duck out on this map," Vivi said.

"So that tells us something, right?" Ian said.

"It tells us that this area probably means something to him. The other cities were probably cities of convenience," Nick interjected.

"So he probably travels?" Carly asked.

"Yes, but most people do these days," Vivi answered.

"But not usually with shackles or whatever he's using to restrain his victims," Ian pointed out.

"Fair enough." Vivi turned toward Ian as he pulled his eyes from the board. "Ian?" she said, a signal that he needed to tell his team what he wanted them to do next. He gave a sharp nod, then spoke.

"Okay, Carly and Marcus, dig into what we have in the files and see what you can find. See if you think we can, or should, eliminate any of these women. Wyatt, work with Nick on Jessica Akers and Rebecca Cole. Look into their phone records, last movements—see if you can find any connection between the two women or anything they shared that might put them both in the sights of this killer. Vivienne?"

"I think Daniel and I will head up to Albany to meet with Sam and go over the evidence again," Vivi said.

Ian nodded and followed them down the stairs. "Can I talk to you a minute?" He gestured with his head toward his office. Vivi glanced at Daniel who was watching them much like his mother might.

"Daniel, why don't you head out to the car? You can drive. I'll be out in a minute," she said.

He gave her a look of glee that told her he knew as much about his mother's matchmaking hopes as she did. She gave him a pointed look back and he had the good sense to turn around and leave. Following Ian into his office, Vivi perched on the edge of his desk. He picked up a pen and rolled it between his fingers. Then, setting it down, he tapped his fingers on his desk before looking up.

"Rob is booked tonight and for the next several nights. I assume Nick's going to need a place to stay. Why don't you stay with me?"

His expression was so intensely neutral that it told her more than any other look might. He had made light of his nightmares earlier, but she was under no delusions that he wasn't bothered by them. And, by asking her to stay with him, he was inviting her into his nighttime hell. It might not have happened last night, but the more often she stayed with him, the more likely it was that she would see him fall apart. Not an easy thing for a man like Ian to stomach.

And yet, he'd asked. It confirmed what she already knew, that their night together was more than a one-night stand. They'd seen too much of each other in those hours to think it was just about the sex. What it was, or where it was going, she didn't know, and she doubted Ian did either. But he seemed willing to see.

When she nodded, he let out a small breath, a tiny but unmistakable sign of relief.

"When can we expect you back?" he asked.

Vivi looked at the clock, it was close to lunchtime, though it hadn't been that long since they'd had their late breakfast at Frank's Café. "We'll be back around five. After we reconvene here, I'll head to The Tavern and pack up. Work for you?"

They agreed and she left to meet Daniel. He was waiting for her—hands in his pockets, grin on his face. In many ways, he was just like his mother.

"So, you and the Sheriff?"

"He's the Deputy Chief of Police, Daniel."

"So, you and the Deputy?" He grinned wider and followed Vivi as she started walking down the street toward her car. She got about ten feet before remembering she'd told Daniel he should drive.

"My mother will be very happy to hear about this," he said.

"Have you eaten lunch?"

"What?"

She repeated herself. When Daniel shook his head, she turned around and started walking back toward Main Street.

"You're changing the subject, Dr. DeMarco."

"I'm getting some ice cream before we go." It wasn't lunch, but she needed something to distract Daniel.

"I'm lactose intolerant," he said.

She gave him a look as she pushed the door open to What's The Scoop. "They have sorbet."

"You're avoiding me," he pointed out the obvious.

"I don't have to avoid you, Daniel. I'm your professor—and the only reason you're on this case, I might add. You're brilliant, cute, and I love you to death, but if you bug me about Ian, I'll sic Nick on you."

"Oh, hello again."

Vivi turned to see the young woman from the day before, emerging from the back with a smile. Leaving Daniel to ponder her good-natured attempt to get him to back off, she moved to the counter.

"Meghan, right?" Vivi asked.

The girl smiled and nodded. "Thanks for coming in again. I heard about that poor woman up on the Mayfield's land. Are you helping Mr. MacAllister with the case? Not that he couldn't handle it on his own," she hastened to add, "but it would be nice if he had some help since he's always helping everyone else."

"Yes, I'm working with him, so you may be seeing a bit more of me. I'm Vivi DeMarco, please call me Vivi," she said as she shook Meghan's hand. "And while I'm sorry to be here for the reasons I am, I'm glad to have the chance to come back. Your wild blackberry ice cream is amazing," Vivi added. Meghan smiled at the compliment.

"I'm working with Deputy Chief MacAllister too," Daniel interjected, stepping forward and holding out his hand. Meghan eyed him with curious suspicion but held her hand out and shook his. "I'm Daniel Westerbrook. One of Dr. DeMarco's students."

Meghan turned a questioning look to Vivi. "I have a few PhD students I take on. Daniel is one of them. He lives in the area, so he offered to come down and help," Vivi explained.

The young woman's blue eyes swiveled back to Daniel. "Meghan Conners."

He might not be as subtle as Ian or some other older man, but Vivi recognized the look in Daniel's eyes. And smiled.

"What can I get for you both?" Meghan asked.

Vivi ordered her wild blackberry while Daniel ordered chocolate sorbet, chatting with Meghan all the while. By the time they got back to Daniel's car, he'd dropped the subject of her and Ian altogether, just as she'd hoped, and they spent the time it took them to get to Albany in the more interesting pursuits of university gossip and a discussion of the possibilities of the case.

But the drive back from the labs was much less engaging. After spending three hours with Sam, they were mostly silent on the nearly forty-five minute drive. What Sam found, or didn't find, was weighing on their minds, and approaching Windsor and the police station made the whole situation more real again. They knew what they had and what they didn't. And while knowing— even knowing what they didn't have—was usually better than not knowing, it also had a way of taking away some of the hope. Hope that maybe they'd find something that could be used to stop a man who kidnapped, tortured, and killed young women.

CHAPTER 13

IAN LOOKED UP FROM HIS desk, from the files he'd been poring over, when he heard the door to the station open. He could see Sharon gathering up her things and getting ready to switch the dispatch over to county before heading home for the night. As he watched her, Vivienne and Daniel came into view. He'd sent Marcus out on patrol, but Wyatt, Carly, and Nick were still upstairs. Rising from his seat, Ian glanced at the calendar on his desk. For everyone's sake, especially the women who might become the targets of their killer, Ian hoped they could wrap things up quickly.

He met Vivienne and Daniel in the lobby and, after locking the doors behind Sharon, the three of them trudged up the stairs. Carly and Wyatt looked up expectantly, while Nick only spared a glance before returning his attention to the phone call he was conducting. The man hadn't been half bad after Vivienne had left. He'd been head down, nose to the grindstone most of the day—his superficial, irritating charm only making an appearance when trying to cajole information from people. Like the phone records he was currently trying to sweet-talk out of someone at the phone company. They had obtained the warrant, so his request wasn't out of the blue. And both Jessica Akers and Rebecca Cole had used the same provider, so that made things a bit easier. But given that Jessica's last call was over three years ago, the phone company was giving them a two-day ETA on her records. Nick was trying to knock it down to twelve hours.

Vivienne and Daniel went to the board to look at the new information the team had posted throughout the day. When Nick ended his call, tossing his cell down with a muttered curse, everyone came to attention.

"Looks like you made some progress," Daniel commented.

"Did you solve the case, Viv, luv? You always do, you know." Nick's chide didn't come out like one, but as Ian started to call him on it, Vivienne raised a hand and shook her head.

"Don't bother. He gets cranky when a case doesn't move as fast as he wants."

"Does it ever move as fast as you want, Larrimore?" Ian posited the rhetorical question.

Nick shook his head, then grinned. "I wasn't easy to live with, was I, luv?"

Vivienne rolled her eyes. "I wouldn't know, Nick. We never lived together. Now, focus on the case, as I'm sure you did all day while I wasn't here, and stop trying to get a rise out of Ian—"

When Vivienne snapped her mouth shut and pursed her lips, Ian knew she'd realized her mistake. She'd just acknowledged the personal nature of her relationship with the Deputy Chief of Police to the entire room. She cast him an apologetic look then motioned him to get things started. Which he was more than happy to do.

"All right. Vivienne and Daniel, why don't you give us an update on what you found up at the lab. Then we can go over what we found today."

Vivienne moved to the front of the room and perched on a table. She looked exhausted. After everything that had happened last night, the physical and the emotional ups and downs, it didn't come as a surprise to Ian.

"We don't actually have all that much to add. The slivers that were found on both Jessica and Rebecca come from plywood, the same type of plywood. But it's a common variety, so that in and of itself doesn't tell us much.

"What is interesting about them," Vivienne continued, "is that they both had trace absorptions of exhaust. The sliver found in Jessica had a higher concentration, but both had the same chemical makeup."

"Which means?" Carly prompted.

"The wood was kept in a car or truck for a while before the women came into contact with it," Daniel provided.

"Could it have happened during shipping?" Carly pressed.

"Depending on the shipping method, it's possible. But in this case, the chemical makeup leads us to believe it was a gas-fueled car or truck," Daniel answered

"As opposed to a diesel truck," Wyatt said.

Vivienne nodded and continued. "Maybe he's transporting the makeshift tables in his car until the right time."

"Or, maybe his car is where he holds them," Carly suggested.

Ian looked at Vivienne, who was looking at Carly, her head cocked to the side. "You have a good point, Carly. It's possible he could have set up his table and shackles in a car, or more likely, a van or truck," she said.

"So it couldn't be diesel but would still need to be big enough for him to move around in," Carly added.

Vivienne nodded and Ian considered this option before weighing in.

"If that's the case, I'd wager it's a van rather than a truck," Ian said. "They're easier to move around in, and it's easier to conceal things in the back."

"Okay, so maybe we can add that to the board?" Vivienne said.

Wyatt got up and wrote "Van?" on the board behind her.

"What else did you find, Vivienne?" Ian asked.

"Dirt," she responded.

"Soil," Daniel corrected her.

"Soil, then," Vivienne said, rolling her eyes. "And only on Rebecca. Jessica's remains were too contaminated, too old. Everything we found on her, with the exception of the sliver, was consistent with her dumping spot. Rebecca, on the other hand, had soil on the tips of her right fingers and the bottoms of her heels that was inconsistent with the soil in the well."

"Which means?" Ian asked.

"We're not sure. But…" Vivienne's voice drifted off.

Ian watched as a distant expression stole across her features. She was making connections and coming up with ideas.

"It might give more credence to our theory of a van," she said.

"In what way?" Ian asked.

"Well, at first I was thinking she might have gotten soil on her fingertips and heels from being dragged, but now I don't think so. The mechanics don't work," Vivienne answered.

"How's that?" Wyatt prompted.

"Here, let me show you. Ian?" She waved him over. "Put your hands under my arms, as if you were going to drag me and take a few steps back. I'm going to let my body go, so be prepared for the weight."

"Yeah, I think I got it," Ian responded to her warning before thinking about it. His mind had instantly gone to how easily he'd held her weight the night before. Judging by the look on her face, her single arched eyebrow, and the smile that played at the edges of her mouth, it must have come through in his tone.

"I'm going to step back now," he said, clearing his throat. And he did. And she made her point. By the time Vivienne was close enough to the ground where both her heels and her fingertips dragged, he was hunched over like Igor. No one would drag a dead body around like that, at least not far. Not even a psycho serial killer. It was too awkward and too uncomfortable.

"But this," Vivienne said, standing upright and then moving toward a table. "Makes more sense." She lay down on the table and positioned herself in a reasonable facsimile of how they imagined Rebecca and Jessica were shackled. Her heels rested against the tabletop and her fingertips brushed against it over her head.

"But if he keeps them shackled on the same surface as the wood sliver we found, why aren't there slivers in her fingertips or heels?" Wyatt asked.

"Because she was probably kept on the ground, or close to it," Carly answered standing up. Ian turned toward his officer as she approached the table. Vivienne propped herself up to see better. Nick was sitting forward, a crease between his brows.

"Why do you say that?" Ian asked.

"A couple of reasons." Carly paused and studied Vivienne before motioning her to scoot down the table. Vivienne moved down until her feet and ankles were hanging off the edge. "It's possible that the shackles aren't part of the table, but attached to the ground, in which case, her wrists and ankles might hang off the edge of the wood."

Ian frowned in thought, impressed with her report. "Good point, Carly."

"It is a very good point," Vivienne echoed. "And, I think, if we're on the right track, probably a correct point. It would explain why there aren't slivers in her fingertips, and it also makes it easier for the killer to clean up."

"Remove the board, burn it, replace it with a clean one, and *voila*, you have no biological evidence and a clean place for your next victim." This came from Nick, who sat back and crossed his arms as he spoke. "And then there's the rape aspect of it," he added.

Ian wasn't going to like where this was going. Especially when Nick got up and moved to Carly's side.

"And that was going to be my second point," Carly said, her voice contemplative.

"Meaning?" Wyatt asked.

"The mechanics of it." Ian's voice was flat as it dawned on him what Nick was alluding to.

"Yeah," Nick said. "If her wrists and ankles are hanging off the board, the board can't be that big. And it's a lot easier to rape a woman when you aren't worried about falling off the ledge. Not to mention you'd have better leverage."

"Which means, if she was restrained this way," Vivienne spoke, lying back down for visual impact—one that Ian could do without, "then chances are she was close to the ground, making it easier for him to do his thing and better for her to collect trace soil evidence on her fingers and heels."

"Okay, time to get up, Vivienne," Ian said, breaking everyone's intense focus on her. Seeing her lying there, in the place of Rebecca Cole or Jessica Akers, was giving him the cold sweats.

"So, it looks like what we might have is a van that has the space for a plywood board and the right setup to hook up shackles," Ian summarized.

"And space for him to do what he's done to these women," Vivienne added.

Ian frowned at the reminder, then spoke. "I want everyone to keep an open mind because what we're talking about here makes sense, but there could be a hundred other options we aren't considering. But if we are on the right track, we're probably looking for a large, industrial-style van. The kind with no windows, like electricians use, not a minivan or commercial passenger van," he added.

He gave everyone, including Nick, a pointed look. What they were saying did make sense. But they were dealing with someone who killed women for some unknown reason, and he didn't want to rely on "good sense."

"So anything else, Vivienne?" Ian asked. She shook her head and slid to the edge of the table. "Okay, Carly and Nick, do you want to go over what you all found today?" The two looked at each other, and Carly gave Nick a nod to go first.

"We are tracing the last moves of both women, which is obviously easier with Rebecca—who has only been missing a little more than a month—than with Jessica. Still, we've tracked down some friends of both. Colleagues in the NYPD will be interviewing them and collecting evidence as time permits. They'll send everything to Sam as soon as possible.

"In the meantime, we're working on getting the phone and bank records. Again, easier for Rebecca, harder for Jessica," Nick provided.

"What about Jessica's mother? Will she be coming up?" Vivienne asked Nick.

Ian saw a look of frustration pass over Nick's face before he answered. "No, she won't be coming up."

Vivienne raised her eyebrows at this.

"Jessica's mother blames her for her father's downfall. She didn't exactly say her daughter got what she deserved, but she was very nonchalant about the remains. She gave me the name of a funeral home to release them to when we're done. Said they'd take care of everything." Nick didn't bother to hide his disgust.

"When you talked about notifying her mom, it sounded like it was going to be devastating. Her response isn't in line with that at all," Vivienne pressed.

Nick frowned. "Yeah, well, when Jessica went missing, it was before General Akers's fall from grace. Before *Mrs.* General Akers was ostracized from society and her entire life fell apart. She's had a lot of time to reflect and blame someone. I guess she's blaming Jessica."

"Nice," someone muttered.

"Any more we can do or is everything moving along?" Ian asked.

Nick shrugged. "If you can produce some phone records, that would be great. Other than that, we've got all the requests in, and we're just sitting on our hands for a day or two."

"Any estimates on when we might start to see things?" Ian pressed.

"Your guess is as good as mine," Nick answered. "A couple of days for the physical evidence to be collected and sent to the lab by NYPD, a day or two for the records, maybe a few more for the interviews. I may go down there and do a few myself, depending on how things go."

"Okay, Carly?" Ian asked, swinging his gaze to the officer. "What about the other women?"

"I talked to most of the case officers for the women we have on the list. Two I had to leave a message for. One is, well—" Carly's eyes went to Vivienne for a moment, and she looked uncomfortable. "Well, he didn't want to talk to me about the case, but he said you needed to call him, Dr. DeMarco."

Ian's eyes tracked to Vivienne. She frowned. "Call me Vivi, and why does he want to talk to me? Who is it?"

"Lucas Rancuso. Boston PD," Carly supplied.

Vivienne let out a deep breath then a quiet curse. "The three women in Boston?"

Carly nodded.

"I'll call him tonight or tomorrow," she said.

Carly looked at Ian. He raised an eyebrow in question.

"Ah, Viv," Nick sat back, glee in his voice.

"Shut up, Nick." She glared at him before turning back to Carly. "Lucas and I are longtime friends. Those three cases we're looking at in Boston didn't ring a bell when we first started talking about them, but now that I know they were Lucas's cases, I remember them well."

"And why does he need to talk to you, Vivienne?" Ian asked.

She sighed. "Because when Lucas tied the three missing persons cases together, he didn't like how the women looked like me. One of them was even a professor at the same university where I teach. He's a good friend of the family and has been for years. He won't like that I'm looking into them, and he'll want to know what I'm doing and that I'm okay. That's all. Like I said, I'll give him a call later and get us the information we need."

She gave Ian a reassuring look, communicating to him that'd she go into it more later. He nodded and waved Carly on.

"So, have you found anything interesting, Carly?" Ian asked.

Carly contemplated a piece of paper she was holding before answering. "I think there are a few women we can eliminate from our list." Indecision was clear in her voice—not indecision about her opinion, but about bringing it up. There was a lot to lose, for the women, if she was wrong.

"Walk us through it, Carly," Vivienne coaxed.

Carly nodded and stepped up to the board. "This woman, Amy Clayton, was in an abusive relationship and there was some evidence that her boyfriend was involved in her disappearance. He's a rich real estate broker and lawyered up right away, but the case officer said they had some evidence that he'd taken her by force in his car. They just didn't have enough to arrest him.

"And this woman," Carly said, pointing to one of the pictures, "Jolene Henderson, has three kids. None of the other women have kids."

"What did the case officer have to say?" Ian asked.

"That she was a hard-working woman who went missing during Katrina."

"Okay. Who else?" Vivienne asked.

"Francis Buckley was a prostitute. It doesn't fit since all the other women were attractive, successful women. Francis was attractive, at some point, but not successful and definitely from a different socio-economic strata than the other women."

"That's good. Any more?" Vivienne prompted again.

"The last one I think we can eliminate is Sarah Kirk. She looks the part in many ways, but she was thirty-three when she went missing ten years ago."

"Most of the women on the board are about that age. Give or take five or so years," Wyatt pointed out.

Carly shook her head. "No, most of the women would have been thirty-three or thirty-four *this* year. All of the women were born within a year of each other."

Vivienne stood and went to the board, scanning each of the profiles. Nick got up and followed. By watching the two, Ian knew Carly had stumbled onto something.

"Well, shit," Nick said when he reached the end.

"You can say that again," Vivienne uttered.

"Guys?" Ian prompted.

"Carly is right, and I can't believe we missed it," Vivienne shook her head, still studying the board.

"What does it mean?" Ian pressed.

"It could mean our killer is what Vivienne likes to call a relational killer," Nick supplied. Everyone turned to her for an explanation, including Nick.

"A relational killer is a term I use," Vivienne said. "It's not official. But what it means is that the victims have a relational resemblance to the killer. An example might be something like a killer whose victims are all single fathers whose children are the same age as the killer. Which means that, as the killer ages, so do the fathers, or victims. The profile of the victim changes because it's related to something external."

"And in this case?" Ian asked.

"I would wager that it's about the age of the killer, so, as he ages, the victims age. Which would explain why the latest victim is thirty-four, but this victim," Vivienne said, pointing to another photo of a woman who was reported missing five years ago, "is only twenty-nine. It's not a variation in his victim profile, it's a central part of it."

The news hit Ian with the subtlety of a sledgehammer.

"So you're saying to me that the age parameters we put in when conducting our database searches are completely irrelevant?" Ian asked, overwhelmed by the possibilities.

"No, age is very relevant," she answered, "Just not in the way we were originally thinking about it. We were using age to define the boundaries, assuming his victims, like the ones we think we've found, are between the ages of approximately twenty-eight to thirty-five. But now we can use age to show us the path he's taken. The good news is this can give us a lot more information about him, specific information. The bad news is, because we don't know his age or the age he started killing, we need to go back far enough to the extent that it would have been impossible for him to commit the murders."

"How far back?" Ian demanded.

"To be on the safe side, thirty-four years. Something about that date triggered something in the killer. He might have started then," Vivienne answered.

"Thirty-four years," Ian repeated, stunned at the potential enormity of it.

"But we only need to look for women born in these two years," Vivienne said, writing them on the board. "It will eliminate a lot of women. And I'd recommend starting the year this woman was killed," she said, pointing again to their twenty-nine year old. "And go back year by year, looking for women of the right age. I doubt he's been killing for thirty-four years, and my guess is we'll find fewer and fewer victims as the women get younger and younger."

"Why?" Wyatt asked.

"Because of the sexual nature of the crimes," Vivienne answered. "I don't think this is a parent/child thing, not with the kind of rape we saw with Rebecca. I think he has some sort of identification with the victims as *women*. And he's probably an adult around the same age, give or take ten years."

Ian took in the information and forced himself to be open, to listen to Vivienne, to her experience. But it was overwhelming. How in the world was he, with his small-town force, supposed to solve this kind of case? Then again, there was always the FBI. He could call them in, and with Vivienne as his backup, he knew they would respond.

By unspoken agreement, everyone in the room moved to implement this new plan, looking through over three decades of missing persons reports for women born during those two years. But Vivienne came toward Ian and met his gaze.

As if she'd read his mind, she spoke. "We can call in the FBI, Ian, and they'll send people. Good people. But they'll probably hire me anyway. I'm not saying don't do it, because I think at some point, we're going to need to. But I am saying don't discount yourself and your team. You have me, and Nick, too. Use us to get us as far as we can go and then we can call for help. It's not as though we don't have the resources. We do."

"What if someone else dies while we're spinning our wheels?" His biggest fear. What if pride kept him from calling in the big guns and another woman died? There was enough death on his hands; he didn't want any more.

"We're not spinning our wheels, Ian. If I thought my colleagues in Quantico could do this better or faster than we can, I wouldn't hesitate to call them in. But I'm not convinced they can. I know what their case load is, Ian."

He ran a hand over his face and through his hair then crossed his arms over his chest. "I can't take that chance, Vivienne."

He could feel her studying him, debating what to do next. He knew she wanted him to believe he could lead his team through this. But he just wasn't there; in his mind, the risk was too high.

"How about this? Tomorrow morning we'll call my colleague in the FBI behavioral science group. We can run through everything with him and see what he has to say. He's a good guy and will give you his honest opinion."

Ian looked down at her, searching her face. He wanted to feel good about the fact that she believed in him. But this was big; these were the lives of unknown numbers of women. If someone could do the job better than he could, they should.

"Why are you pushing?" he asked.

Vivienne pursed her lips and looked away for a moment. Her gaze landed on the window but he got the sense that she wasn't seeing what was out there. Finally, she looked back.

"Just trust me. All I'm asking is for you not to call the FBI in tonight. To wait to talk to John tomorrow. And after you talk to John, then you can decide whether you want to bring them in."

"Won't it be too late at that point? I mean, if I talk to him, we'll be discussing not just a serial killer, but one we are pretty sure has crossed state lines. Won't he *have* to come in at that point?"

"Just talk to him tomorrow."

Again, Ian searched her eyes for some answer. But all he saw there was a question: would he trust her for this little bit of time? He glanced at the clock and noticed how late it was. Even if he called them tonight, the likelihood of them doing anything before tomorrow wasn't high. He looked back at Vivienne, whose gaze hadn't left his face. He sighed. Tonight, tomorrow, it wouldn't make a difference. He nodded his agreement.

"Thank you," she said, her voice soft. He wasn't sure what she was saying thanks for, but he nodded again.

"Are you hungry?" he asked.

"And a little tired, plus I could use a shower."

He smiled at the image. "Why don't you head back to my house? I'll finish things up here and then meet you there. I'm scheduled for patrol tonight, though, so I'll be out from eleven to seven."

She nodded then turned to say her goodbyes to the team. Daniel and Nick opted to leave with her. Within five minutes, the three were gone. Ian stood at the window and, for a long time after they'd disappeared from sight, he watched the streets and the growing shadows.

***

Vivi pulled up alongside Ian's house and saw a dog bound out of the woods. She paused before opening her door, watching as the pup danced and spun toward the car wearing a goofy dog grin. He had a thick, gray coat and when he approached her window she noticed his yellow wolf-like eyes. If it hadn't been for his huge ears that stuck straight out at right angles, the lock of wayward fur on his head, and the grin, she might have been worried.

But when he finally settled, the dog sat beside her car door with his tail slapping against the ground. He stood as she opened her door and climbed out of the car, his enormous tail wagging his body. Vivi gave him a friendly scratch, wondering whose pet he was, then headed for her trunk to grab her bag.

She had just slipped the bag's strap over her shoulder when she heard Ian's Jeep approaching. Surprised he was home so soon, she waited. Obviously curious himself, the dog plopped himself at her feet, or rather, on her feet and waited with her, his tail making an occasional sweep of the ground.

As soon as Ian climbed out of his car, the pup jumped up and barreled toward him.

"Hey, Rooster," Ian said, bending down to give the dog a good rub. "How's my boy?"

"Is he yours?"

Ian looked up. "Yeah. My folks watch him when I have long

days, but he's mine. Rooster, meet Vivienne. Vivienne, this is Rooster." He stood and walked toward her.

"Rooster?"

"He hardly ever barks now, but when I first got him, when he was a puppy, he used to howl every morning when the sun came up."

Vivi smiled. Given the thick fur that stuck up on his head, the name was fitting in more ways than one. "How old?"

"He's not quite eight months old."

"He's going to be a big boy," she said.

Ian inclined his head. "So, my mom is here," he added.

Vivi blinked. Her bag dropped back into the trunk. "Your mom is here?" she repeated, looking around for a car she might have missed.

"Yeah, she called and said she was going to walk over and drop off some food for me."

"I see." Vaguely, Vivi noted that Rooster's head was bobbing between them as they spoke.

"You don't want to meet my mom," Ian said.

She didn't. Not because she thought the woman was going to be mean or scary, but because it all seemed too sudden.

"It's not that exactly," she hedged.

Seeing him standing across from her, arms crossed, feet apart, Vivi knew he was trying to figure her out.

"If last night hadn't happened, would you still be hesitant to meet her?" he asked.

Vivi shook her head. "No, but last night did happen, and, well…" her voice trailed off.

"She's not scary, Vivienne. She's actually pretty nice."

"I'm sure she's lovely."

"Then?"

She sighed. "Look, what it comes down to is, if there isn't a dead body involved when I meet someone, I'm socially awkward." And she was. She never knew what to do at parties or bars, so she rarely, if ever, went to them. She was good with colleagues and family, with them she was comfortable. With others, well, that was another story.

"You're perfectly social." As if to support his owner's statement, Rooster stood and nudged Vivi's hand, his tail showing his excitement.

"I'd like to point out that we met over a dead body," she countered, absently rubbing Rooster's head fluff.

Ian sighed. "Come on, let's go." He grabbed for her bag with one hand and reached for her hand with the other. She let him take her hand, but snatched her bag strap back.

"If you're going to make me meet your mother, I am *not* going to meet her carrying an overnight bag into your house."

Vivi knew women who could waltz in like they owned the place, but that kind of behavior wasn't part of her makeup. Her parents—her very Catholic parents—and family had always drilled in respect for elders, and while they weren't blind to the shenanigans all the kids got into, there was a firm divide between the things you shared with your parents and elders and those you did not. Sex lives fell firmly into the latter. And walking into Ian's house with an overnight bag was just as good as walking in and telling the woman to her face that she was sleeping with her son.

Ian gave her a look before shutting her trunk, sans bag, and dragging her into his house, Rooster trailing in their wake. Again, Vivi had a fleeting thought that she should know how to handle this better. But the truth of the matter was, there were too many unknowns, about her life, about Ian's, and about their place in each other's lives. With a start, Vivi realized she wasn't too unlike Ian and his ever-present plans. She didn't call them plans, but evidently, she preferred things in black and white.

When they entered the kitchen through the back door off the laundry room, all Vivi could see was an open refrigerator. Ian anchored her by his side and spoke.

"Hi, mom."

"Oh hi, honey," came a surprised but pleasant voice from behind the door. "I brought you some chili and a few other things.

Oh, hello." A form appeared as the door shut. Vivi didn't miss how Ian's mother's eyes went from Ian to her and then back again.

"Mom, this is Dr. Vivienne DeMarco. Vivienne, this is my mom, Ann MacAllister."

"Dr. DeMarco. It's nice to meet you. Please call me Ann."

"Mrs. MacAllister. It's nice to meet you, please, it's Vivi." They both spoke at the same time, then smiled. Vivi stepped forward and the two women shook hands.

"So, you're leading the charge to solve these horrible deaths?" Ann asked.

"I'm helping Ian in every way I can," Vivi corrected. Ian's mom had the same soft green eyes as her son, and they darted between Ian and Vivi, landing on their intertwined hands more than once. His mother's hair, though now mostly white, held shades of brown and red, like Ian's, and had the same thick curl to it. Ann was shorter than Vivi, rounded with age, and, like her son, carried an air of practicality about her. And not that Vivi had any doubts about Ann's character, but it was nice to see that she also loved dogs, which was obvious when Rooster headed to her side and she gave him a good, long scratch behind his ears with a familiar gesture.

Ann gave a small smile. "Well, I'm glad he has the help. It's such an awful thing. Nothing like this has ever happened here before."

The cynic in Vivi suspected more had happened in this area than people knew or admitted, but she nodded in agreement.

"Anyway," Ann said on a breath, "there is food in the fridge. I can take Rooster again if you like. And don't forget Brianna and Chris will be here tomorrow night. They'll both want to see you if you can spare the time?"

Ian wagged his head and looked at Vivi. "Brianna is my sister and Chris is my nephew. They live in New York City and are visiting for a few days," he explained. Turning back to his mom, he answered. "You can leave Rooster here. I may drop him off tomorrow, though. And I'll make time for Chris. Brianna, we'll see," he added with good-natured affection. Ann rolled her eyes.

"Well, it was nice to meet you, Vivi. I'll let you two get back to your evening." When Ann's eyes fell again to her hand in Ian's, Vivi tried to pull away, but Ian tightened his hold.

"Thanks, mom. We appreciate the food. And thanks for taking care of Rooster. I'll give you a call tomorrow about Chris."

At that, Ann bid them goodbye and disappeared out the door. Rooster followed her as far as the laundry room before turning back to the two of them as if to ask "what now?" Vivi turned to Ian.

"That wasn't so bad, was it?" he asked, tugging her toward him and sliding his hands into her hair, pulling out her ponytail as he worked his way over her scalp. She tilted her head back to give him better access. Rooster ambled back into the room and sank to the floor.

"I feel like I'm going to throw up."

He chuckled. "She's not that bad, it was fine."

Vivi let her head fall against his chest and, as she relaxed for the first time all day, she realized how tired she was. Ian held her close as he brushed a kiss across the top of her head.

"I need to change out of my uniform. Then we can dig into some of the food she brought."

"What time do you have to go back out?" Her voice was muffled against his chest.

"I don't. I rearranged the schedule a bit. I called in our part-time officers for most of the patrol work. Marcus, Wyatt, Carly, and I will take turns being backup, but none of us will be on patrol for the next few days. I wanted to keep everyone on this case. At least until we have a better idea of how far we're going to take it."

"Good call," Vivi said. "They may not have the experience, but I think they did a good job today. Especially Carly." They stood for a little while longer, enjoying the inertia, before she spoke again. "I smell like the lab. I need to shower."

"Now that's something I could get into."

Ian's arms had tightened around her and his voice was quiet but deep. Rooster rose and bumped against them as if he, too, wanted in on the embrace. One of Ian's hands dropped down to Rooster's head, but he kept the other firmly around Vivi. She smiled. "I'm sure you could get into it in more ways than one. But if you do, it might be a while before we eat. Just saying."

He smiled back. "Food is overrated."

CHAPTER 14

SEVERAL HOURS LATER, IAN SAT on his porch with Rooster at his side, watching the night. Vivienne was inside making a call to Lucas Rancuso. Ian wasn't sure what to make of that situation but trusted her to tell him what he needed to know.

Rooster's head popped up at the same time Ian saw headlights cut up his driveway. On instinct, he felt for his weapon and came up short. In his effort to reintegrate into civilian society, Ian had become very intentional about leaving his weapon locked up for the night. He tried not to think about it too much—tried not to think about how vulnerable it made him feel. But especially at times like this—when he was going to have an unexpected visitor—it was hard.

He stood and planted himself at the front of the porch as the car made its way toward him. It came to a halt and, even as his body tensed in anticipation, two laughing people, a man and a woman, spilled out. Rooster made a low sound in his throat—not really a growl, but not a fully committed bark either.

Wrapped up in conversation, the two visitors seemed almost oblivious to Ian and his dog, though they would be seemingly hard to miss standing on the well-lit porch. From what he could see in the dim light, the man and woman looked to have the same color hair and same relative builds as each other. Their skin color was also similar, as was their bone structure. He'd peg them as siblings, but in the dark, it was hard to tell.

The couple came to a stumbling halt at the bottom of his steps. Two sets of green eyes took him in. Then the woman smiled.

"You must be Deputy Chief Ian MacAllister. We believe you're sleeping with our cousin."

Ian blinked. Rooster, the faux guard dog he was, was already doing his happy-to-have-visitors dance, waiting for Ian to open the screen door.

The woman's smile widened as she linked her arm through the man's. "I'm Naomi and this is my twin, my *younger* twin, Brian. We're Vivi's cousins. On her dad's side." She spoke as if that explained why they were on his doorstep, or even how they had found his house.

The man grinned, an identical gesture to his sister's. "Yes, we're the younger, funner versions of Vivi," he chimed in. "But then again, we're not burdened with IQs of 163 like Vivi, are we, Nano?" he joked.

Naomi laughed. "Thank god, no. So, is she here?" She cocked her head to the side and gave him an expectant look.

Rooster pressed his nose against the screen as Ian regarded the two for a long moment. Neither seemed at all bothered by his scrutiny.

"Vivienne," he finally called over his shoulder.

After a short wait, Vivienne appeared on the porch behind him, still carrying her cell. "Yeah?" He felt her pause, then take another step forward. "Brian? Naomi? What on earth are you doing here?" She glanced at Ian as she moved forward to unlatch the porch door. Rooster bounded out and greeted the two by jumping up and down and spinning in circles.

"Our parents were worried so, of course, they sent us. *They* wouldn't want to appear to be interfering, you know." Naomi laughed as she hugged Vivienne then stopped to give Rooster a good rub and a kiss. Brian stepped forward to do the same, forgoing the dog-kiss, though.

Vivienne turned to Ian and, rather awkwardly, introduced him to her cousins. He couldn't get a read on whether or not she was pleased to see them. It was clear they were all close and she liked them; it was less clear if she wanted them there.

He ushered everyone inside and into his living room. Once they were seated, Ian offered his guests some wine, which they accepted. Glasses in hand, he, Vivienne, and her two cousins sat across from each other in a somewhat awkward tableau. Rooster found a spot on the floor at the end of the couch, the only one who seemed thoroughly pleased with the situation.

"So, not that I'm not happy to see you, but why are you here?" Vivienne asked again, looking at Naomi.

"Mom and dad were worried about you," Naomi said.

"Everyone is worried about you," Brian piped in.

"So they sent you?" Vivienne asked.

Brian and Naomi shot each other furtive looks in response.

"Oh, no." Vivienne sat back. "Who else is here?"

"Travis," they said in unison.

"Another cousin, sort of," Vivienne clarified for him. "Not blood related, but his mother and my mother were best friends and our fathers, all of ours," she said with a gesture encompassing the twins, "were on the force together."

"But of course, he would *never* want to show up on a doorstep uninvited," Brian tacked on.

"He's a bit formal," Vivienne explained.

"Stuffy," Naomi corrected.

"Both far nicer adjectives than I would use," Brian added.

"He's not that bad," Vivienne spoke, turning toward Ian. "He's just not quite as laid back as the rest of us. He's a location scout for a couple of big-name movie directors. He isn't around us as much as we're around each other, so he's not always as comfortable."

"And, he has a thing for you, Vivi," Brian pointed out.

"Maybe when we were, like, ten years old, Brian. Now he actually has a life of his own." Vivienne tucked her feet under her and took a sip of wine. "How long are you guys staying for?"

"As long as you need us," Brian said.

"Or as long as we think you need us," Naomi added.

"And, no offense, but what I if I don't need you at all?" Vivienne said.

Both Naomi and Brian looked at her for a moment, then turned their eyes toward Ian. It didn't take a genius to figure out what they were doing, and he didn't mind. They could judge him all they wanted, try to figure out if he was good for their cousin. While it would be nice to be accepted by Vivienne's family, the only person in the room whose good opinion he cared about was Vivienne's.

After a long moment, Naomi's eye's jumped back to Vivienne and she grinned. "We're planning an attack on the Pentagon tomorrow."

"At the same time as we go after the CIA and NSA headquarters," Brian added. "It's going to be massive fun, but we can do the planning and testing from anywhere and this place looks nice enough."

"So, you're going to stick around?" Vivienne asked, not sounding quite as excited about the prospect.

Both twins waggled their heads and spoke in unison. "Probably."

"And Travis?" she said.

"He is doing some scouting for a period piece. He figures this area is as good as any other in the Northeast," Naomi answered.

"Excuse me," Ian interjected. Perhaps he was a little slow but the words had taken a minute to sink in. "Did you say you're planning an attack on the Pentagon?"

The look the twins gave him could only be described as one of devious delight. He looked at Vivienne. She looked skyward and gave a small shake of her head.

"They aren't crazy," Vivienne said. "They get hired by the government to test its electronic and technical security. If Brian and Naomi find a weakness, it gets fixed and then they get hired again to test the system. These two probably do more work for the government than I do. And I *know* their security clearance is higher."

He glanced back at the easygoing, carefree pair. It was hard to believe that the Pentagon trusted them to break into their systems. But, then again, they didn't look the part, so maybe they were perfect.

"Uh, okay," he said.

"You're a good sport, Ian MacAllister," Brian stood as he spoke. His sister followed. "So, we'll leave you two to, well, you know," Brian continued with a grin as he moved toward the door. Vivienne uncurled from the couch, and she and Ian rose to walk the twins out, Rooster at their heels.

"What are your plans, Vivi?" Naomi asked when they reached the porch.

"I have to go to Boston tomorrow." This was news to Ian and he shot her a look. Her eyes met his for a brief moment before turning back to her cousins. "Lucas Rancuso had the cases from the Boston area that we want to look into. I spoke with him tonight and he's going to give me the information, but he wants to see me first."

Vivienne's gaze stayed on her cousins, but theirs switched to him for a moment before returning to her.

"Well then, breakfast tomorrow?" Brian asked.

Vivienne nodded. "Let's meet at Frank's Café at nine o'clock. Bring Travis so I can see him. I'll head to Boston after that and you can all go back to your lives."

After a quick round of goodbyes, Naomi and Brian were in their car and headed down the drive. Vivienne stood in the cool night air with her arms wrapped around herself, watching them go.

"I'm going with you to Boston." Ian softened his declaration by wrapping his arms around her from behind and pulling her against him. She was about as pliant as he expected. But it wasn't negotiable as far as he was concerned. Like it or not, it was his case, and while asking his officers to place calls to gather records and files was one thing, sending Vivienne out on her own was entirely different. Especially when the victims, both actual and presumed, looked like her and were the same age. No, he most definitely had no interest in letting her out of his sight for any length of time.

**

Reluctantly absorbing the warmth of Ian's body behind her, Vivi stayed still. He had every right to go to Boston with her if he wanted to. It was his case. And, truth be told, she wouldn't mind the company—it wasn't the most exciting stretch of the turnpike. But if she walked into the station with him, between her cousins and everyone she knew and worked with on the force, including Lucas, she may as well be advertising their relationship in neon lights. It wasn't that she wanted to hide it, but over the past few days—even before she'd come to him in her short dress and high heels—there was a little something about him, something private and safe, that she didn't want to lose. Maybe it was selfish, but he was hers. And she wanted the time they had together to be hers. If their relationship went anywhere, she knew it wouldn't always feel like this. So, for now, after having lost so much, she wanted to hold onto something of her own.

Ian shifted behind her. She closed her eyes and inhaled a deep breath of night air. The sweet scent of fresh-cut hay lingered in the air. The crickets were starting to do their cricket thing and the sounds of frogs echoed up the valley. They would go to Boston tomorrow. He would meet her colleagues. He might even meet some of her family.

But they would come back here. They would come back to his house, to this porch, and it would be the two of them again, wrapped in the night and peace of the valley. The realization that whatever happened in the day—whoever they met or didn't meet, whatever they learned or didn't learn—would all be tempered by this quiet made acceptance easier.

Vivi sighed and relaxed into his arms.

"You know, my cousins would probably be felons if the government hadn't given them a productive way to use their devious intellect."

Ian's chuckle rumbled against her back. "Yeah, I can see that. I can definitely see that."

"You might meet more of them tomorrow."

"Family or felons?" he asked.

"Since we're headed into BPD headquarters, probably both."

She felt him shrug. "I'm okay with that."

Leaning back into him, she closed her eyes again and listened to the nighttime symphony. "Yeah, I am, too," she said softly.

A few more minutes of peace passed, then Ian asked, "Were they serious about offering to help? What if you said you needed them, what would they do for you?"

"Anything I asked," she answered.

"I kind of get that, but what would you ask them to do?"

"They can pull up any electronic data you can imagine, and some you can't. From social networking to phone and bank records to dating sites. That's the kind of thing they do. But listen to me, Ian, you're a good cop and we have a good team. If there is something specific you think they can help us with, we can ask, but they shouldn't be brought in just because."

He let out a deep breath and stared off into the night sky. "I know, you keep saying that, Vivienne, but this is my first rodeo. I want to catch this guy before he kills any more women. If your cousins can help, what harm can that do?"

She turned in his arms to face him. "They can help when and if you want them to. I'm not saying don't use our resources, I'm saying you need to place some value on the resources you have— namely, you."

Ian seemed to mull this over for a while before looking down at her. His hands moved up her back and he wrapped them in her hair. And her heart broke a little when he finally spoke. "It's hard to have faith in something you know is so flawed."

She knew he wasn't as flawed as he thought, but she didn't want to argue with him. Yes, PTSD could ruin a person's life, but Ian wasn't just living his life, he was living it successfully. He had nightmares, he worried about people's safety all the time, he was constantly reaching for his gun when she knew he'd deliberately taken it off. But he was also hunting a killer, leading a team of smart, capable people, and even keeping a sense of humor. He might not have faith in himself at this particular moment, but she did. And she'd have to show him it was well placed.

"We'll call, John, in the behavioral science unit tomorrow. Let's see what he has to say and we can go from there," she said.

His eyes locked on hers. "And if he says they're coming?"

She inclined her head, giving him what he wanted, her acquiescence. "Then we find another B&B where they can stay, because they aren't staying here. And in the meantime, why don't you take me to bed and I'll let you show me how good you are."

It took less than a second for Vivi's words to sink in, and Ian gave her a cocky look. "There's good and then there's wheelhouse good, honey."

***

Despite not getting much sleep the night before, Vivi awoke rested and ready for the day. Either she was more like Ian than she thought or he was rubbing off on her—she found herself going over the plan for the next few hours, ticking everything off, and putting everything in place: call John, meet her cousins for breakfast, drive to Boston, see Lucas, pick up the evidence, and then head back to Windsor. It would be a long day, but being able to add the files of the three Boston women to their growing collection would, she hoped, give them an exponential amount of additional information. And the more information they had, the better their chances of discovering *something* that could help them find the person responsible for the deaths of Jessica and Rebecca.

Rising from the empty bed, she threw on one of Ian's t-shirts and walked into the kitchen. He was sitting at the table filling out paperwork. Rooster was sprawled on the floor beside him, resting his head on what looked like a well-loved stuffed toy and a small blanket. Ian's uniform shirt was unbuttoned and he wasn't wearing his gun, but he didn't need either to command authority. He may have been questioning his ability to perform the duties of an investigator, but he was still a leader, still in charge, still shouldering the responsibility.

"Are you ready to call John?" Vivi asked.

He looked up from his paperwork, and she didn't miss the sweep of his eyes over her. She arched her brow, then winked at him, making him smile, before she walked over to pour a couple of cups of coffee. Bringing them both back to the table, she grabbed her cell from the counter before sliding into the seat across from the Ian. Rooster must have become accustomed to her already, as he simply raised his head and watched her until she sat, then dropped his head back down and closed his eyes.

"Ready?" she asked.

"As I'll ever be."

She hit speaker, then speed dialed John's number. It rang twice before her colleague picked up.

"Levitt, here."

"John, it's Vivienne DeMarco."

"Vivi, it's good to hear from you." She could hear the surprise in his voice. John was the only person she'd talked to at the Bureau about her decision to take some time off, the only person she'd told, until Ian, about the manic behavior that had consumed her after her parents and brother died. His surprise wasn't unexpected.

"Everything all right?"

"I'm fine, I'm doing okay," she answered. "Unfortunately, I happened upon a young woman who wasn't so lucky. I'm here in Windsor, New York, with Ian MacAllister, the Deputy Chief of Police, and we're working an interesting case. It's Ian's first here as law enforcement, but he's been a Ranger for over a decade. We thought your opinion might be helpful."

"Sure, anytime. Why don't you tell me about it and we'll see what we have."

So they did, or rather, Ian did. Vivi sat back and listened as he gave John the details in a succinct, but thorough, overview of what they'd found—who the victims were, the serial killer theory, and the possible additional victims. John interjected a few times—

asking questions, clarifying who was who—and when Ian finished, Vivi could all but see John leaning back in his chair, frowning in thought, and maybe running a hand over his bald head.

"You've found yourselves in quite an interesting situation. But let me ask you this, are you calling me because you want the Bureau involved?"

Vivi looked at Ian, waiting for him to answer. He caught her eye and held it for a long moment before answering.

"Truth be told, sir," he started, "I'm not sure. I'm not opposed to federal assistance if it will help catch whoever is doing this, but I also don't want to take you away from cases that might be more in need of your attention. I think we're going to need you at some point, but being new to this, I'm not sure at what point that will be. Vivienne's been telling me to wait but was gracious enough to humor me and set up this call."

John grunted. "Vivi is a smart woman, and you don't strike me as someone who just fell off the turnip truck. You're right, if you do verify victims in other states you will need to officially notify the FBI, but right now, you only have two confirmed victims, both in New York, both in your jurisdiction. You're doing all the right things to discover if there are more. With Vivi there to help, and you mentioned Nick Larrimore, who, despite being somewhat of an arrogant prick, is a great agent, you're doing exactly what we would do."

Vivi took a sip of her coffee to hide her satisfied smile; John had said what she'd hoped, what she'd expected him to say. Ian shot her a look, not of defeat, but of good-natured acceptance.

"We're pretty busy here now, anyway," John continued. "But if you keep doing what you're doing, by the time we come in, if we come in, you'll have friends for life for doing most of the grunt work, I promise you that."

Ian thanked John for his time and promised to keep him updated. They were getting ready to end the call when John interjected.

"And listen to me, MacAllister, when I say that what made you a good soldier will make you a good investigator. I know it may seem like different skills, believe me I know. I spent seven years as Marines Special Forces before coming back and getting in with the Bureau. But those instincts you have as a soldier—your ability to assess a situation and people, knowing that sometimes the most obvious way out isn't the best way out—will all serve you well. It's your intuition that made you a good soldier, not the other way around. And that intuition will make you good at this job too."

Vivi studied Ian as his eyes stayed glued to the phone lying on the table. After a moment he mumbled a thank you, which John acknowledged with his own indecipherable grunt, and the two hung up. Ian toyed with the phone for a moment before raising his eyes to hers and holding her gaze.

"You knew he was going to say that, didn't you?"

She shrugged, rose from her seat, and slid onto his lap. "I had a good idea he was going to say that, and I figured you needed to hear it from someone with whom you are not involved." She wrapped her arms around his neck and leaned in to nibble on his earlobe. His arms came around her.

"So, we're "involved," are we?"

She trailed soft kisses down his neck. She loved the soft, musky scent he used after shaving.

"So coy, MacAllister. It doesn't become you."

She could feel his throaty chuckle against her lips.

"No, it doesn't, does it?" Ian stood, lifting her with him. She gave a little yelp of surprise, then realized where this was going as he headed to his bedroom.

"We have to meet my cousins in forty-five minutes and I haven't showered yet," Vivi protested as he laid her down on his bed and came down over her. Unbuckling his pants on the way.

"That gives us twenty minutes. Twenty-five if you shower fast." He said, reaching for a condom.

He slid into her and she shuddered at the feel of him. At his strength and the rawness of who he was as a man.

"Maybe thirty minutes if I don't wash my hair," she murmured.

***

Ian followed Vivienne into Frank's Café fifty minutes later—they'd made good time considering they'd also dropped Rooster at Ian's parents' house. The twins, seated next to each other, were having a spirited debate about something, and another man, maybe a few years older, sat opposite them, watching their discussion with a detached expression. Figuring it was the-cousin-who-wasn't-a-cousin, Travis, Ian understood in an instant what the other three had been talking about the night before. His khakis were pressed, his shirt wrinkle-free, and he even had a sweater tied over his shoulders. Ian would bet that Brian wouldn't be caught dead with a sweater tied over his shoulders. Travis looked out of place with his cousins, but to Ian, he looked like a lot of the weekenders, with nothing much else distinguishing about him.

When Ian and Vivienne approached the table, all three stood for hugs and handshakes. Vivienne introduced Ian to Travis and then settled in with her cousins. Ian headed over to say hello to Frank and place an order for Vivienne and himself. When he came back to join the table, the four of them were midconversation.

"Not a chance," Vivienne was saying with an emphatic shake of her head.

"You know you want to," Naomi prodded.

"There are a lot of things I want in life. This isn't one of them," Vivienne retorted.

"I'm kind of on your side on this one, Vivi," Brian chimed in. Then, with an apologetic look at Ian, he added. "Naomi is trying to get Vivi to dish on your sex life. Vivi is holding her ground, I'm sure you'll be happy to know."

He shot Vivienne a look and she gave him a what-can-you-do-it's-family shrug. He opted not to weigh in on the discussion, knowing the less he said, the better.

"Welcome to the zoo." Travis's comment was sardonic, but a hint of a smile touched his lips as he looked at Naomi and Vivienne. "I'd say this isn't normal, but it is."

"I have a sister, I remember what she was like with her girlfriends. Though sometimes I wish I didn't," he said as he sat down beside Vivienne.

"So, how are things going?" Brian asked, changing the subject.

"Since last night?" Vivienne arched an eyebrow at him. "Fine. We're headed to Boston today to pick up a couple of files. Other than that, nothing new."

"You're going with her?" Brian asked. Ian picked up an undercurrent of surprise in Brian's voice, but didn't react other than to nod.

"Are you going to stay the night? See some of the family? They'd love it," Travis said.

Vivienne shook her head. "It's not in the plan. It depends on what Lucas has to say, but we're planning on coming back tonight. What about you, what are you up to these days?"

Travis shrugged. "I've been driving around, checking places out. You know how much my mom loves it here, so I've been here before with my folks quite a bit, but I never looked at it from a scouting perspective. It's a preliminary trip, but there are definitely some places I'm going to follow up on." Then, turning to Ian, he asked, "Do you know if any movies have been filmed in the area?"

Ian shook his head. "I don't think so, at least not recently. But we do have an active arts community and a lot of actors and movie folks have summer homes around here."

Travis seemed to contemplate this, then made a noncommittal noise.

"Is that a bad thing?" Ian asked.

Travis wagged his head. "Depends. Some directors and actors don't like to have movies filmed in their backyards, so to speak. Then again, if they are committed to the area, they would probably support the money it might bring in to the local population."

"Bringing money into the area would definitely be a good thing. If you're looking for anything in particular, let me know. My family has been here forever and I know the area as well as anyone," Ian offered.

"Thanks, I might take you up on that," Travis responded.

Frank called their order and, after he and Vivienne had retrieved it, it was obvious the twins wanted to revisit the case. Vivienne must have noticed too and spoke as she slid into her seat.

"It's an ongoing investigation, guys. We can't talk about it."

"Not true, you can talk about some of it," Brian pointed out, leaning forward.

Vivienne speared him with a look. "Fine, ask a question. If we can answer, we will."

"Actually, I don't want to ask questions, but I do have a few opinions," Brian said.

Ian looked at Vivienne. She kept her eyes on Brian as if debating whether or not to ask. She sighed and Brian grinned at her silent acceptance.

"So, I was thinking about where you found Rebecca and the house she stayed in—"

"Whoa, hold up," Ian interjected, holding a hand up to stop Brian. "How do you know where she was found? Or where she stayed?"

Four sets of eyes turned on him. And stared. He looked at each of them before letting his own gaze fall on Vivienne in question. She pursed her lips.

"Uh, remember what I told you about the twins bordering on being felonious? Well, sometimes that border is a little fuzzy." He stared at Vivienne for a moment, wondering if she'd just admitted that her cousins had committed a crime.

"You'll never be able to trace it," Brian piped in as if reading his thoughts.

"Or prove it," Naomi added.

"So you might as well let it go," Vivienne ended. His eyes narrowed.

"Isn't there something about 'the fruit of the poison tree' or something like that?" Ian pointed out.

Vivienne bobbed her head. "Yes, but as long as the information they give you wasn't gained through illegal means, you can still use it for evidentiary purposes."

"But you just said the border for them is fuzzy."

"But they are also adept at skirting the right side of the line," Travis added.

Ian regarded everyone at the table, then threw up his hands in defeat before pointing a finger at the twins and issuing a warning. "Fine, go ahead. But if you do anything, and I repeat *anything*, to screw up this investigation, you will regret it. You aren't the only ones who know how to skirt the law." He fixed them both with a hard look. Naomi's eyes went to Vivienne, Brian looked at him in surprise.

"Wow," Brian said with a glance at Vivienne. "I think you may have found a good one this time, Vivi."

"It's kind of hot when he goes all Ranger on us," Naomi added with a wink and a grin.

Vivienne shot Ian an apologetic look. He wasn't quite sure what to say. Usually men cowered when he spoke like that. Her family laughed it off.

"On that note, I think you should look at the houses around where Rebecca stayed," Brian picked up from where Ian had cut him off. "From the images I saw, there are a couple of other houses on the street, but they are tucked back and probably wouldn't have noticed much. However, there are two houses, one to the south and one to the east, that sit up on hills and have good views of the place she was staying."

"You don't actually think they might have seen something? It's about as likely as someone from the road seeing something," Ian said. All this cloak and dagger stuff—Ian couldn't believe what he was hearing. Or not hearing. Because what he wasn't hearing was a good lead.

Brian and Naomi shared a look. "Take it for what it's worth," Naomi finally said.

Ian looked to Vivienne. She was watching her cousins with a contemplative look, a small frown touching her mouth. Huh.

"Vivienne, we should head out." Ian rose from his seat and reached for her empty plate to bus the table. She looked up at him, then murmured her assent. Ten minutes later, after quick goodbyes and promises to keep in touch, Ian and Vivienne were headed out of town.

"What's the story with the 'tip' from Brian and Naomi?" he finally asked. Remembering the look the twins had shared and Vivienne's concentration on their suggestion, he knew he must have missed something. Like something they weren't saying.

"Shit," he continued, not waiting for Vivienne to answer. "They know something about those houses, don't they?"

Vivienne bit her lip, then inclined her head. "Probably."

"Do I want to know?" Did he want to know what they knew or how they knew it? "Never mind," he said with a shake of his head. "I'll—I guess I'll just look into it. Canvassing the neighborhood is a routine procedure, one we hadn't thought to expand beyond those closest."

"I think that would be a good idea."

"Your cousins are good at what they do?" They left the Taconic Parkway and merged onto I-90, headed toward Boston.

"Very."

"So I should listen to them. What they say and what they don't?" he asked.

Reluctant acceptance tinged her answer. "Probably."

CHAPTER 15

IAN THOUGHT HE WAS USED to scrutiny. After being in some of the places he'd been and doing some of the things he'd done, he was pretty comfortable with it all. But walking into the Boston Police Department headquarters made his skin feel tight and his fingers twitchy. He didn't have to see everyone to know he and Vivienne were being watched as they made their way toward the back of the main room, a large, open space filled with desks and cops.

When they reached the back, Ian was glad to see they were headed into an office. An office with shades drawn and the door closed. The scrutiny would continue, but he wouldn't have to see it, at least not from all directions.

"Come in," a gruff voice called out in answer to Vivienne's knock. She cast Ian a look before opening the office door and stepping inside. Following closely on her heels, Ian shut the door behind him and got his first look at Lucas Rancuso.

Wearing a jacket and tie, he sat behind a desk, hunched over some files. He looked up as they entered, and a lock of thick, black hair fell into his eyes—eyes lined with dark circles. He considered the two of them for a heartbeat before rising.

Now, Ian wasn't a tall man, but he wasn't short either. Rancuso, on the other hand, was a giant. Easily six and a half feet tall, he towered over Vivienne who had wordlessly stepped forward and into a hug.

"I'm sorry I didn't call," she mumbled. A look of pain crossed the big man's sharp features, but he shook off her apology. Then he turned his eyes to Ian.

"Ian, this is Detective Lucas Rancuso. Lucas, this is Deputy Chief Ian MacAllister from Windsor."

As Rancuso studied him, Ian studied the detective. After the initial surprise at the man's size waned, Ian took in his rumpled clothes and gaunt features, factors that made Rancuso, who was probably only a few years older than Ian, look much older. No doubt, he was an imposing man, but he was also, clearly, running on fumes. Ian stepped forward and offered his hand, and after a beat, it was received in a firm shake.

Gesturing to them to take the empty seats in the room, the detective rounded back behind his desk and sat. Placing his hands flat on his desk, he spoke. "So, you want to look at a couple of my cold cases?"

Ian nodded and rattled off the names of the three women they were interested in, though he knew both Vivienne and Carly had covered this in their conversations with Rancuso as the case officer. And the detective wasn't really listening anyway; he was not so subtly taking Ian's measure.

Not taking his eyes off of Ian, he leaned back in his chair and said, "Tell me what you know and what you think."

The drill wasn't new and Ian easily tapped into his training to deliver a succinct, complete report of what they had found, what they were looking for, and what they thought the likely outcome was going to be.

"You're former military, aren't you?" Rancuso asked when he was done.

Ian gave a short nod. "Ranger, twelve years." An unreadable look passed between Vivienne and her friend.

"So you think it's a serial killer?" Rancuso sat forward and placed his hands back on his desk.

"I don't want to, but yes, we think it's likely, Detective," Ian answered.

Rancuso studied him again for a long moment, before picking up some files. "Call me Lucas, and I'm glad. Not that there might be a serial killer out there," he clarified, "but that you think so.

When these three women went missing," Lucas handed the files to Ian as he spoke, "I warned Viv about it. I didn't like it. We only found one body, and then it stopped so we didn't officially take the serial killer position on the cases. But I always thought it was likely."

"What bothered you most about these cases?" Ian probed.

"Other than the fact that they all looked like Viv? Were professional women like Viv? Were the same age as Viv? And that two of them went missing from places Viv frequents?" Vivienne made a half-hearted sound of protest at his side. She'd obviously heard all this before and had dismissed his concern, but now that Lucas had a second chance, he wasn't going to let it go.

Ian was starting to like the guy. "Other than that."

"It was three women in a six-month time frame. The similarities in the victims were too strong to ignore, but there were also other things."

"Like?" Ian prompted.

"Like, all three women had multiple phone calls to a burner cell phone in the few days leading up to their disappearances. Different numbers for each woman, but the same pattern. Two of the three mentioned to friends that they were seeing someone new, but no one had any details about who this new person was. The last one went missing walking home from a restaurant where she was attending a big office holiday party. The second went missing after giving a lecture on Emily Dickinson at the university. And the first woman? Also on her way home, from a fundraising event for the children's hospital."

"All public places where it was easy for someone to blend in," Ian finished. He sat back in his chair and thought about his two victims, Jessica and Rebecca. They didn't have enough information about the final movements of the women, but he could easily see the similarities. Jessica was a nurse at a busy emergency room in New York City and Rebecca worked in theater—both places a man could hide in plain sight. As for the burner phone calls, he'd be sure to look for those when the phone records showed up.

"This isn't all you have, though, is it, Lucas?" Vivienne asked with a gesture to the files Ian held. Lucas shook his head.

"No, we have boxes down in storage. It all happened nearly two years ago, and with no movement on the case, we boxed everything up and took it down to the crypt."

"Can we have access?" Ian asked.

"I *have* access," Vivienne pointed out.

Lucas shot her a look. "I'll give you all the access you need. We can have the paper files copied for you to take, and we'll send you anything we have that's electronic. Between the two, you'll have all the lab and evidence reports including the autopsy results. But there are hours of video in the boxes too. We can copy those, but it might take a little more time."

"I want to know more about the videos you have, but I also want to hear more about how the one body was found." Ian sat forward and rested his elbows on his knees.

"Fluke, as usual," Lucas answered. "She was the first to go missing and the only body we found. She'd been dumped in Walden Pond, out by Concord, about ten miles from here. A man brought his dog by a few days later and played a little water fetch with him—which isn't allowed. The dog stirred things up enough that the body floated up."

"Powerful dog," Ian commented.

"He was a big boy, about a hundred and twenty pounds, but more to the point, he happened to be charging in and out of the water right where we think she must have been dumped."

Ian frowned and nodded. "Of course, the perpetrator couldn't very well bring a boat into the state park, not to mention how obvious that would be, so he had to dump her relatively close to the shore."

Lucas nodded. "She was only about twenty feet out, but the pond isn't that deep. She was weighted down with rocks tied to her ankles and wrists, but two came loose. And then, with the help of a rambunctious dog, the jostling was enough to bring her close to the surface. Once the guy recognized what he was seeing, he called it in right away."

"And they say the only kind of real luck is bad luck," Ian said.

Lucas grunted. "Too bad her body didn't tell us enough about who killed her though."

Ian concurred with that. "What about the videos?"

"We have video surveillance from various spots around the university lecture hall, as well as from the fundraising event—not inside the event, but it was at a hotel so there were cameras in the lobby and out front by the valet parking. We don't have any video from the office party, but there are traffic cams on the two corners nearby, so we have that footage as well."

Ian was impressed. "How many hours?"

"A little over a hundred, total."

Okay, he was less impressed.

"And someone's been through it before?" Ian asked.

Lucas wagged his head. "Yes, but we were pretty short staffed about that time. I'm not saying we would have missed anything obvious, but it's possible that if there was something subtle it might not have caught our eye. We also had three different techs reviewing the footage."

"So, if John Doe Murderer showed up in all three as a regular looking guy out for a nighttime stroll, he probably wouldn't have been noted," Ian commented.

Lucas's jaw clenched as he shook his head. "I wanted to put the same person on it, but the captain had other plans."

Ian knew a thing or two about not getting what you wanted from a superior.

"So, can we?" Ian said, rising from his seat. Vivienne had been unusually quiet during the meeting, but she stood as well. Rancuso took the lead as the three made their way down to the evidence lockers, signed in, and began the search for the evidence.

Forty-five minutes later, Ian was leaving the copy room with his last stack of papers. The videos would take some time because they had to be done by a tech in the evidence lab and Ian and

Vivi would have to sign the evidence out then be at the mercy of finding a tech with the time.

"Does he know?" Ian heard Lucas's hushed voice as he came closer to the table holding the evidence box. He slowed his steps.

"No," Vivienne answered. "Of course not."

He heard Lucas let out a long breath.

"So, how are you? Really, Viv?"

Ian stopped walking, waiting for her answer. "I'm okay. Well, not okay, but better than you might think, better than I was. What about you? I am sorry I didn't call, Lucas."

"I'm fine," the man responded.

Ian recognized the universal male brush-off tone.

"I thought you were going to take some time off," Lucas pressed.

"I was. I did. A little over a month."

"Wow, a little over a month. I thought the plan was the whole year."

The sarcasm in Lucas's voice was plain as day. This was news to Ian—Vivienne had never mentioned taking an entire year off. He frowned and wondered why.

"We both know a year would never have worked. And besides, what could I do? I *found* a body, Lucas," Vivienne said.

"You could have left it to the police like most normal citizens do," came his dry reply. "But then, of course, you met Mr. Highlander." Given what Nick had intimated the day before, Ian figured that at some point there must have been something going on between these two. But Lucas's voice held more amusement than sarcasm, and no jealousy that Ian could detect.

"I'm *not* talking about Ian with you."

"Of course you will. You always do. Maybe just not today."

"We're done with this conversation. We can talk about the other stuff later. I'm going to see if Ian is ready," Vivienne said.

"I'm ready," he said, stepping around the corner. Surprise and a hint of guilt or wariness flashed in both sets of eyes. "I have the last of the files here," he said, holding up a stack of papers. "Let's get everything back in place, then find a tech to copy the videos. After that, we should be good to go."

Vivienne and Lucas nodded and began wordlessly putting things away. An awkward silence fell over the group as they worked and so, after a minute or so, Ian he broke it. "I called Nick while I was waiting for the photocopies and a copy of the phone records mysteriously appeared this morning—four hours before the official copies were emailed in."

"Naomi and Brian," Vivienne gave a put-upon sigh. "Sorry about that. Like I said, felonious minds, good intentions. Don't be surprised if you end up with more stuff from them."

Ian shrugged. "If you can remind them to keep it legal, I'd appreciate it. You convinced me not to involve them, but if I can't stop them from giving us information, it would be helpful to at least get information that will stand up in court."

"Good luck stopping Naomi and Brian. And if you do find a way, please share," Lucas said, offering his first smile since they'd arrived.

Ian had to laugh at that. He doubted there would be a way but hoped maybe Vivienne might have some ideas. After resealing all the boxes and getting them back in place, the three made their way upstairs to the lab. And after another forty-five minutes, they secured the promise of one intimidated tech to make the copies as soon as she could—the next day.

Ian didn't want to leave Vivienne alone, but he reluctantly agreed to let her stay the night and bring the videos back to Windsor as soon as they were done. He hated it, but it made the most sense. He couldn't afford the time away from the office. And she had her own apartment to stay in and could spend the evening assuaging her family. To make the situation even remotely acceptable, she agreed to stay in the lab and watch the videos until Lucas could bring her home. She protested, but both he and Lucas were adamant and, after realizing they wouldn't budge, she not-so-gracefully capitulated on the condition that Lucas would let her borrow his vintage Porsche to drive to Windsor the next day.

With no one entirely happy about the situation, they packed Ian's Jeep with the paper files, he planted a very possessive kiss on Vivienne, and they said their goodbyes. He watched Vivienne and Lucas in his rearview mirror as he drove away. Seeing them standing on the sidewalk, side by side, he couldn't ignore his gut feeling that whatever they'd discovered about their killer so far was only just the beginning.

CHAPTER 16

Vivi pushed back from the computer screen, and rubbed her neck. She'd spent eight hours the day before and four today poring over videos, hoping to see something someone might have missed—something to help them ID their killer. But she was pretty sure the only thing she was catching were kinks in her neck and crossed eyes.

She hit pause and allowed herself to think about where she was. She'd spent the night in her own apartment in the North End, and she and Lucas had shared dinner at what used to be one of her favorite family restaurants in that Italian part of town. But since the death of her parents, Vivi hadn't spent much time in Boston, and it didn't feel much like home anymore. She hadn't been lying when she told Ian that she'd jumped on every plane she could to stay as far away from her memories as possible.

The department had given Vivi a leave of absence and told her to come back whenever she felt up to it. And she hadn't felt up to it yet. Not even now, sitting in the building. Now, she wished the tech who had promised to copy the videos would hurry up and finish the last one so she could get back to Windsor.

Lost in thought, she jumped when the door banged open and Lucas came striding in. At the sight of his grim expression, Vivi's heart dropped. And when Nick came in behind him wearing a similar look, it leapt into her throat.

"Oh god," she said, and as if from a distance, she saw her hands start to shake. "Ian?"

Nick stepped around Lucas and spoke. "He's okay."

Vivi could hear the "but" in Nick's voice, and staring at him, she waited for the other shoe to drop.

"But there was an accident. A car accident."

She started to slide from her seat, but Lucas was there to stop her fall. "He's okay, Viv. He's going to be okay."

For a moment, Vivi felt nothing. Numb to what they were saying, numb to the memories that were assaulting her head. She couldn't feel anything so she let them batter her—images of her parents' car, of the blood all over the seats, of the state trooper standing on her parents' doorstep saying he was sorry for her loss.

Her head started to pound with the kind of headache that can only be brought on by soul-wrenching loss. She felt Lucas force her head between her knees and heard him telling her to breath. Somehow his voice penetrated the crushing numbness and slowly she began to breath, began to hear what they were saying.

"He's okay, Viv," Nick was saying. "He was wearing his seatbelt, thank god. He's in the hospital in Riverside. I don't know everything, but I know he was conscious when I left to come here."

He was conscious, that was a good thing, right? But she was a doctor, she knew how things could go from bad to worse in a heartbeat. She heard the sound of the door opening, the shuffling of feet across the floor and back again, and then the door closing. Lucas took one hand from her neck, but left the other rubbing her head. She managed to bring herself to look up. He was reading a piece of paper.

"I had someone look into it when Nick arrived," Lucas told her. "Ian went into surgery for his wrist, but he's out now, awake, and doing fine."

She stared at Lucas for what felt like forever before the words sunk in. "He's doing fine?" she repeated. Lucas nodded.

"I need to..." her voice trailed off.

"That's why I'm here, Luv. I'm here to bring you back to Windsor. My car is out front."

"The videos?" she heard herself ask.

"Done, I'll have them packaged and ready for you by the time you get to Nick's car," Lucas said.

The only thing she could do was nod. A few minutes later, she found herself in Nick's car heading west to Ian.

***

The car ride was silent. She felt Nick's worried looks every now and then, but she ignored him. Focusing on the fact that Ian was okay was the only thing that kept her together for the two and a half hours it took to get from Boston to Riverside. But of course, it wasn't just the thought of losing Ian that affected her; it was knowing, all too well, what that kind of loss felt like.

Nick parked in front of the hospital and followed her in. They stopped at the reception desk and were directed to the fourth floor. When they stepped off the elevator, a pretty blonde woman approached them.

"You must be Vivienne?" she asked with a soft smile. Vivi nodded. "I'm Jesse Baker, the Hospital Administrator, and more importantly, I'm a friend of Ian's. He asked me to go through his charts with you, so you'll know he's going to be okay. And while I'm doing that, I'll have a nurse shuffle his family out so that, when you see him, you'll know exactly what's going on and can have some privacy."

Vivi figured she was still lingering in a state of shock, because before she knew it, she and Jesse were seated in a private room, and Vivi was reading Ian's charts and looking at his X-rays. She'd thought that the first thing she would want to do when she arrived was see Ian. But somehow he'd known she would need this. And it did, in fact, calm her nerves and stomach a bit to know precisely what his injuries were. And, more to the point, to know his injuries weren't life threatening. He'd had a pin put in his right wrist, but it would heal fine. He had a couple of cuts and scrapes and a minor concussion the doctors were monitoring, but all in all, he'd come out mostly unscathed.

"Thank you," she said, looking up from the last of the papers and handing them back to Jesse. "Can I see him now?"

Vivi felt comforted by what she'd read, yet she couldn't stop the memories and images flying through her head. And the closer they came to Ian's room, the more she wanted to turn and run. She wanted to run and scream and fight and cry about nothing and about everything. But she forced herself to put one foot in front of the other and follow Ian's friend to his room.

"He's right in there. I'll leave you to your visit, but if you need anything, please let me know." And she was gone, leaving Vivi staring at a closed door. Thinking of Ian and the efforts he'd made to make this easy for her, she braced herself and stepped in.

Vivi stood against the wall as the door clicked shut beside her and Ian's eyes sought hers. She took him in—his hospital gown, the temporary cast on his wrist, the cuts and scrapes on his face, and the stitched-up gash on his forehead.

"I'm okay, Vivienne."

He might be okay, but she wasn't. She bolted into the bathroom, slammed the door, and vomited.

The stress, the anxiety, and the memories had tied her stomach into knots, until finally her body gave way and tried to purge it all physically. By the time she was done she was shaky and pale, but in an odd way, she felt stronger. Pulling herself up off her knees, Vivi searched in the bathroom cabinet and came up with a foam toothbrush. She brushed her teeth and rinsed her mouth the best she could, then braced herself, again, to see Ian.

She walked out of the bathroom and let the door close behind her. This time she looked at *him*, not his cuts or bruises or the cast, but him, his eyes, his face. She opened her mouth to speak, but he cut her off.

"If you apologize for that, I might get mad."

She pursed her lips and searched his eyes. Taking a step forward she spoke. "I am sorry," she held up a hand to stop his protest. "Not for that," she said with a wave toward the bathroom. "But I'm sorry it's hard for me to be a good friend right now."

A look of sadness came over his expression, and he held out his left hand to her. She came forward, took it, and sat beside him.

"It brings up a lot of memories, Vivienne. Believe me, if anyone here knows what the power of memories can do to you, how it can bring you to your knees, it's me."

"We're quite a pair, aren't we?" she asked.

"We do have our fair share of baggage." Ian smiled at her as he raised his hand and traced her jaw.

"How are you? Really? I mean, I talked to your friend—"

"Jesse," he supplied.

"Yes, Jesse, and she gave me the medical prognosis. And thank you for setting that up. But how are you feeling?"

Ian wagged his head an inch or two then winced. "A bit banged up. I'm on pain meds now, but I'm sure I'll be sore tomorrow. Nothing too bad to keep me down for too long."

Vivi let out a deep breath and touched his face. "What happened?"

A cloud passed over his expression. "I'm not sure. My tire blew, and the next thing I knew I was crossing lanes, and my Jeep was flipping down a ditch."

Her stomach rebelled again at the description, but she willed it into submission as Ian continued.

"There was a car in the other lane. A couple of kids. Thank god they were paying attention and not texting or talking on the phone. They were able to avoid me, more or less, although, I hear they hit a tree in the skid."

"Oh, Ian." Vivi knew how much that would pain him, knowing the kids could have been seriously hurt.

"I'm told they are both okay. One has a single broken rib and the other a banged up head. But god, Vivienne, it could have been so much worse."

She squeezed his hand. "I'm glad it wasn't. For any of you involved."

"Yeah, me too. It could have been a lot worse for me, too. I'd gone to breakfast with my nephew, and he told me to buckle up, so I did. I was dropping him at my folks' place when I got a call."

For a lot of law enforcement officers—and, more to the point, Vivi thought, a lot of soldiers—buckling up wasn't a given. And, once out of the habit, like any habit, getting back into it was hit or miss.

"Was anyone with you?" she asked.

"In the car? Just me and Rooster—who is also fine. He's at the vet getting his foot stitched for a glass cut, but he's okay otherwise. Marcus and Carly were behind me and saw most of it. It was on a curve, so by the time they came into view, my Jeep was already rolling down the hill."

"And your family?"

"I think I might have scared a few years off my mom's life."

"At least," came a voice from the door. Vivi spun around to see Ann MacAllister entering the room, followed by two more adults, presumably Ian's father and sister, and a child.

"Mrs. MacAllister," Vivi said, trying to pull her hand from Ian's. In response, he made a deliberate show of letting her go.

"Ann, please, remember?" The older woman said as she stepped further into the room to shake Vivi's hand again.

"This is my husband Richard, my daughter Brianna, and my grandson Chris," she said, nodding to the others. "Kevin, my son-in-law, stayed in the city," she added.

"Chris." After greeting the others, Vivi knelt down to meet him at eye level. "I have something to say to you." His eyes shot up to his mom, who was watching the exchange with maternal curiosity. When Chris's eyes fell back to Vivi, she continued. "I really hope that your mom and grandma and grandpa are spoiling you rotten today. You helped keep your uncle safe, and for being so smart and brave, I think you deserve a treat or two, and at the very least, I wanted to be sure to say thank you."

His eyes widened. "What'd I do?"

Vivi smiled. "You reminded your uncle to wear his seat belt."

"You should always wear your seat belt." Chris sounded confused as to why this would be such a big deal.

"You're right, you should always wear your seat belt." Vivi agreed. "Did your mom and dad teach you that?" He nodded. "You have smart parents, Chris. Be sure to listen to them." She heard Brianna give a little snort, and Vivi looked up and grinned at Ian's older sister.

"But your uncle wasn't wearing one today, and you reminded him to put it on. If you hadn't been there or, more importantly, if you hadn't said anything, he might be more hurt than he is now. So, thank you for saying something, Chris. I'm sure glad you did, and I'm pretty sure everyone else here is too."

His eyes followed her as she rose, then traveled to his mom's face. "Does this mean I can get some ice cream?"

Brianne laughed. "Yes, especially if Dr. DeMarco is treating. You can have as much as you want."

"Of course, I'll treat," Vivi said with a smile as she rose. "I'll leave you with your family, Ian," Vivi said, turning back to him. "Nick is waiting for me. We'll head to the station, and I'll update everyone on where we are. I have the videos." Then a thought occurred to her that made her stomach turn. "Are the files in your Jeep?" It would make sense, since he'd been out for an early breakfast and probably hadn't had time to drop them at the station. She could always ask Carly or Marcus to retrieve them.

But Ian shook his head. "I dropped everything off last night. It's upstairs with all the other things we've gathered—including more reports that came in from the folks Carly was reaching out to."

Vivi nodded. "Good. I'll catch them up, they can catch me up, and by the time you're out of here we should all be on the same page."

"Except me." Ian looked so miserable about being left out, she couldn't stop herself from crossing back to him and laying a hand on his cheek. He took it in his free hand and pressed a kiss into the palm.

"I'll come back tonight and fill you in. How does that sound? When are they going to release you, anyway?" she asked.

"That sounds good, especially if you sneak in some real dinner. They want to hold me for one night," he said, not at all happy.

"And I threatened to go public with some of his baby pictures if he didn't listen to the doctor," Brianna interjected. Vivi turned and smiled.

"How about I take you *and* Chris to ice cream later this afternoon, and you can bring his high school pictures? Baby pictures are always cute, but I find the truly cringe-worthy ones are from about seventh grade to tenth grade," Vivi laughed.

"I like how she thinks, Ian." Brianna gave her brother a smile and turned to Vivi. "You have a deal. How does four work?"

Vivi glanced at the clock. It would give her a couple of hours at the station to touch base with everyone. She nodded. "Perfect, I'll meet you at What's The Scoop."

Ian groaned behind her.

"I'll bring you a banana split when I come back," Vivi added with another smile.

"Okay, deal," he said, instantly halting any complaint he was about to lodge. Vivi wanted to bend down and kiss him goodbye, or at least show some sort of affection toward him. But modesty wouldn't let her take such a public action. So she said her goodbyes, and with one last look at the very much alive Ian, she breathed a sigh of relief and left him to his family.

***

Ian watched the door close behind Vivienne and knew he didn't have long to wait. Sisters were so predictable.

"Ian's got a girlfriend," Brianna teased in a sisterly, singsong voice as she approached the bed and perched beside him. "I like her."

"I like her, too," Chris chimed in.

"She promised you ice cream, of course you like her," Ian chided his nephew.

"No," Chris said. "I like her 'cause she called me smart. And she's pretty." Everyone laughed at that.

"Mom's not so sold, and Dad hasn't said a word," Ian pointed out.

His sister waggled her eyebrows. "And is it to the point that you *care* what mom and dad think? Besides, mom likes to withhold her judgment on *everyone*."

"I'm cautious, that's all," his mother argued. "But I do like her, she seems like a lovely person. It just hasn't been long and it seems like you went from never dating anyone to living with someone. It's just a surprise."

"Whoa there, baby brother. You're *living* with her?" Brianna's eyebrows would have disappeared into her hair if they'd gone any higher.

"You didn't tell me this, Ann." Ian's dad finally joined the conversation. Just as it was about to spiral out of control.

Ian held up his hands the best he could, trying to fend off any more comments. When it was clear everyone was paying attention to him, he spoke.

"Look, Vivienne and I are involved," he said, repeating what she'd said the day before. "We don't know where it's going, but neither of us is a player. On the other hand, we both have a lot of things we're dealing with, and I don't just mean this case. The circumstances that we met under are unusual and this whole situation is bizarre, so we're not pledging our undying love to each other. We're letting it play out and seeing where it goes."

"While you're playing house." Unfazed at his glare, Brianna grinned.

"Yes, she is staying with me, and that's all I'm going to say on the matter."

Both Brianna and his mom opened their mouths to comment, but his dad cut them off. "I think she seems like a very nice young woman and I'm glad you've found someone you're interested in spending time with. I look forward to seeing her again and getting to know her better—when and if you decide that's what you'd like."

Ian's mouth twitched into a small, satisfied smile. His dad had a way of ending a conversation that brokered no arguments.

"So, do I still get to have ice cream?" Chris asked—the simplicity of his concern taking some of the tension out of the room.

"Of course you do, honey. I don't think Dr. DeMarco would promise you ice cream and then not follow through on that promise. That doesn't strike me as the kind of person Vivi is."

Ian met his sister's knowing gaze and gave a small nod of acknowledgement. Vivienne was most definitely not the kind of person to back down from a promise.

***

Several hours later, Vivi was pulling out of Ian's driveway with a clean uniform for Ian and Rooster's stuffed toy and blanket at her side. Earlier, Ian had called to tell her that the vet needed to keep Rooster overnight and asked her to drop off the dog's comfort toys on her way back down to the hospital. She'd spent several hours at the station, and with the strain of the day, all the driving, and the stress of the case, she was looking forward to giving Rooster a good rub at the vet's and then spending some quiet time with Ian. Granted, the hospital wasn't the ideal place to spend time together, but at this point, she'd take what she could get.

Vivi followed the directions to the vet that Ian had given her and pulled into the nearly empty parking lot. After grabbing Rooster's toys, she walked into the office and found the reception desk empty, so she rang the bell on the counter.

Within seconds, a tall man in a white coat, whom Vivi assumed to be the vet, walked out. He was unusually good looking, with dark brown hair and eyes that matched, and looked to be about Ian's age, maybe a year or two younger.

"I'm Dashiell Kent," he said, striding forward with his hand outstretched.

For a split second Vivi found herself just staring at him. It wasn't that she was attracted to him—she wasn't—it was just that his face was the kind a woman couldn't help but admire. But then he smiled at her—the kind of smile that was more self-effacing than arrogant—as if he was aware of his looks but found them more amusing than anything else, and the moment was gone.

She smiled back and shook his hand. "Vivi De Marco. Ian sent me with a few things for Rooster. How is he?"

Dr. Kent waved her toward the back. "Come with me and you can see for yourself. In general, he's doing okay," he said as they made their way through a few doors. "We stitched the paw, but then his hip seemed to be bothering him. We dug around and found a couple of pieces of glass embedded pretty deep. Given Rooster's thick coat, we did an x-ray to make sure we knew where all the pieces were, and then we had to put him to sleep for a bit so that we could dig them out. He's good now, but because he was put under, I wanted to keep him overnight just to be sure he handles the anesthesia."

They'd arrived at the kennels, and Rooster was the only dog in occupancy. He was lying on his side with a cone over his neck to keep him from chewing on his stitches. His tail thumped against the kennel floor as she approached, but he didn't move much more than that.

"But he'll be okay?" Vivi asked, reaching for the kennel door.

"Rooster will be fine. He's tired now, but I'm glad Ian had you bring his things by. It's always helpful to have reminders of home when in the hospital. For animals as well as people."

Vivi placed Rooster's blanket and stuffed toy beside him, then ran her fingers through the thick fur on his head, rubbing the spot behind his ears. "I wonder what he was doing in the car with Ian in the first place?" she pondered, mostly to herself.

"Ian had an appointment for Rooster's shots this afternoon," Dr. Kent surprised her by answering. "He takes very good care of this guy," he added.

Vivi didn't doubt that, but there was something in Dr. Kent's tone that hinted at something more. She turned an inquisitive eye on him, even as she continued to massage Rooster's head.

The vet shrugged. "Ian found Rooster abandoned on the side of the road the first week he was back from Walter Reed. By my estimate, Rooster wasn't even six weeks old. I'm not sure who needed whom more, but they both helped each other heal and survive, that much I do know."

Vivi hadn't known that but had no problem seeing Ian nursing Rooster back to health, maybe even bottle-feeding him. It had probably been something Ian needed more than he knew—a reason to get up in the morning, a reason to push through each day. Yes, he'd had his job, but having a job is different than having a living thing depending on you.

Vivi leaned down and gave Rooster a big kiss. "You get better, Rooster, and Ian and I will be back to pick you up tomorrow, if Dr. Kent says it's okay," she said against his fur.

"Call me Dash," Dr. Kent said. "And if he keeps recovering the way he is, he should be more than ready to be home tomorrow."

Vivi gave Rooster one last kiss, then took a step back as Dash locked the kennel door. "Call me if you have any questions or just want to know how he's doing," Dash said as they made their way back toward the front of the building. "Ian and I went to school together. He's a few years older than I am, but it's a small town. If there's anything I can do for either of you, please let me know."

Vivi stopped at the front door and looked at Dash Kent again. His face was still striking, but more to the point, she saw a friend of Ian's—yet another person who cared about him. "Thank you," she said. "We will."

After leaving Rooster and stopping by Frank's Café for some dinner, Vivi arrived at the hospital and peeked her head into Ian's room.

"It's safe," he said.

"I didn't want to interrupt," Vivi countered, entering the room. It was partly true, she didn't want to interrupt him if he were with the doctor or his family, but by the look on his face, she knew he knew that wasn't the primary reason.

"You're afraid of my family." Ian smiled as he held out his good hand to her.

"Not afraid, it just seems premature to be at the "meet the parents" stage of the relationship, that's all," she said, putting down the bag she'd brought and coming to his side.

"Too late for that, and besides, nothing about our meeting or being together has been normal. I think abnormal is probably our normal."

She inclined her head. "You do have a point. How are you feeling?"

"Better, less sore. They let me get up and walk around this afternoon despite being on pain meds. I think it helped get the blood flowing again. They said I can even take a shower tonight."

"That sounds like an exciting night."

"Not nearly as exciting as a few nights ago." His hand came to rest on her thigh. Again, she wasn't inclined to argue.

"Be that as it may, I did bring some entertainment," Vivi said.

"And food, if my nose is still working."

"And food. And some clothes, a clean uniform for you for tomorrow," she added, pointing to the bag. "But no ice cream. What's The Scoop was closed, but I'll promise you some for tomorrow if you're good," she said, leaning down and brushing a kiss against his lips.

"I'm always good," he countered with his own smile. One that faltered when she pulled away and stifled a yawn. "It's been a long day for you, hasn't it?" His hand curled around hers. Her eyes watched his bigger, rougher hand entwine with hers.

"Probably not as long as yours."

In truth and in different ways, it had been a long, tough day for both of them. Physically for Ian, and, well, for her the emotional roller coaster she'd been riding almost all day wasn't something she was going to stand in line for again, if she could help it.

"Anyway, let's eat. I brought a laptop and a copy of a few of the surveillance videos. I figured this is our best shot at dinner and a movie these days."

Ian chuckled. "Like I said, abnormal."

She unwrapped the food as he pulled the table over the bed. It probably wasn't the big meal he craved, but Vivi hadn't wanted to load his stomach down given he'd just had surgery. Ian didn't seem to mind too much, and while they ate, Vivi updated him on what they'd gone over at the station that afternoon, which wasn't much. The only new development was that Carly was able to eliminate one more woman from the list of possible victims. Charlene Wycoff, one of the missing women, had a two-million-dollar insurance policy and a brother champing at the bit to have her declared legally dead. The cops were trying to keep the case open, but without more evidence to support their belief in the brother's involvement, they were running up against a brick wall.

"So, how much of the video did you watch yesterday?"

Vivi gathered up their wrappers and napkins and, after tossing them into the garbage, pulled out her laptop. "I went through about twelve hours of the office party traffic cam videos between yesterday and this morning. But I haven't seen all of it," she added, "or any the videos from the fundraising event or the university."

She plugged in the computer, popped in a disc, and pulled the table back over the bed. Tucking herself in alongside Ian, she hit play. A darkened intersection popped up on the screen. The image quality wasn't HD, but it was enough to see cars and people. Snow banks lined the streets and pedestrians hurried by wrapped in thick coats and hats.

"I take it this is the one of the street cams near the office party?" Ian asked. "Any identification of people is going to be a bitch," he added.

Vivi grimaced. "I know, winter gear is good at doing its job, but it sucks for us. Still, we can see what crops up and who knows what kind of cars or vans we'll see."

"Did you see any vehicles that might fit what we're looking for in the video you watched?"

"Two. I noted the time stamps and Nick is looking into them," she said.

They watched a few hours of video in a quiet that was occasionally punctuated with commentary by one or the other. They saw three more vehicles that were worth looking into, and Vivi dutifully noted each one, texting the information to Nick as it came up.

But by ten thirty, Ian was waning. And when Vivi found herself checking on him more than the video, she decided to stop for the night. Ian's eyelids had drifted closed and every few minutes the arm he'd wrapped around her would twitch, reliving some memory.

She eased herself from his side and, as quietly as she could, packed up her computer. When she was ready to go, she paused by the bed and took a moment to study this man she'd really just met. The bruises were growing more prominent on his arms and face, but the cuts and scrapes and the gash on his forehead had been cleaned since she'd seen him earlier in the day.

She felt a wave of anxiety wash over her when she allowed her mind to think about how he'd gotten those injuries. But she also realized that anxiety wasn't the strongest emotion she was feeling.

She reached out and brushed a finger across his forehead, then traced his jaw, pausing over his cheek. She'd been overwhelmed by her own fears and memories for most of the day. But now, standing here looking at Ian, watching his chest rise and fall with each breath, she gave thanks that he was okay to whatever god that would listen. Not because she wouldn't have been able to stand yet another loss, which was probably true, but because the world would have lost another good person if anything worse had happened. And the world needed all the good guys it could get.

CHAPTER 17

VIVI HAULED HERSELF OUT OF her car, more tired than she'd realized, and made her way to Ian's back patio. She missed Rooster's greetings, which were so much more pleasant than arriving alone at the dark house that seemed to loom in the night in front of her. She let out a little sigh and fumbled with the key. Her imagination was already getting the better of her. Ian's house was a cute, colonial-style bungalow. It didn't "loom" anywhere. Especially not with its white sides glowing in the moonlight and flowers hanging from little baskets, no doubt a gift from his mom.

She entered the quiet house and flicked on the light before shutting and locking the door behind her. How many countless times had she walked into her own dark, empty apartment, or a hotel room, and not felt even a hint of unease? Even when she was working the ugliest of ugly cases.

But pausing in the kitchen, absorbing the silence, she felt it now. The thought of heading into The Tavern and bunking with Naomi crossed her mind. Her cousin would love it. Only Vivi couldn't bring herself to do it, to leave Ian's house—a house that, just two nights before, she'd felt so safe in.

She glanced at the bottle of wine, recorked two nights ago, and thought about knocking back a glass or two and crawling into bed. Then, as a gust of wind came over the hill and rattled the trees, she could no longer deny what her instinct was telling her—now was not the time to be alone. She could ignore it and, chances were, she would be fine. But if she did ignore it, and something happened, she'd have to live with all the what-ifs, and god knew she had enough of those already.

Without leaving the kitchen, Vivi pulled her cell from her purse and dialed Naomi.

"You're up late. I heard about Ian, how is he?" Naomi said when she answered the call.

"He's going to be okay. He has to stay at the hospital tonight. What are you up to?"

"Um, nothing."

"Naomi."

She let out a breath. "I persuaded that cute, young Officer Granger to let me make copies of the surveillance videos. I figured I could run them through our facial recognition programs. It's not linked to a database, so it won't pull up data on the people in the video, but it will pull up faces that appear multiple times."

Vivi wasn't quite sure what to make of this news, or her cousin's third insinuation into the case. She flip-flopped for about five seconds between scolding Naomi and being intrigued by what the program might find before she realized she was too tired to care either way at the moment, so she went for denial.

"Want to come for a sleepover?" Vivi asked.

"At Ian's?" Naomi didn't bother to hide the surprise in her voice.

"Yeah, it's quiet here. No Ian, no dog, no sounds of Boston's North End."

"You don't want to be alone after the day you've had."

"And, I don't want to be alone after the day I've had," Vivi conceded.

"Give me five minutes to pack. I'll be there in fifteen." Her cousin didn't miss a beat. Vivi smiled.

"You can bring Brian and Travis if you want, they'll either have to share the queen bed in the guest room, or one of them can bunk on the couch."

"Not that they wouldn't want to, but Brian is already asleep, and I don't know where Travis is. We had dinner together, and he said something about wanting to see the light from some hill or something. So it's just me."

"Just you is perfect. I'll have a glass of wine waiting."

Vivi hung up, looking forward to seeing Naomi. Walking through the rest of the house and turning on a few lights here and there made her feel even better. She poured herself a glass of wine and picked up her cell again, calling Kiera this time. Not only was it good to hear her other cousin's voice and touch base, it was a perfect way to pass the time until Naomi showed up, precisely two minutes early.

"Kiera says hi," Vivi said, placing her cell on the kitchen counter.

Naomi dumped her bag on the floor and plopped herself down at the kitchen table with a grin. "That's nice. I talked to her today, too. So, we can cut through the chitchat about the baby. Pour me a glass of wine and spill all the details on Deputy Chief of Police MacStudly."

"I don't know what you're talking about. There are no details," Vivi said, but couldn't hide the smile tugging at her lips.

"You suck at lying. Always have. Brian and I, on the other hand, are masters. Which also makes us good at spotting lies. So bring that bottle over here and don't even think of sugarcoating anything. He's hot, he looks like he has the goods, and he looks like he likes giving them to you. Now, tell me all about it."

***

The morning sun and fog drifted through the tree branches, creating an almost surreal, dreamlike effect. Which wasn't helped by the headache Vivi now sported thanks to Naomi's insistence on not only finishing the bottle of wine already open, but opening a second. They'd talked long into the night about Ian, about life, about work. They hadn't talked like that since Vivi's parents and brother had died. And though she wished they hadn't had so much to drink, Vivi didn't regret calling her cousin over. She did regret that it had taken her so long to reach out to her own family and that she'd only done so because she'd had a sudden case of the heebie-jeebies. But she'd learned her lesson and made a promise to herself to value the family she still had.

With these life thoughts floating in her mind, Vivi pulled her car to the side of the road and killed the engine. Ian stood about forty feet away, his uniform crisp, his wrist in a cast, staring down into a ravine—the expression on his face unreadable. Her heart ached for him, for the sense of responsibility she knew he felt for the kids involved, for the confusion the accident had brought into his life. And for what she knew he was being forced to accept— that safety wasn't a promise in life, no matter where you lived. He might have left one kind of danger behind him in Afghanistan, but that didn't mean the world couldn't or wouldn't come up with something different to lie at your doorstep.

Climbing from her car, she approached Ian in silence. When she got to his side, she too looked down. The ravine wasn't much of one, more of a steep slope ending in a swollen creek. But it was long enough to allow a car to roll a few times. And seeing the scarred land and brush, Vivi could trace the path Ian's Jeep must have taken when he had flipped over this embankment. Glancing at the creek, she gave a double thank you that he hadn't landed upside down in the water. Even though the seatbelt had saved his life during the roll, if he'd landed upside down in the water, it was high enough that it could have drowned him if he hadn't been able to get his belt unbuckled.

She felt sick to her stomach.

Forcing a deep breath in, she turned to Ian. "When I called this morning, the hospital said you'd checked out. You weren't at the station. I thought you might come here, but how did you get here?"

He glanced up at her, and she saw the shadows in his eyes. "One of the doctors dropped me. I figured I could call someone when I needed a ride back to the station."

His voice sounded reasonable enough. Too reasonable.

"Tell me about it."

He didn't speak for a long time, and when he did, his eyes never met hers. He relayed the events, as he remembered them, leading up to the accident.

"I was driving, sirens on, to the call out on Hancock Road. Carly and Marcus were behind me by about a half a mile. I came around this corner," his left hand came up to trace his route, "and as I was about here," he pointed to a spot, "my front right tire blew. My Jeep swerved into the other lane, and when I saw the oncoming car, maybe I overcorrected, I don't know, but I ended up down there." He turned and looked back down toward the creek. Vivi looked at him.

"And the kids?"

"That tree there." Ian's answer and accompanying gesture were instant. Vivi eyed the tree and could see faint scarring along the bark. She studied the road and imagined Ian driving fast to make it to the call. Between the tightness of the curve and the additional speed, it was no wonder his car shot outward when the tire blew. And there were enough rocks at the edge of the ravine that, if his tires hit them with enough speed as he was skidding from the blowout, they could cause the Jeep to tip and flip.

But something in his face, in the way his jaw ticked, told her he wasn't reliving the accident. His mind was somewhere else, somewhere worse.

"Ian?" Vivi put a hand on his shoulder, then let it fall down his arm until she twined her fingers in his. He looked up and into her eyes, and the memory of him—of that moment when the thunder had ripped across the sky and he'd pressed her up against the tree, protecting her body with his—came to mind. That moment when she'd caught a fleeting glimpse of his fears. And his shame.

"Ian."

His expression shuttered and he turned away. Pulling his hand from hers, he walked the few steps to the edge of the ravine and looked down again.

"Your hair is down today," he said.

A car passed them, interrupting the quiet of the morning, and she debated whether to let the issue slide. She didn't want to, but where would it get her? Here in this public place with Ian already feeling exposed, she doubted any conversation about what he was thinking, or more to the point, what he was feeling, would go anywhere good. But she couldn't leave it. She had to try to take some of the pain away. But maybe the best way to do that, in this moment, was to let him have his space. She hoped.

"Chris and your sister came by this morning," she said. "I wasn't quite ready to leave yet and hadn't pulled my hair back. He told me I looked pretty, like a princess, and that I should leave it down. He's a hard kid to disappoint." Vivi couldn't help but smile remembering her conversation with the little boy. Thankfully, her smile was contagious and she saw the hint of one touching Ian's lips.

"He's a boy with good taste," he said, walking toward her.

"Maybe it runs in the family."

"It definitely runs in the family." Ian wrapped his good hand in her hair, tilted her head up, and covered her mouth with his. The kiss ended in laughter when a car full of kids drove by hollering, "Go MacAllister!" to cheer Ian on.

Still smiling, Vivi pulled back and rested her cheek against his chest. He held her there, his lips brushing the top of her head.

When the honking stopped and the sound of the car faded, she looked up. She wasn't going to let him ride this out alone. But for now, they had a job to do. They'd talk later.

"I've always loved a man in uniform. Want a ride?" she offered with a mock-lascivious look.

"If you ask me, I think you prefer me out of uniform."

"Ian!" she smacked him playfully on the chest, though the gesture had no real effort in it since she couldn't argue. He let out a bark of laughter and pulled her tighter into his arms, his cast pressing into her back.

"Maybe I should leave you out here. I bet I can convince your team to let you walk."

"Nah, well, maybe," he conceded then sighed. "I hate to say it, but we do have a couple of murders to solve."

She answered with a sigh of her own. "Yes, yes we do."

***

Ian walked into the station with Vivienne, on the phone with Daniel, right behind him. Sharon looked up, an expression of concern flitted across her face, then stayed.

"Are you sure you should be in today?" the receptionist asked.

He lifted a shoulder. "Don't have much of a choice. What's the update?"

"Marcus, Carly, and Nick are upstairs. Wyatt is out with Teddy, cleaning up a car accident out on 203," Sharon said, referring to one of their part-time officers.

"Vic's going to have a fit when he sees the bill for the part-timers," Ian muttered.

"The mayor will back you. He already stopped by this morning to make sure you know that. He wants this cleared up. Nothing like this has ever happened here, and he doesn't like that it happened on his watch."

"That and he's my uncle," Ian said.

Sharon grinned. "He is that."

Ian let out a little laugh and, as Vivienne hung up her cell, he motioned her up the stairs, asking if there was any news from Daniel.

"No. They're running some more sophisticated tests on the wood and dirt—" Vivienne was saying.

"Soil." Marcus, Carly, and Nick all interjected as they hit the landing.

Vivienne let out a put-upon breath and cast Ian a look. "Soil," she corrected. "But nothing yet. Daniel is more interested in the bodies, so he's spending some time researching and brainstorming some other tests he might be able to run."

"To look for what?" Ian asked as he approached the board,

looking for anything new that might have been posted in the last twenty-four hours while he was in the hospital.

"A variety of things. Other objects that might have been used on the body, elements that might have been absorbed into the bones or body tissue. Things like that."

He opened his mouth then closed it. "I don't want to know. Not unless they find something."

"Good choice, if you ask me," Vivienne said.

"So, how are you, boss?" Carly asked. His two officers were looking at him with genuine concern.

"I'm okay. A little sore. But thanks for pulling me out. I'm glad you all were behind me. If you or those kids hadn't been there to see it happen, it could have been a while before anyone found me."

To his right, Vivienne was going through one of the boxes he'd brought back from Boston. Her back was to him, but he saw her straighten at his comment and he gave himself a mental kick in the ass. She didn't need to hear that.

"Yeah, we're glad we were there too. It's weird though. Those tires were only put on about six months ago, but I guess sometimes those things happen," Marcus commented before going back to his papers.

"I'm just glad it wasn't any worse," Carly added.

"You and me both." Ian replied, turning in time to catch Vivienne and Nick sharing a look. He watched them for a heartbeat before they realized his attention. Vivienne went back to her box.

"Whatever happened with the call you were on your way to?" Vivienne asked as she pulled out a file and opened it on the table.

"Wyatt went." Marcus answered. "It was a report of multiple gunfire. It's not too unusual around here, though this time of year, it's less common than in hunting season. People shoot on their own property for practice all the time, but because it was a report of multiple shots fired in rapid sequence, we wanted to check it out."

"Did he find anything?" Nick asked.

"No, couldn't even find the caller, but if I weren't local and heard gunshots, I'd probably hightail it, too," Carly answered.

"Anyone mind if I open a window?" Vivienne asked suddenly. Nobody did, so she crossed the room to do just that. Ian didn't miss the piece of paper she slid in front of Nick. Without being obvious, Ian watched as the agent folded the sheet, put it in his pocket, and stood.

"I'm off to see the felons. If anyone needs me, you all know how to reach me," Nick said. And he was gone. When Ian's eyes sought Vivienne's, she looked away.

"Felons?" Carly asked.

"Naomi and Brian," Ian supplied. "Not actual felons, I feel obligated to point out."

"But they could kind of pass as some," Marcus interjected with a grin. "I ran into one, Naomi, at Frank's. Said she'd spent the night with you, Vivi, and was on her way back to The Tavern. I think Frank might actually be in love. Not real love, mind you, since he's like twenty years older," he added as an aside.

Now this was news to Ian. Not that Frank might be in love, but that Naomi had spent the night with Vivienne. He certainly didn't mind and was actually glad she'd had someone with her. But the fact that she hadn't mentioned it made him wonder if maybe Naomi's visit was more than just a girls' night in. Again he turned to Vivienne.

Avoiding his look, she cleared her throat. "Carly do you have any updates?" she asked.

Both Carly and Marcus stood. "Yeah, and I don't think you're going to like it," Carly answered.

Ian's gaze lingered on Vivienne a moment longer before he turned back to his officers. "But I'm not going to be surprised, am I?" he said. He could hear the inevitability in Carly's voice.

"I wish, but no," Marcus responded.

"All right," Ian said, stepping to the front of the room. "Lay it on us."

"Turn the board over, boss," Marcus said. "It's all there."

CHAPTER 18

"YOU GOTTA BE FUCKING KIDDING me." Ian crossed his arms and stared at the board. The newly updated board of death. They'd started with eighteen women, three confirmed dead and the other fifteen missing. The last time Ian had looked at the board, Carly had eliminated five of the victims, bringing the number down to thirteen women who fit the profile.

This board had twenty-one women on it. Girls, some of them. And went back over fifteen years.

"There were a few earlier than this woman, or, uh, girl," Carly corrected herself, pointing to the first picture on the board. Amanda Corlis, seventeen, found raped, strangled, and murdered in a summer resort town in southern Maine. She was probably getting ready to go to college. "But they only had one or two similarities so I didn't include them," she added.

"Shit." Ian ran his good hand over his face. "So, how many of these women are missing and how many confirmed dead?" Ian couldn't believe he was hearing those words out of his mouth. This wasn't Afghanistan, asking for "confirmed dead," while standing here in his small, quiet town was more than surreal.

"Ten in total are confirmed dead. The remaining eleven are missing, presumed dead," Marcus answered. His voice sounded about how Ian felt.

"And do we have the files?" Vivienne asked.

Carly nodded. "I was able to track down everyone I needed yesterday, and we have all but one, but that one should be here today."

They all stared at the board for a long, silent moment. Ian

thought about turning to Vivienne and asking that she call in the Bureau. But as he studied the board, a pattern emerged in his mind. A plan.

"We need timelines," Ian said.

His officers looked at him with a combination of curiosity and eagerness in their expressions. Vivienne's face said something more along the lines of "you know what we need to do, now tell us." That she didn't bother to hide that little bit of "I told you so" brought a faint smile to his lips.

"A couple of timelines. Of the women we know are dead, we need to know when they went missing and the estimated times of death," Ian continued.

"To get an idea of how long he holds them," Marcus interjected, speaking more to himself than anyone else.

"But we also need to know more about where they were last seen. If they were seen at a bar on Friday night and reported missing on Saturday, we'll have a more reliable sense of when the clock started ticking for them," Ian kept talking.

"But if they went missing from somewhere where it's harder to lock down a time, like if they went camping by themselves or something like that, then we need to take that into consideration," Carly added, catching on.

Ian nodded. "We also need to know where they went missing from and where the bodies were found. If there is any pattern there, it might give us an idea of how far he takes them from the grab sites. And it might also help us know where to look for the other women, depending on what we find." Both Carly and Marcus moved into action—pulling up their computers, calling off dates and locations, examining the files.

"Ian?" Vivienne's voice held a note of concern.

He swiveled his eyes from his officers to Vivienne. He could tell by the look on her face that she'd seen the same pattern on the board he had. He gave an almost imperceptible nod.

"And folks, I hate to say this, but I think we need to work fast," Ian added. Both heads shot up. "When he started his spree, he went after about one woman a year for several years," Ian continued. "But in recent years, his attacks have been getting closer and closer together. If all these women really are his victims, a few years ago he went after two a year. Then there were the three in Boston, all in one year. After that, it looks like there might have been a short break for some reason, but he picked up again a little less than a year ago, and since then he's already gone after two, with Rebecca being the most recent."

"What does that mean? Other than the obvious, I mean," Marcus asked.

"It means that he is devolving," Vivienne answered. "Whatever it is that's driving him is becoming more and more of an obsession. To the extent he's losing control over it."

"Isn't that the definition of an obsession? Having no control?" Carly asked.

"That's the definition of an addiction," Vivienne corrected. "With a lot of serial killers, killing itself is a kind of addiction, they get a high from it. But some are driven by compulsion, the desire to commit the act itself, and some by obsession, a desire or need for something else that results in the killing."

"Is there a difference that can help us?" Ian asked, unsure why what drives a killer would matter.

"Maybe."

Ian didn't like the sound of doubt in her voice. "Vivienne?" he prompted.

She sighed. "Compulsive killers can often be easier to identify because the more they kill, the clearer their compulsion becomes to those of us trying to find them. And, at some point, their compulsion can overwhelm other parts of their personality, making it harder for them to hide what they've done."

Ian crossed his arms over his chest. "And obsessive ones?"

"Honestly, they're all over the board. It all depends on the obsession."

The cool breeze and clean scent of spring that blew into the room through the open window was so at odds with the conversation that Ian felt unbalanced for a moment. But watching Vivienne pull her hair back into a ponytail, as if girding herself for battle, brought him back to the here and now.

"What do you think his obsession is?"

"This woman, whoever she is." There was no doubt in her answer as she gave a sweeping gesture that encompassed all the women on the board.

"And what does that mean for us?"

"He'll keep going until he gets her. Whether or not he falls apart before that happens, your guess is as good as mine."

Ian liked the sound of that about as much she did, judging by the look on her face. "When you say "gets her," what do you mean? It sounds like you're talking about a specific woman, but you're looking at all of them."

"Oh, it's definitely a specific woman. And I think he wants her as a lover. And when he can't have her or doesn't get her, he takes out his frustrations on these other women," Vivienne answered.

"Uh, what's the likelihood of him actually being able to be her lover?" Carly's voice was filled with disgust.

"And what happens if he is, will it be over?" Marcus asked.

"It depends on who she is. If she's a celebrity, it's unlikely. If it's just a woman he knows, it's always possible, depending on how charming he is. And, as to your question, Marcus, if only it were that simple. What I've seen is that once obsessive killers actually get their hands on the person or object of their obsession, paranoia sets in and they devolve in a whole different way than, say, how compulsive killers might devolve."

"Meaning?" Ian pressed.

"They are unpredictable. They might kill themselves because they don't think they are worthy. If their object of obsession is a person, they may kill him or her. They might also start to believe that the people around them are starting to judge them, believe them unworthy."

"And take it out on a big crowd of people?" This whole thing started out as a nightmare for Ian and it was only getting worse. At least in Afghanistan they had a general idea of who the bad people were and what they might do. When they would do it, who knew? But at least they knew what to look for.

"I've seen it happen," Vivienne said quietly.

"Shit," Ian muttered, more to himself than anyone else.

"So, is there any way to find out who his obsession is?" Carly posited.

"And do what, use her as bait? Come on Carly, you know we'd never do that," Marcus responded.

"No, we wouldn't," Ian interjected. "But I imagine, like most things, the more we know about his obsession, the more likely we are to find him." He turned to Vivienne, who was nodding.

"If we can find the woman, it's more likely than not the killer will be someone she knows. But that makes it sound easier than it is because she may not know she knows him. It's possible he could be her brother or an uncle or something like that. But it's just as likely to be the guy at the coffee shop who serves her coffee every day, or the male nurse at her doctor's office. But still, if we can find her we might be able to narrow the playing field, so to speak."

"But we don't have to find her, do we, to find him?" Ian believed in Vivienne's work as a forensic psychologist and didn't discount the benefit of knowing the victim, but everything in him screamed to find the killer.

"You're right. It's a bit if the chicken and egg scenario. We can try to find her in order to find him, or we can try to find him directly through the evidence. We don't have a lot of physical evidence in these cases, but we should be tracking both avenues," she answered.

"We may have some more evidence," Carly said, standing and holding out three files. "The families of these three victims have left standing permissions to have the bodies exhumed if it will help find the person responsible."

Ian took one of the files and handed the other two to Vivienne. He flipped it open and saw the face of a young woman smiling back at him. Her long brown hair was blowing in a breeze, and her dark brown eyes sparkled in laughter. She'd been twenty-nine when she was killed. Her body found in an abandoned mine shaft in Virginia, not far from her DC home. Her parents had included a directive in the case file that left no room for doubt, agreeing to the exhumation of their only child if it meant someone might bring the person responsible to justice.

"No parent should have to do this." He slammed the file shut and handed it to Vivienne as well. "I'll leave it up to you as to whether or not you think we should exhume these women."

She nodded in response. "I'll take these files with the autopsy reports up to Sam and Daniel and come up with a game plan." She glanced at Carly, who'd gone back to her place among the files with Marcus sitting beside her reading off information. Turning back to Ian, Vivienne asked, "Can I talk to you for a second?"

Ian inclined his head. He had a few things to say to her, to ask her, but he wasn't sure if this was the right time. Still, he followed her down to his office and shut the door behind them. Vivienne's eyes darted out the window. He crossed his arms and leaned against his desk.

"I have some things I need to do today. I'm going to run these files up to Albany, and then Nick and I have a couple of things to discuss. I'll probably head straight to The Tavern when I get back. He'll be there, and I can also check in with Naomi to see if the facial recognition program has kicked up any faces yet."

Ian wondered if she knew what a bad liar she was. She might be doing everything she said, but there was something she wasn't telling him.

"Do you want to tell me what errand you sent Nick on?" For a moment, she looked like a deer in headlights. Then she turned away and walked to the window, keeping her back to him. He figured it wouldn't be long before she spoke. And it wasn't.

"Do you want to talk about what you were doing out at the accident scene this morning?"

For a moment, his temper flared. That she'd turned the conversation around on him wasn't a good sign. In his experience, if someone evaded a question, they usually had something to hide.

At his silence, she looked at him over her shoulder. And when she turned to face him, he saw his own frustration mirrored in her eyes. He had evaded her this morning in much the same way she was evading him now. But she'd let him get away with it—for the moment. And in her acceptance, in her willingness to let him pick the time and place, he'd found himself knowing that he would do the same for her. His own sense of honor and respect demanded that he give her the opportunity. Even if he hated doing so.

"Later. We'll talk later."

She nodded, walked toward him, and brushed a kiss against his cheek. "I'll meet you at The Tavern tonight. I'll call and let you know when I'll be there." And then she was gone.

CHAPTER 19

IAN'S ARM ACHED IN A pulsing rhythm as he pulled on his jacket and prepared to close up for the night. Vivienne had called to tell him she'd be back at seven, and Carly and Marcus had left ten minutes earlier, leaving a scattering of papers and the smell of coffee behind them. He glanced down at the table and debated whether or not to tidy up. Then training got the better of him, and he began to put the papers in order.

Fingering one of the sheets, he thought it was such a flimsy thing, thin and weightless, to be carrying such a heavy load. He looked at the name on paper, Genevieve Gray, aged thirty-one when she was murdered.

He sighed, finished straightening up, and flicked the lights off. From the other side of the alley, the church security light cast long shadows through the windows and across the room. Forcing himself to leave his maudlin thoughts behind, to not wonder how a room that held so much death could look so normal in the night, he made his way down the stairs, careful not to jog his body or head too much.

Still, the short walk to The Tavern, down his quiet Main Street, did him some good. Whether it was the movement or the familiar scents and sights of his hometown, who could say? When Ian arrived at The Tavern ten minutes later, his arm still pounded but his head felt a bit less fuzzy.

"Hi Rob," he said, entering the bar area. It felt like ages had passed since he and Vivienne had shared their first meal together her second night in town. His eyes traveled of their own accord to the corner table they had shared. It was now occupied by two women. And the sight of their food seemed to awaken the hunger in his own body, his stomach growling loudly enough for him to not just feel it but hear it too.

Inhaling the scent of shepherd's pie and beer with longing, Ian slid onto a bar stool. "Seen Vivienne?" he asked the bartender. Rob gave him a sideways look then gestured upstairs with a nod of his head. Ian sighed; food would have to wait.

He climbed the stairs that creaked as much as his body at this point, and turned toward Vivienne's old room. He knew she was meeting with Nick and figured Nick's room would be a good start.

"You have to tell him, Viv." Nick's voice was loud enough to be heard through the door and Ian stopped short outside the room.

"I will, Nick, but you have to give me some time. *I* need some time."

"Time we may not have, Luv." Ian heard the sound of a notebook or file being slammed onto a desk, punctuating the frustration he heard in the other man's voice.

"I've been doing this almost as long as you, Nick. I know the cost. I know the risk. I *will* tell him. I'm just not going to do it right now, and I'm not going to do it over the phone."

"Then *when*?" Nick insisted.

Ian heard Vivienne let out a deep breath, and she paused before answering. "Tonight. I'll tell him tonight. We have a few things we need to hash out anyway. But in the meantime, do not, I repeat, do not tell anyone, Nick."

"Ahh, luv." That Nick thought Vivienne was making the wrong decision was about as clear as the night sky.

"Promise me." She insisted

"God, you are bloody stubborn. Fine, I promise. I won't say anything until you talk to Ian."

"Until we have a plan," she insisted.

"Viv," Nick all but pleaded. Ian's stomach plummeted to the floor. He didn't know what they were talking about, but he sure as hell recognized the desperation in Nick's voice. And he knew enough about Nick at this point to know the man was not prone to hysterics. If Nick was worried, something bad must be going down.

Ian heard the shuffle of feet and Vivienne's voice. It was so low he couldn't catch the words, but the tone was solemn. Nick must have finally grumbled an assent, because Ian heard Vivienne mutter a thank you. And in the silence that followed, Ian became acutely aware of the feel of his blood rushing through his body—a response to the unknown.

He recognized and acknowledged a moment of insecurity as it washed over him. When she'd said to him, "We need to talk," did she want to talk about *them*? In his gut, he didn't think so. In his gut, he believed that if there was a problem between the two of them, Vivienne would have spoken earlier.

Or maybe that was denial.

Fuck, he thought to himself. His life was already screwed up enough, and in the last few days it had taken a monumental dive into a cesspool. He didn't know what the hell was going on, but as his superior used to tell him, quoting Winston Churchill, when you find yourself in hell, just keep moving. And so he did.

He knocked on the door, and when it swung open, Vivienne stood on the other side looking surprised. "You told me to meet you at seven," he said.

She glanced at her watch. "Oh, I guess I lost track of time. Are you hungry?"

He looked into the room and saw Nick glaring at them from his position behind the desk.

"Everything okay?" Ian asked.

"Everything is, well, everything will be fine." Vivienne walked toward him and, grabbing his good hand, laced her fingers in his. The gesture itself surprised him, but what caught him off guard was the sense of reassurance she seemed to want from him. He gave her hand a quick squeeze and her shoulders relaxed.

"Dinner?" she asked. He had no idea what was going on, but dinner was always a good place to start.

***

Vivi slid into her seat across from Ian and wondered how she was going to eat. Not only had the day been almost as shitty as the one before, but she saw the curiosity in Ian's eyes. Curiosity laced with a hint of suspicion. She would allay that suspicion, but what she knew would replace it was much worse.

Somehow, by mutual but unspoken assent, they made their way through the meal without discussing the case at all. And it wasn't until she saw Ian grappling with closing the door to her car with his casted hand that they started to discuss the day. In a safe way.

"It's been a long day. How are you feeling?" she asked as she pulled out of the parking lot and turned north toward Ian's house.

"I'm okay."

She stopped at the one light in town and used the time to stare him into the truth. He cracked and offered her a half smile. "I'm sore, my head hurts, and I feel like I may not make it all the way into bed before I fall asleep tonight, I'm so tired. Knowing you can't carry me and that I'd have to sleep in the car is probably the only thing keeping me awake right now."

She made a right turn onto the other end of County Route 8 from where Jessica was found. "Did they give you any medications?"

He grunted. "Yeah, but I don't want to take them."

"Taking them because you need them is different than taking them because you want them."

"Yeah, I know. But after the IED attack, I was doped up for weeks and then again all during recovery. It took me months to not feel like I needed the painkillers. I'd rather not remind my body of how good they can make me feel. Especially when they make my brain feel like shit."

She mulled this over for minute. After that first time she'd asked him about his injury, he hadn't brought it up. She spared a glance at him and noticed he was rubbing his thigh.

"Does it hurt now?"

He shook his head. "No, but I also don't want to take the medication, because the doctors told me they'd had to up the level they gave me in the hospital for the surgery. Turns out that, even though I don't crave the drugs anymore, my body still has a high tolerance for them."

"And that scares you." It would scare her. For a man as in control as Ian, knowing his body teetered on the edge of dependency must be disconcerting, at the very least.

"I don't know that scared is the right word. But it's true, I don't like it."

Vivi slowed the car and made a left onto the dirt road that led to Ian's driveway. "Okay, so no meds. How about a shot of whiskey and a hot bath?"

Picking up her right hand, he brought it to his lips and placed a kiss on her palm. "Now that's a treatment plan I could get into, Doc."

She curled her fingers over his cheek and felt some of the tension leave his body. "Then we'll see what we can do."

And, call her chicken, call them both cowards, but the minute they set foot in his house, that's exactly what they did. And despite the awkwardness of his casted arm, the hot bath and whiskey led to where it naturally would, where they both knew it would when they started. And by the early hours of the morning, Ian was sleeping like the dead with Vivi curled up beside him.

With her head on his chest, she absorbed the feel of his heart beating beneath her cheek. The smell of the bath soap, clean sheets, and sex permeated her senses, as did the very solid presence of Ian beneath her. The moon had waned but was still more than half full, and dim shadows lined the walls.

Vivi inched closer, thinking about what she needed to tell him. She wanted him to sleep for hours, she wanted this all to go away. But she knew she was only going to make it worse. Shifting out of his embrace, she slid off the bed and made her way to the bathroom. When she stepped back into the room, she paused and watched Ian as his arm twitched and he threw it over his head. It looked like a sweet, child-like gesture and she started to smile—until she saw the frown on his face. His arm came down again, and his body twisted under the sheets as his head began to thrash back and forth. He was having a nightmare.

He started to mumble. Prayers, pleas, and orders to stop. His body reflecting the agony playing out in his mind. For a moment, Vivi watched, waiting to see if he would wake on his own. If he would wake before her own heart broke at his pain.

When she couldn't take it anymore, she walked to the foot of the bed and called his name. He didn't respond, so she called again, louder, and grabbed ahold of his ankle. When she called a third time, Ian's body went rigid. Then, like a jack-in-the-box, he bolted upright. She jumped back at his sudden movement but kept her eyes locked on his.

His breathing was coming fast and heavy; sweat beaded his face and chest. His eyes were wild and unfocused. And then they landed on her. Vivi watched him slowly, breath by breath, bring the world back into focus. And she saw a look of shame cross his face.

"I scared you." His voice was flat.

She moved to sit beside him and placed a hand on his chest. His heart still thundered under her palm. "You didn't. I didn't want to scare you. I was up using the bathroom. I thought if I got back into bed to wake you, it might startle you when you came to."

His eyes searched hers, looking for any hint that she was lying. Vivi kept her gaze steady, hoping he would see only the truth.

He let out a deep breath and rubbed his left hand over his face. "Was it bad?"

She didn't have anything to compare it to so she lifted a shoulder in response. "What do you see, Ian?"

He flopped back against his pillow and looked up at the ceiling. He was quiet for so long she wondered if he was going to answer at all. But then he reached for her hand and spoke.

"Sometimes I don't remember at all. I just wake up with a feeling of helplessness, like I should have been somewhere sooner or stopped someone from doing something. Other times it's people I've known. Sometimes the dreams are of things that actually happened, but sometimes they aren't. Sometimes they're dreams of people from here, but doing something over there."

She came down beside him and he wrapped his arm around her. "And tonight?"

"Tonight it was those kids. Those kids I hit in the accident yesterday." By his tone, she knew there was more. It wasn't just the kids. He was thinking about the same thing he'd been thinking about when she'd found him this morning at the accident site.

"Ian."

He took in a deep breath. "I heard the pop of the tire and I think my PTSD thing kicked in. I should be able to handle a blown tire, Vivienne. Shit, you should see some of the things I've driven in and through. A popped tire on a well-paved road, even at the speed I was traveling? I should have been able to handle it. But I didn't. And because I didn't, those kids could have been seriously hurt."

Vivi's heart sank. It was time to pay the piper. She couldn't let him think that any longer. What she had to tell him might ease his mind about the accident. But it was going to make everything else a lot worse.

She forced herself to sit up and leaned against the headboard. He rolled to his side and gave her a questioning look. Looking into his eyes, she wished to god there was a way to change what she was about to say, but knowing there wasn't, she dove in.

"About that accident, Ian. It wasn't your fault."

He drew his head back and frowned. "I know it wasn't my fault, but I could have handled it better."

"Maybe, maybe not. I had Nick take a look at your Jeep. He went to the salvage yard this morning."

That got his attention and he sat up too. "Why would you do that?"

"Because I thought the same thing. I thought it was weird that a blown tire would cause you to flip and roll your car. A normal driver, maybe, but I know what kind of training you've had. All the evasive and defensive techniques you've probably had to learn.

And it didn't make sense to me either." She paused and took a deep breath. "And then, when Marcus mentioned the new tires this morning, I knew something was off. So I sent Nick to have a look."

Ian's eyes had hardened in preparation for what was to come. "And what did he find?"

"Your tire blew because it was shot out. By a high-powered rifle—a very high-powered rifle. Nick found the bullet lodged between the tire and the rim. If we search the side of the road, we'll probably find a casing. Unless, of course, the shooter collected it."

When Ian didn't respond, she turned to look at him. A look of disbelief and confusion fixed on his face.

"Someone shot my tire?"

Vivi nodded.

"Why would someone shoot my tire? And that's a hell of a shot."

Her eyes locked on his. He was thinking of the immediate questions, but she knew the bigger implication would sink in. His eyes fell to hers and, second by second, she watched as they began to clear and focus in on her like a laser. When his jaw ticked, she braced herself for the fallout, knowing he'd come to the same conclusion as Nick.

"Because you're his obsession."

CHAPTER 20

"GODDAMN IT, VIVIENNE. IS THIS what you and Nick were talking about at The Tavern?" Ian demanded. She bit her lip and nodded. He vaulted out of bed and started pacing.

"So, what?" he paused and pinned her with a look. "He came after me because he's after you?"

She swallowed. "Yes, that's what Nick and I think. The shot fired at your Jeep was too professional, too good to be an accident. And unless you have any enemies we don't know about, Nick thinks that since he can't come after me, or won't come after me, he's going after you. You need to be careful, Ian."

Ian, who had resumed his pacing, stopped abruptly and shot her an incredulous look. "*I* need to be careful, Vivienne? I told you from the beginning that those women looked like you and you wrote it off. Now we think he's killed over twenty women and you're pretty sure he's doing it because it's you he wants? And *I* have to be careful?"

"Ian." His jaw clenched and she had no doubt he was fighting hard to hold his tongue. Vivi took a deep breath. "Look, Ian. You're right. I wrote you off. I noticed the resemblance, but what were the odds of me finding a body in a place I've never been, buried three years ago, by someone obsessed with me? You have to admit it's pretty far-fetched." He didn't look prepared to admit anything.

"I'm sorry, Ian. What more can I say? Nick came to this conclusion tonight. I'm still not sure I completely buy it. He's convinced me to consider it because there are too many similarities and coincidences. But after your day, after both of our days yesterday, I didn't want to talk about it tonight. I figured it wouldn't make much of a difference if I told you tonight or in the morning. And, at least if I told you in the morning, you'd get a good night's sleep. And I *was* planning to tell you."

"Well, sleep sure as shit isn't going to happen now, is it?"

She sighed. "I'm sorry, Ian. I should have told you when Nick told me."

He paced a few more times, then seemed to come to some conclusion as he stopped at the end of the bed. He opened his mouth to say something, then closed it. After a pause, he started speaking.

"You don't need to apologize, Vivienne. I probably would have done the same thing. And I'm not mad *at* you. I'm—" he stopped. His eyes landed on hers and softened. His shoulders dropped. "This just scares the hell out of me, Vivienne."

All she could hear was the sound of crickets in the fields beyond the house. And the only thing that mattered was this moment. This moment when she could lie and say everything was fine, that she was fine. Or this moment when she could tell the truth to him and herself. She was aware of the rise and fall of her chest, of Ian's eyes watching her.

Then a single tear slid down her cheek. "I know, Ian. It scares me, too."

***

Ian froze for a split second. He'd seen Vivienne cry over her parents and her brother, but this was different. This was her own fear, her own vulnerability. He thought to go to her side, to lie down beside her and hold her, but something stopped him.

Instead, he held out a hand, asking her to come to him. Asking her to make a choice. Telling her that he knew, even in her own vulnerability, that she was strong and capable.

She eyed him for a moment, then rose from the bed and crossed over to him. Her arms wrapped around his waist as his came around her shoulders. She tucked her head under his chin and he rested his cheek on her hair. He held on for a long time, just holding her, feeling her, before he spoke.

"I wish I could tell you that nothing is going to happen to you. I wish I could say I'm not going to let anything happen to you," he said.

"But you can't promise me that, and I'd rather you be honest than make those kinds of promises."

"I wish to god I could, though."

The floor was cool under his feet. If it weren't for the threat on Vivienne, the moment would have been one of perfect peace and quiet. The crickets chirped outside, the house was still, Vivienne was solid and real in his arms. He could feel her breathing against his chest; the shirt she wore pressed against his bare skin and through it he could feel the heat from her body.

"How sure are you?" he asked.

"I don't know. I still can't wrap my mind around it. Nick seems convinced, especially after looking at the Boston files and talking to Lucas."

"I bet Rancuso wasn't happy."

Vivienne let out a soft laugh. "You can say that again. I think the only thing keeping him from storming out here is the fact that he doesn't have any leave and is in the middle of a triple homicide."

"I'm sorry he's caught such an ugly case, but I have to say, I think we have enough outsiders in on this already."

Vivienne drew back and looked at him. "You know there was never anything between Lucas and me, right?"

"Even if there was, there isn't now. But my guess, from the way he talked to you, is he's like a brother to you. Or more like a brother-in-law, right?"

She drew even further back in surprise. Then her eyes turned wary. He sighed and pulled her back to bed with him. Once they were tucked under the sheets, he spoke.

"I figured, he and your brother?"

Vivienne sat up on her elbow to study Ian's face. Probably looking for some sort of censure or judgment. She wouldn't find any, he wasn't hung up on people's sexuality. Well maybe Vivienne's, but that had already been established.

She let out a breath and tucked herself back in beside him. "Yes, he and my brother had been together for over six years when Jeff died. No one knew except me, my parents, and Lucas's parents. They were waiting for the "don't ask, don't tell" law to be repealed, and then were going to get married."

"And they just missed it." Ian hadn't known Vivienne's brother, but any couple prevented from getting married, only to have one die before they could, was tragic.

"They did." Vivienne was quiet for a long moment and then Ian felt her smile. "The funny thing was, Lucas was planning on it. He always said that he would walk into the bull pen after getting married, announce it to everyone at once, then tell them that if anyone had any objections they could meet him in the alley after work."

Ian laughed, he could easily see the guy doing that. "Do you think he would have had any takers?"

"I doubt it, but it would have been interesting."

Then something occurred to Ian. "When your brother died, Lucas had to mourn in private, didn't he?" Adding to the tragedy.

Vivienne nodded against him. "Yeah, he did. We spent a lot of time together right after Jeff died. A lot of folks probably thought he was comforting me in more traditional ways, and we let them think that. It was easier than anything else."

"That's why you said you were sorry for not calling him?" he asked, recalling something Vivienne had said when they'd first met Lucas in Boston. Again, she nodded.

"I don't know if I forgot, or if it was denial. But I should have called him on the anniversary of my brother's death. I know I have my whole family to count on. They know what I lost. But only Lucas's parents and I know what he lost."

Ian pulled her tighter to him. He wasn't ready to call it love yet, but the woman at his side had *something*. And whatever it was, it was calling to him, telling him that he, and she, were exactly where they should be.

"So I don't suppose there is anything we can do about my accident and you being the target of the obsession tonight, is there?" he said.

Vivienne shook her head, tickling his nose with some of her hair. "Nick can give you the particulars tomorrow. We should probably do it with Lucas on the phone, if he can get the time."

"He's going to have a hard time staying away."

"I know, but he's already skating on thin ice so, unless he wants to lose his job, he doesn't have a choice," she responded.

"Because he's taken so much time off this year?"

"And because, even when he's there, he isn't always there, if you know what I mean. For all intents and purposes, he lost his spouse. And, as if that isn't enough to deal with, he has to pretend everything is fine."

"That's shitty."

"No kidding," she agreed.

"Maybe he can come out and take my job."

Her head popped up. "You're still second guessing yourself?"

He thought about that for a long moment, then finally shook his head. "No, actually, I'm not. It's just that I kind of fell into this job and never really gave it any thought. It hasn't been until recently that I've thought about it at all. It was just something I did, like brushing my teeth and putting my socks on in the morning. I think that maybe, when this is all over, maybe I should think about what it is I want to do with the rest of my life."

Vivienne snuggled back down. "Maybe, when this is all over, we can take a trip to Tahiti and you can do all the thinking you need."

He smiled, liking the sound of that. "That your plan, DeMarco?"

She leaned forward and kissed him. "One of them, that's for sure."

He gathered her close for a moment, then grunted and rolled

out of bed, dislodging her from his arms. "I'm not going to sleep any more tonight. Why don't you get some rest and I'll watch some more of that video footage."

She eyed him from under the covers as he pulled on a pair of sweats over his boxers. "Ian?" He turned at the door. "Why don't you bring the laptop in here, and we can both watch. I'm not sure I'll be getting much sleep either."

**

The next morning, Ian and Vivienne headed to the vet to pick up Rooster. Dash had called the day before, offering to keep Rooster one more night and administer his shots this morning, rather than make Ian bring the pup back in. Ian had missed his dog the night before, but given how he and Vivienne had spent their night together, he thought perhaps the pup had been better off in the kennel.

"Have you talked to Naomi recently?" Ian asked as they made their way through town. "Not since she came out to the house when you were in the hospital," Vivienne answered.

He glanced over at her, turning left toward Dash's clinic. He'd forgotten about Naomi spending the night. "Want to tell me why she came over? Not that I mind, but since you didn't mention it, I'm curious."

She took a deep breath. "You're not going to like it."

"I don't like any of this."

Vivienne inclined her head. "Fair enough. When I got back to your place that night, something didn't feel right." She told him about her instinct and why she'd opted to call her cousin.

"What about Travis and Brian—not that I'm discounting two women together," Ian said over her grumbled objection. "But it seems to me that if you were going to rally the troops, you'd rally all of them." He fumbled with the turn signal as he made a right turn. Driving with his cast wasn't easy, but it was doable.

"Travis was out. Brian was asleep. I didn't need protection, I wanted company."

He mulled this over for a long moment as he drove. Instincts were never disregarded in his line of work. He didn't want to scare Vivienne any more, but he made a mental note to have Nick go scout around his property and see if he saw anything out of place. Which reminded him of Nick.

"Is Nick going to be in today?"

Vivienne nodded.

"Good, I want to know what he found. Exactly what he found." He gave her a pointed look.

"Hey, don't look at me. I've told you everything I know. Nick took what he found up to Sam yesterday. He might have more information today." The hint of guilt in her voice made Ian smile. She didn't need to feel guilty anymore, but the fact that she did assured him that Vivienne knew how important it was to him to know about anything that concerned her safety.

"Does anyone else know?"

She shook her head. He played a couple scenarios over in his mind then gave a quick nod. "Good, I'd like to keep it that way, if you don't mind."

He could feel her eyes on him, studying him. Slowly, she nodded. "You don't want anyone to know not just about the cause of the accident, but about what we think about you being targeted because of me."

"I want whoever it is we're hunting to think we're still chasing false scents. And, make no mistake, Vivienne, we are hunting. We know he's in my territory, we know he's close enough to know about us. That, in and of itself, narrows things down a bit," he said as he pulled into a parking spot at the veterinarian's.

When he switched the ignition off and Vivienne didn't move, he turned to her. "Vivienne?"

It took her a heartbeat or two, but she swung her gaze to his. "I hadn't thought that far ahead, Ian." He didn't know what she was talking about, and it must have shown on his face. "I mean, I get Nick's theory about me being the target, although I still find it hard to believe. But even accepting that, I hadn't let myself think about what that really means."

Ian clumsily unclipped his seatbelt and turned to face her. Taking her hand in his good hand, he raised her palm to his lips. He knew where this was going and it wasn't going to be easy. Not for anyone, but especially not for someone like Vivienne who "fixed" things for other people, who based her career and life around helping to bring closure and some sort of peace to everyone she worked with.

"If he's here," she continued, looking straight out the front window. "And you were a target, then anyone close to me could be a target." He felt her hand contract in his in protest of what she herself was saying.

But she took a deep breath and shook her head. "But that's not right. If he's obsessed with me and it's sexual in nature, it makes sense that he'd only go after you."

Her eyes met his again and she added, "So, the good news is, most people around me are safe. The bad news is, you're not."

He thought about going all macho and saying he could take care of himself. But for him, the number one priority wasn't keeping himself safe, but keeping Vivienne safe. She'd object if he told her this so he said nothing on the matter.

"The other good news is that he's on my turf now," Ian added. "He may have dumped one body here and killed one woman when we weren't on the lookout. But we are now. And while I may not know everything there is to know about police procedure, believe me, I know how to hunt."

Vivienne's eyes searched his and Ian knew some of the feral, primal emotions he felt were clearly displayed on his face. But he hadn't been lying and he hadn't been talking about hunting deer.

She nodded, leaned forward, and brushed a kiss across his mouth. "I'm glad you're on my side, Ian."

"I can say same the same for you, Dr. DeMarco." She gave him a small smile and squeezed his hand before opening her door and sliding out.

They liberated a lively Rooster from the kennel and, after dropping him off at Ian's parents', headed back into town. When they entered the station, Wyatt was filing some paperwork and Carly was in an office on the phone.

"Hi boss, Vivi," Wyatt said, closing a file drawer. "Had some paperwork from last night to finish up."

"Anything I should know about?" Ian asked, taking off his jacket and hanging it up on the rack outside his office. He was never a big fan of his uniform, but even with his arm in a half cast, he much preferred this short-sleeved uniform to what he'd had to wear in the desert.

Wyatt shook his head and his eyes trailed to the cast. "How's it feeling?"

Ian shrugged as Carly exited the office. "Carly," he said with a nod. "Anything new we should know about?"

"No, not since last night. Daniel stopped by early this morning to talk to Nick, then left for Albany. Nick's upstairs doing something, and Naomi popped by earlier and brought everyone some bagels and mochas from Frank's. What's the plan for the day?" Carly asked.

"We need to get the timelines up on the board, or in the computer so it can graph it out for us. After that, let's see what happens," Ian answered.

He ushered everyone upstairs where they found Nick hunched over at one of the tables—a folder in one hand, a pen in the other—madly scribbling something. He looked up at their arrival, but did nothing more than offer a gesture of acknowledgment before turning back to his file.

Grabbing a mocha and ignoring the bagels, Ian turned to the board. He wanted timelines, knowing they would help establish a pattern and, when they caught the guy, would help establish guilt. But the name of the game had changed and Ian hadn't been making nice when he'd said he was hunting. All his old instincts kicked in and he could feel the familiar sense of anticipation growing, his senses sharpening, and his focus honing in. Up until now he'd been playing defense. That wasn't the case anymore.

After making the appropriate comments and spending enough time on the details, Ian excused himself and, asking Nick to accompany him, headed back down to his office—ignoring Vivienne's questioning gaze.

"Viv told you," Nick stated as soon as the office door closed behind him. Ian stared at the other man. Nick cocked his head.

"The man is a dead man, he just doesn't know it yet," Ian said.

"You were very good at your job, weren't you, guv?"

Ian inclined his head. "Yes."

"So what now?"

"Now, I want you to look into Brian, Travis, and Vivienne's Uncle Mike," Ian directed.

One of Nick's eyebrows shot up.

"After she told me last night, neither of us were going to go back to sleep, so we watched some more video. All three of them were at the university; all three of them were at the fundraiser."

"What does Viv have to say about that? Surely she noticed?" Nick asked.

Ian wagged his head and sat down. "Her uncle sometimes guest lectures at the university, Naomi and Brian do security for it, and Travis was scouting."

"And the fundraiser?"

"It's one their whole extended family was involved in." Ian's voice was flat, and judging by Nick's expression, he found it about as convenient as Ian did, but a knock at the door prevented him from saying anything. Ian sighed, then called for whoever it was to enter.

"The information on the two houses you requested," Carly said, holding up a file and stepping into the office. "One is owned by Simon Willard. He's a widower and an author. The other is owned by Timothy Howell. He's unmarried and a master wood-worker," she added, handing the documents to him.

Ian flipped the file open and scanned the information. He could see Willard coming up on Naomi and Brian's radar. If he was a famous author, he probably did writing tours and traveled around. But a local woodworker? And then he saw it. Timothy Howell volunteered regularly with a low income housing organization—something that could take him all over the world.

"Thanks, Carly. I'll follow up on these." She eyed them both before nodding and leaving, closing the door behind her.

"You want me to take those, too?" Nick asked, gesturing with his head to the file in Ian's hand. Ian shook his head.

"No, if our board is anywhere close to being accurate, the killing started right around the time Vivienne was seventeen. I want you to look into all the people who might have known her since then. Not people she met in the last five or ten years, but people who have known her that long."

"Ah, guv, you know Viv started college when she was sixteen, right?"

Ian blinked. He hadn't known that. He knew she must have started early in order to have finished everything by the time she was twenty-eight, but he hadn't realized it was that early.

"Shit."

"She turned seventeen a few months after she started," Nick offered. Ian looked up.

"So maybe it was someone she met her first year?" he suggested. Nick lifted a shoulder. "Maybe."

"Then find out." Ian issued the order easily. "Look at her professors, the kids in the classes, see if any of them crop up in her life over the years. If he's obsessed with her, I'd have a hard time believing he's stayed completely in the shadows all these years."

"Right, got it. Look into three of the people Viv trusts most in her life as well as her entire college class. When shall I report back?"

Ian met the man's sarcasm with a flat look. "It's Vivienne."

Nick sighed. "I'll see what I can do. Call in some favors. I assume this is between you and me?" Ian nodded. "Don't you want to know about the shots fired at your Jeep?"

"Not unless it's going to tell me who this son of a bitch is?"

Nick frowned. "Probably not, but it does tell you he's a good shot."

"Military background?" Ian asked.

"Possibly."

Ian considered this. It would be easy enough to add it to the list of factors to consider, and he told Nick as much. Nick seemed to agree and didn't put up much fuss, so within two minutes, the agent was out the door, headed somewhere more private to do his digging. And Ian was left in his office with only a file and the sounds of Vivienne and his officers moving around upstairs.

***

Vivi looked at the murder board, at the women's faces, their names, and the times and dates of their deaths. Something niggled in her mind, but she couldn't get it to focus into a coherent thought. And, since she'd agreed to keep the others in the dark about her possible involvement, she couldn't talk it out with anyone. On a sigh, she gave up and hoped that, in trying not to try so hard, it might come to her.

She picked up her cell and dialed Naomi. "How's the recognition program running?" she asked without preamble when her cousin answered.

"Well, hello to you, too. I assume, since you didn't call last night, Chief McStudly kept the boogeyman away. Not that I was worried."

But she was, Vivi could tell by the tone of her voice. "I'm sorry I didn't call you yesterday. It was a long day, to say the least." She felt an almost overwhelming urge to tell her cousin everything, but calling on years of training, she managed to bite her tongue. "But I'm back at the station and I was hoping your miracle computers might have come up with something?"

"Mmm, maybe," Naomi answered, as Vivi heard the clack

of the keyboard in the background. "Brian was double-checking some things, but he should be done in an hour or so."

"Is he there with you?" Vivi moved to the window facing Main Street and looked down on the small town. And frowned. Daniel was walking up the street. She glanced at her watch. It was only nine o'clock. According to Carly, he'd gone to Albany that morning—to be back already would have made it an awfully short trip.

"Hello-o?" Naomi's voice cut into her thoughts.

"Huuh, oh, what did you say?" Vivi asked.

"I was saying that Brian stepped out for a little while. Not sure where he went. I saw Travis this morning. I think he went to some bar last night, intent on scouting, but maybe had a bit too much to drink. Anyway, he was going to head down to New York today and will be back tomorrow."

Vivi heard Ian's footsteps on the stairs and saw his head appear over the rise. Turning her back to Carly and Ian, who'd started talking quietly, she continued her conversation with Naomi.

"Okay. What are your plans?" she asked her cousin.

"Vivienne?" She turned around at Ian's voice. At the look on his face, she froze.

"Naomi? I'll call you back. Or you call me when Brian gets back. I have to go." Not taking her eyes from Ian, she ended the call.

She saw him swallow before he spoke.

"We have another body."

CHAPTER 21

VIVI GESTURED TOWARD THE STAIRS with her head. "Tell me about it on our way there." And in an instant, she and Ian and his two officers were back down in the main station room, gathering their tools of the trade and a few extra items Vivi thought they might need. When Daniel walked in, they were headed out. Without asking, he turned and walked with Carly, climbing into the backseat of her police car as Wyatt slid into the front.

Vivi and Ian went to his Jeep and as soon as they exited the parking lot, he began telling her the sparse details.

"It's Meghan from the ice cream shop."

Vivi's heart broke. "How? When?"

He shook his head. His good hand clenched and unclenched the steering wheel while his casted hand lay in his lap, his fingers curled tightly over the edge of the plaster. "We don't know. All we know is she was at work the day before yesterday. The shop was closed yesterday so no one thought anything of it."

"What about her mom or the baby?"

Again, Ian shook his head. "I don't know, Vivienne. I don't know." He made a fast turn onto one of the county's innumerable dirt roads with Carly right behind them.

"And who found her?" Vivi asked.

"Rich Caston. He owns a construction company but has a lot of property. He and one of his boys were up four-wheeling this morning and found her in a gully."

She could tell Ian didn't know much more; there wasn't anything more to say. Within minutes, they were bouncing up a track intended for the much smaller ATVs, but Ian was so focused, Vivi doubted he noticed.

She was out of the car before Ian had even put it in park and jogging toward where an older man stood waiting for them. His eyes were cast down and his hands gripped his worn hat. He looked up when Ian and Vivi approached.

"She's down there," he said quietly with a gesture behind him. Vivi walked to the edge of the gully and looked down. With Ian beside her, she took in the body of the young woman.

Lying naked on her stomach, it looked like Meghan had been rolled down the hill. Vivi looked at Ian to point this out, to point out they'd want to protect the crime scene, but his eyes were already tracking up the hill in recognition of the same idea.

Vivi turned her attention back to Meghan, her arms were raised above her head, one leg bent out. Bruises marred her backside, but there were no obvious fatal injuries. Vivi started to head down the hill. Ian stopped her with a hand on her arm.

"I need to get down there," she said. "I'll go first, scout the area, and then you can come down with a camera." Ian looked at her and the surrounding area, as if assessing the threat to her, then let her go.

With caution, she made her way down the hill—looking carefully, every step of the way, for evidence or anything that might tell them something about what had happened here. When she reached the bottom, she stilled about two feet from Meghan's head and studied the area up close. Her eyes fell to Meghan's wrists, which bore the same signs of shackling, then traveled up to her elbows. Her arms were splayed in such a way that Vivi could only see the insides of her elbows and not the outsides, not the part where they had found the slivers on Rebecca. Vivi was focused on the soft skin of Meghan's inner arm, lost in thought, when she froze.

"Vivienne?" Ian called. By the worried tone of his voice, he must have sensed her changed state. She said nothing, but continued to stare, not sure if she had seen what she thought she had. And then, again, she saw it.

"Jesus," she shouted and stepped toward the body. Kneeling down she felt for a pulse. "I think she's alive, Ian." He was beside her in an instant, waiting for her to determine one way or the other.

When she felt the faint pulse under her fingertips, everything seemed to jump to Mach speed. As if from a distance, Vivi heard her own voice confirm the presence of a pulse. She heard Ian barking orders and together, bracing Meghan the best they could, they turned her over. A shock blanket made its way down to them. Daniel was at Vivi's side, offering assistance. Their crime scene would be shot to shit, but nothing mattered more than keeping Meghan alive.

What seemed like forever passed before an ambulance arrived. Vivi and Daniel, with help from Ian and the EMTs, moved Meghan to the gurney as gently as possible. Heedless of the fact she wasn't licensed to practice in New York, she started giving orders to the EMTs even as they rushed Meghan into the ambulance. Climbing in after them, Vivi caught one last look at Ian. His face was grim, he was pulling out his cell and he was pushing Daniel in after her. Then the doors closed, and she focused on the woman before her, praying that she could shift the delicate balance of life in the young woman's favor.

Meghan managed to stay alive during the ambulance ride. Still at her side, Vivi monitored her vitals as the EMTs unloaded her. When they entered the emergency department, nurses flocked to Meghan's side, and Vivi felt herself being pulled away. She fought to stay but slowly became aware of a hand on her arm, holding her back. She looked down at the slender fingers then up into the face of Jesse Baker, the woman she'd met just a few days before. Ian's friend.

"We have a doctor waiting for her. Ian called. Dr. Martinez is very good."

Vivi blinked, then regained her senses. Of course she couldn't take care of Meghan. Aside from the practical issues, like not having hospital privileges, she was an ME, not an emergency doctor. She could handle herself in an emergency situation and had many times before. But with a qualified emergency doctor on hand, it made more sense for her to turn over the reins. But there was one thing she couldn't let go of. She met Jesse's gaze head on.

"Meghan may have been raped in addition to what was done to the rest of her body. She is a crime scene. Can you tell Dr. Martinez?"

Jesse seemed to regard Vivi for a moment before the import of her words sunk in. Then she nodded and turned toward the room Meghan had disappeared into, talking as she walked away. "I'll tell Dr. Martinez, and we'll put a sexual assault nurse in there to gather and document evidence. We have the locker downstairs. We'll be sure everything is taken care of by the book."

Vivi let out a small breath as Jesse disappeared. It was the best she could do without being in there herself. Now all she could do was wait.

"Dr. DeMarco?"

Vivi turned to find Daniel standing behind her looking shell-shocked.

"They'll do the best they can, Daniel," Vivi told her student. She didn't know what Meghan's chances were. It hadn't looked good in the ambulance, but then again, Vivi knew Meghan was a fighter.

"I don't understand. She doesn't look a thing like the other victims. And—"

"Daniel," she cut him off with a look of warning. No one knew they were after a serial killer and she didn't want it to get out, not like this. His eyes widened and she felt his pain. Apparently, Daniel had been spending more time than she knew with the pretty, young store owner.

"Viv, luv." She looked up to see Nick striding toward her. Taking her somewhat aback, he pulled her into an embrace. "Ian doesn't want you alone," he whispered in her ear.

She'd almost forgotten a killer was obsessed with *her*. With an understanding nod, she pulled away.

"Vivienne?" Jesse came back down the hallway toward them.

All three stood with bated breath. "I don't have any information on her yet, they're just getting started," she spoke as soon as she reached them. "But I made it clear what you need and they'll do their best. Believe me, they'll do whatever they can to help you investigate who did this. It may be a while, so I wanted to offer you a room to wait in. We have one that isn't being used right now."

They all agreed and shortly she, Nick, and Daniel were ensconced in a small room that somehow managed to feel a million miles away from the hustle of the emergency room. Knowing Ian wouldn't call her, wouldn't want to interrupt her if she were working on Meghan, she pulled out her cell and dialed him.

"Is she alive?" he asked without preamble.

"For now. She made it to the hospital. Jesse made sure that everyone working on her knows to do the best they can to save her and preserve any evidence. Now we're waiting. What about her mom and son, Ian?"

"Marcus and Carly are on their way over to their house. I'm not sure why her mom didn't report her missing, since I don't think there's a day that goes by without Meghan helping her out," Ian answered.

"I don't like the sound of that," she said.

"Me neither, but I'm not going to invite speculation. We'll have to wait until we hear from them to know. Nick there?"

Vivi mumbled an affirmative then asked about the scene.

"There are tire tracks we're casting. Maybe a couple of boot prints, but it's hard to say how old they are. Could be from the owners. I think they might be, but we'll see."

"Why do you think they are from the owners?" she asked.

Ian let out a deep breath. "I think whoever dumped her pulled up to the edge of the gulley, opened the doors, and tossed her out. Judging by the tire marks, that is."

Vivi recoiled at the callousness of the image. She'd seen a lot of ugly things in her work, and for good or for bad, it still got to her. With nothing much more to report on either end, they hung up, promising to call if anything new developed.

"She doesn't look like any of the victims," Daniel repeated. He was slumped in a chair, eyes cast down, shoulders hunched.

Vivi looked at him, then at Nick, who was watching the younger man. Nick's eyes transferred to hers, and she gave him a small nod.

"You're right, she doesn't."

Daniel's gaze shot straight to Nick's. "Then, why her?" he demanded.

"Because he's crazy. His mind is fucked up. She was in the wrong place at the wrong time. Who the hell knows?"

It wasn't what Daniel wanted to hear. And when his eyes shot to Vivi's, she saw the boy she met all those years ago. She wished she could fix this for him, but this was the world he was walking into. He'd already lost his sister, and while she didn't want him to get used to it—no one should get used to it—he would need to figure out how to cope. They all had to figure it out at some point.

"I'm going to get something to drink." Daniel stood abruptly then stalked out. With a look at Nick, Vivi finally sat.

"Is this his first real case? First time he's seen a body somewhere other than the dissecting table?" he asked.

Vivi thought of the remains of Daniel's sister they'd found and shook her head. "No, but this is the first active crime scene he's been to. It doesn't help that he has a bit of tendre for Meghan."

After that there was nothing left to do but wait. Daniel came back with his coffee, and every now and then Nick pulled out his cell. But other than that, the room was silent for close to two hours. Just as Vivi was contemplating going in search of someone, her cell rang. Glancing at the number she answered.

"Where are you?" she asked.

"Do you need me?" Ian replied.

"No, we're fine. Still waiting. No word."

Across the line Ian was silent for a heartbeat. "I called in some assistance from the sheriff, and we're almost done with the evidence collection. I'm going to leave Marcus and Carly here to finish up and head back to the station. There are a few things I want to check into, and I need a better computer than my cell phone."

"Sounds good. I'll give you a call when we hear something, and we can figure out where to go from there. Any news on her mom or the baby?" Vivi asked.

"Yeah, well, at least that was good news. Meghan was supposed to head down to the city for a seminar associated with her online classes. She'd arranged for a neighbor to come in and care for both her mom and the baby, which is why she wasn't reported missing," Ian answered.

"So they're both okay?"

"They're not physically hurt, but as for okay? This is going to be rough on that family given everything else going on." Vivi couldn't agree more and hoped that, like in a lot of small towns, the community would come together to help. But that, of course, remained to be seen.

"Let me talk to Nick." Ian's voice interrupted her thoughts, and with a look, she handed her cell over. Nick's gaze shifted away from hers.

"Yeah…no…yeah…you have what I have…no. Yeah, of course I'm staying. We'll call before we leave." Nick ended the call and handed Vivi's cell back without a word.

"Any interest in telling me what that was about?" she asked.

"No." He didn't hesitate. There were a hundred and one reasons Nick might not want to talk about his conversation with the Deputy Chief of Police, but Vivi trusted Ian to tell her what she needed to when she next saw him. She sat back and looked at her watch. It was hard to believe less than two hours had passed since they'd all rushed out of the police station. She sighed.

"So you're going to take 'no' for an answer?" Daniel's tone was bordering on a belligerence Vivi knew was based in fear.

"Yes," she said.

His jaw ticked. "Well, I'm not. What did Ian say? What does he have?" He directed his questions to Nick.

"Nothing that concerns you, Daniel." Nick answered.

"If it involves this case, if it involves Meghan, it's my concern," Daniel insisted.

Nick yawned and stretched his arms overhead before answering. Vivi thought his nonchalance was a bit overdone, even if he was trying to make a point.

"Look, Daniel, I like you. You seem like a good kid, and you're one of Viv's students, so you can't be all dumb. But this is your first rodeo, you don't get to call the shots, you don't get to demand information," Nick said.

"Like hell—"

Daniel cut himself off when Jesse knocked on the door and entered the room. Vivi figured the woman sensed some tension, because she stopped a stride into the room and cast her eyes across all three of them before focusing in on Vivi.

"You're the only law enforcement officer officially on this case, according to Ian, so you're the one we'll talk to. What I can say to all of you is that her mother was well enough to make it here and is sitting with her now."

"So Meghan's alive?" Daniel stood. The hope in his voice was almost painful.

Jesse inclined her head. "Alive, but in a coma. That's all I'll say. Dr. Demarco?" Jesse opened the door and gestured Vivi out, leading her down the hall to another small room where a woman was removing her scrubs and washing up. Her head came up as they entered.

"Abigail," Jesse said, "this is Dr. Vivienne DeMarco. She's working with Ian on trying to sort out what happened to Meghan. Dr. DeMarco, this is Dr. Abigail Martinez. I'll leave you two to talk."

When Jesse was gone, Vivi turned to Dr. Martinez.

"Call me Abigail, please. I'd shake your hand, but, well, you'll have to forgive me," she said as she stepped on the foot pedal and started to wash the soap off her hands and forearms. "Meghan suffered severe trauma to the head as well as an attempted strangulation. The trauma was a beating—maybe by an object, but more likely, in my opinion, by a fist—that was concentrated on her face."

"Was she raped?" Vivi asked.

Abigail shook her head. "Surprised us, too. Given the state she was in when she arrived, I was all but certain we'd find evidence of rape. But we didn't. She's pretty banged up in a couple of other places—her left arm, both sides of her rib cage, and her lower spine."

"Damage from the strangulation?"

"Yes, but nothing she can't recover from. Like I said, it's the head trauma we're worried about. The beating was so severe she has a broken jaw, two shattered cheekbones, and a fracture that originates at her right temple and runs up to the top of her skull. And there is significant swelling around the brain," Abigail supplied.

She dried her hands and turned to face Vivi. "Even if she makes it, we won't know for a while if there is any permanent damage," she added.

"And what chances are you giving her?"

Abigail's head cocked to the side. "I wouldn't tell her family this, but maybe thirty percent. As you know, these first few days will tell us a lot about her ability to recover from the injuries, but we'll still have to wait to see if she comes out of the coma."

Vivi considered what she was hearing, and for more than the obvious reasons, she didn't like the sound of it. In front of her, Abigail Martinez must have been thinking along the same lines as she let out a deep sigh.

"Whoever did this to her had a lot of rage. Maybe at all women, but I'd bet my retirement there was something specific about Meghan." She paused, then shrugged, and shook her head. "I'm not a psychologist, but if you ask me, anytime a person's face is attacked the way Meghan's was, there's got to be some underlying psychosis there."

Vivi was a psychologist and couldn't agree more. So, after making arrangements to collect additional evidence from Meghan and gather the evidence already collected by Abigail and her team, Vivi thanked the doctor and made her way toward Meghan's room.

In the hall, Nick met her with an evidence collection kit and a promise to be nearby. She gave him a brief overview, making sure he understood the seriousness of Meghan's condition so he could convey the information to Daniel. And while she knew there was always the chance she might find evidence on Meghan that could help break the case open, it was with a heavy heart that she prepared to violate the young woman's body one more time in the name of justice.

As Vivi approached the room, she spotted Jesse gazing in Meghan's window, a look of sadness etched on her face. In silence, Vivi came to her side. Looking in, they saw a thin, still form lying under blankets with a myriad of wires protruding from underneath, all attached to machines that beeped, moved up and down, and flashed numbers. At Meghan's side was a frail-looking woman sitting in a low-slung chair. Wrapped in a big sweater, the woman sat still, her back straight, her hand grasping Meghan's. Her mother. Vivi sighed.

"Do you have children?" Jesse asked.

Vivi thought about all the times she and Ian had been together in the past few days. They'd always used a condom, but stranger things had happened. "No," she shook her head. "You?"

"Yes, two boys. My oldest is a junior in high school this year, but when he was a freshman, Meghan was a senior." Her voice was distant but strong. "He didn't know her well but when she got pregnant, well, it's a small town and an even smaller high school. Everyone knew."

"That must have been hard for her," Vivi said.

"I'm sure it must have been, but she never let that show in public. She settled down and was always sweet and kind. Believe me, I'm the last person to condone teenage pregnancy, but I've always respected her, how well she handled everything. I know when my kids were young I didn't parent with as much grace as she does."

"I'm sure she's had her moments."

Jesse gave a soft laugh. "I'm sure she has, but now that I'm on my own, I have even more respect for her. My husband was killed in a fire in his office building a year ago." The last was added almost as an aside, like she'd just remembered she wasn't talking to someone born and raised in the area.

"I'm sorry. I haven't lost a spouse, but my parents and my brother both died last year. Separate incidences, one car accident and one insurgent attack in Afghanistan." It felt strange to say the words aloud to a virtual stranger. But though Vivi was still aware of the wrenching pain that gripped her when she thought of her family, it was tempered by something. By what, she didn't know, but looking at Meghan and then at Jesse, maybe, she thought, maybe she didn't have to feel so alone.

"I'm sorry," Jesse said softly.

Vivi lifted a shoulder. "Yeah, me, too. But we do the best we can do."

Jesse nodded in understanding. "Yes, we do. And if Meghan is even a tiny bit the fighter I think she is, she's going to pull through. And she's going to want to see whoever did this to her brought to justice."

"So, I should go in and do my thing?"

"I already told her mom you would be coming in. She's expecting you."

CHAPTER 22

IAN HEARD THE DOOR OPEN and looked up from his desk to see Vivienne and Nick walk in. The day was still young from an hours perspective, but from an emotional one, well, it had run the gamut and both of them looked it.

"In here," he called. Without a word, they veered from the stairs and walked into his office, closing the door behind them.

"Did Wyatt make it down to the hospital?" he asked.

Vivienne nodded and handed him a brown paper bag—he could feel the warmth from the grilled sandwich inside. "I figured you hadn't had lunch either," she said, opening her own bag. "I gave Wyatt everything I collected and what the hospital did too. He and Daniel are running it up to Albany now. Daniel was supposed to be there already, but he stopped for breakfast before heading up this morning, then saw us leaving the station and hopped in the car with Carly and Wyatt. The wisdom of allowing him to do that is something I'm still debating," Vivienne added as she sat down with a heavy sigh and took a bite of her sandwich. Nick came to stand behind her, giving Ian a look.

"I don't suppose there was anything obvious?" Ian asked, opening his lunch. He hadn't thought much about food since leaving his house this morning, but now that it was in front of him, he was starving.

Vivienne shook her head. "I wish. We won't know exactly what we found until Sam can run all the tests, but I didn't see anything that struck me immediately as being a key piece of evidence.

It's possible, in the scrapings I took from her nails, there might be skin, but I couldn't tell."

"And how was she when you left? Did her mom make it in?" Ian asked.

"Yes, she was there. Very quiet woman. Meghan was hanging in there. It will probably be a while before we understand the full extent of her injuries," Vivienne answered.

"Before she can tell us anything." Ian put his sandwich down and rubbed a hand over his face.

"If she can tell us anything," Nick interjected. "So, where do things stand, guv?"

Ian rose from his chair and walked to the window. The world on Main Street was going about its business, but he knew in most of those shops, shops owned by locals, people were talking.

"Marcus and Carly are trying to trace Meghan's movements prior to the attack, interviewing neighbors and the like," Ian answered.

"What about her car, Ian?" Vivienne asked.

"We found it at the train station in Riverside. Her mom said she was supposed to take the train, so we went there first and there it was. No signs of a struggle."

"Do you think she was snatched from the station?"

Ian considered Vivienne's question, then lifted a shoulder. "Who knows? And before you ask, there is no surveillance, so no video to look at. It's possible she actually made it to the city and was taken from there."

"You know what train she was supposed to be on, I assume you're looking at video from New York?" Nick half asked, half suggested.

"The train went into Penn Station and yeah, we have a request for the video. We should have it later today or tomorrow morning, and we'll go from there."

"Yay, more video," Vivienne said. Her tone might have been dry, but Ian didn't doubt she would be the first one to volunteer to review it. He let his eyes drift back to Main Street. An older woman was coming out of the bank with a little girl in tow. They stopped to talk to a man who owned one of the shops a few doors down. The woman laughed and the little girl pulled on her hand, wanting to go. Ian knew it was time.

"How do you both feel about a field trip?" he asked, turning to Vivienne and Nick. They glanced at each other before shrugging their acceptance.

"I want to check out Simon Willard and Timothy Howell."

"Who are they?" Vivienne asked. Ian looked at Nick before answering.

"They own the houses your cousins thought we should look into. We're trying to dig up more information on them, but I think it's time for a visit. Given their proximity to where Rebecca Cole was staying, we can fudge our reasons a bit."

"You want me to go because you want to see how they'll react to seeing me. See if they give anything away," Vivienne said, crumpling up her wrapper and shoving the remains of her lunch back into the bag.

He hated that she didn't even ask. That she just stated it, like a fact. He hated even more that he was asking her to do this.

"That's a bit daft, guv, don't you think? Dangling her out there like that?" Nick's chummy words didn't hide his opinion.

"Nice of you to care, Nick. But that's why I want you there. I can take care of Simon or Timothy, but if anything does go south, I want you there to protect Vivienne."

"How about protecting her by not putting her on the doorstep of a possible suspect?" Nick retorted.

"I don't need protection," she interjected. Both men snorted. She rolled her eyes. "Oh right, this is one of those ridiculous guy things, isn't? Is this the 'I must protect the woman' version or the 'I need to know you're taken care of to do my job' rationale? Which one are you aiming for here, Ian?"

"Probably both, Vivienne."

She sighed. "At least you're honest."

"Why don't I protect her right here, and you go interview the two men?" Nick offered.

"Because he needs to see how they react when they see me. And he probably wants my professional opinion, too," Vivienne answered for him.

"Not to mention, I'd like for you to meet them and see if either seems at all familiar," Ian added.

Nick opened his mouth to say something, then closed it and shook his head. "This is seriously messed up, but you know I won't let you go alone, so let's get it over with."

***

Ian took in the house of Timothy Howell as they pulled up the driveway. A dog came bounding out of one of the outbuildings, reminding him to call and check on Rooster. His pup had seemed fine when they'd dropped him off at his parents' earlier, but the accident had still been an ordeal for the young dog.

"Nice view," Nick commented, as he exited the car. Ian and Vivi joined him beside the vehicle, and from where they stood, they had an uninterrupted view of the front of the house where Rebecca Cole had stayed. They were far enough away to foster a sense of privacy, but it would be easy to see when someone was home and, with binoculars, what they were doing.

A man wearing overalls and wiping his hands on a rag walked out of the building the dog had just come from. He was of average height with light brown hair that was receding a bit at the front.

"Can I help you?" he asked as he approached the group. Ian watched Howell take them all in. And he didn't miss how the man's gaze lingered on Vivienne for a moment too long.

Ian stepped forward. "Timothy Howell?"

"Yes."

"I'm Deputy Chief of Police, Ian MacAllister and these are my colleagues Dr. DeMarco and Agent Larrimore." Howell nodded and looked at Ian.

"I'm sure you've heard about the woman we found a few days ago. She was staying at that house," he pointed behind him as he spoke.

"Sure, everyone's heard about that."

"Given your view of the place, did you ever see anything, hear anything?" Ian asked.

"Hear anything? I'm a ways away, I doubt I would hear anything," Howell answered.

"Sounds travel around the valley sometimes," Ian offered.

Howell frowned. "No," he answered with a shake of his head. "I saw lights on and off, of course, but nothing that unusual."

"No cars, trucks, or vans coming or going?" Ian pressed.

Howell shrugged, and his eyes darted to Vivienne before he answered. "Not really. I travel a lot this time of year, building houses down south or in warmer climates. I'm usually here more in the summer, running workshops, teaching classes, that sort of thing."

"You ever been to Boston?" Ian asked.

The question seemed to take Howell by surprise, which was Ian's intention.

"Of course, hasn't everyone been to Boston? It's only a few hours away."

"And New York?" Ian saw suspicion creeping into Howell's eyes, and the man physically drew back.

"Of course."

"When was the last time you were in the city?" Ian pressed again.

"Is this the point in the conversation when I ask if I'm a suspect?"

"Routine questions," Ian replied to Howell's obvious irritation.

"I was in the city a few days ago. I got back the day before yesterday. I was working on a townhouse down in Tribeca," Howell answered, his voice curt.

"Do you recognize this woman?" Ian asked Howell with a

gesture to Vivienne. Out of the corner of his eye, he saw Nick straighten.

Howell looked at Vivienne, his eyes trailing all over her. Ian's skin was crawling, but he knew he showed no signs.

Finally, Howell looked back and answered. "No, but she does remind me of my ex-wife a bit. Same dark hair, same," his eyes went back to Vivienne for a fleeting moment, "same build."

"Thank you, Mr. Howell. Will you be around if we have any more questions?" Ian stepped back.

Howell shrugged. "I'm scheduled to be here for the next month."

"Good," Ian nodded. "We'll be in touch."

Back in Ian's Jeep, Vivienne was the first to speak. "Well, that was gross."

"Gross, but useful," Ian commented. "Unless the guy is a very good actor, he's never seen you before. On the other hand, he did say you look like his ex-wife, and there didn't seem to be any love lost there," he added as he turned out of Howell's driveway

"Ian, there are two more houses you can see from here. I know they weren't on Naomi and Brian's list, but maybe they're worth checking out?" Vivienne pointed out as they passed a break in the trees that allowed them a different view.

Ian scanned the area and saw the two pieces of property she was talking about. He didn't know who currently lived at the locations, but he knew one used to be the family farm of a friend of his dad's.

He phoned in to the station and asked Carly to look up the names of the owners. As they made their way to Simon Willard's house, she filled them in on what was popping up on her computer.

"Both houses are owned by out-of-towners," Carly said. "Both are from New York. The house up on Cobleskill Road is owned by Schuyler and Lilly Adams." They heard the click of the keys on her keyboard before she continued. "Looks like he's a lawyer and she's a designer, interior. There is a picture of them on his website, they look to be in their mid-to-late-fifties. No kids are mentioned in the bios of either. Big donors to the children's cancer research hospital."

Sometimes it was amazing what they could learn just running a public search.

"Thanks, Carly. What about the second house?"

Again they heard the keyboard click away before she answered. "Kyle Reardon and Roger Blake. One's a doctor, the other an architect."

"A couple?" Nick asked.

"Kyle's bio says he likes to spend time with his partner at their summer home in the Hudson Valley but doesn't mention who that is. Roger's bio says nothing."

"I'd wager yes, then," Vivienne said.

"And so, unlikely to be someone we're looking for," Ian added, saying goodbye to Carly and ending the call.

"Let's talk to them anyway and see if we can find anything out. Maybe they saw something," Nick interjected.

Ian agreed and turned into Simon Willard's long driveway.

While they waited for him to open the door, Ian scanned the area from the porch. Like Timothy, Simon had a clear view of the house where Rebecca had been staying, only his was from the side, looking toward the garage doors. His view also took in the field and tree line where they'd found her body. If he wasn't the man they were looking for, maybe he had seen something.

Ian was about to mention this to Vivienne when the door swept open, revealing an older gentleman with a long face and brown hair gone mostly gray, wearing a sweater vest over his long-sleeved shirt. Rapidly the man's eyes went from him to Nick then landed on Vivienne. Simon Willard straightened away from the door.

"Vivienne DeMarco, what a surprise."

CHAPTER 23

IN A SPLIT SECOND, BOTH Ian and Nick flanked Vivi without making a sound. She studied the man but for the life of her couldn't place him.

"Do we know each other?" she asked.

Simon Willard chuckled. "No, dear, of course not. But my wife, my late wife, was a big fan of yours. If she were still alive, she'd be speechless seeing you here." It seemed to dawn on him that something was unusual about this visit, and he frowned. "Not to seem inhospitable, but what are you doing here?"

Ian took a half step forward and introduced himself. "How do you know Dr. DeMarco, Mr. Willard?"

The man's fingers gripped the door handle, but he answered. "My wife was one of her professors her first year in college. I remember Claire coming home and telling me about the sixteen-year-old prodigy in her class."

"What did she teach?" Vivi asked.

"Psychology, for years. Professor Claire Downs. Perhaps you remember her?" he suggested.

Vivi did, she remembered her well. "Her class got me interested in psychology. Until then I was pure, hard science. She was an excellent teacher." She looked at Ian as she spoke, making sure he understood the man was telling the truth, at least about this.

Simon beamed. "She'd be thrilled to hear you say that."

"I hadn't heard she'd passed away. I'm sorry to hear that," Vivi offered her condolences.

Simon inclined his head. "Thank you. We moved here about

five years ago, ironically because I had cancer and we wanted a slower, quieter life. I'm clean as a whistle now, but she passed away from cervical cancer."

"I understand how you might know of Dr. DeMarco from your wife, but may I ask how you recognize her now?" Ian asked.

"Oh, Claire followed her career out of curiosity for years. She used to say a student like you," he said with nod in Vivi's direction, "came along once in a lifetime. So she kept track of you. And when you started giving your own lectures, she would go. Occasionally, I went with her. In fact one of your lectures was our last trip into Boston before she died."

Ian seemed to be weighing all this, while Nick stood silently beside her. He hadn't moved an inch but she could feel the tension radiating from his body.

"Can I ask what this is about?" Simon finally asked when Ian offered nothing.

"You have a good view of the farm across the way," Ian said. Simon nodded, waiting for more. "Do you know the woman who used to stay there?"

Simon swallowed, "The woman who was found in the well a few days ago, right?"

Ian nodded.

"Well, I saw her on occasion," he said. "Saw the lights from the house, of course. But no, I can't say I knew her."

Simon Willard wasn't telling the whole truth. He didn't strike her as the rape, torture, and kill kind of man, but then again, she'd seen stranger things.

"You seem unsure about that, Mr. Willard," she pressed.

He opened his mouth to say something, closed it, and then opened it again. "I didn't know her," he repeated.

"This is a murder investigation, Mr. Willard. Even if you didn't know her, if you know something you should talk with us," Ian said.

Simon's eyes went to Ian. A look of sadness passed through

them before he spoke. "Would that I could tell you something about her death, Deputy Chief MacAllister, but I know nothing."

For some reason, maybe it was the tone of his voice or the way his hand seemed to slump on the doorknob, but Vivi believed him. He might not be telling them the truth about everything, but she did believe that he didn't know anything about Rebecca's death.

They thanked him, and once seated in the car, Ian expressed the same sentiment. He asked Nick to look into the old man to tie up loose ends, but no one thought they would get any more out of Mr. Willard.

Vivi called to check on Meghan on their way toward the main road. When she hung up, both men were looking at her, Nick over the back of his seat and Ian through the rearview mirror. She gave a shake of her head, there was nothing new to report. Their visits had netted nothing, Meghan was still in the ICU, and they had two dead women and no plan.

"Why don't we swing by those other two houses before we head back to the station?" Vivi suggested. Both were weekenders but maybe someone was home. With no other better plan, Ian headed in the direction of the closest of the two houses.

Kyle Reardon and Roger Blake's home was empty, but as they pulled up to Schuyler and Lilly Adams' property, they spied a truck parked in the open garage and a man, much younger than mid-fifties, digging a hole in the garden. Beside him sat a sapling ready for planting.

He stopped what he was doing, straightened, and watched as they parked and climbed out of the car.

"Mr. Adams?" Ian said as they approached. The man was much too young to be the same Adams Carly had mentioned, and his eyes were watchful, darting between the three of them.

"Yeah," he answered. He had one gloved hand on his shovel and the other on his hip. He didn't look threatening, but he certainly wasn't welcoming either.

"Mr. Schuyler Adams?" Ian clarified.

"Nope, wrong Adams. I'm Joe Adams, Schuyler's son."

Nobody stepped forward to shake hands. "Can I help you?" he asked after a moment of silence.

"We're investigating the murder of the woman who used to stay at that house," Ian started waving toward the home that was visible, barely, from where they stood.

"Yeah, I heard about that. I think it's the first time I've ever heard of something like that happening up here," Joe said.

"You'd be right, we haven't ever seen a murder like that before. How long have you been up here?" Ian asked.

Joe's eyes dawned in recognition of what was happening, which told Vivi two things—he had past experience with law enforcement and he wasn't all that surprised to find them at his door. She expected one of two reactions from him based on the expression on his face, flat denial of everything or hostility. But he surprised her by taking an altogether different tack.

"I just got here this morning." Just the answer, nothing more.

"Where did you come from, Mr. Adams?" Ian inquired.

"Brooklyn, where I live."

"And have you been up here much in the past few weeks?"

He brushed a piece of hair off his forehead with the back of his hand. "No, I haven't been up here all winter. My stepmother, Lilly, asked me to come up and check on the house and garden for her. Some of her family were here last week and they aren't known for being overly considerate. She wanted to make sure everything was in order before she comes up for Memorial Day weekend with my father." His sudden chattiness could have been nerves, but Vivi sensed it was more relief, relief at knowing that the time frame they were talking about was something he could account for.

"So, someone was staying here recently?" Ian clarified.

He nodded. "Lilly's two sisters and her mother. They usually come up every spring and shop, go to the spa, pretend they are more than what they are."

"Meaning?" Vivi prompted.

He shrugged. "They aren't very nice to Lilly. She's made a different life for herself than the rest of her family. Better in some ways, in others, well—" Whatever he was going to say, he stopped himself. "Anyway, her family has always mooched off of her, expected her to pay their bills, buy their clothes, provide them with vacations and things like that because she can afford it."

"Because she married your father?" Nick asked.

"Yes, no, well, in part, yes," Joe answered. "She was actually left quite a bit of money from her father's side of the family. They left it to her and not to the rest of the family, which is why they feel entitled."

"And she feels guilty enough to let them feel that way," Vivi finished. Joe nodded.

"And then she married my father, and, yes, money is not an issue for them," he added.

"Do you know when they were here?" Ian asked, bringing them back to the issue.

Joe shook his head. "I thought they were supposed to be gone a few days ago, but when I got here, I think they might have just left this morning."

"What would make you think that?" Nick asked.

"There were water beads in the shower, a few crumbs on the counter. Nothing too out of place, or nothing I wouldn't expect knowing someone was here, it just seemed like they were here more recently than a few days ago is all."

Vivi took a mental note of this, then filed it away. They could easily check up on that fact, especially since Ian was already asking for their names and contact info. Joe went into the house to look it up. A few minutes later he came jogging out with his gloves tucked in his pocket and a piece of paper in his hand.

"Those are quite some cuts you have on your hand," Nick commented, as Joe handed Ian the sheet of paper. His casual comment was anything but.

"I work with rocks, wood, saws, and anything else that someone might want in their garden. I can get pretty banged up," Joe answered, shoving his hands in his back pockets.

"You a landscaper?" Ian asked.

Joe nodded.

"You've mentioned your stepmother. Does your father know you're up here?" Ian asked.

Joe's jaw tightened before he answered, but Vivi would wager his reaction wasn't in response to Ian's suspicious tone.

"It's possible he knows. We're not that close," Joe answered.

"Or close at all," Vivi posited.

"Or close at all," Joe agreed with a curt nod. "My father is, well, he's not an easy man to like. My life isn't what he expected of his only child, and to be fair, in my younger years I tried my hardest to make it that way."

"But now?" Vivi pressed.

Joe shrugged. "Some people aren't meant to get along, he and I are some of those people."

"How long have he and your stepmother been married?" she asked.

"It will be ten years June sixteenth."

"That's pretty exact," Nick said.

"That's because the day they got married was the day I quit drinking and doing drugs. Lilly is, she's too good for my father, but I'm glad she doesn't think so because, without her, I have no doubt I'd have been dead long ago."

"More of a parent than your own father?" Vivi said.

"More of a parent than most parents these days," was his answer.

"And do you recognize Dr. DeMarco?" Ian asked. The question, coming from out of the blue seemed to give Joe pause. He studied Ian before his eyes slid to her. His gaze didn't crawl over her, like Timothy Howell's, but stayed focused on her face. A small frown touched his lips.

"You look a little familiar but I don't think we've met. Or at least not since I've been sober. Have we met?" he asked. She suspected the concern she heard in his voice was more about what he might have forgotten than about what it might mean if they did know each other.

Vivi shook her head. "Not that I can remember."

Joe studied her for another long moment before turning back to Ian. "Anything more I can help you with? I need to get this tree in today," he said, with a gesture to the sapling.

Ian shook his head and they made their way back to the car. As they drove away, Vivi glanced back to see Joe watching them, hands on his hips, unmoving, and alone.

"What do you think?" Nick asked.

Wanting to give Ian the space to answer, she sat back and said nothing. Several minutes passed before he spoke.

"His animosity for his dad is pretty clear, but I didn't get the sense he was lying about anything. We can easily call his step-mother and verify his story. I want to check out the cousins, too."

"And the fact that he thought someone else was in the house recently," Nick added.

Ian inclined his head. "That, too."

"You ruling him out?" Nick asked.

Ian shook his head. "At this point I'm not ruling anyone out until we have some definitive evidence that they aren't involved. I'll have Carly run some more background info on all of them."

"You may want to ask Naomi and Brian for help on that, too," Vivi suggested. "Carly can search the official sites, but if you want someone to dig around the net, legally," she added, "they can do it better and faster than anyone else. And since you aren't likely to get warrants for any personal records or information, their computer skills might come in handy."

"We'll see," was all he said.

Vivi suggested heading straight back down to the hospital, but Ian wanted to drop Nick off at the station. When they arrived, they found Naomi and Brian waiting for them in the parking lot.

"Nick, why don't you run Vivienne back down to the hospital. Marcus is already there and can bring her home when she's done," Ian said, surprising her.

"My cousins are here. Why don't I take a look at what they brought, then we can head down together?" And, even before he answered, she knew what he was going to say. He was back to not sharing.

"I'll take care of it," Ian said, closing the door on any discussion. "I have access to all the facial recognition databases that we can run the pictures through and I can work with Carly on the background information on the men we talked to today. Why don't you head down, check on Meghan, then maybe, if there's time, head up to the lab to see how Sam and Daniel are coming along? I know you say he's good and I don't doubt it, but it would make me feel better to have your eyes on the evidence collected from Meghan."

It was late in the day, and having her run up to Albany wasn't what Vivi thought Ian really wanted to accomplish with his suggestion. "Ian, what's going on?" she asked.

"Nothing, I just want to use our assets the best way we can. Keeping you here to do work Carly and Wyatt can do doesn't make a lot of sense," he responded.

And again, she could tell he wasn't telling her everything. She studied his green eyes for a moment, and in them she saw not defiance but a question. She didn't know what was going on but she knew he was asking her to go with it for the time being.

Confused but trusting him, she nodded. And before she knew it, she was parked in Nick's car and headed south to Riverside.

***

"Where's Vivi going?" Naomi asked as her cousin sped away with Nick.

"We have a file from the facial recognition program," Brian interjected. Ian looked at Vivienne's cousins and hoped like hell Brian wasn't involved in any of this. Glancing at the file they'd handed him, he wondered if they'd included their own pictures. They didn't know he'd already seen them in all three of the videos. He supposed if they'd removed their own pictures, they might have a problem. But even if they were included, that still wouldn't answer the question as to whether or not Brian was a killer.

Ian took a deep breath and flipped the file open. In it were nine eight-by-ten pictures. Three men and two women he didn't recognize, plus Naomi, Brian, Travis, and Vivienne's uncle, Mike. At least they hadn't tried to hide anything.

"Come in," he said with a gesture toward the station. They followed him in as he led them, not upstairs, but to his office.

"Everything is upstairs, why are we coming in here?' Naomi asked. Ian didn't say anything until he was standing behind his desk. He laid the folder down and looked up. Both twins were looking at him expectantly. Vivienne's safety was the most important thing to him, but even so, he debated how blunt he could be with her family. He was about to say something when Brian spoke up.

"He has to question us, Nano," Brian said, using the nickname for Naomi Ian had heard him use before.

"Us?" she said, although the surprise Ian heard in her voice sounded somewhat forced.

"Well, probably more me, since they know it's a man involved in the attacks. Is that right, Ian?" Brian said.

"That's ridiculous," Naomi responded, crossing her arms, doing a good impression of being put upon.

"Yeah, it is, but he doesn't look like a man who is going to take no for an answer. And my face, my picture is in that file," Brian pointed out.

Naomi's eyes narrowed on Ian's face, challenging him. He didn't mind and he wasn't going to back down.

"Can I ask where you were four weeks ago when Rebecca Cole went missing?" he asked Brian, not backing down.

Brian's eyes skittered away, and Ian's heart sank. "I, uh, I can't do that?"

"And might I ask why?" Ian crossed his arms over his chest.

Brian gave him a self-deprecating smile. "Okay, this is going to sound very cliché, but it is the truth. I can't actually tell you where I was because it's a national security issue."

The only reason Ian gave the statement any credence was the goofy grin Brian was unsuccessfully trying to fight. He looked like a kid who couldn't believe what he was saying. He didn't look like someone trying to hide something.

"Is there anyone who can confirm you were on the job without providing more details?" Ian pressed. Brian and Naomi shared a look.

"Here," Brian said, writing down a number with no name. "Call and ask for Justice."

"Justice?" Ian repeated.

"I know, terrible name, isn't it? I thought it was made up when we first met, but it isn't," Naomi said.

Ian's eyes bounced from twin to twin. Reaching for the paper, he looked at the number. He couldn't place the country code but it was definitely foreign. "Do I need to account for any time difference?"

Both the twins smiled and answered simultaneously, "No."

He took a deep breath. "Okay, what about three years ago then?" He rattled off the dates between when Jessica Akers went missing and when the road was repaved.

"May I?" Brian asked, lifting his ever-present laptop. Ian nodded and Brian popped open his computer and began keying something in. Within a minute, he sat back.

"I was in Okinawa and Hawaii during that time. We were testing some communications systems."

"That proof?" Ian said with a nod toward the computer.

"Yes, for what it's worth. Our invoice to the government with credit card charges noted. You can check with them too, if you want to be certain I'm not making this up. I also have the trip report but I would have to redact it before I showed it to you so it's probably not worth it," Brian said.

Ian's gaze slid over the invoice and he scrolled down to see the accompanying charges. If it could be believed, Brian was nowhere near the eastern seaboard when Jessica Akers was kidnapped and killed.

"I had to look into it," Ian said, raising his eyes to meet Brian's. The perennial cheerful twin grinned.

"No worries, mate. I don't like the idea of you thinking I might be capable of doing what was done to those women, but I appreciate that you have to do your job and, to be honest," Brian added, confirming what Ian had suspected, "it's not like it wasn't expected. Naomi was just testing you, seeing if she could get you to back down. We're both glad you didn't, especially considering all the women look like Vivi and were even born at the same time."

"Brian!" Naomi admonished. "You don't need to worry him."

Brian raised an eyebrow at his sister. "You don't think he hasn't noticed? No one else on the force would know Vivi well enough to know when she was born, but you do, don't you, Ian? You know Vivi fits the profile to a T, don't you?"

For a fleeting moment, Ian thought about denying it. But what good would that do. It would be a lie and a blatant one at that. He let out a long breath and ran his good hand through his hair.

"Yeah, I do know. *We* know. Which is why I need to check on everyone in this file." He tapped the manila folder sitting on his desk.

"And why you sent her down to the hospital before she could talk with us," Naomi mused out loud. After a moment, she asked, "So, is Brian cleared now? Because if he is, we would like to help Carly do some background work on everyone else the computer found."

"You haven't done that already?" Ian asked, doubting they'd been so circumspect.

"We wanted to, but the computer just finished running the program. We figured we'd run these pictures over to you, then go back and do our own work. But you got here at the same time we did, so we haven't had a chance," Brian answered.

Ian took a good, long look at the siblings, weighing whether or not he could believe what they'd told him, about the pictures but also about Brian's whereabouts. Instinct told him they were good, but he didn't want Vivienne's safety at risk because of his gut.

Without a word, he sat down and dialed the number Brian gave him. The line picked up and he asked for Justice. Two minutes later, his mind cleared of any doubt, he followed Vivienne's cousins up the stairs.

***

"You hustled me down to the hospital, and I didn't even get to ask what Naomi and Brian found," Vivi said into her cell as she and Nick walked into the hospital.

"Sorry about that. There were nine people who showed up in all three locations. Three men we're going to run through the database," Ian answered.

"What about the others?"

"Four are your family members and the other two are women. We may run them too, but for now we're focusing on the three men."

The elevator doors glided open, and Vivi stepped out into the ICU. "What about the folks we met today?"

"I'm going to check all of them out, too. We'll see if any of the guys show up in the system and Naomi and Brian are going to do some internet magic to see if they can find anything," Ian answered.

"Are you including Joe's father, Schuyler?" she asked, holding Nick back. She wanted to finish this conversation before they checked in on Meghan.

"Yeah, I am."

"I think that's a good call. It doesn't sound like he's in the area, but he definitely has access," she said.

"And Joe thought someone was at the house," Ian added.

"Speaking of which, any updates on Lilly Adams's cousins?"

She could hear Ian let out a frustrated breath. "No, no answer at any of the phone numbers we have for them. If I don't hear from them by tomorrow morning, I may call someone local and ask them to check up on them."

Vivi smiled. "I think that's a good plan."

Ian chuckled. "Yeah, yeah, yeah. Go check on Meghan and let me know how she is. I need to talk to Nick, but Marcus will bring you back when you're done."

"Where are you sending Nick?"

He paused for a moment before answering. "You mentioned feeling like you weren't alone the other night, when you were at my place and I was in the hospital. I want Nick to go up and check out the property. I haven't had a chance to get out there, but I think it's worth at least having a look to see if anything is out of place or disturbed."

That thought made her heart skip a beat—and not in a good way. She opened her mouth to tell him she'd probably been imagining things, that it would be a waste of Nick's time. But then reality set in.

She let out a huff. "As much as I hate to admit it, because the thought makes me sick, that's probably a good idea—and one I should have thought of earlier. If he was there and he did leave any traces, they'll be harder to find now."

"Don't be so hard on yourself. You told me Nick is good. If something is there, he'll find it. You've been busy taking care of other things."

She had, they all had. They ended the call, agreeing to talk again before she left the hospital. She hadn't taken four steps toward the nurses' station, when her cell rang again. Glancing at the number, she answered.

"Daniel, where are you?" she asked.

"I'm at the lab with Sam." His voice was tight.

"Are you sure that's a good idea?"

"Meaning?"

Vivi sighed and made a mental note to herself to incorporate more of the real world into her work with her students in the future. "How are you holding up?" she asked instead.

Daniel ignored her question. "We have the blankets and materials used during transport, surgery, and cleanup. The hospital did a good job of labeling everything with where it was collected from and during what stage—surgery, cleanup, etc. We started with the wipes used to clean her face. It was," his voice broke for a moment then he cleared his throat. "Her face took the brunt of the assault so we're going to look to see if maybe some of the perpetrator's blood got mixed in with some of hers. We're running blood typing and DNA on each swab."

That was a monumental task, but a good one. If Meghan was beaten by a fist, chances were her face was their best bet for any trace biological material of the attacker. "Can you have someone in the lab send all the photos of her to Ian's computer? I probably won't make it up to Albany tonight, but I would like to have a closer look at the pictures of her injuries."

Daniel agreed, and after making plans to talk later, they hung up. Within minutes, Dr. Martinez showed up to give Vivi and Nick an update, which was brief. Meghan was still in a coma and her condition was still serious. Vivi hadn't expected anything else at this point, but at least Meghan was considered stable.

"Her mother is here if you would like to talk to her." Dr. Martinez offered.

Nick shrugged and spoke, "I need to go do a few things. I assume Marcus is standing guard?" he asked Dr. Martinez, who nodded. Turning back to Vivi, he added, "I know Ian called in some help from the Riverside police, and they'll be providing someone to relieve Marcus in about an hour. Why don't you go see Ms. Conners and then head back with Marcus. I'll leave as soon as you're in the room."

If Dr. Martinez thought it strange that Nick was lurking and basically playing hot potato with her by handing her off to Marcus, she didn't show it. She turned her gaze back to Vivi, who inclined her head in agreement.

Before entering the room, Vivi looked in to see Meghan's

mother, right where she'd left her earlier. Looking small, frail, and utterly lost, she sat beside her daughter.

Vivi gave a soft knock before sliding the door open and stepping inside; once it snicked back shut, the only sound in the room was the beeping of the heart monitor. Vivi looked at Meghan again, her face swollen and bandaged. She had an oxygen tube under her nose, but at least she was breathing on her own.

"She's a much better person than I ever was," Ms. Conners said, her voice muted with fatigue and sorrow. "She's stronger, smarter, more loving. You should see the way she loves Davey."

Vivi walked to Meghan's side and rested a hand on her arm, waiting for Ms. Conners to continue, knowing she needed to talk, to keep her daughter well and happy, if only in her own mind.

"And, good lord, is she a worker. Works harder in a week than I did most of my life. I don't know where she got that from. Not me and definitely not her father." She paused and Vivi watched as a single tear fell from her eye. "Or maybe she did get it from us. From knowing what she didn't want to be."

"You know she was taking classes right?" Ms. Conners asked, finally raising her eyes. Vivi nodded. "She ran that shop and was almost done with her associate's degree. She was going to get her bachelor's degree next. She *is* going to get her bachelor's degree next," she corrected herself.

"And what does she want to do?" Vivi asked.

A ghost of a smile touched the older woman's lips. "Ice cream. She's good at it. Have you ever had it?"

Again, Vivi nodded and agreed.

"She wants to get a degree in business and grow her ice cream business. Maybe not quite the next Ben and Jerry's but something like that."

"She was on her way to New York City, what class was she taking down there?" Vivi asked.

Again, a faint smile crossed Ms. Conner's lips. "That was a design class, interior design. It counts toward her degree, but isn't part of the business degree. She took it because she plans to open more stores sometime down the road, and she wanted to know about design so she could do it herself and not hire others. 'Mom,' she used to say, 'No one knows better than me what I want my customers to experience when they come into my shop.' So she took the class." Meghan's mother's voice cracked and faded.

Vivi looked down to give her a measure of privacy. Tracing a line down Meghan's arm, Vivi paused at the marks left by the bindings. They looked a little different than what they'd found on Rebecca, but then again, Rebecca's body had decomposed enough that a comparison wasn't really viable. Vivi gave a mental sigh. The good news was Meghan had survived; the bad news was that with a live body they couldn't get as aggressive about evidence as they could with a dead body. She had swabbed the cuts earlier, but doubted that, without more invasive techniques, they'd get enough to confirm a material match in the kind of bindings used on the victims. But Vivi didn't mind giving that up as long as Meghan lived. She knew no one did.

"Ms. Conners?"

The woman looked up.

"I'm going to head back to the station now. Please, if there is anything I can do to help you or your family, will you let me know?" Vivi reached into her pocket and pulled out a business card.

Meghan's mother stared at the card for a moment, then reached for it. "You're with the FBI?" she asked, reading the title. "I didn't know Ian had called in the FBI."

"I consult with them, and I was on this case as a favor to Ian before Meghan was involved," Vivi answered.

"You think whoever killed that poor woman in the well did this to my daughter?"

Vivi had assumed someone had spoken to her about this, but judging by the look on the woman's face, this was all news to her.

"We think it's a possibility, yes. There are a number of similarities that lead us to believe we are looking for one person."

Ms. Conners's eyes went back to Meghan for a moment then flitted back to Vivi. "She wasn't supposed to live, was she?"

Like Meghan's mother, Vivi's eyes traveled to Meghan's battered and bandaged face. Her mind flashed back to that morning, to finding Meghan's bruised and brutalized body lying naked in the gully. The blood pressure machine whirred to life, beeped, and revealed a steady number. Meghan might have been left for dead but she was fighting.

CHAPTER 24

THE STATION WAS BUZZING WITH activity when Vivi and Marcus arrived. Sharon had gone home for the day, but they could hear feet shuffling on the floor above, chairs being moved around and scraping against the hardwood, and voices. Hoping Ian and his team had found something, she and Marcus trudged upstairs. The toll of the day was definitely wearing on her.

"Vivienne," Ian said, as she stepped onto the landing. "Meghan?"

At his question, everyone paused and looked at Vivi. "Same, serious but stable. She's a fighter though. I bet we'll know more tomorrow."

"God, I hope so," Carly muttered.

"Amen to that," Brian added.

The room wasn't all that small but was packed with people. In addition to Carly, Ian, and Wyatt, Naomi and Brian were there. With her and Marcus joining the crew, and Nick coming in right behind them, it made for tight quarters. Even so, the murder board was tidy and next to it stood a new one, covered with pictures of men. Seven of them to be exact. Three were the men she'd met with Nick and Ian earlier in the day. The other four were identified as Schuyler Adams—Joe's father—Mike Ross, Kirk Hancock, and Lee Grant.

"I take it these other three are men from the videos?" Vivi asked, stepping closer to have a good look. Ian came up beside her and confirmed her assumption. He stayed silent as she examined each picture, trying to recall if she knew them, if she'd met them anywhere before.

"Ross and Hancock look a little familiar, but it might be because I met them at the fundraiser," she said. "Grant isn't ringing any bells, but that doesn't necessarily mean anything. Where are you with the background searches?"

"A few showed up in the system and we can talk about that in a minute," Ian said. "We were just wrapping up for the night here, but I want to go over everything with you when we get home. Marcus?" The officer turned, as Ian called his name. "Have Carly catch you up and then you guys can head home for the night. Wyatt, you're done, so go home and get some sleep. It's going to be a long day tomorrow, folks. Daniel and Sam should have some physical evidence by ten or eleven, or so they've promised, and I think we all need to try to get as much rest as we can before then."

He paused and made a point of looking at each one of them, to make sure they not only heard what he was saying but were actually listening too. Apparently satisfied, Ian continued. "Tomorrow morning we'll reconvene here and review all the evidence against what we dug up today on each of these men. Based on that, we'll decide if we have a viable suspect and enough to take to a judge for a warrant."

To Vivi's surprise, even Naomi and Brian started putting away their computers. Then again, she didn't doubt that they would head straight back to The Tavern and pick up where they'd left off. Which reminded her, "Have you guys seen Travis?" she asked.

Both her cousins shook their heads. "No," Naomi said, sliding her computer into a bag. "But he said he was going down to New York today. I think he found some places up here for one of the films he's scouting for and wanted to meet with the director. Why?"

Vivi shrugged and handed Brian the folder he was reaching for. "No reason. I just haven't seen him much and was wondering what he was up to. I feel kind of bad that he was sent all the way out here to check on me and, other than breakfast, I haven't even been able to give him the time of day."

"You didn't ask us to come here, the parents sent us," Brian interjected. "And besides, last time I saw him, he was happy as a clam. He's come up here a few times with his parents, but he was saying this is the first time he's really been able to take the back roads, if you know what I mean."

Vivi knew exactly what Brian meant and gave a small laugh. Aunt Mary, Travis's mom, was *not* a "chill" kind of person and Vivi was pretty sure the word "relax" was not even in her vocabulary. She kind of envied Travis at this moment and wondered what it would be like to be driving around looking for pretty places rather than studying a murder board. Like she'd been trying to do after the debacle in Seattle.

"Anyway," she said, grabbing a stack of files from Ian, "If you see him tomorrow morning before you come in, ask if maybe we can try to catch lunch or something."

Naomi and Brian nodded as they finished gathering their things. Once they'd headed out, Vivi realized the place was empty—with the exception of her and Ian. She watched as he made a last pass around the room. His shoulders sagged a bit under his uniform and, as her eyes traveled down his body and over his clothes, wrinkled and muddied from the activities of the day, a wave of fatigue washed over her. She yawned.

"Tired?" he asked, walking toward her.

"I think it's sympathy fatigue. You look like you could use a good night's sleep."

Ian stopped in front of her. After tucking a strand of hair behind her ear with his good hand, he rested his palm against her neck, his thumb tracing her jaw.

"I don't think I've ever told you how beautiful you are."

His comment threw her for a moment. It was out of the blue and spoken so matter-of-factly that the raw honesty of what he felt when he looked at her was made clear. Not one to handle compliments well, had it been less sincere she would have turned away in embarrassment. But as it was, she offered him a smile and touched her lips to his.

"Thank you," she said. And taking a moment, she leaned against him as his cheek came to rest on her head.

"We have a long road ahead of us, Vivienne," he said, his voice quiet. "It feels like the momentum is picking up, like we have more leads now, but we still have a long way to go before whoever is doing this is locked up for good."

She nodded against him. It was true, even if he made an arrest tomorrow, it could be months before a trial. Evidence had to be sorted, compiled, reviewed, and evaluated. It *was* a long process, much longer than the television shows portrayed. And she was glad he didn't expect a magic bullet. But even so, living just one day thinking someone was obsessed enough with her to kill other women and target those close to her had taken a toll on both of them. For her, for Ian, and for all the women who had died, Vivi hoped tomorrow would bring some progress, some real progress, and they might find themselves a real, viable suspect.

"Guv?" Nick popped his head in. "I'd say I hate to interrupt, but I don't, so I won't. I want to be caught up on what you lot found today."

Vivi stepped away. Catching her eye, Ian cocked his head in question. She shrugged in response.

"Did you find anything today?" Ian asked.

"If I did, does that mean you'll invite me home for dinner and a debrief?" Nick asked.

"Maybe." Ian crossed his arms.

"Maybe," Nick answered. Ian glared at him. Nick sighed.

"Yes, I did. All jocular antagonism aside, we do have some things to talk about."

Vivi watched as Ian held Nick's gaze as some form of silent, male communication occurred. After a moment, Ian turned his gaze back to her; then he let out a long breath.

"You think there's enough food in the freezer or should we stop and pick something up?"

***

Ian watched Vivienne as she walked out of the bedroom, phone to her ear, Rooster at her heels. They'd stopped at his parents' to pick up the dog, then headed home for a quick shower and change of clothes before Nick joined them. Vivienne was now on the phone with Sam, getting an update on where he was with the evidence.

"You two seem awfully cozy," Nick said, taking a sip of his beer.

Ian didn't bother to answer.

"I never lived with her, you know. Close, but as you Americans like to say, no cigar."

Nice, just what he needed tonight, a reminder that the man having a friendly dinner with them had once been one of Vivienne's lovers. He didn't feel threatened by Nick, but he was feeling extremely possessive and protective of Vivienne. The protective part didn't surprise him so much, the possessive part did. He was pretty sure it was an altogether new feeling for him.

"Yeah, you fucked that one up," Ian said, hoping to close the door on where this was heading—it was not a conversation he wanted to be having.

"She told you, didn't she?" Apparently, he wasn't going to be that lucky.

Ian slid a pan of lasagna onto a pot holder on the kitchen table. "How you dismissed her and then used her theories to work a case, taking credit for them? Yeah, she told me. She may trust you as an investigator, but don't believe for a second that she trusts you as a friend."

After pouring himself a glass of milk, Ian caught Vivienne's attention and gestured with his good hand to her empty glass, silently asking what she preferred. She pointed to the wine from across the room, even as she continued her conversation, and he set a glass on the table for her. He would love a glass himself, or a beer, but not now, not while there was someone still out there after Vivienne.

"She reduced me to a school boy, you know," Nick said.

Ian looked up from dishing out a helping onto Vivienne's plate.

"I half-hated her because she's so damned smart, smarter than me by a long shot. And I was half in love with her. Like some kind of punk teenager, I couldn't handle the conflict so I solved the problem by making it go away. If she hated me, problem solved," Nick explained, taking the serving spatula from Ian.

Ian raised an eyebrow. "I hadn't realized we'd reached this level of sharing." He was pretty sure Nick was exorcising his own guilt, but as far as Ian was concerned, he was doing it with the wrong person. He didn't give a rat's ass what had been going through Nick's head when he and Vivienne had their falling out. He thought it was a dick move, but Nick's loss was his gain.

"Sharing what?" Vivienne asked, joining them at the table. Rooster followed her in and flopped his body on the floor beside her seat, looking ever hopeful for a scrap. Ian shot a look at Nick, letting him know this one was all him.

"What a fuck up I was all those years ago," Nick answered, sliding a huge portion of lasagna onto his plate.

Vivienne looked startled for a moment then turned to look at Ian—to check on him was more like it, to make sure he wasn't upset. He shrugged.

"You're here with me and not him," Ian commented.

"That's very straightforward, MacAllister," Nick drawled.

"Life's not all that complicated, Larrimore. Not unless we make it that way. Or someone else does," he added, in reference to their current situation. "Any news from Albany?" he asked, changing the subject as they dug into the meal.

"They've got DNA running on all the swabs collected from the hospital," Vivienne started. "So far about half have come back as only Meghan's. They'll be running them through the night, or rather Daniel will be running them through the night, so we should know by tomorrow if there is any blood other than hers in the mix. They focused on biological evidence today, since it takes the most time. Tomorrow, they'll start on the other evidence, like her car and clothes. They'll see if they can find anything similar to what we found on Rebecca, and of course, the car will be dusted for prints and vacuumed for particles."

"How is Daniel?" Ian asked.

"Holding up. Sam said he's a machine, but a meticulous one, which is a good thing. I think, given Daniel's past, he's probably the last person to do anything that might compromise evidence, but it was good to hear Sam's confidence in him, especially on this case." At Nick's questioning look, Vivienne filled him in on the kidnapping and death of Daniel's twin sister.

By unspoken agreement, they finished their meal in silence, and once the dishes were clean, all three made their way to the living room and sat down. The files of the men—of the potential suspects—lay on the coffee table. As Rooster dragged his soft toy and blanket into the room, Ian picked up the top folder and handed the first picture over to Vivienne.

"We'll go through all the faces Naomi and Brian found and then go from there. Your Uncle Mike was in all three videos, as were Brian and Travis." He handed her the three pictures.

"We already knew they were in all three locations, so this isn't new. Who else do you have?" She dismissed them, and though Ian had already cleared Brian, the other two were still in the running as far as he was concerned. A look at Nick told him they would talk later, and so, choosing his battles, Ian moved on.

"Mike Ross is forty years old and lives in Boston," he started as he handed her another picture. "He comes from a wealthy family and doesn't seem to do much these days but float around the fundraising circuit and hold a figure-head position at his family's business."

"Which is?" she asked.

"Wiring, but special wiring used by defense contractors. Not very glamorous, but very profitable," Ian answered.

"I think I know that name, now. I'm pretty sure Collette, Naomi and Brian's mother, has a friend with the last name of Ross. What do you know of his family?" Vivienne asked.

"Father's name is Christopher, mother's name is Leanne. He has two sisters, Susan and Jenna," Ian provided. "Do any of those names sound familiar?"

"Yes, I think Leanne Ross does sound familiar, but you could ask Brian and Naomi. Did they say anything about him today in the station?"

Ian shook his head. "No. They saw the photo but they were working mostly on the local potential suspects we have. If he was the same Ross you think he might be, would they have said something?"

Vivienne nodded. "Most definitely. If they recognized him."

He paused then asked another question. "The Ross family seems to run in different circles than families from the North End, how would the twins' mom know them?"

Vivienne gave a little snort. "Because their mother is about as Boston Brahmin as you can get. Her family was and is loaded. She was an only child so she inherited everything when her parents died. She's married to Tony, one of my dad's brothers."

"There's got to be an interesting story there," Ian said with a smile.

"My dad, Uncle Mike, and Uncle Tony are all cops, and one night Uncle Tony was walking the beat and saw some guy getting a little too aggressive with a young woman. He stepped in, and he and Collette fell in love that night and have been in love ever since. Believe me, Uncle Tony is the butt of many a family joke, especially since they moved into her family's Beacon Hill mansion after they got married. The twins were raised there. You're right it is a different world than the North End, but there you have it."

That was a new twist, something unexpected. Not that he thought it would solve the case, but it was possible Vivienne would have encountered Mike Ross at some point in her younger years. But he wasn't sure what to think about the twins not recognizing him if he was a family friend.

"Anything else about him?" she asked.

"Yeah, he applied to the police academy when he finished college. He started but never made it through. We don't have the records yet on why he didn't make it," Ian supplied.

"If he was there for any length of time, he would at least have a familiarity with weapons," Nick pointed out.

"Chances are he also hunts. A lot of families like his do," Vivienne added. "Do we know where he is now?"

"No, I'll see what Naomi and Brian can find tomorrow and we'll go from there. This," Ian said, handing her the second picture, "is Kirk Hancock. He showed up in our records because he has a military background. He's a former Marine, Special Forces. His record was minimized, but reading between the lines, Nick and I figure he probably does a lot of the same kinds of things I used to do."

"The kinds of things my brother used to do," Vivienne added.

"He's not from Boston but since he's been out, he's been consulting with defense companies, two of which are located near Boston. Back at the station you said he looked familiar to you, any more thoughts on that?" Ian asked.

Again, Vivienne studied the photo, frowning. A stray lock of hair fell forward against her cheek. He brushed it back behind her ear, earning him a small smile that shot straight to his chest. He never had any doubts about Vivienne, although he knew they both had questions—about themselves, each other, and them as a couple. But in that moment, all his questions were answered and he knew what it felt like to be certain of someone. The rest they would figure out along the way.

"I feel like I've seen his face before, but not like this," she said, holding up the picture. In it, Kirk Hancock was wearing a suit, his clean-shaven face smiling at someone with whom he was talking.

"In what way?" Nick asked.

She shook her head. "I don't know. It's the smile I recognize more than anything else."

"Any chance he was a friend of your brother's?" Nick asked. Vivienne cocked her head and studied the picture again.

"My brother did send me pictures every now and then. If you scruff him up, he'd look the sort Jeff would have worked with. Ian?" she said, raising her gaze to his. He knew what she wanted to say but wouldn't in front of Nick. Lucas would have a better idea if her brother knew Hancock. Acknowledging her suggestion, he took the picture back and said he'd handle it. Before Nick could ask what "it" was, Ian handed her the last picture.

"Lee Grant. Thirty-eight years old. He's a search and rescue professional based out of North Carolina. He has no weapons experience we can find, but he's from the rural south so chances are he knows his way around a rifle."

"He definitely doesn't look familiar," Vivienne said with certainty.

"You said that at the station, but I don't want to rule him out quite yet," Ian said.

"Why?" she asked.

"Because," Nick interjected, looking at the file of information on him. "He's been to a lot of the same disaster sites you have. Has worked with some of the same agencies. Going by this," he said, holding up the paper, "he's had ample opportunity to get to know you. Whether you know it or not."

Vivienne's eyes went from Nick to Ian, then back to Nick again before she spoke. "Fair enough," she said, handing the picture back to Ian. "You're right, I don't know him, but that doesn't mean he doesn't know me. Or think he does anyway. What else do you know, Ian?"

"He travels a lot. There is a SAR training facility in Maine where he teaches, so he's been in the Boston area. All the other areas where the women are missing or dead have all experienced a disaster of some sort or another that would require SAR assistance. We'll work on seeing if we can get anything to line up tomorrow."

Done with the men in the videos, Ian moved on to the local men, Joe and Schuyler Adams, Timothy Howell, and Simon Willard.

"I think we can rule Timothy Howell out. He's a bit of a creep, but if he taught the workshops on his website, there are more than a dozen of the women on our board he couldn't have had contact with, including the missing and murdered women in Boston," Ian said.

"How do we know this?" she asked.

"Naomi and Brian pulled up all the cached information from the past several years from his website. He does teach and work all over, but most of the dates didn't line up with anything on our timeline," he responded.

Vivienne seemed to mull this over before putting the file down and picking up the next. "Schuyler and Joe Adams?"

"Now there's a pair," Ian said. "Joe's story pretty much aligns with what he told us today. He was in the military, though, right out of high school. Didn't handle it very well and started drinking and doing drugs. He was in and out of rehab for a few years before finally getting clean for good. Since then, he's gone to landscaping school and now runs a small but successful company. He does most of the work himself."

"Healthy body, healthy mind," Vivienne commented.

"Avoiding idle hands is probably more like it," Nick interjected.

"Either way, there is nothing on record about him for the last several years," Ian continued. "Naomi and Brian dug up some Facebook pages with pictures of him. He doesn't have a page, but he has friends that do. The pictures are all benign—ones of him running the Boston Marathon, fishing with some friends, that kind of thing. No pictures of him drinking or doing anything dumb."

"Any pictures of him with women?" she asked.

"One, she was petite and blonde. The name tagged was Stephanie Moyer, she's a kindergarten teacher in Brooklyn," Ian answered.

"So, are you ruling him out?" Nick asked.

Ian shook his head. "Not yet. He has weapons training and access and familiarity with this area. He also travels a lot for his job and, as far as Naomi and Brian could dig, some of his trips aligned with our timelines of missing and murdered women."

"That's not looking good," Nick commented.

Ian inclined his head in agreement. Still "not looking good" was a far cry from being a viable suspect.

"His dad is even more interesting. Also military background, but he was Naval Academy and then JAG corps. When he got out, he practiced in Boston and made a ton of money as a criminal defense attorney," Ian said, handing her another file.

"Joe said his dad's current wife is his stepmother. What about his first wife?" Nick asked.

"She died in a suspicious car accident when Joe was ten. She came from a small town in Mississippi and wasn't exactly the kind of wife an up-and-coming attorney wanted as he climbed the social ranks."

"What were the circumstances?" Vivienne asked, closing the file.

"By all accounts, she never drank," Ian started. "Not even socially. According to the report Lucas emailed us, that was actually one of the issues between them. It was hard for him to schmooze at cocktail parties when his wife was a teetotaler. But when she died she had blood alcohol level of .12, way more than the legal limit."

"Where had she been before that?" Vivienne asked.

"At a house she and Schuyler had rented for the summer on the Cape. All three of them had been down there. Schuyler drove back early with Joe, claiming he needed to work. She followed several hours later but never made it."

"Any indication she lost it? Maybe got tired of being married to a jerk and stopped by a bar on her way home?" Nick suggested.

Ian shook his head. "A neighbor saw her leaving, waved to her as she drove away. There wasn't time for her to stop anywhere before the accident."

"And did they go through her things at the house? Did they find any alcohol?" Nick asked, sitting forward.

"They did. She was a juice drinker. There was vodka in her orange juice, both in the carton in the fridge and in the bottle she'd brought with her in the car."

"And what did Schuyler have to say about that?" Vivienne interjected.

"That she was depressed."

"That's it?" Nick asked, disbelief clear in his voice.

Vivienne made a little noise to his right. "He's a successful defense attorney. He would know that the less said the better. Let me guess, he said all the right things, cooperated just enough with the police, indicated his wife had problems other people didn't know about, but acted appropriately shocked at her death?"

Ian nodded. "According to Lucas, who wasn't the investigating officer but knows the guy who was, Schuyler's response was strictly textbook. It seemed genuine in every way, except how scripted it felt. Still, they couldn't gather enough evidence to prove anything, so the case was ruled suspicious and left on the shelf. So to speak."

"And Joe?" Vivienne raised the next obvious question.

"His father refused to let him be interviewed. And since he wasn't a suspect and was only ten years old, they opted not to press the matter."

"Any chance the father was covering for the son?" Vivienne tossed the question out.

"That possibility was raised in the report, too. According to people who knew Joe at that age, he wasn't a normal kid. What that means, I don't know. So it's a possibility, but I have a hard time believing a ten-year-old could be that devious. It seems like if a kid his age wanted to hurt his mother, there would be other ways he would do it."

And he believed that. He wasn't totally discounting the possibility that Joe was involved in his mother's death, he just didn't think alcohol would be how a kid would have done it.

"Okay," Vivienne said. "What about Simon Willard?"

"Now, he's an interesting cat. If it weren't for his squirrely reaction to Rebecca Cole's name, I would take him off the list, too. He has no record, no documented weapons experience, and Naomi and Brian found nothing to suggest any unhealthy proclivities. Not to mention the fact that he looks like he might have a heart attack if he had to carry someone up the hill to the well we found Rebecca in."

"But?" Nick said.

"But I didn't like how he reacted, so we're looking into him more. I don't think he's the doer, but he may know something."

"So that's it on the potential suspects," Vivienne said, closing the last folder and leaning back on the couch. "What about you, Nick, what did you find today?"

Nick's eyes landed on Ian, questioning what he was allowed to say in front of Vivienne. Ian realized he'd forgotten to tell Nick that Vivienne was aware of at least one of the tasks he'd given him. "I mentioned I'd sent you up on the property to have a look," Ian said, giving Nick some guidance on what to talk about, which did not include investigating Vivienne's entire life since entering college.

"A cigarette butt and a shoe imprint. Anyone you know traipsing about your property or smoking?" Nick asked Ian.

"The Caufields hunt up there in the fall, they might have been up looking for a place to put a hunting blind. The father smokes. I can call them in the morning and ask if they've been up recently," he answered. "What about the footprint?"

"Men's size eleven," Nick replied. "Even if the Caufields have been up, I doubt the shoe is one of theirs—unless they wear dress shoes?"

That got Ian's attention. Beside him, Vivienne crossed her arms and rubbed her hands as if warding off a chill.

"Dress shoe?" he repeated.

"Yes, not a leather bottom, no-tread dress shoe, but close. I took a cast and have it, with the cigarette butt, in my car to take up to Albany tomorrow. I'd wager it will be something like a boat shoe or a dress shoe with a fine, rubber sole."

"Definitely not the kind of shoes the Caufields would wear," Ian muttered.

That bit of news gave them all pause. And something to go on. It might not be much, but maybe it was something.

"I want to go to Albany tomorrow with Nick. Ian, do you mind?" Vivienne asked.

He did, he'd rather she be with him. But as possessive as he was feeling, he couldn't throw rationality out the window altogether. It made sense that she go where the evidence was.

"You want to check on Sam?" he asked.

"Mostly, I want to check on Daniel. Sam can update me, I can go over everything with him, and then Nick and I can come back and report in. Sound like a plan?" A teasing smile touched her lips and he looked skyward.

"Yes, it sounds like a plan," he repeated.

Vivienne and Nick agreed to leave at seven the next morning and, ignoring Vivienne's curious look, Ian walked Nick out to his car.

"Did you have a chance to look into her family?" he asked without preamble once the door had shut behind them. It was a cool, spring night. The air was clean and the sky was clear, but the wind was picking up and he could see a storm off in the distance.

"Probably not as much as you would like, but I think we can eliminate Mike. He doesn't travel. Rather, he doesn't fly, not even to see his daughter Kiera in LA. If he goes on vacation at all it's to North Carolina or Florida and he drives. He's never flown and as far as I could tell, has never been to New Orleans, or Seattle."

"Okay, that's good." Ian then filled Nick in on what he'd learned about Brian.

"Glad to hear that because he was a bit of an enigma to me. Lots of holes in his life, not long ones, but flights out of the country and then back in via somewhere else. If he does that kind of work for the government, that would make sense."

"And Travis?" Ian asked as they reached Nick's car.

Nick made a vague gesture with his head. "Also a bit of an enigma. He travels a lot, but it's to be expected with his job. I found nothing in his background to indicate he's anything other than what Viv thinks he is or what he portrays himself to be, but there was also nothing in there that would eliminate him from the suspect pool."

Ian thought this over for a moment before speaking. "Okay, we'll keep Travis on the list. At least we eliminated four men today, Simon Willard, more or less, Timothy Howell, Brian, and Mike. That leaves us with Hancock, Ross, Grant, and the Adams men."

"And Travis."

"And Travis," Ian repeated.

"How are you going to handle that one with Viv?"

His stomach sank. "I'm hoping I don't have to. We'll see what the lab finds and what Naomi and Brian turn up overnight. Maybe by tomorrow we can narrow the field even more."

Nick nodded and climbed into his car. Ian stood in the dark of the night, breathing in the familiar scents as he watched the car disappear down his driveway. When the headlights vanished, he turned toward his house. Inside, he could see Vivienne moving around, putting away the last of the dishes. She looked at home and comfortable.

She'd been through so much over this past year, she deserved to be safe, to feel a sense of place and belonging. At that thought, Ian felt a rueful smile tug at his mouth. Because he deserved those things, too. He didn't just deserve them, he wanted them. And most of all, he wanted them with Vivienne.

CHAPTER 25

VIVI ROLLED OVER IN BED, propped herself up on her elbow, and peered over the chest of the man sleeping next to her to see the clock.

"Relax," Ian said without opening his eyes. "I texted Nick last night and suggested you guys go to Albany after debriefing with the team. That way you can be there with them to walk through where we are. They kind of like you," he added, toppling her onto his chest. "So do I."

"I like you, too. But I could have made it to Albany and back in time for the powwow at nine," she said, pushing herself off Ian and rising from the bed.

"Maybe, but I also know Daniel is champing at the bit, and Sam will want your attention, and the cast of the shoe will need to be run through the database, and then you and Daniel will want to test the cigarette for DNA, and then, if you find it, you'll want to run it through the database to see if we have a match somewhere…"

"Okay, okay," Vivi said with a laugh. "I get your point. Now, get your lug of a body up, so we can get to the station on time."

"You love this body, admit it," Ian teased, heading for the shower. Vivi didn't answer, didn't have to, but she watched as his naked form disappeared into the bathroom. She wanted to join him but didn't. Showering together seemed like a reasonable way to save time, but it wouldn't. Instead she pulled on a shirt, padded out to the kitchen, started some coffee, and fed Rooster.

With the nighttime storm come and gone, it was a perfect spring morning. Hearing the shower running, Vivi took a moment to step out onto the front porch. Dew made the green fields sparkle in the early sun and a light fog hovered in the small valleys off in the distance. Taking a deep breath, Vivi inhaled the clean smell, realizing, not for the first time, that her decision to stay and help Ian had been a good one. He was good for her—steady, strong and, like her, flawed. He made her feel a part of something good, something important. Something other than an investigation.

Since coming to Windsor, she'd started to see herself as something more than her job. Until now, she had always felt her value was measured by how much work she did, how many murderers she caught, how many families she reunited. Yes, she'd always felt connected and loved by her family, but here she was beginning to feel that her value on this planet, for the short time she was alive, was made up of many things. Her work was part of it, but so was being part of a community. And that feeling was beginning to feel like it was worth a lot to her.

"Vivienne?" Ian said, coming up behind her. "Everything okay?"

She turned her head and looked at him. Standing there on his porch, uniform on, hand in a cast, hair still damp—he made her smile.

"It's a beautiful morning and I'm glad I'm here to enjoy it." His eyes searched hers for a moment, but she didn't need him to say anything. So, with a kiss on his cheek, she took herself off to the shower.

The team was already upstairs when she and Ian walked in. Naomi and Nick were huddled over a computer. Brian, Carly, and Marcus were sitting at a table reviewing files, and Wyatt was standing by the murder board studying it. Everyone looked up when they entered the room.

"Well, the good news is, if we find a fingerprint on the cigarette, a few of our suspects will be in databases to compare it to," Nick said, starting the ball rolling. "Mike Ross would have been fingerprinted when he applied to the police academy. Kirk Hancock and both of the Adams men will be in the military database. Hancock probably has a DNA sample in there too, but depending on the kind of work he did, both his fingerprints and DNA might be blocked. From a routine match," he added when Naomi opened her mouth. Vivi knew all too well that a blocked record would be no problem for Naomi or Brian to navigate.

"And Lee Grant?" Wyatt asked, still standing at the board.

"Sometimes agencies will collect data on SAR professionals, but often it's voluntary so we should look into that," Vivi answered. Downstairs they heard the door open and close and the murmur of voices. Vivi glanced at Ian to ask if he was expecting anyone when they heard footsteps on the stairs. Ian shook his head as Sharon appeared in the doorway.

"Dr. DeMarco, Naomi, and Brian, your friend Travis is here. He said he wanted to pop by and say hi to everyone but doesn't want to disturb you."

Neither Naomi nor Brian moved, making Vivi shake her head and chuckle at their pigheadedness. The twins liked Travis, everyone did, but he was so different from them—he just wasn't their favorite person to spend time with.

"Oh, no, don't get up," Vivi said to her family members. "No need to trouble yourselves, I'll pop down and say hi."

Both twins grinned at her.

"And I'll make plans for the five of us for dinner," she added. Without waiting to see their faces, she followed Sharon back downstairs.

"Travis!" Vivi exclaimed as he came into sight. He was looking as put together as ever but was sporting a black eye. "What happened to you?" she asked, giving him a kiss on the cheek.

He gave a rueful laugh. "One of the directors I went down to the city to see is renovating his brownstone. I wanted to run a few things by him, and he wanted to work on his house, so I joined him. He was doing something on the second floor and I was below him on the stairs when he kicked a scrap of wood out of his way, and it came flying down."

She touched it, inspecting the damage. "Does it hurt?"

"When you touch it, yes."

Chagrined, Vivi stepped away. "So when did you get back?"

"Late last night. I heard about the young woman, Vivi. I'm sorry about that. Makes these seem a bit trivial," he said, holding up a white box. "Mom said when she talked to you the other day, you were missing Lucia's cannoli, so she overnighted some to me to deliver to you."

A smile touched Vivi's lips. Her family, all of them, liked to fix things with food. Taking the box with a thank you, she lifted the lid and took a deep breath, inhaling the memories.

"Meghan is strong and hanging in there," she added, closing the lid and bringing her mind back to the present. "I talked to the hospital this morning and she's still unconscious, but her vital signs are stronger."

"Good, I'm glad to hear that. Look," he said, running a hand through his hair. "I don't want to disturb you, but since I'm here and we're rarely in the same place at the same time, I was hoping we might be able to get together?"

"I was telling Naomi and Brian that we should make dinner plans—or, tomorrow's Sunday and I've heard there's a great brunch place down by Housatonic. Either of those work for you?"

"Brunch tomorrow would be better. I still have some sites to scout today and then I want to get a decent night's sleep. Should I pick you up?"

Vivi shook her head. "No, we'll come to you guys at The Tavern and then we can head down there together. You don't mind if Ian comes, do you?"

"Of course not," he answered. And, after agreeing on a time, Travis left and Vivi made her way back upstairs. Not without some glee, she informed the twins of their upcoming brunch.

"Did I miss anything?" she asked, turning to Ian who was now standing next to Wyatt examining the pictures.

"I eliminated Mike Ross," Naomi spoke up. "When Ian filled us in about who you thought his mother was, we checked with mom. Turns out he was at a fundraiser with his mother when Meghan was attacked, and they sat at the same table as our mom and dad. He was also out of the country when two of the three victims in Boston went missing. We didn't recognize him because mom and Leanne Ross aren't that close. They tend to just see each other on the circuit so to speak," she added.

"Any updates on Meghan?" Nick asked.

Vivi sighed and repeated what she'd told Travis. "Can we eliminate anyone else?" she asked.

All eyes went to Ian as he thumbed through a stack of papers in a file. Finally he spoke. "No, I don't think so, not at this point. Naomi and Brian confirmed that Kirk Hancock is in the area having meetings with legislators in Albany, we can't find Lee Grant, and we know Joe Adams is here."

"What about Schuyler?" Carly asked. Everyone looked at Naomi, who let out a frustrated breath.

"I can't seem to find him," she said. "I've looked at all his social media sites, his friends' social media sites, his law firm's site, the sites of his clients, and a few other places that I won't mention. He's had no activity on any sites, credit cards, or anything. He did have a large cash withdrawal from his bank about two weeks ago, though."

"Large enough to sustain him from then until now?" Ian asked.

"Depends on how he is living, but I'd say yes," Naomi answered.

Vivi watched Ian process this information. "Keep digging for both Grant and Schuyler Adams," he said. "The others we can find if we need to, but I don't like not knowing where two potential suspects are."

"Vivienne, why don't you and Nick head up to the lab now? We'll keep plugging away down here on all this," he said with a wave toward the board and the pictures. "By now Daniel is either passed out from fatigue or so wired on coffee that you might need to talk him down a bit."

"And relieve Sam," she added with a smile.

Ian cocked his head in agreement, but said nothing. Nick moved to her side and she caught a shared glance between the men.

"Let's go, luv. Evidence to process and all that," he said, taking her arm and leading her out before she could say anything.

"What's going on?" she asked when they were seated in Nick's car.

"Same ol', same ol', as you Yanks say. He just doesn't want you alone." Changing the subject, he asked, "Are you going to stay here when this case is over?" The question startled her. It hadn't ever really entered her mind that she would leave Windsor, which was probably an answer in and of itself. But she wasn't ready to share that yet.

"I forgot my computer at the house," she said instead. Nick looked at her, then turned right, toward Ian's rather than left toward the Taconic Parkway.

"You like it here," he pressed.

"Yes."

"And you like Ian."

"Yes." She wasn't going to encourage him.

"He's good for you, you know."

"Yep," she agreed, hoping he'd drop the subject, but she wasn't so lucky.

"He's not intimidated by you, your intelligence, and accomplishments."

Vivi thought that statement was more reflective of Nick than Ian but opted not to pursue that vein of thought. "He's an Army Ranger, they aren't that easy to intimidate."

"That's bullshit and you know it, Viv. Yeah, I'm sure it's true in Iraq or Afghanistan or Sudan or any of the other hellholes we send our troops to, but this is different and you know it."

She did know it but still didn't want to discuss it.

"He's solid, Viv," Nick continued. "He may have his issues, but he's a good man," he added as they pulled onto Ian's driveway.

Vivi studied Nick's face as they pulled up to the house. Despite his flippant nature, there was a sincerity in his tone that was unmistakable.

Vivi started to say something but stopped when her cell rang.

Hitting the answer button as she climbed from the car, she heard Ian's voice.

"Vivienne, where are you?"

"Almost to your door. I forgot my computer and wanted to pick it up before we head to Albany."

"Get back in the car and get to the Adams' place. I'm headed there right now with Marcus. Carly and Wyatt are behind us."

"Why? What's going on?" she paused at the back porch.

"They just got to processing Meghan's car, and they found a hand print."

"Joe's?"

Ian paused. "Yes, how did you know?"

In the background through the phone, she could hear the sirens of the police car, and she could all but see the two of them rushing to apprehend the man. The breeze lifted the end of her ponytail and somewhere in the distance she heard a hawk.

"Because I'm looking right at him," she said.

CHAPTER 26

To say the situation wasn't good was an understatement, Vivi thought to herself as the man emerged from the shadows of Ian's patio. With the new evidence from Meghan's car, he was the new number one suspect—the only suspect with any solid connection to one of the victims—and, judging by the look of him, he knew things were bad. His hair was matted and wet; he had dried blood from a gash on his cheek smeared down his face, a black eye, and a goose egg visible from eight feet away. In his hands he carried a gun and a pair of bloody handcuffs. But it was the wild look in his eyes that most caught Vivi's attention.

She sensed Nick moving wide and to her right. That he hadn't already shot Joe was a bit of a mystery, but maybe Nick sensed the same thing she did. Besides the obvious, something wasn't quite right.

"Ian, I'm putting the phone down now." His protests echoed across the static as she slid her cell, still on, into her pocket and focused her attention on the man swaying on his feet in front of her.

"Joe? Are you okay?" she asked, testing his response. She wasn't sure what to expect from him; between the situation and his appearance, he could have any range of responses from coming at her full tilt to falling to the ground and passing out.

His head tipped, as if he didn't understand the question. Then he took a staggering step toward her. "Dr. DeMarco."

"Stay right there," Nick ordered. She raised a hand, signaling Nick to back off.

"Joe, tell me what's going on. How did you get here?" Keeping her voice modulated and calm, she took a step forward, ignoring Nick's warning. There was something familiar in Joe Adams's eyes; call her sentimental, but she didn't feel like she was looking at a killer. Nick didn't seem to share her observation as he ordered Joe to drop the gun.

"Nick, stand your ground and let me do this," she said. Never taking her own eyes off Joe, she watched as his gaze bounced between her and Nick as if he were unsure where he was or what they were doing there. Which wasn't a good sign.

"Joe," she said, wanting to bring his attention back to her. After a moment, it worked and he appeared to settle into a stance that seemed attentive to her. In the distance she could hear sirens and knew Ian and the others were nearby. If she didn't get Joe talking now she was sure the chaos of noise and people that would soon surround them would drown—or chase—out any coherent thought in his mind.

"Joe, tell me what happened. What happened to Meghan? What are those?" she asked, indicating the items in his hands.

He looked down at his hands, then opened his palms, like a child who is caught holding something he shouldn't be.

"I'm sorry," he stammered, raising both his hands toward her. The gun was resting in his palm, the handcuffs swinging from his fingers. An offering. Not a threat. "I'm so sorry," he said. That was the familiar thing she had seen in his eyes—sadness and sorrow.

"I'm so sorry," he whispered again, motioning his hands toward her. The sirens were getting louder, Nick was talking to her, and Joe was pleading in silence for forgiveness. Maybe she was wrong, and he had attacked Meghan and those other women. Everything about the situation added up to that conclusion, and she'd been so wrong before in Seattle.

"Please, Dr. DeMarco." As Joe took a step toward her, she saw tears in his eyes, and she froze in indecision, in self-doubt.

"Viv," Nick commanded.

"Joe, did you hurt Meghan Conners?" she asked, trying to get her feet under her, trying to understand what he was telling her. She needed to know if she was wrong. Her gut still said he didn't look like a killer; everything else said otherwise.

"I—"

He never finished the sentence. A shot rang out and Joe Adams pitched forward, a look of shock in his eyes that Vivi knew she would never forget.

***

Ian watched from the cruiser as Vivienne hit the ground. Before Marcus even pulled to a full stop, Ian was out the door moving to her side, gun drawn.

"Vivienne!" He heard the panic in his own voice. He'd been in any number of tense situations, but his heart had never stuttered the way it did when he'd heard the shot and seen Vivienne drop. He heard Nick order him to stop and take cover, but there was no way in hell he was going to leave her out there. Trusting Nick and the others to cover him if need be, Ian reached her side and dropped to cover her.

"Vivienne? Are you hit?" Even as he shielded her from god knows what, he was running his hands over her body checking for any injuries.

"It's not me, Ian. Ian!"

Her voice penetrated the haze of his mind and he pulled back to look her in the face.

"It's not me, Ian. The shot got Joe. I dropped on instinct. I'm fine. Well, fine as I can be, knowing someone is out there shooting at us. I assume it wasn't you or one of the team."

He heard what she was saying, even understood it, but the truth was that nearly everything else was drowned out by the tremendous relief flooding every inch of his body and soul knowing she was okay.

"Ian." She gave him a little shake. "Are you okay?"

He blinked. "Of course, I'm fine. I'm pretty sure you took

about ten years off my life and I feel like I'm about to throw up, but other than that and the fact that there is another shooter out there," he acknowledged, "I'm fine."

"Okay, then maybe we should find some other cover?"

Of course they should. And he should have of thought of that. Assessing the situation in a flash, he noted Nick behind one of the cars, Joe Adams lying head toward them on the ground, a pool of blood seeping onto the grass, and Marcus and Carly also safely behind the squad car. His patio was to their left. Ian offered a silent question to Vivienne and she nodded. He called to Nick to cover them then grabbed her hand. The two of them lunged up and bolted toward his house.

Shoving Vivienne behind him, he tucked her up against an external wall. No shots rang out.

"Nick?" he called out.

"A single shot fired from the woods. It hit Adams in the back. Can you tell if he's dead?" Nick answered back.

Ian felt Vivienne peer around from behind him. She didn't like being there, but he was not going to let her into anyone's line of sight. "There's a lot of blood, judging by what I can see from here," she said to Ian. "It's hard to tell where the bullet hit, but if he is alive and we don't get that blood to stop flowing, he won't be for long."

There was an ambulance waiting for them at the bottom of Ian's driveway. He'd had Marcus call for one when he heard Joe Adams was at his house. But he didn't want to call it up the driveway until they knew the area was clear. He relayed Vivienne's opinion and the information about the medics to the team.

"Nick?" Ian called.

"Ready when you are, guv," came the reply. That he didn't need to ask what they were going to do spoke volumes about how much Ian now trusted this man.

"Marcus, Carly, cover us. We're headed into the woods. Once we're there, if it looks clear, call the ambulance up," he barked the orders out. And then, speaking to Vivienne, he added, "Once we're clear, go do your doctor thing and see if he's savable. I don't really care one way or the other, but it's cleaner if we have him around to confess. Do you want my backup gun?"

He felt her shake her head behind him. "No, I've got one," she answered, reaching down to an ankle holster. For a brief moment, he allowed himself to smile.

"That's kind of hot, you know," he said.

She let out a soft laugh and nudged him. "Unknown shooter in the woods, suspect bleeding out—focus, MacAllister."

"I have to wonder why I've never seen that before, I mean given that we've been living together and all."

"You don't want to know, at least not while you're wearing a uniform."

"And I can guarantee the next time I'm out of this uniform, I won't care."

When she laughed at him again, he knew then and there that, when this was all over, it would be just the beginning for the two of them. They were good together, right together. There was no other way to describe it.

"Get back to work MacAllister. And be safe."

He turned and gave her a quick kiss before signaling to Nick and barking another order to Marcus to leave their radios on. A few seconds later, he was running toward the woods with Nick to his right. At the edge of the tree line, they paused and listened. Hearing nothing, he motioned Vivienne out to tend to Joe then turned to Nick. Entering the woods together from about where they estimated the shot must have been fired, they fanned out. Moving silently into the thick, the two men looked for any signs of movement or retreat—including broken branches or footprints.

Ian estimated they were about three hundred yards in when he lost sight of Nick. He wasn't all that worried, knowing the man could take care of himself, but still, thinking it might be better to stay together, he paused. Straining to hear any sounds that didn't belong, his heart rate kicked up. He and Nick were quiet, but not that quiet, and he should at least be able to hear Larrimore making his way through the woods. But he heard nothing.

Taking cover in the newly budded ground shrubs, the peculiarity and the familiarity of the situation hit him. Not in a million years would he have thought to find himself hunting like this—hunting a human—in his hometown, on his own property. And yet, other than the foliage and the humidity, it was the same thing he'd done for years in the service. The instincts came roaring back and he'd never been more grateful.

With adrenaline coursing through his veins, his movements became all but silent as he made his way toward where he and Nick had first split. About a hundred yards back he picked up Nick's trail and started to make his way toward his partner. He paused to listen every few steps, occasionally picking up what he thought might be the sound of branches and leaves being brushed aside.

Catching an unfamiliar sound, Ian halted mid-step. His foot had barely touched the ground when he heard Nick grunt and two shots ring through the woods.

"Larrimore!" Ian shouted, breaking cover.

"Here," came the strong answer. "Whoever he is, he's down," Nick added.

Hearing those words, Ian no longer cared about making his presence known and ran the remaining few yards to his colleague. Nick was standing, gun at his side, a steady trickle of blood flowing from his temple, looking at the crumpled body of a man.

"You okay?" Ian asked.

"I have a hard head. He hit me with a branch after I disarmed him, but I'll be fine. Any idea who that is?" he asked, gesturing toward the body. The man could have been anyone, lying face down in the dirt.

"His gun?" Ian asked, wanting to make sure that on the off chance the man wasn't dead, they wouldn't get shot at when they turned him.

"It's over there," Nick pointed with his own weapon to a spot about ten feet away. Ian could see the dark barrel buried in the leaves. "But believe me, he's dead. I all but blew a hole in his chest." Ian glanced at Nick's gun. It was definitely the caliber to do the job.

"Roll him?" Ian suggested.

Without another word, both men approached the body and crouched down. Ian grabbed the man's jacket-clad shoulder and pulled it toward him. The body flopped over and Ian stared down, more confused than ever.

"Ian?" his radio crackled on his belt. Vivienne. She would have heard the shots. She'd be worried.

"We're fine, Vivienne. The shooter, or who we think is the shooter, is down," he answered.

"You don't sound too certain about that, Ian. Is he still alive? Do you need the EMTs?" she asked.

Ian shook his head even though she couldn't see him. "No, he's definitely dead."

There was a beat of silence before Vivienne asked, "Are you not sure it's the shooter then?"

"I don't know what to think at this point. But all I can tell you is we're looking at the body of Schuyler Adams."

CHAPTER 27

STANDING IN THE HALLWAY OF Riverside Hospital, Vivi understood the annoyed acceptance she heard in Ian's voice. The news Dr. Martinez had just delivered about Joe Adams wasn't good.

"Given his injuries," Vivi stepped in to support Dr. Martinez and take the brunt of Ian's frustration, "he probably won't be speaking for a while. The bullet went through his left lung, barely missing his heart. The trauma caused his other lung to collapse, and he lost a lot of blood. If he survives, it will be a miracle. That he didn't die instantly was only because our shooter was half an inch off in the wrong direction."

Ian ran a hand through his hair. Nick was leaning against the wall looking nonchalant, but Vivi knew better. Tensions were high. They had evidence and a good suspect for the attack on Meghan, but with both Meghan and Joe not able to talk and Schuyler Adams dead, a sense of frustration over the lack of closure hung in the air. Ian liked his plans. He liked things neat and tidy. But he wasn't alone in wanting clear answers on this.

He sighed and finally looked ready to accept that it might be a while before they knew anything definite. "How is Meghan?" he asked.

Dr. Martinez smiled. "I'm happy to tell you that at least she is looking better. Not talking yet," she said, raising a hand to stave off the next question. "But she's responding to stimuli much differently today than before, and in a good way. We're more optimistic about her than we have been since she was brought in."

"At least that's some good news. Maybe she can enlighten us in a day or two," Nick said.

Dr. Martinez wagged her head. "Maybe, but in the meantime, you all look like you need to get some rest and maybe clean up," she added with a nod to Vivi who was covered in Joe Adams's blood from when she assisted the EMTs. "If you have any questions, you know you can call us anytime."

Vivi watched the woman leave and silence descended on the room, the kind of silence that was heavy with fatigue and frustration. The three of them were still in their same positions when Jesse Baker walked in several minutes later. She paused at the door and swept the room with her eyes before landing her gaze on Ian.

"Collin Grey from the Riverside police sent a couple of officers over to keep an eye on Joe Adams. I assume that's something you requested?"

Ian nodded. "We don't have the manpower to keep someone on him, so I asked for help from the other local agencies. I hope that's not a problem?"

Jesse shook her head. "Of course not, and if you let us know who's coming, we can be sure to check IDs, etc. I'm not sure what we would be able to do if someone tried to impersonate a police officer, but having our staff check IDs does add another layer of protection. We all know what happened to Meghan and those other poor women, and if there is anything else we can do, please let us know."

Vivi smiled. Community. Real community. And she felt a part of it, a part of something for the first time in a long time.

"Thanks, Jesse," Ian said. "The state troopers are going to help out, as is the Sheriff's office. Wyatt is back at the office and will be coordinating the watch. I'll have him send you a list of the officers you can expect to see."

Jesse nodded then turned her gaze to Vivi. "How are you?" Vivi knew she must look worse than she felt, with her shirt soaked in dried blood, and she said so. Jesse looked like she wasn't sure if she believed her, and in a moment of honesty, Vivi could kind of see her point. There was still too much up in the air to feel any sort of triumph for having caught Meghan's attacker. What was Schuyler's role, if any? What was Joe's tie to the other women? What was his tie to her?

"I'll be okay," she added. And she would, maybe not now, but eventually. "Thank you for asking."

Jesse's eyes went to Ian again before she nodded and left. Something in the exchange must have caught Ian's attention, because he was suddenly beside Vivi, reaching for her hand.

"We should go. Riverside PD is here, we've briefed them, and they're good. There's nothing we can do right now. Marcus and Carly are taking the evidence up to Albany, Wyatt is running more background checks at the station with Naomi and Brian, and you're covered in Joe's blood. Let's go home, you can shower and change, we'll get something to eat, and then we can head back to the station if we need to."

A smile crept across her face. They still had a lot to do, and as always, Ian had a plan.

But, several hours later, they didn't head back to the station. Instead, the station came to them. Not literally of course. But Vivi sat with her legs curled beneath her on the couch and a glass of wine in her hand, while Naomi and Brian spread a series of files out on the coffee table, and Marcus and Carly pored over the evidence analysis on a laptop. Three of the part-timers were on patrol and Wyatt was supposed to be heading home, but Vivi suspected he'd show up on the doorstep any minute. Ian and Nick were grilling dinner for everyone out back.

"We can already place Joe in the same areas as three of the murders," Naomi said.

"And we're not counting the ones within driving distance of New York, like Windsor and Boston. We figure those could be done in a day so we may not be as likely to find things like credit card statements or airline tickets. We're looking at the ones in Seattle, New Orleans, Savannah, and such."

"Where have you placed him already?" Vivi asked, taking a sip of her wine. Brian gave her the names of three women they'd had posted on their board.

"It's his blood on the handcuffs," Marcus announced. "Sam sent an analysis, and, well, it's his type anyway. And Meghan's. They're running DNA but won't have it back until tomorrow. His prints were on the handcuffs, but we knew they would be."

All the evidence was stacking up against Joe. Stacking up in a way Vivi couldn't dispute, but there were too many unanswered questions for her to feel any measure of comfort.

"I wish I knew what his tie was to me, or if it's really about me at all."

At that statement everyone looked up at her. And then she remembered she hadn't actually mentioned Nick's theory about her being the killer's obsession to anyone other than Ian. So she did, relaying Nick's impressions and their thoughts on Ian's car accident not being an accident at all.

"His tire was shot?" Carly repeated.

Vivi nodded. "Nick collected the bullet from the tire. I was planning to have a look at it today in Albany before Joe appeared at the house."

"Sam mentioned something about a ballistics test, but I didn't follow up since I didn't know what he was talking about. That'll teach me to let things slide," Marcus added in a muttered voice.

"Hmm," Naomi said, holding up one of the files.

"Did you find something?" Vivi asked.

"Maybe. Maybe something Uncle Mike can help with," Naomi suggested as she handed the file over to Vivi. "Schuyler Adams was a criminal defense attorney in Boston for years before moving to New York. His bio says he lectured at the law school where Mike lectures. Let's give him a call and see if he ever heard anything about the Adams men or even if he ever met Schuyler."

Vivi agreed and dialed the number. Putting the phone on speaker, she greeted her uncle when he answered, then filled him in on the day, and launched straight to the question.

"Do you know Schuyler Adams or anything about him?" she asked.

"I do. He was a big-time attorney for a while. The kind of guy that we cops hated but also admired. But then his wife died and something changed. It wasn't long after that, he and his son left and moved to New York. We used to guest lecture together sometimes," her uncle answered.

"Meaning?"

"Meaning the criminal law professor liked to bring in the cop and the defense attorney for a little round of dialogue for his students. Schuyler and I did it together a couple of times. Come to think of it," Mike paused. "Come to think of it, you met him once, Vivi. And his son."

Vivi sat up. Ian and Nick walked into the kitchen at that moment and must have sensed something. Their banter died down, and they quietly placed the food on the counter and joined everyone in the living room.

"I did?" she asked.

"Yes, the spring before you started at the university yourself," Mike's voice had taken on the tone of one recalling a long-forgotten memory. "You had admissions and wanted to check things out so you came with me to campus one day. You walked around a bit while I lectured, but then you joined me at the end. I introduced you to Schuyler and his son, Joe. If I recall, the kid was a couple of years older than you, and his father was quick to point out your achievements in not a very nice way. I thought he was a bit daft about it, but what do I know? I mean you're exceptional, Vivi, but his son seemed like a good kid—was headed off to college himself as far as I knew—so it didn't make sense to have his dad harping on him. You weren't a good comparison for most college-aged kids, I mean you being sixteen at the time and all."

"Do you remember the meeting, Vivienne?" Ian asked.

She frowned. "Now that Mike mentions it, vaguely. But obviously not enough to remember the Adams men specifically."

"It was two months later that the young girl we think was the first victim was killed," Carly said, her eyes back on the laptop.

"Could you have brought to the surface some sort of latent rage toward his father?" Ian asked.

"And he took it out on women who looked like me as a way to annihilate what his father thought he should be? It's possible, but I need to think about it a little more." She thanked her uncle who, as always, told her to stay safe and hung up. She sat back and took another sip of wine.

"Something isn't sitting well with you, is it, Vivienne?" Ian asked.

It wasn't, but she couldn't quite put her finger on it. "I don't know, Ian. Maybe we should eat, and I'll try not to think about it so hard and see what comes into my head."

"Maybe when we know more about him, about the evidence and how he lived, it will make more sense. If it ever makes sense." Ian held out a hand and helped her off the couch. "In the meantime, I think you're right. It's been an intense day for everyone. Let's eat, maybe blow off a little steam, and we can go from there."

By the time they climbed into bed that night, they still didn't have anything from Joe's apartment, but between his whereabouts, his cloudy past, and the physical evidence, it wasn't looking good for him. They had even found the truck they believed was used to transport Meghan on the back part of the Adams property. It had been cleaned but was still being processed in Albany.

Pushing the details from her mind, Vivi didn't find it all that hard to shut down that part of her brain. Not with Ian beside her. When she curled up alongside him, he wrapped his good arm around her and pulled her close.

"That gun in my ankle holster is unregistered," she said, smiling. His chest rumbled with a soft chuckle, as she traced her fingers along his skin. "A friend got it for me a while back when we were traveling in some less than hospitable places. Not sure why I kept it, but I did."

Ian rolled toward her and ran a fingertip down her cheek.

"You know I could arrest you for that." She arched a brow at him. "But, like I said, I'm out of my uniform now, and I definitely have other things on my mind."

She smiled and pulled his lips toward hers. "I was hoping you'd say that."

CHAPTER 28

FOR GOOD OR FOR BAD, Ian let Vivi sleep in the next morning. He had gotten up early, showered, made coffee, and headed into the station, but she had taken it easy and was now sitting on the front porch, in a pair of his boxers and one of his t-shirts, enjoying a cup of the coffee he'd left brewing for her.

She was absorbing the quiet when she heard a car pull off the road onto the driveway. A few seconds later, Nick's rental appeared.

"There's coffee in the kitchen if you want some," she offered with a gesture of her head when he joined her on the porch.

"Don't mind if I do."

A few minutes later he was seated in another chair beside her, boots propped up and a steaming mug in hand. "This place suits you, Viv."

She inclined her head. "I agree, it does."

"So, are you going to stay?" he asked, picking up the conversation he'd tried to start the day before.

She couldn't say she hadn't given it much thought, because she had. In between everything else they were thinking about and dealing with, she had thought of little else.

"Don't complicate things, luv."

"Meaning?"

"Meaning, you're thinking too hard. You're thinking about your job and your family and the fact that you've only known MacAllister a few weeks."

"I shouldn't think of those things?"

"You know you're one of the smartest people I know, Viv.

309

One of the smartest people *you* know. But you're also annoyingly intuitive, luv. It's really not cosmically fair, come to think of it, that you're not some weird savant on either end of the spectrum—being either scary smart *or* eerily intuitive."

"What are you getting at, Nick?"

"If you're smart enough to do the things you do, you're smart enough to figure out how to make your life and Ian's life into a life that works together. And, judging by the way you two look at each other, I think it will be disgustingly easy, actually, if you decide it's worth it. So, is it, Viv? Is it worth it?"

It was, but she didn't say so. She gave a small nod and heard Nick exhale as if he'd been holding his breath, waiting for her to make the wrong choice. And now that she had made the right one, he could finally relax. She smiled to herself; it was funny just how much a little breath could tell her about how much Nick cared about her. Despite everything, or maybe because of it, he wanted her happy.

They sat together in companionable silence, finishing their coffee. Just as she was rising to get ready to head into town, Nick's cell rang.

He glanced at the number, then mouthed "Sam" before answering. Vivi stood listening to Nick's half of the conversation, and it didn't take long to know there was a snag in the investigation. Whatever it was, it had to do with the handcuffs, and while Nick didn't look overly alarmed, his look of concern wasn't what she wanted to see.

"Well?" she asked, as soon as he hung up.

"There's a third partial print on the handcuffs. Sam doesn't have enough to get a full match, but what he does have could match with Schuyler Adams."

"That's not all that surprising. Our best guess right now is that he discovered what his son was doing and was trying to stop him. Trying to kill him was a bit much, I think, but if he thought his son was responsible, and we know he had a temper, it's not out of the question. And it might have been the handcuffs he found that clued him in. If he picked them up, it wouldn't be unusual to find his prints on them."

"And his DNA?" Nick added.

Her stomach sank. "What kind of DNA, and where did Sam find it?" If it was sweat DNA, her reasoning might still be valid.

"Epithelial DNA. In the locking mechanism."

"Like what we'd find if someone not used to using handcuffs got their finger pinched when locking them around someone's wrist. Shit." That bit of information definitely threw a monkey wrench into their theory. She needed more from Sam, but unless they could come up with a very good reason Schuyler's skin cells would be where they were, it was looking like it was the father, not the son, who went after Meghan. And maybe they had it all backward. Maybe Joe discovered his father's secret and was trying to tell her. And then his own father tried to kill him to stop him.

Her mind raced through what they knew and she grabbed her cell.

"Viv?"

Ignoring Nick, she dialed Ian. When she didn't get an answer, she hung up and called Sam back.

"Sam," she said without preamble. "We sent you some pictures of Schuyler's injuries. Can you run them by your team and see if we can get an idea of what might have caused them?"

"I can tell you right now they were caused by someone's hands. And small hands at that," he answered.

"Hands the size of Meghan Conners?" she asked.

Sam paused for a second then answered. "We'll run some comparisons, but I'd say that's a possible scenario."

"You think it was Schuyler who went after Meghan, don't you?" Nick asked after she hung up.

"I think it's definitely something we need to look into. Did you see Ian this morning? He needs to know this and decide if he wants to ask NYPD to search Schuyler's home and office."

"I ran into him, the felons, and Travis at Frank's this morning. He was waiting for the evidence from Joe Adams's apartment to arrive before heading up to Albany. The four of them were having breakfast together."

Vivi tried Ian's cell and, again, no answer. Tapping the phone on her hand, her mind raced. Something *was* off; something didn't fit. And then she knew.

"Shit." She headed into the living room and began going through the files.

"What?" Nick said, following close on her heels.

She focused on what she now realized had been bugging her all along. She pulled out photo after photo of the victims and lined them up on the coffee table. When she had nine photos out, she stepped back. Her heart sank and she felt ill. They'd been wrong, very wrong.

"What do you see, Nick?" she asked, pointing to the pictures. Some were photos of discolored flesh, others were of clean, white bones. All of them were wrists. Nick leaned down to take a closer look. He picked up one after the other and, after examining the last, looked up.

"I should have caught it sooner, Nick. Hell, I was even the one to noticed it in the first place," she said.

"Viv."

"Whoever did this to these women," she said, gesturing to the photos, "he never, not once, used handcuffs. With the exception of our first victim, without fail, he restrained them with shackles, Nick. Thick, metal shackles. Whoever killed these women is still out there."

CHAPTER 29

"We need to find Ian," Vivi said, calling out to Nick from the bedroom. Tugging on a pair of jeans and a t-shirt, she glanced down at her boots. On any other day she wouldn't think twice about pulling them on, but she was beginning to feel a sense of urgency. And she'd been around long enough to know not to ignore her intuition. Casting her boots aside, she slipped on a pair of sneakers and, after checking her weapon, she strapped on her ankle holster and slid the gun inside. She hoped she wouldn't need it, but she'd rather have it and not need it than the other way around.

"I'll drive you into town, and we can check for Ian at the station, then head to Frank's. In the meantime, you can keep trying to reach him on his phone," Nick said.

She tried two more times on their drive in; it wasn't like Ian to not answer. But then again, if he was back out on patrol for some reason, there could be any number of explanations for why he wasn't answering, from being in a location with no coverage to being in the middle of something else—like dealing with a car accident or policing his town.

All three officers were at the station when they arrived, but none of them had seen Ian since he'd gone off with the twins and Travis for breakfast. Walking down Main Street toward Frank's Café, Vivi called Naomi.

"Are you guys still at Frank's?" she asked.

"Uh, no. Brian and I are here at The Tavern working. Ian went with Travis to scout some of the local farms. He said he had a few hours before the evidence from Joe Adams's apartment arrived, and it was a nice day, so they headed out somewhere. Why?"

"Because I can't find him," Vivi said and then told Naomi her new belief that Joe Adams was not the serial killer and that they needed to keep looking.

"Call Travis, and in the meantime, I'll try to track Ian's cell. If it's still on, I should be able to find it."

"Is that legal?" Vivi paused.

"Do you really care?" her cousin countered.

"Just let me know," she replied.

"I will. And by the way, you should know we had a very interesting breakfast with Deputy Chief MacStudly. He kind of likes you, you know. As in, I think he'd like to take you to the church, if you know what I mean." Vivi could hear the grin in her cousin's voice.

She also had no problem envisioning her cousins interrogating Ian on the subject. She felt a little bad for him, but then again, he had chosen to go with them to eat, so he'd gotten what he'd deserved. And there *was* a little girly part of her that liked hearing what Naomi said.

"Nice, Naomi. I'm glad to hear your interrogation techniques are still getting you results. Now, please go find him, so I can check to make sure he hasn't gone into hiding from you all."

Naomi laughed. "Not hardly. He doesn't hide from anything. But I'm on it. I'll call you back as soon as I have anything."

Vivi and Nick headed back to the station, calling Travis on their way and not getting an answer. When they arrived, they updated Wyatt, Marcus, and Carly. None of the information they'd accumulated upstairs had been removed, so they all made their way back up to see if, on what felt like their thousandth viewing, they might discover something new.

She stared at the information on the board, intentionally focusing not on the images of the women, but on the data scribbled on the white background. Sometimes she could find patterns this way. Something fluttered in the back of her mind when she let her eyes fall on the date the second victim disappeared. She couldn't quite grasp it though and was moving on to the third when her cell rang.

Travis's number popped up and while she was glad to get ahold of at least one of the men she was looking for, she wished it was Ian on the other end of the line. She hadn't bothered to ask Carly or any of the others to try and trace Ian through his car since she knew he was with Travis—at least in talking to her old, family friend, she might get the information she needed.

"I just saw you called. I left my phone in the car when I stopped to take some pictures. What's going on?" he asked after they'd said their hellos.

"Naomi said you and Ian went off together to look at some potential sites. Is he with you?" she asked.

"No, he's not. I dropped him at the hospital. Have you tried his cell?"

"Yes, and he's not answering." Frustrated, she let out a deep sigh. "I've called him three times in the past forty minutes," she added.

"It's probably only been a few hours since you've seen him, so please tell me you aren't pining for him already. You hardly know him all that well, anyway," he responded.

Surprised at Travis's interpretation—or misinterpretation—of the situation, Vivi paused for a moment before answering.

"We've had some evidence come in that changes things for the case we're on, and I need to find him. What time did you drop him off at the hospital?" She kept her voice intentionally cool, reminding Travis that there were bigger issues at stake than her love life.

She heard Travis sigh and knew he felt bad. "Sorry, Vivi. That was uncalled for and I know you better than to think you'd act like some love-sick teenager. It's been a long few days. I dropped him off about fifteen minutes ago. Maybe he's in a location where he can't use his cell?"

She ended the call quickly, not wanting to get into a longer discussion with Travis at the moment. But as she turned her attention back to the board, his words kept floating in her mind. *You hardly know him all that well anyway. I know you better.*

Like gears coming together, thoughts suddenly began to fall into place. She looked at the dates of the victims again. Victim one, raped and strangled in southern Maine—July. Victim two, June of the next year. By the time she reached victim six, she felt like she was going to throw up.

"Viv?" Nick said from beside her. She looked away from the board. Everyone in the room had stopped what they were doing and was now staring at her. She opened her mouth to say something and was, thankfully, cut off by the sound of her own cell. She wasn't ready to voice her thoughts yet. She wasn't ready to let herself even think them.

"Vivi?" Naomi's voice cut through the haze.

"Yeah?"

"I have Ian's cell at some farm out about four miles as the crow flies from his house. I pulled up the satellite maps and it looks like there's a barn there. It looks to have been built recently and not at all the kind of place Travis said he was looking for, so I don't understand what Ian would be doing there."

Vivi's heart sank. "Can you tell if his phone is moving?"

"Not if it's moving a couple of feet here or there, but if he moved more than, say, thirty feet or so, I would see it."

"And has it? Moved?"

"Vivi, what's going on? Is something wrong?"

"Just answer me. Has his phone moved since you located it?"

"Uh, no."

When she'd lost her brother and her parents in the same day, there had been no fear, just the searing pain of loss and sorrow because it had all come as a surprise. But she knew that what gripped her now was an entirely different kind of emotion, a sense of panic and terror she had never, in all her life, experienced before. Because she knew very well what could happen next.

Think, she ordered herself. Forcing in a deep breath, she tried as best she could to focus. There could be any number of reasons

Ian's phone wasn't moving, but of the two that came to mind, neither were any good. Either the phone was on Ian and Ian wasn't moving, or the phone had been tossed. That it was simply lost wasn't a viable option in her mind, since she knew he clipped it to his belt and it would never just fall off.

"Okay," she took a deep breath. "Give me a second." Turning to Nick she motioned to his cell. "Call Jesse Baker at Riverside hospital and see if Ian is there." Without question, Nick did as she asked. While he was on task, she returned to her call with Naomi.

"Naomi, can you tell me where Travis's phone is?"

"Uh, sure, but why?" Vivi heard the question even as she heard Naomi clicking away on her keyboard, but her attention was on Nick whose eyes kept darting in her direction.

"Thank you, Jesse. No, everything is fine. Yes, please do let us know if he shows up." Nick ended the call and looked at her with a shake of his head. "No, he hasn't been by since we left yesterday."

"Vivi?" Naomi brought her attention back to the phone. "This is really weird but Travis is with Ian. Or, at least according to what I'm seeing, their phones are together. I mean, I know they're supposed to be together, but Travis is looking to scout locations for a Revolutionary War–era movie. What would they be doing in a barn made of corrugated metal?"

That was the question Vivi didn't want to think about.

***

"Viv, talk to me," Nick ordered as they followed the directions to the barn Naomi had sent them. Marcus, Carly, and Wyatt were in the cruiser behind them. Vivi felt a sense of urgency to the core of her bones, but at her orders there were no sirens. If Travis and Ian were in there, she didn't want to make the situation worse by ratcheting up the tension. Nor did she want to give Travis any cause to do what she was certain he intended.

"It's Travis we're looking for, Nick. He's the one who killed all those women, the one who went after Ian last week." God, it hurt to say those words. She could feel Nick's doubt, and she could hardly blame him. She hadn't quite wrapped her mind around it either, but she knew she was right.

"Travis?"

"Yes, he said something to me on the phone a little while ago. He said he knows me better and that I hardly know Ian at all."

"He has a point, Viv. It seems an awfully big leap from that to him being a serial killer and Ian being in danger. And you do think Ian is in danger right now, don't you?"

"I do. I think Travis is obsessed with me and is going to do something to Ian I don't even want to consider, because he knows how Ian feels about me, he knows what we mean to each other. And, as to the other, as to being a serial killer, his words kept bothering me, and then when I looked at the dates the victims had all gone missing, I realized that, for those I could remember, Travis and I had had very similar arguments just before each of them."

"As in, you would do something, the two of you would argue, and then he'd go out and kill someone?"

"I think it's probably more complex than that, but that's what I'm working on right now. I think after every argument he'd go out and kill someone who looked like me."

"Because he couldn't have you. Or control you." Nick went silent for a moment as he sped along the country road, driving like he'd lived there his whole life. "I might be able to buy that, but tell me why the arguments would spur the behavior? "

"The only two things Travis and I ever argued about were men and me doing things he didn't agree with, usually things that took me away from Boston."

"Away from him and out into a world he couldn't control, which left him feeling helpless and impotent."

"That's my thinking."

"Viv, you know this all still sounds a little crazy. Not that you may not be right, but if you are, it's going to devastate your family."

"I know, Nick. Believe me, I know. I can't," Vivi paused and intentionally reined her emotions back in, "I can't think about that right now. Right now, I just want to be sure Ian is okay. If I'm wrong, then I'm wrong. But if I'm right, the conversation Ian had with Travis and the twins this morning could have pushed Travis over the edge."

"What conversation was that?" Nick asked, pulling onto the long, gravel driveway that would take them closer to the barn.

"Naomi said Ian was talking long term, maybe even marriage. If it is Travis, he's already taken a shot at Ian, and that was just because we decided to stay in the same house. If his mind is so tainted, so unhinged, that he'd do that, I don't even want to think about how he might handle the idea of me getting married."

Nick pulled to the side of the road, still a good distance from and out of sight of the barn. The others pulled up behind them.

Nick put a hand on her arm, stopping her from getting out. "Viv, luv, I don't think you're the right person to be going in there. If it's you he wants and you who sets him off, if you walk in there and aren't able to hide your fear or feelings for Ian, it may set things in motion in a way you don't want it to."

Vivi knew this, it was actually her worst fear right now—well her second-worst fear, her first being that Travis had already taken out his frustration on Ian. But it had to be her because she was pretty sure that, at this point, she was the only person who had any chance of reaching Travis. Once he understood that she and the entire team suspected him, he'd have nothing left to lose and she was hoping, that his feelings for her, no matter how warped, would slow him down enough that one of the others would have a chance to intervene.

"It has to be me and you know it. I know I'll be a sitting duck when I walk from here to the barn. I'll be out in the open and exposed. We don't know if he has a weapon, but we should assume he does and that he's not afraid to use it. I'll need you to cover me and lead the rest of the team. I won't be able to carry a weapon, because I don't want Travis to see me as a threat."

Nick's jaw ticked. He didn't like it, but at this point, there was no other way.

"Fine," he finally conceded. "But you don't go in until I get the others on the ground and in a position where they can assist if it comes to that." They climbed out of the car and met the three officers. Motioning them all into a copse of trees, Nick started issuing orders. Nick would cover Marcus as Marcus scoped out the barn. Once they had a general idea of the layout, Nick would put folks in place and only then would Vivi be allowed to move toward the barn. The wait was torture, but she knew it was the right thing to do, for her and also for Ian.

Using a scope to look through a window, Marcus spotted Ian inside, lying on his side with his feet and hands bound. As this bit of news crackled softly over the radio, Vivi's stomach plummeted; it crashed even more when Marcus reported that Ian wasn't moving. Vivi forced a breath in and told herself he wasn't moving because he was tied up, not for any other reason. So focused on maintaining control over her own self, she didn't even notice that Nick had already processed Marcus's intel and positioned Carly and Wyatt.

"Give me forty-five seconds to get into position then start walking toward the barn," he directed.

Vivi nodded at the order.

"And so help me god, do not let anything happen to you. MacAllister would never forgive me and, as much as I hate to admit it, I kind of like it here and wouldn't mind coming for a visit or two, which isn't as much fun when you're on the police department's shit list."

Despite everything, a smile crept onto her lips. "Thanks, Nick."

He gave her one last look, nodded, then vanished into the woods. Vivi glanced down at her watch and began to plan what she might say to the man she had played with as a child, the man she had grown up with and thought of as family. The man she now believed killed so many women because of her.

CHAPTER 30

LYING ON THE PACKED DIRT floor, Ian's body felt twice its normal weight. Disjointed thoughts floated through his mind including an abstract awareness that his hands and feet were restrained. The various times and ways he'd used duct tape throughout his career flashed in random images in his head. He could feel the slow rhythm of his heart, much too slow to be healthy, and he could feel the familiar effects of a prescription painkiller.

Vaguely, he remembered drinking a flavored water Travis had given him in the car. He thought he'd pulled out his cell to call Vivienne, but couldn't say for certain. And he had no idea what had happened—or how much time had passed—between drinking the water, which must have been laced, and semi-waking up on the ground just now.

Some latent instinct from his days as a Ranger must have kicked in; he had managed to keep his breathing intentional and slow and he hadn't opened his eyes yet. Travis, if it was Travis who had done this, would likely think he was still unconscious. Ian wasn't sure what he was going to do about the situation—he wasn't thinking that clearly yet—but given that he was still alive, he was hoping that by playing dead he might stay that way long enough for the fog to clear.

"Vivi! What are you doing here?"

Travis's voice and, more to the point, his question, did more to focus Ian's mind than probably anything else could have. *Shit*, he had no idea why he was where he was, or what Travis had to do

321

with the price of bread, but whatever it was, it wasn't good and he didn't want Vivienne anywhere near it.

"I'm looking for Ian," she answered. Judging by their voices, the two were standing a bit away and maybe in another room. Choosing to take the risk, Ian cracked an eye. When he didn't see anyone, he opened both and tried to assess his situation. He was lying on the floor of what looked like a hay storage barn. Being spring, it was empty but, taking a deep breath, he recognized the scent of alfalfa and timothy hay.

There was a large door, and though it was open and Ian could see the field beyond, he couldn't see either Travis or Vivienne.

"I told you, I dropped him at the hospital, did you check there?" Ian heard Travis say.

That didn't make much sense, but Ian figured he could sort that out later. What he needed to do now was focus on getting his hands free.

"I did check, he wasn't there, and, since you're here, I thought I would ask you. Since you know me so well, it shouldn't come as a surprise to see me here."

Vivienne's voice sounded strained—terse but also nervous.

"Look, I apologized for snapping at you earlier, Vivi. Really, I'm sorry. It's just been a hard few weeks, is all. I'm not sure what to tell you about Ian," Travis responded.

"Other than I don't know him all that well," Vivienne said.

The conversation wasn't making any sense to Ian, but he was following it even as he did his best to work the duct tape against his cast in the hopes of starting a tear.

"Well, you don't, Vivi. You never do," Travis countered.

"Have you noticed Travis, the only times we fight it's always either about someone I'm seeing or because I'm making a decision to do something you think I shouldn't?" Vivienne pointed out.

"We don't fight all that much, Vivi, so I don't get what you're trying to say."

"I'd say, over the last eighteen years or so, we've had at least twenty-one fights. Is that about right, Travis?" Vivienne asked.

Ian froze. *Twenty-one*. That wasn't a number Vivienne had pulled out of her hat. That was the number of potential victims they'd identified. Ian began to double-time his efforts.

"I don't know what you're talking about, Vivi," Travis hedged.

"I think you do, Travis. And I think I want to see Ian now. After all, you know me better than to think I'm going to walk away from this barn without seeing him."

Ian felt the start of a tear in the tape as the two came into view. Vivienne was leading, and for a split second, his eyes met hers before he went limp and feigned unconsciousness.

"What did you do to him?" Vivienne's voice came closer to him as she spoke.

"Don't go near him, Vivi. I swear to god I will kill him."

In that moment, Travis's voice went dead flat—no inflection, nothing. Just the monotone speech of a man speaking with disinterested certainty. Ian fought the urge to open his eyes and see how Travis planned to do the job. It was possible Vivienne was between him and Travis, but he couldn't be certain.

"With his own service revolver. Nice Travis. Very clever. And what did you do to him?" Her voice was coming closer to Ian as she spoke, and he had no doubt she was speaking more to feed him information than for any other reason. And then he felt her fingers on his neck, checking his pulse. "You drugged him, didn't you? Probably with the painkillers the hospital sent home with him, or something similar. Is that right?"

She was putting herself between him and Travis, and though he didn't want her there, he wouldn't have expected anything different. That was why it came as such a surprise when she stood and walked behind him, exposing both of them to Travis and his weapon.

"Don't touch him again, Vivi." Travis issued an order, but his voice had changed again. It was thin and high-pitched, and to Ian it sounded on the verge of hysterical. And Vivienne calmly ignored him.

"I want to look at his hands, Travis. He had surgery a few

days ago, and I'm a doctor, remember. You know me better than to think I wouldn't want to check on him. But I won't touch him."

More than a few times, Vivienne had referred to how well Travis knew her. Ian didn't understand the reference at all, but it was beginning to sound ominous and a harbinger of something to come.

"He should be dead already, but the stupid bastard didn't drink enough of the water."

Vivienne nudged Ian in the back with the tip of her shoe. "Oh, you didn't know? Ian has an unusually high tolerance for pain medication. Comes from back in the day when he was recovering from an IED attack. He was a Ranger you know. An excellent marksman, too."

Vivienne's tone was goading Travis, but Ian sensed she was trying to tell him something, too. And when she nudged him in the back again, it clicked into place. Doing his best to keep the rest of his body still, he wiggled his fingers until he felt her ankle. And the gun in her holster.

"I swear to god, Vivi, I will shoot him if you don't move away," Travis said.

"You're not going to shoot him while I'm standing here, Travis. After all, everything you've done, you've done for me, haven't you?"

A terrible silence fell across the barn. Even the birds seemed to stop chirping in the field.

"Not for you, Vivi. *Because* of you."

Ian knew in that instant that Travis had reached the point Vivienne referred to as devolved. His voice was shaking and, though Ian hadn't opened his eyes, he had no problem picturing Travis's expression: tight, white, and livid.

"Because I know you, and you—you don't seem to ever even *see* me," he continued. "You never call me, you never listen to me, you never ask my opinion. And when I offer it, you never give it any credit. You never stop by and visit. You, the perfect specimen, top of your class in everything you do. You are so caught up in yourself that you never—" Travis cut himself off, but Vivienne finished his statement.

"I never noticed that you were in love with me. That you wanted me the way a man wants a woman."

"I don't," Travis spat.

"You do. And when you can't have me or when I do something that takes me completely out of your life, you look for a substitute you can control. Another woman you can take out your anger and frustration on. At least twenty-one times since I turned seventeen, Travis. Twenty-one women you've tortured and killed because I treated you like family."

Vivienne's voice had a calm certainty to it that almost, but didn't quite, hide the sorrow Ian knew she was feeling. Sadness for the victims, but also for what this would do to her family.

Ian's fingers closed around the gun. He opened his eyes to see Travis raising his weapon, his hand eerily steady for someone so close to the edge.

"I was going to make it look like he'd killed himself, succumbed to his PTSD and all that shit. Now, I guess I'll have to make it look like murder-suicide."

It was such a preposterous statement that it, more than anything, told Ian how far into his own mind Travis had gone. Making himself believe things that couldn't ever be true.

"You know that's not how it's going to work, Travis." Vivienne responded. "You've left enough DNA in this barn that you may as well post a neon sign proclaiming your guilt. Not to mention that you can't possibly believe I came here on my own."

"Vivienne," Ian warned. With every word out her mouth, every word that reminded Travis of just how beneath him she was, Travis was raising his weapon higher and higher. But he paused when Ian spoke and his eyes darted down. With a clear head and a clear sight, Ian met and held his gaze. Vivienne's small gun was in his hand and Ian knew he had a clear shot, but he was also certain that if Travis was good enough to shoot the tire of his Jeep, he was good enough to get off at least one shot before Ian had the chance to fire.

"Naomi has already placed you and Ian in real time in this barn together. I told Nick everything on my way here. He'll call Lucas and execute a search warrant on your home. What will they find? What trophies did you take from all those women, Travis?"

"Vivienne." Ian's tone was short; Vivienne was going too far. Travis was clearly on the edge and Vivienne kept pushing.

"Nothing," Travis exploded. "They won't find anything. What would I want with them when I was done?" he demanded. "They weren't. They were nothing but cheap imitations. Oh, for a moment, for one tiny moment, I could pretend they were you and everything was as it should be. But then I'd open my eyes and see them. See them for who they really were. Just little fakes, pretending to be you."

"And that made you angry." Ian finally understood the dangerous game Vivienne was playing. Until this point, until she'd pushed him to this point, he hadn't actually admitted to doing anything other than to drug him. As a Ranger he hadn't needed to think about things like evidence and prosecution. As a seasoned law enforcement officer, Vivienne knew otherwise. Every bit of information they collected now would help build the case against Travis. Of course, if he ended up with a good lawyer, he'd plead insanity, but Ian knew Vivienne wasn't going to plan for that. She wanted evidence. She wanted a confession.

"Of course it made me angry," Travis erupted. "They weren't you. How could they possibly be you?" Suddenly Travis dropped his hand, and Ian watched as the man deflated in front of them. "How could anyone possibly compare to you, Vivi?"

Ian knew the sad, lost look in Travis's eyes made Vivienne pause. He glanced up in her direction and saw her own sadness reflected in her eyes. This whole situation was almost more than she could handle. On top of everything else she'd gone through in this last year, she'd now been betrayed by someone she loved and told that she was the reason twenty-one women were dead. Ian wanted to reach out and hold her, pull her close to him, and take her away from it all. But with the gun in his good hand, he settled for wrapping the tips of his other fingers around her ankle. It was all he could do without risking alarming Travis.

"And so you killed them. Because they weren't me," she said quietly.

Travis nodded.

"You know it's all over now, right, Travis? I can't let you get away with killing all those women."

"I did it because of you, Vivi."

Vivienne stepped away from Ian. She moved toward Travis but stayed out of the line of fire. Not that Ian had ever had any doubt, but she was one cool customer—competent, in control, and calm.

"Why don't you give me the gun and we can talk about it a little more?" She held out her hand as she took another step forward.

"I don't want to talk about it anymore."

"Then we don't have to talk about it anymore. Just hand me the gun or toss it away and we'll both walk out of here."

Travis looked at the gun in his hand. Ian could feel his pulse in his throat—it definitely wasn't sluggish anymore. He'd been able to move himself into a better position and, at this point, felt confident that he could get a shot in before Travis, but he'd prefer not to. For Vivienne's sake.

Slowly, Travis took the weapon in his other hand and made to hand it, butt-first, to Vivienne. Ian saw her let out a tiny sigh of relief as she took the last step forward and wrapped her hand around Travis's. Ian flicked his gaze to the other man's eyes and saw a look he recognized all too well.

"Vivienne!" Ian called as a shot rang out.

He leapt up and forward as Travis crumpled to the ground. Eyes wide with shock, Vivienne stood and watched, her hand still hanging in the air where moments before it had been holding Travis's.

"Ian, I—" her voice a hoarse whisper. "Oh god."

He caught her as she lunged toward Travis. Despite everything, he was still the boy she'd known her whole life, still the man she considered family.

"There's nothing you can do, Vivienne." Ian held her back even as he became aware of Nick and his officers swarming into the barn.

"I have to try, Ian. For Mary, his mom. I have to try." Her eyes were wild, and he couldn't even begin to imagine what she was feeling at that moment. But he did know there was nothing she could do. Travis had all but blown the top of his head off with Ian's service revolver. He was dead before he hit the ground.

"Vivienne." Ian took her by the shoulders and forcibly turned her away from the body. "Vivienne, listen to me." He waited until she stopped straining against him. "Trust me, honey, there is nothing you can do, and this isn't how you want to see him."

Her eyes searched his for a good long moment before her shoulders dropped from the weight of it all. "Oh god, Ian." And the tears began to fall.

"I know, Vivienne. I know." He didn't know everything or anything of what she was feeling, not yet anyway. But he pulled her against him, knowing for certain that they would sort it all out, together.

CHAPTER 31

VIVI STOOD AND STARED AT the pictures of the women whose lives Travis had ended—their names still written below their faces, along with the dates of their disappearances or, if known, their deaths.

"Vivienne?"

Ian stood in the doorway wearing jeans and a t-shirt rather than his uniform. He'd been checked out at Riverside and given a clean bill of health, despite having ingested a risky level of pain-killers in the water Travis had given him. The only physical mark on him was his wrist that had been rubbed raw when he'd broken through the tape. Her eyes traveled to the bandage.

"It's fine," he said, stepping into the room. "How are you?"

She lifted a shoulder. It wasn't a question she could answer now. "Did you call Lucas?"

He nodded. "He's executing the search warrant on Travis's apartment today. He was also able to confirm that Travis often rented vans to cart around camera equipment as part of his scouting job."

"I chickened out and sent Naomi and Brian home to tell his parents, Mary and Josh, and the rest of the family."

Ian came to her side and stood, a solid presence in her life.

"Jessica Akers," she said, looking at the picture of the young woman. "I went to Haiti just before she was killed. Travis didn't want me to go. The earthquake had just happened, it was such a disaster." She gave a small shake of her head remembering the destruction, the lives lost, and the people she had tried, but failed, to save.

"Vivienne," Ian said softly, telling her she didn't need to go on. But she did.

"Rebecca Cole," she said, touching the picture. "Travis was in Seattle when I had my meltdown. He wanted me to go back to Boston with him. I agreed, but when I woke up in the morning, I knew Boston wasn't where I was supposed to be. So I left him a note and took off to LA to see Kiera. He flew back to the east coast and, a few days later, Rebecca went missing."

She moved down the line. "These three women," she pointed to the three women from Boston who had all gone missing in a relatively short period of time. "I got engaged just before the first one went missing."

"Engaged?"

She turned and smiled at Ian's tone. It was a heavy smile, but a smile. "For about a week. Actually, Travis was the one who made me realize that my fiancé was more interested in politics than me. My family isn't financially powerful, we're all working stiffs with the exception of Naomi and Brian's branch, but we've been around a long time and we're very well connected in both the Irish and Italian communities. Travis pointed it out, and we fought, but then I realized he was right and ended the relationship."

"And didn't take up with him," Ian finished, explaining the rapid disappearance of the three women.

"And this young girl," Vivi moved to the front of the line. Their first victim. "This was the summer I lost my virginity. My family was vacationing in Maine. I met Aurelio, an Italian exchange student. He was older, and I spoke Italian, and it was one of those summer things. Brian and Travis overheard me and Naomi talking about it."

She stared at the photo for a long time before speaking again. "You know, a few days ago when Brian said Travis had a thing for me and I brushed him off saying he might have when we were ten? I've been thinking about our lives, and we were closer to fifteen when Travis got up the nerve to say something to me. Not ten. But we were practically family, Ian. It's not that I didn't take him seriously in general, but he was like all my other cousins, so I figured he was just messing with me."

"I don't think it would have mattered if you had taken him seriously, Vivienne. Do you think it would have changed things?"

She looked at the photos and knew logically that a man capable of doing what Travis had done would have been triggered by something else at some point in his life if she hadn't been the trigger at fifteen. It might not have been the specific twenty-one women on the board, but it would have been others. Still, her heart wasn't ready to accept this.

"He's a good shot, you know. That's how he got your tire. He didn't join the police like his dad, but he was brought up with guns and with shooting, like the rest of us. He used to laugh and say the skill gave him something to talk about at Hollywood parties." Wanting to change the subject, *needing* to change the subject, she asked. "How is Meghan?"

"She and Joe both woke up and are talking. They're stable and a full recovery is expected for both."

This was news, good news. "Ian, that's great. When did this happen?"

"Just as we were leaving the hospital ourselves. If I had told you then, you would have wanted to stay. I thought we needed some time away. Marcus and Carly are there with her."

"Was it Schuyler?"

Ian nodded. "He's the father of her child. Meghan didn't know that her instructor for the class she was taking in New York was Schuyler's wife. But when Schuyler saw Meghan at the class one day, he was convinced she was coming at him through his wife and was planning on blackmailing him or something."

"A child out of wedlock is hardly a cause for murder," Vivi pointed out.

"In his mind it is, especially given she was seventeen when she got pregnant and he was planning a run for office in the next state election. If she had come forward, which she said she never had any intention of doing, his aspirations and his reputation wouldn't have survived."

Power, love, or money. It always came down to one of those three. "And Joe?"

"He came to class one day to meet his stepmother and found her chatting with Meghan about Windsor, about the coincidence of them both living there—if only part-time for Lilly. He says that when Meghan pulled out a picture of her son, Joe thought he was looking at a picture of himself at the same age. And when she said the father wasn't involved, he knew his dad well enough to want to look into it. And so he did."

"And how did he find out the truth?"

"He didn't, but he suspected, and so he came up here to talk to her. He knew from his stepmother that Meghan was a struggling single mom and he told Marcus that if his father was the father of Meghan's child, he wanted her to have some help, financial help, from the family. He also admitted to hoping that, if it were true, he might be able to build a friendship with her and his half brother."

Ian paused for a moment, then let out a long breath and continued. "Joe didn't say he was starved for familial attention, but that was the sense Marcus got. His life with his father was so cold that it wasn't until his stepmom came along that he realized what a real family relationship could be. I think he hoped he might be that family for Meghan and her son."

Vivi sighed. "So he was just trying to help."

Ian nodded. "And then he heard about Meghan and found the handcuffs and the gun in the garage. He was coming to tell us about it when his father caught up with him."

"They fought and he went to your house because it was less obvious than the police station and he probably thought his father would be looking for him there, or somewhere between their house and the station," Vivi posited.

Ian nodded again. "But we figure Schuyler must have followed him instead."

"And tried to kill his own son." Vivi shuddered. So much violence in such a small town. "This is going to be hard on the town, Ian."

"I know. But right now I'm not thinking of the town, or the fact that Vic, the real Chief of Police, will be back in two days." He reached out for her and she stepped into his arms. Wrapping her own arms around him, she rested her head against his chest.

"It's not over by a long shot, Vivienne, but we got the bad guy. We'll turn over all the evidence and let the prosecutors do their thing. And we can begin to get on with our own lives."

For a long moment, they simply stood there in the upstairs room of the police department. Vivi could hear the birds outside the open window and the occasional sound of a car or voice of a passerby floated up from the street below. But most of all, she could hear Ian's heartbeat. She closed her eyes and savored it.

"I'm staying, Ian," she finally said. He hadn't asked, but she wanted him to know.

He pulled back to look at her. "You're staying?"

"Here, with you," she clarified.

"Here?" Ian paused, but she knew it wasn't because he didn't want her there. He wore an expression that told her she'd upended one of his plans and he was reassessing.

"I know you want me to stay, Ian."

That snapped him out of it, and he braced her face between his hands. "God, yes, I want you to stay. I was just thinking that I would have to spend some time convincing you. I had all these arguments planned out about different ways we could make it work. I guess I don't need to use them now?"

Vivi smiled and went up on her toes to touch her lips to his. "No, you don't. I haven't worked out the specifics of my jobs, but I'm not actually that concerned about it. I'll officially quit with the Boston PD, but I can still teach a day a week and I can still consult with the FBI. Maybe Sam will want me in the lab or something. I figure, we're two smart people, we can figure it out. We also have a dinner date we need to schedule with the governor," she added with a grin, reminding him of that brief call so many days ago.

Ian stared at her for a beat, then dipped his head and kissed her the way she needed to be kissed, a kiss that held all the emotion of what he felt for her and the promise of what was to come.

When he pulled back, he traced his thumb down her cheek and smiled. "That's not much of a plan, Dr. DeMarco, but I definitely like it."

ACKNOWLEDGEMENTS

THE ONLY REASON I AM lucky enough to be able to write *A Tainted Mind* is because I have the support of so many great people. The entire Booktrope team, including my Book Manager, Sophie Weeks, deserves a big round of applause. In addition, my editor, Julie "Where's Rooster?" Molinari, gets big kudos for getting this book into shape from cover to cover. And seriously, if you like Rooster, thank her.

A lot has changed since *The Puppeteer* was released, not the least of which is that we have moved from the Puget Sound area to Northern California. While I'm glad to be back in my home state, we left behind an amazing group of friends who have brought, and will continue to bring, so much joy to my life. So here's to the families of Bridle Trails that I am honored to call my friends— your support over the years means the world to me. More special shout-outs go to Meghan for everything you've done to support me, including swapping closets, and to Cathy and Jenee for providing food, advice, feedback, and lots of good times (with more to come). And to Sarah (we'll always have our block), Lisa (we expect to see you in a month), and Jere (I'm sure Liam left his glasses at your house so I'll just have to come get them)— you know what you mean to me and I miss you all every day.

And last but not least, to my mountain movers and my family—thanks for supporting and celebrating this life with me.

Keep reading for a preview of Tamsen Schultz's

THESE SORROWS WE SEE
WINDSOR SERIES BOOK 2

Sorrows are something Matty Brooks knows a thing or two about. Having grown up in the projects of New York City, she's seen her fair share. But as an adult, and successful author, Matty is all too happy to leave that life far behind.

Secrets aren't something Dr. Dash Kent knows much about. As a small town vet with deep ties to his community of Windsor, New York, life has always been pretty straightforward. Until Matty Brooks comes to town.

Redemption is what Brad Brooks wants. As Matty's half brother, he's ashamed of how his family treated her — how they cast her out. But when the olive branch he extends turns deadly and Matty stumbles into Brad's biggest secret, she finds herself cast back into a world of violence and deceit. Now redemption is easy; survival is the hard part.

CHAPTER 1

MATTY BROOKS LET OUT A long-suffering sigh. It was loud enough for her friend on the other end of the cell phone to hear over the wind and noise created by Matty's new, sleek convertible. She was driving north on the Taconic State Parkway toward a small town called Windsor, a few hours upstate from New York City. She should have stayed in the city. Having been born and raised in urban areas—first New York, then DC—she was a city girl, by birth *and* by preference. But she hadn't stayed and she knew why—even if she didn't want to share that reason with her best friend. And so, opting to be obtuse, Matty answered the question Charlotte posed, if not the one she'd really been asking.

"I desperately need an expert in modern Chinese political history, Charlotte. That's the only reason I agreed to come up here, to the middle of nowhere, and dog-sit Brad's brood for a few weeks."

"Bull," came her friend's answer. "There's something bothering you. Are you having problems writing? Is your mom okay? Did Brad say something to get you to drive all the way up there?"

Her writing wasn't going as well as it usually was at this stage; she had a draft of her fifth book due to the editor in four weeks and she was behind schedule. Her mom had made no attempt to hide what she thought of Matty house-sitting for Brad. But it was the last question Charlotte asked that made Matty most uncomfortable.

Brad, her half brother, hadn't really said anything persuasive to get her to come up. Under normal circumstances, if they had been a normal family, that might not be so unusual. But she and Brad had spoken exactly three times in her life—once when she was seventeen, once at their grandmother's funeral, and once, this last time, when he'd called to ask her if she would come dog-sit for him while he was away for three weeks. He had called her several times in the past few years, but she hadn't answered. Why she had picked up the phone yesterday she didn't know, and why she had even entertained the idea of house- and dog-sitting for him, let alone agreed to it, she could no more explain than quantum physics.

But he *had* promised her an expert on modern Chinese political history—something she needed in order to finish the research for her next book. She'd tossed the request out more like a challenge than anything else when he'd asked what he could do to get her to agree to come up. Of course, Brad, with his family connections, knew someone. A classmate of his from Princeton, now the head of the Chinese department at one of the universities in Boston, was a friend and had a house in the Hudson Valley too. He'd be happy to make the introduction.

Matty didn't *really* need Brad to find an expert for her. She had enough of her own connections—especially at this point in her career—to find an expert in DC herself. But he had given her a reason, if a flimsy one, to say yes. And so she had. Though she still wasn't sure why.

"Everything is fine, Charlotte. I promise. You can imagine my mom isn't too happy, but she'll get over it. And it's not like Brad is going to be there or I'll be spending any time with him. I'm just staying at his house and watching the dogs. Besides, it's kind of pretty up here, in a bucolic kind of way," she added, taking in the view of a lush, green valley as she rounded a bend in the road. "It will be good for me to be up here, away from everything, while I finish this draft."

Charlotte made a noise and Matty knew that, although her friend wasn't buying it, she had decided not to press the issue right now. "Just be sure to wear bug spray," Charlotte said—her way of conceding, if only for the moment. "They have a lot of ticks up there. The kind that carry Lyme disease," she added. "And it's supposed to be hotter up there this week than it is down here, so be careful."

Matty smiled. No doubt Charlotte had researched everything there was to know about Windsor the moment Matty had told her she was going.

"Yes, Mom."

"And call me—or your mom—every day. I don't like the idea of you staying in a country house in the middle of nowhere all by yourself."

"But you don't mind that I stay in a city mansion in the middle of one of the most dangerous cities in the US all by myself?" Matty teased.

"You're city wise, Ms. Brooks, not country wise. Besides, they had some trouble up there a few months ago, caught some serial killer. He ended up shooting himself before they could arrest him."

Matty frowned; Brad hadn't mentioned that. Not that it changed things all that much. "People get killed in DC every day. I'm sure the serial killer was just one of those fluke things. Did he kill a lot of people?" she couldn't help but ask.

"They think about twenty-one women, but only two bodies were found in Windsor. The rest were all over the country."

"And the small-town police force caught him," Matty pointed out; it was an assumption, but a fair one, she thought. "I'll be fine."

"Just call me," Charlotte issued the order before hanging up. Matty smiled, thinking of her over-protective friend. Charlotte's reasoning wasn't always logical, but the two of them had known each other practically since birth and had been looking out for each other almost as long.

Matty pulled off the Taconic, turned left, then made an immediate right, following the directions Brad had e-mailed her. Based on the road sign she saw, she was heading away from the town itself, but her half brother had assured her that, while it might look as though the roads could wind to nowhere, it was, in fact, the right way.

But before driving too far, she was forced to stop behind a

truck and trailer waiting to make a left turn into a gas station. Noting that the station had a mini-mart—always a good thing to know—she let her eyes wander to two men who were talking out front. One wore a beige uniform of some sort and was leaning against a huge SUV that had lights on top and the head of a goofy-looking dog hanging out the window. The other man, with his hip hitched against a massive blue diesel pickup, was clad in boots, jeans, and, despite the August heat, a long-sleeved shirt that was rolled midway up his forearms. Matty let out a little laugh; she definitely wasn't in Kansas anymore—or the city, to be more precise. Maybe it was the size of the two trucks flanking the men or the fact that the man not in uniform wore clothes that were utilitarian rather than stylish, but there was no doubt in her mind that the next few weeks would be very different from her urban life. She just hoped it was in a good way.

Following Brad's directions over a railroad bridge and along a road that, on a good day, could be called one and a half lanes, she passed farmhouse after farmhouse. It all looked like something out of a Norman Rockwell painting to her—too wholesome, too quaint to be real. In fact, it was so charming she actually reminded herself of the recent serial-killer incident Charlotte had mentioned just to make the place seem a little less perfect. A little more accessible.

Quelling her rising doubts about the wisdom of her decision to come here, she passed through what Brad called Old Windsor, a "town" that consisted of Anderson's Bar and Restaurant, a post office, and a general store. Exactly another seven-tenths of a mile down the lane, she turned left onto a dirt road. There she paused for a moment and consulted the directions for the umpteenth time. According to her half brother's e-mail, the road was shared with his neighbor and Brad's house was located at the end. An end she couldn't see from where she sat, though if she craned her neck, she could make out a weathervane and what looked like the top of a barn.

Two mailboxes were perched at the side of the road—a simple black box and, next to it, a rather more colorful one. Painted hot pink with a white roof, the second box resembled an old school-house, complete with a tiny chimney. Matty assumed the pink one was the neighbor's. Brad hadn't said anything about his neighbor, but if the mailbox was anything she could go by, she guessed its owner was decidedly un-Brad-like and therefore someone she needed to meet.

The undeniable beauty of the place, the clean and quiet air, and the interesting mailbox all served to quash the remaining doubts she harbored about making the trip. In fact, as she made her way slowly up the road, she was actually beginning to think this little journey had been a good decision, albeit an out-of-character one for her. And then, as she came around a slight bend and Brad's property came into view, her heart actually fluttered a little bit. She might not care much about her half brother, or even know him well enough to know if she cared, but his home made her feel like she was stepping back into the warm embrace of history.

Continuing up the drive, she came alongside an enormous red barn on her right. She had no problem envisioning generations of farmers moving in and out of the structure, tending to livestock, storing hay, and doing all sorts of other things farmers did. She braked for a moment beside the building and took it in. She'd never seen a barn of this size before. Scratch that, she'd seen polo barns and more modern barns of this size, but she'd never seen a historical barn of such stature. And it *was* old—she could tell from the wood siding, which was well tended but weathered, and the slight tilt to the entire building.

Unbidden, a smile touched her lips, and what little tension was left in her since she'd agreed to come to Windsor slipped away. She eased her foot off the brake and continued up the road. Also on the right, the house was positioned so that the drive came up parallel to the entrance rather than straight on. The two-story wooden farmhouse was built on a hill with what looked like a stone foundation. It appeared that the view from the other side was of a vibrant, sweeping, green pasture that seemed, from her perspective, to go on for miles.

The house itself was built in the Greek Revival style. Clean lines dominated the exterior and the big, paned windows were lined with shutters. There was enough architectural detail to provide some depth and the soft cream color, highlighted with earthy tones, made it inviting as well as stunning. There was also a freestanding garage facing the gravel parking area in front of the main house. Though built in the same style as the house, judging by the materials, it was probably the newest building on Brad's property.

But the beauty of the architecture aside, it was the gardens that made the place seem magical. Lush, green fields surrounded the property, but well-tended planting beds and paths had been created, and they meandered around the land closest to the house. In those beds and along those paths were flowers of every color, style, and height that she could imagine. Inhaling a deep breath scented with fresh-cut grass, humid air, and roses, Matty acknowledged that never in her life had she seen such spectacular gardens outside of an arboretum. Not even in her own yard.

From Brad's e-mail, she knew that the main entrance to the house was actually a small door that led into the kitchen—toward the left side of the house—even though a more traditional grand entry graced the center of the building. And as she pulled to a stop by this side entry, she could hear the cacophony of Brad's dogs inside. She'd been told there were five and, by the sound of it, they were a vocal five.

She stepped onto the small flagstone patio in front of the door and found the key under a pot of dahlias where Brad had said he'd leave it. She would have taken a moment to appreciate the sweet little café table and chairs set up on the patio, a perfect place for an early morning cup of coffee, if it hadn't been for the melee she heard inside. With a small laugh at the big noise, she opened the screen and unlocked the door. When it swung open, she was immediately accosted by noses, tails, and furry bodies.

Laughing aloud at the chaos, she managed to push her way inside to the kitchen. Not pausing to look at her surroundings just yet, she dumped her purse on a table and went down on her knees to greet the dogs. Not surprisingly, the yellow Lab, Bob, was right in her face. Rufus, the Great Dane, was nosing her head while Lucy, a wiry little mutt, was springing up and down from all four of her short, dainty legs. Roger, the Newfoundland mix, was gently sniffing Matty in curiosity, and Isis, the gorgeous Ridgeback, was standing back, assessing the situation. It was a motley crew, but she knew from Brad that all of them were rescue dogs and had come to him in various ways over the past two years.

She stayed low to the ground, petting all of them and letting them check her out until, with the exception of Lucy who seemed in a perpetual state of wiggliness, they all quieted down. Rising, Matty glanced at the water bowls lined up against one of the walls and was pleased to see the dogs hadn't run out of water while waiting for her. She was about to take a closer look at the house when the dogs suddenly burst into renewed chaos and all ran to the door. The noise caught her off guard and her heart rate leapt in response. She didn't know what they were barking at but figured that with five dogs, sudden chaos was probably something she was going to have to get used to. At least she'd get some cardio workouts in without actually having to exercise.

When she opened the screen door to let the animals out, all but Isis went tearing down the driveway. In the quiet of their absence, she could hear what had set them off—the telltale sound of a diesel pickup truck. And judging by the increasing volume, it was headed up the drive in her direction.

Frowning to herself, Matty walked out onto the patio as the truck she'd seen at the gas station on her drive in pulled into a small parking area by the barn. The dogs surrounded the driver's door and, when the lanky man in the long-sleeved shirt and jeans stepped out, the barking stopped—even if the body wags continued. She had no idea who he was, but at least it looked like the dogs knew him and, judging by the way the man rubbed heads, scratched ears, and patted shoulders, he knew the dogs.

When she stepped from the shadows and into view, the man's head came up and in that instant she experienced something she never had before. The moment slowed and everything around her faded into a dull presence. She recognized the sound of birds and sensed a breeze against her bare throat, but she didn't really hear or feel them. Everything inside her, for one brief moment, stilled and focused only on this man in front of her—on his eyes that were locked on hers.

And then Isis pressed her cold nose to Matty's bare thigh and the world fell back into place.

With a little shake of her head, she moved off the patio; the man straightened away from the dogs as she walked toward him. She'd already noticed his form, but hadn't realized how tall he was—two or three inches over six feet, if she had to guess. She'd place him in his early- to mid-thirties and, given his wiry build, which she thought suited a man, she'd bet he had been a very skinny kid. But it was his eyes that caught and held her attention, eyes that didn't stray from hers as she made her way toward his truck. They weren't an unusual shade or anything like that, but they were a rich, dark—very dark—brown that matched his hair almost exactly. Hair that was a little longer than was fashionable, at least in the city, and that curled over the tops of his ears.

"I'm Dr. Dashiell Kent, Brad's vet. I'm here about the cows," he said, holding out his hand. Matty took it in hers and immediately noticed not just the rough texture but the dry heat of his palm.

"Hi, I'm—wait, did you just say *cows*?" she repeated, dropping his hand and looking around. She hadn't seen any on her drive up and Brad had most definitely not mentioned any cows.

He inclined his head. "Yes, six of them. Brad probably put them in the barn."

Her stomach dropped. Dogs she could handle, but cows?

"Is Brad here?" Dr. Kent asked, moving to the back of his pickup. He let the tailgate down and began pulling out supplies of some sort.

Matty shook her head. "No. I'm Matty Brooks. I'm Brad's half sister. The more honest and forthcoming half, obviously. He asked me to dog-sit for him but sure as hell didn't say anything about cows." It dawned on her that she didn't know this man from Adam and perhaps she should watch her language. He didn't look like a prude, in fact, if the vibes she was picking up from him were anything to go on, he was probably about as nonprudish as she was, but still.

He smiled as he reached for a wicked-looking needle. "Well the good news is, especially this time of year, the cows are easy to take care of. I just need to give them a vaccination, and then I'll turn them out into the pasture. They don't need to be fed since the grass is good, but you may want to keep an eye on their water. It will refill automatically, but in this heat it's always good to check it occasionally to make sure the refill mechanism hasn't broken."

His words were meant to be comforting but somehow they weren't—what if something happened to one of the cows? She would never be able to tell if one was sick or hurt unless it was actually hobbling on three legs—or dead.

"Wait," she said as his words sunk in. "You said the good news is the cows are easy to take care of. Does that mean there's bad news, Dr. Kent?"

"Call me Dash," he answered. "I don't know if I'd call it bad news, but I'd guess if he didn't tell you about the cows, he probably also didn't tell you about the cats, rabbits, and chickens," he continued.

Matty stared at the man for a long moment, waiting for him to laugh and say something like "gotcha!" But he didn't.

"That son of a bitch," she muttered then cast a look at Dash to make sure she hadn't offended him.

He laughed even as he continued prepping his shots. "I've heard worse, believe me. Brad really didn't tell you about the other animals? That's not like him," he continued, not waiting for her reply, "he's pretty meticulous about their care."

Matty shook her head. Mostly in dismay.

"And he didn't leave you any directions or instructions or anything?"

She started to shake her head again then stopped. "Actually,

I just arrived a few minutes before you did. He might have left something for me, but I haven't had a chance to take a look."

Dash held up a second mean-looking needle and tapped the container of liquid with a free finger. "Why don't you go inside and see if he left anything for you. I'll take care of the cows, let them out, then stop by. If he didn't leave anything for you, we can walk through what you'll need to do. If he did leave something, have a look and if you have any questions we can go over them."

It seemed wrong to leave him to handle six cows on his own, but as he filled a bucket with water from some tank on his truck and then arranged his supplies in a tidy box, he looked like a man who knew what he was doing.

"Are you sure?" she asked, still feeling a little guilty about leaving him to his own devices.

He smiled and she noticed he had a dimple in his left cheek. "Yeah, I got it. Brad's cows are pretty docile and the shots are quick. You go on and I'll be up in about ten minutes."

She gave him one last look before nodding and turning back toward the house. Isis and Bob trotted after her while Lucy stayed behind. Roger and Rufus, having assessed the situation and moved on several minutes earlier, were already crashed out on the patio; neither even bothered to raise their heads when she walked by.

Fifteen minutes later, Matty looked up from where she sat at the kitchen island to see Dash at the screen door.

"Come in," she waved him in.

"My boots are filthy."

"I'm not feeling so inclined to care much about Brad's floors these days."

Dash let out a little chuckle as he stepped into the room. "Those the directions?" he asked, nodding toward the paper in her hands.

"All four pages of them," she answered.

"*That* sounds more like Brad. Do you have any questions? Anything I can help with?"

She took one last look at the typed, single-spaced text. "I tried to call him but I'm sure it won't surprise you to hear he didn't answer," she said, not without a bit of wry sarcasm. Then she shook her head and set the pages down. "And why on earth would anyone want rabbits? I mean they're cute and all, but you can't cuddle them and he only has two, so it's not like he's collecting angora or anything."

"Brad's an interesting guy," Dash said, crossing the room and coming to a stop a few feet from her.

Matty arched a brow. "That's an interesting comment."

"It's not a commentary, just an observation. Where is he, by the way?" Dash asked, his eyes not leaving hers.

"I don't actually know," she frowned. And thinking back to the conversation she'd had with him, Brad hadn't really left her an opening to ask. "He didn't say and didn't really give me the opportunity to bring it up. He just asked me to come up for a few weeks and watch the dogs."

"From where?" he asked, leaning his hip against the island and crossing his arms.

"DC," she answered. "I'm a city girl. Dogs I can do, and the cats won't be too bad, but cows, chickens, and rabbits will be a new one for me."

"Well, here," he pulled a card out of his shirt pocket. Reaching for a pen on the counter, he scribbled on the back. "If you have any questions, just call me. Brad takes good care of his animals. My guess is that the biggest problem you'll have with them is what to do with all the eggs his chickens are producing this time of year."

"I should be so lucky," Matty said, taking the card and noting the cell number he'd added.

"You'll be fine. Once the surprise of it all has worn off, you'll be able to kick back, relax, and enjoy the country, cows and all."

"I think I'm going to start now. Brad says I'm welcome to any of his liquor," she said, holding up the last sheet of paper. It was a weird thing for him to write, he didn't even know if she drank. "A gin and tonic and a cool bath sounds just about perfect after my long drive. Care to join me?" She meant in the drink, but the side of his mouth ticked up and she realized how ambiguous her question sounded.

"I'd love to, but I have a few other calls I have to make. I'll take a rain check, though."

And she knew he wasn't just referring to the drink. It hadn't been her intention to suggest they share a bath, but now that it was out there, albeit only playfully so, she couldn't bring herself to think it would be a bad idea. But rather than comment, she simply inclined her head and rose from her seat to walk him out. He offered again to be a resource for her should she need it and, a few minutes later, was climbing into his truck and heading back down the road. Matty, deciding to skip the drink, stood on the patio for a few minutes listening to the sounds of the country around her. There was a sense of peace and calm about the place.

She just hoped she didn't ruin it by accidentally killing one of Brad's animals.

***

Dash eased his truck to a stop at the end of the dirt road that Brad's house shared. Pulling out his phone, he dialed a familiar number.

"Hey," his sister Jane answered.

"I just met her," he said without preamble.

"Met who? Oh!" she said, the realization dawning. "Really? You met her?" she repeated, beginning to laugh.

"Yes and it's not funny."

"Yeah it is. After all those years of you saying it was never going to hit you, it's kind of funny. I'm looking forward to the next month or so, it's going to be so interesting," she added, not bothering to hide her enthusiasm.

"Nice, thanks for the support. I'm a little freaked out."

"Yeah, it's like that. So, what are you going to do about it?" she asked.

"Avoid her," he answered even as he thought of the cell number—his personal cell number—he'd added to his card.

"Like that's going to work," she retorted.

"I know, but at least it might buy me some time to get used to the idea. I feel like I can't breathe."

"Oh, you're such a drama king. It might be scary as shit when it hits, but it works out fine. That's the way it's always been," he sister responded, none too helpfully. "What's she like?" she added.

Dash thought about Matty, about how concerned she was about doing the right thing for the animals and how relatively in stride she took the shit her half brother had dumped on her. Which, if he let himself think about *that* particular turn of events, was unusual too. Brad wasn't usually a "shit- dumping" kind of guy. Usually, Brad was the exact opposite. He frowned.

"Well?" his sister pressed, bringing his mind back to Matty.

He thought of the way she'd looked with her long, black hair, light brown eyes, and a face and complexion that hinted at a Latina heritage somewhere in her genealogy. And her curves—it would have been hard to miss those as she'd stood in front of him wearing a pair of short shorts and a tank top. Matty Brooks was not a waif and for that he was truly grateful.

"I'm not talking about it," he answered.

"Because that will make it more real," she taunted.

"You don't have to sound so gleeful."

"I'm your sister, of course I do. I can't wait for Mom to find out."

"But she won't find out from you, Jane," Dash warned. Lord knew what would happen if, or when, his mom found out about Matty.

"Oh please, Dash," Jane brushed him off. "You know how it works. It's the same for *everyone* in the family, and you've just acknowledged you're no different. You and this woman, whose name I don't even know, will be married within a month. I guarantee it. It's our family curse, or blessing, depending on how you look at it, so you may as well just embrace it and tell the parents. It's not like you'll be able to keep it a secret for long."

And that's what he was afraid of—because Jane was right. For as many generations as they could go back in their family, not a single person had had a period of more than a month between meeting the person they would spend the rest of their life with and marrying them. He'd always chalked it up, back in the early days, to arranged marriages and just a different kind of lifestyle. And then, with the more modern generations, he'd just thought the family promulgated the tradition because it was kind of fun and quirky. But after what had just happened to him when he'd met Matty Brooks, he wasn't so sure anything was made up. Because the feelings that had overloaded every one of his senses had been very, very real.

"Fuck," he muttered.

"You'll get there."

"I'm hanging up, Jane."

"Okay. I'll be up for the pancake breakfast in a couple of weeks. I look forward to meeting my new sister-in-law."

"You suck, you know."

"You love me. Good-bye." And she hung up.

He'd been hoping for some sympathy. He should have known better. And, unfortunately, the one thing he could agree with his sister on was that it was most definitely going to be an interesting month.